THE
FROST
TOUCHED
QUEEN

COPYRIGHT

Cover design courtesy of Jay Aheer
Editing courtesy of Rumi Khan
Proofreading courtesy of Pixie Styx Editing
Formatting courtesy of X-Factory Designs

ISBN: 9798379202002

For more information, visit:

@IvyFoxAuthor

THE
FROST
TOUCHED
QUEEN

BY

IVY FOX

"The king is dead. Long live the Winter Queen in the north!"

Unfortunately, those jubilant shouted-out wishes over my role as queen of the Kingdom of Aikyam were short-lived.

All because three pesky kings stand in my way.

King Levi in the east.

King Teodoro in the south.

And the rebel king in the west, Atlas.

They want my crown.

My throne.

My birthright.

So instead of trying to dismantle their plots to overthrow me, I do the unexpected.

I offer up marriage instead.

A trap of my own making that will ensure I remain on top.

Because make no mistake, there can only be one ruler of this kingdom—*me*.

TABLE OF CONTENTS

To the ones who parted from this life and left us alone to pick up the pieces of our shattered hearts—we shall meet again.

AUTHOR NOTE

Dear reader,

First of all, thank you so much for purchasing The Frost Touched Queen.

If you've read the blurb then you already know that this book is a royal reverse harem romance, which means our Winter Queen doesn't have to choose between her love interests.

Please also note that this is NOT a fantasy romance.

Although the medieval setting might hint to that genre, this romance has no paranormal tones or magic to speak of.

If that is what you're in the mood for, then I'm afraid this book won't scratch that itch.

What you can expect is a strong heroine that isn't afraid to put her men on their knees.

Expect loads of hot, smutty moments in these pages as some scenes might be too hot for your e-reader.

But with all my books, also expect a heavy plotline that will not come to its conclusion until the final book in this duet.

Secrets. Lies. Miscommunication (*our queen can be quite a stubborn hothead, what can I tell ya*)

And so many betrayals, that at times you'll find yourself not knowing who to trust.

Oh, and it wouldn't be an Ivy Fox romance if I didn't bring on the angst.

Angst galore!!!

Hope you're ready for it. *wink*

Also, I do not consider this book to fall in the dark romance genre, but there are some subject matters and scenes that may be triggering for more sensitive readers.

If you are on the fence, please read reviews or join my readers group on Facebook – Ivy's Sassy Foxes and ask for feedback.

I would like to also ask one small favor of you, if I may.

Reviews are life for an author. I treasure each one since they enable other readers to find my book babies. If you can spare a few minutes to write one after you've finished The Frost Touched Queen, I'd be forever grateful.

These reviews also help other readers decide if they should take the plunge in reading these types of books that have a trigger warning to them. And ladies, this book definitely does.

If you're okay with all that I've mentioned above, please proceed, and get ready to fall in love with the wonderous Kingdom of Aikyam.

Much love,

Ivy

Aikyam Kingdom

North

Current Ruler: Queen Katrina of Bratsk
Parents: King Orville of Bratsk and Queen Alisa of Bratsk
Capital: Tarnow
Season: Winter
Royal Seal: Blue Rose

East

Current Ruler: King Levi of Thezmaer
Parents: King Krystiyan of Thezmaer and Queen Daryna of Thezmaer
Capital: Arkøya
Season: Spring
Royal Seal: Green hydrangea

South

Current Ruler: King Teodoro of Derfir
Parents: King Yusuf of Derfir and Queen Nahla of Derfir
Capital: Nas Laed
Season: Summer
Royal Seal: Golden sunflower

West

Current Ruler: King Atlas of Narberth
Parents: King Faustus of Narberth and Queen Rhea of Narberth
Capital: Huwen
Season: Autumn
Royal Seal: Orange Marigolds

I leant upon a coppice gate
When Frost was spectre-grey,
And Winter's dregs made desolate
The weakening eye of day.
The tangled bine-stems scored the sky
Like strings of broken lyres,
And all mankind that haunted nigh
Had sought their household fires.

The Darkling Thrush by Thomas Hardy

N othing survives winter land.
Flowers cannot bloom, nor can they flourish in the bare
frozen earth.

Rivers refuse to run downstream, preferring to turn to stone,
ensuring they trap the very life that swims underneath.

All that was, is, or could be, is shrouded under a cloak of white
snow, patiently waiting for the swallow's song to return and breathe life
back into them.

All but one waits for such blessed tidings.

For there is one soul that thrives among the harsh winds of winter.

Frost chills the blood in her veins, while a crown made of icicles is
placed on top of her royal head.

She is the queen of the north, ruler of all the kingdoms.

To her, men must bend the knee, or suffer damnation.

For fire is not the only weapon used to burn through one's enemies.

Ice can be just as deadly.

The urge to suck my teeth in annoyance is overwhelming, yet somehow, I manage to keep my expression completely blank and emotionless as my father's most trusted advisors continue on with their never-ending spiels.

They're no longer your father's advisors.

They're yours now.

Remember?

My hands that have been strategically placed on my lap, begin to clench around the fabric of my gown, my back molars grinding at the cruel reminder as to why these high lords answer to me now and not to their true king—my father is long dead, his crown now heavy on my head.

Thankfully, none of the men standing before me in the royal hall take much notice of my sudden melancholy.

And why would they?

They're far too busy loving the sound of their own voices, each one pitching their own solution to solve my kingdom's problems, to pay me, their rightful queen, much mind.

The gods better give me patience, because if they shower me with strength instead, I'll silence each and every last one of these useless buffoons once and for all just to spare me the sound of their irritating ongoing tangents.

"We should order a draft, Your Majesty," Monad, my chief of arms, shouts from the top of his lungs, making sure that his voice is loud enough to be heard above everyone else's who is currently residing in this great hall. "Order every man between the age of fifteen to fifty to enlist in your army and march east as fast as we can. I bet my last gold coin that once King Levi hears that our army's numbers match his own, he'll think twice before marching over our borders."

Inwardly, I roll my eyes, while making sure my cold expressionless demeanor remains intact. The last thing I need is for everyone in this great hall to realize how his suggestion of a draft grates on my nerves.

Of course, war is Monad's answer to everything.

A man who has not only made it a sport of killing on the battlefield, but also earned his lands and prestigious title from it, must spend every waking minute picturing the next time he's called to arms. I wouldn't be surprised if he snuggles happily into his warm bed late at night, excited to be lullabied to sleep with dreams of wielding his sword to the loud sound of drums and the foul stench of blood and decay infiltrating his nostrils.

A man such as Monad only knows peace with the suffering of others. And while the whole Kingdom of Aikyam might regard me as having a block of ice where a heart should lie, I'm not as bloodthirsty as my so-called trustee advisor. Unlike Monad, I'm not too eager to send young peasant boys and old feeble men to battle and die in my name.

Contrary to public opinion, my people's lives are precious to me. Monad's, not so much.

I doubt I'd shed a tear if I saw Monad's head on a spike—be it mine or my enemies'.

"That might solve our problem in the east, but what do you say about our troubles in the south?" Adelid, my father's cherished best friend and brother-in-law, chimes in, pulling my attention toward him and away from the man who dreams of wearing his chain mail armor again. "Excuse my naivete, Monad, but how are we to feed our soldiers as well as Her Majesty's subordinates if the south keeps *misplacing* their shipments of food to us? I doubt starving soldiers win wars."

Monad's face instantly turns beet red, but he's clever enough not to raise a hand or vicious word against my uncle in response. If there is a man in this room that I trust, it's him. As did my father before me. And every adviser here knows that Adelid's counsel is the only one that I really pay attention to.

Still, he's failed to give me a solution.

In fact, the only thing Uncle Adelid has managed to do is alert everyone in this great hall of another pesky problem I need to fix.

My body stiffens when the large room grows eerily quiet, every pair of eyes directed at my throne, looking to me to offer Adelid an answer, since it's apparent Monad cannot. A low ringing sound worms its way into my ears, my skin starting to itch with each passing second that I'm unable to give a worthy response.

My tense muscles only relax when someone in the back of the hall decides to break the awkward silence in my stead, successfully pulling the crowd's attention off me and onto him. "My queen, if I may be so bold to add in a word," my treasurer, Otto, proclaims hesitantly.

Grateful for the distraction, I wave him over, the crowd of men immediately parting to give Otto ample room to approach my throne at the head of the great hall.

But when he finally reaches me and drops a knee with his head bowed down in respect, it takes him a good three minutes to stand back up straight. And when he does finally manage to do that simple task, the poor man's face turns so sickly pale with how everyone is impatiently staring at him, I'm afraid he'll pass out before he actually says what's on his mind.

"Go ahead, Otto. Say your piece. Her Majesty is waiting," Uncle Adelid says curtly when my treasurer looks like he's two seconds away from regurgitating whatever he had for breakfast.

Even though my uncle shares everyone else's impatience with Otto, I'm not as intolerant.

Unlike every man here, it's a well-known fact that Otto is not one to enjoy notoriety or attention of any kind. In fact, I don't think he likes dealing with people in general, preferring to keep company with his ledgers and books. It's a trait that I empathize with.

Men have a tendency to lie and make themselves larger than they really are.

Numbers are not as misleading.

They just are.

Factual.

Purposeful.

Honest.

How many men here can boast to possess such attributes?

That's why I wait patiently for him to collect his thoughts, giving him time to gather his courage to say what he has to. Unfortunately for Otto, there are others who are getting restless and irritated with him trying to conquer his anxiety and nerves of public speaking

"Otto, for all that's holy, just blurt it out, man," Monad curses, showing that patience was never his strong suit.

"Your Highness," Otto stammers bowing his head again, unable to look me in the eye, or anyone else's for that matter, "how are we to go to war with King Levi in the east or demand that King Teodoro deliver his food shipments to us from the south, when we are unable to pay for any of it?"

"What do you mean?" I ask, confused, my brow arching up high on my forehead. "We have coal and iron to trade, or if that isn't an option, then I don't see why we can't mine diamonds and gemstones from our mountains to offer our compatriots in exchange for their services."

"My queen," Otto mumbles, his voice trembling with fear as he approaches even closer to my throne. "We rely on materials brought from the west to mine as well as their fleets to ship our coal and iron to the other kingdoms. Unfortunately," he continues, his voice cracking, looking every which way instead of meeting my fixed gaze. "King Atlas has… well… has nulled all contracts with us and will no longer be providing us this service."

My upper lip curls in aggravation.

"Did King Atlas give us an explanation as to why he feels he should go against his queen's orders and break a contract that had been forged for decades?" Adelid interrogates, looking just as angry as I feel.

Otto shakes his head, taking a step back away from me, worried that I'll punish him for young King Atlas's defiance.

"This is mutiny, Your Highness! Mutiny! We must respond in kind!" Monad shouts, punching the air with his clenched fists.

My nails tap on the arm of my throne, contemplating what action will serve my people best, while the rest of the room murmurs amongst themselves. The only thing that pulls me out of my deep thoughts is when I hear an all too familiar accusation being hurled out, succeeding in setting my teeth on edge.

"None of this would be happening if King Orville were alive. A woman should not rule. She'll damn us all! She will ruin us!"

"Who said that?!" Uncle Adelid calls out in outrage, after hearing the same thing I did.

The room grows instantly quiet, no one daring to come forth to out themselves or the culprit behind the slur. Their refusal to condemn the man who said such a thing only serves to show that I have yet to win their loyalty. Deep down, I know that half the room is silently rejoicing in my embarrassment, while the other half wishes they had been brave enough to say those words aloud themselves.

Not wanting to prolong this meeting a minute longer and suffer such humiliation, I stand up from my throne and pretend that the curse didn't reach its target—my pride.

"You have given me much to ponder on, my lords. I shall retreat to my quarters and think long and hard on the matter. Rest assured that your queen will give you all a resolution before the week's end and put a stop to these pesky trials and tribulations, once and for all. You have my word."

I don't wait for them to bow and pay their respects, preferring to leave the wretched hall before I do something that I'll end up regretting. Images of cutting out the tongue of the villain who accused me of being an unfit ruler and force-feeding it to him swarm through my head as I speed through my castle's halls. Even at this unladylike pace, my hurried steps never falter, needing to put some distance between me and all the lords who believe they can do the job of ruling my kingdom better than I can.

My handmaiden, Inessa, rushes silently behind me, trying her best to keep up with me as I dash outside, needing fresh air to clear my head. It's only when I step foot into my winter garden, filled with my kingdom's traditional blue roses, that I'm finally able to take a fortifying breath. Inessa stands guard, leaving me to roam the garden freely on my own, giving me the space and solitude I need to simmer my rotten temper.

I should have stayed.

I should have stayed in that hall and gave Monad carte blanche to find the culprit who had the audacity to insult me.

My father would have stayed.

Even if he had to torture every last man in that hall, he would have stayed behind and made an example of them all.

But what did *I* do?

I ran before they made a murderer out of me.

Damn the gods!

Maybe the coward who said such a slur wasn't that far off. A man wouldn't have hesitated to splatter the hall's walls with innocent blood just to expose him for the coward that he is.

But alas, I'm the one who seems to be lacking all the required skills I need to rule the kingdom my father left me. A fact that has been made evidently clear with the way my vassals have all suddenly turned against me.

King Levi to the east marching with his army of thousands, all pillaging my lands and making camp on my borders, is his not-so-subtle way of intimidating me. Everyone knows Levi sleeps in his armor—a true born soldier—and like Monad, it seems he's foaming at the mouth for a fight, poking at me to see if I'll give him one.

Then there is Teo.

The king of the south has shown his true colors by sending his pathetic excuse of an envoy to try and convince me that he has no clue as to why we haven't received the last three food shipments, but that my debt to him must be paid in full before he'll even consider sending me anything else. He'd rather see my people starve than forgive my debt.

And then there's King Atlas. The rebellious king in the west. The last I heard, he had been sailing the world with his fleet. But now it seems the prodigal king has decided to return to rule, and his first action is to defy me by claiming that our contracts are now null and void.

These arrogant kings would have never dared to go against my father's wishes if he were still alive. They'd bend the knee, with their tails tucked in between their asses, begging for mercy before they even thought of defying him.

It was always his way.

The people of Aikyam loved my father just as much as they feared him.

He ruled our lands with an iron fist and an open heart for over forty years and no one dared go against him in all that time. It's only been six months since he fell ill and died, and already my reign is showing cracks.

All because I'm a woman.

And a woman has never reigned over the kingdom since its existence.

How will I ever be able to fill the role of being my father's successor when my own kingdom is in cahoots to dethrone me?

I may be a young queen, but I'm no fool. That's exactly what's happening here.

As much as I dislike the man, Monad was right in his observation. This *is* mutiny. The other kings coming at me, from all directions and all at once, is a way of testing my resolve. To see if I'm worthy of my crown. If they find that I'm not, they will do everything in their power to take it from me and make it theirs.

They'll need to pry it out of my cold dead hands before I ever let them take my birthright.

It's the sudden sound of crushing snow behind me that pulls me away from my hectic thoughts and urges me to spin around to see who my uninvited visitor is.

"My apologies, my queen. I did not know you'd be here," Salome rushes to say, immediately curtsying in my presence, the skirt of her dress soaking up the snow.

"Stand, Salome. There is no need for such decorum when we are alone. I've told you as much." I try to smile, but it comes out as flat as my temperament.

Salome rises to her feet, her forehead wrinkling in concern.

"You look upset, dear. Help me water these roses and take your mind off whatever is troubling you." She smiles warmly.

"I doubt tending to roses will lift my spirits, but I'll help you just the same, even if only to enjoy your company," I reply, grabbing one of the watering pots from her hands. "How is Elijah?"

"Oh, as can be expected for a six-year-old. Can't keep still. Always getting into mischief instead of cracking a book open and learning his letters." She sighs with a shrug.

"Father was like that, too. Preferring action to words," I retort sympathetically.

"True." She frowns. "But sometimes I just wish my Elijah took more after me than Orville. Life would be simpler if he knew his place."

I don't say anything to that.

Being the bastard son of a king is a double-edged sword. My sweet little brother might live in a castle and bear my father's likeness, but he'll never have his name or hold a respectable place in court. That responsibility falls only on my shoulders as the only legitimate heir—a fact I know half of my court wishes they could change. They would rather have a male child on the throne, one they could manipulate and mold to satisfy their every whim, than a woman who has always known her own mind.

"I see that I've said more than I should. You look upset again," Salome says with a worried expression on her face when she realizes my mood has turned once more.

"No. I'm fine." I shrug off. "I'd rather you tell me what my brother has been up to than think about anything else."

Salome's face lightens up as it always does when I call Elijah my brother. It's who he is to me, even if we don't share the same mother.

After mine died, my father found comfort in Salome's arms for a while. I admit that, at the time, I was bitter that my mother could be so easily replaced and forgotten. But when Elijah was born, all those thoughts that Salome wanted to take my mother's place held no room in my heart. I had a little brother, one that I would die to protect. Especially since I saw how cruelly bastards were treated in my own castle. My brother would never suffer the same fate. Not while I was around.

My father wasn't as careful with the way both Salome and Elijah were treated, though. To him, I was the only one worthy of his name, title, and respect, so no matter how many paramours shared his bed or bastards he fathered, they meant nothing to him. After I took Elijah under my wing and publicly claimed him as my kin, Father made it a point of hiding his affairs from me. If there were more brothers and sisters born from his indiscretions, he made sure that I didn't get wind of it. One bastard brother was all he would tolerate for me to dote on. No more.

I wish he had been different on that account. Maybe if he had, then I wouldn't catch myself staring into every child's eyes in my court, wondering if they have the same blood coursing through their veins.

Thankfully, Salome indulges me in taking my mind off my woes by telling me how my little brother has been faring as we water her beloved blue roses. She tells me about all his adventures, such as climbing the castle walls or stealing horses from the castle's stables to race with his friends on a dare. I live vicariously through my little brother, laughing away at his unruly antics, reminded of how at his age, I had the same curious rebellious streak.

"It's nice to hear you laugh again. You haven't been doing much of it lately," Salome says with a shy grin to her lips.

"Not much to smile about, let alone laugh, I'm afraid." I frown, remembering that while my little brother is living his best life, I'm stuck in rooms conversing with old men who think they could rule better than me.

"Hmm," she mumbles. "I heard there was a council meeting today. I take it that things didn't go as well as you would have liked?"

I nod, trying to push that horrid meeting from my thoughts.

Salome wraps her hand around my wrist and gives it a soft squeeze.

"Pay them no mind. You are your father's daughter, Katrina. There is nothing you can't do if you put your heart and soul into it."

"Easier said than done when all I see are foes coming at me from all directions," I grumble bitterly, but when Salome's smile stretches wider instead of offering me words of sympathy, my forehead creases in confusion. "Did I say something funny?"

"No, dear. I was just thinking about something your father used to say."

"My father, like his men, loved the sound of his own voice. He said many things, Salome. Mind narrowing it down for me?" I arch a teasing brow.

"Fair enough." She giggles. "He used to say that a smart man keeps his friends close, but a wiser one keeps his enemies even closer. If your enemies are coming for you, then maybe it's time *you* went after them, too."

"Go after them?" I laugh bitterly at the absurdity. "And how do you suggest I do that? I have no army to speak of. No money to pay or feed one even if I did. How am I supposed to go after my enemies when it feels as if the noose around my neck keeps tightening with each pull they make?"

"You may not have an army, but you have your mind. And a woman's mind can be a frightful thing if she so wishes it to be," she advises poignantly. "Go and seek out your enemies and let them feel how cold it is to stand in your shadow. Make them kneel before you and pledge their undying love to their true ruler in front of the masses and all to behold," Salome explains before plucking a blue rose to hand over to me, pride and fearlessness in her gaze. "And if they should not, show them what the north can do to those who refuse to submit to the Winter Queen. Make examples of them all, before they make *you* one."

"Winter Queen?" I raise a brow at the mention of the title my people christened me with after my coronation. "I sound terrifying."

Salome shakes her head and smiles with pride in her gaze.

"No, dear. You sound like a queen. And it's time you remind everyone of it."

I twist and turn in my bed, sleep a sullen stranger that refuses to pay me his visit. Salome's earlier counsel keeps me awake, as I stare at my ceiling, wondering how I'll ever live up to the fearless Winter Queen she envisions me to be.

But her words aren't the only ones that rummage through my mind. The man who accused me—in my own court, no less—to be an unfit queen, also plagues my thoughts.

Two very different people who hold polar opposite impressions of the person that I am, yet I have no idea who is right and who is wrong in their assessment.

The only thing I know to be true is that I *am* my father's daughter. Which means I can't lie around here and wait for someone to fight my battles for me. And by the way things are going, a battle is starting to feel unavoidable.

Levi.

Teo.

Atlas.

All three deserve my wrath for their part in my troubled sleep.

I'm not a fool. These crown games all come down to one thing—who holds power and who is forced to relinquish theirs.

How am I to show these kings, and my kingdom, that I'm not one to be trifled with? That I can lead as well as my father did before me? Or any man for that matter.

War is not an option, but neither is having my people starve, which they will, if I don't have the means to feed them. I need to make an example of their insolence while still being able to rely on their patronage, but how?

These questions keep me up until the rays of dawn begin to filter through the curtains of my bedroom window, alerting me that a new day has commenced.

Since rest is no longer possible, I get up from my bed, throw on a robe, and wrap the belt around my waist, even though I am far from cold with the fury that bleeds out of me.

On bare feet, I walk over to my window and stare at the white-covered mountains on the horizon, wondering how long they will keep danger at bay.

In my mind, I picture Levi's soldiers marching over them, their swords raised high and aimed at my heart. I'd willingly let them cut it out of me if I thought it would spare the lives of my people. But it wouldn't. Not if Teodoro insists on starving every commoner and lord alike. Even if Levi took the crown from me and placed it on his raven head, Teo would never accept Levi as his rightful ruler. And as for Atlas? Who knows where his allegiances lie.

No.

Aikyam has always had but one ruler—the north, and it will remain that way as long as air still fills my lungs.

I must find a way to punish all three kings while somehow keeping them obedient and loyal to me.

But again… how?

It wasn't always like this between us.

Once upon a time I called these three wretched kings my best friends. Even though it seems like a lifetime ago, I can still recall when they were just boys, eager to experience life to its very fullest, with no thought of dethroning me whatsoever.

It was a simpler time then.

A time where this castle was filled with the echoes of their joyous laughter.

Their families would travel, far and wide from their rightful lands, and come north to pay their respects to their true king. I remember standing by this precise window, waiting impatiently for their arrival. It was the highlight of my year, knowing they would spend a whole month within these walls. As an only child at the time, I eagerly awaited those days where I could bask in their friendship and companionship. None of us talked about how one day I would rule them all or even cared for that matter. We were equals then, even if there were obvious distinctions in our personalities.

Levi, being the oldest of us, took his responsibility of making sure none of us came to any harm very seriously. Especially when it came to me and Atlas. Me, because I was the only girl in the foursome, and Atlas, because he was always so sickly back then.

Atlas…

He was such a little thing the first time I saw him. Even though he was just a year younger than Teo and I, Atlas always looked smaller and frailer. I can still vividly recall how Levi looked like a grown-up to us, always standing tall and stoic, watching over little Atlas as he tried to keep up with my and Teo's mischievous antics.

Which were very frequent.

Teo had a knack for always getting into trouble, almost as if he thrived on the chaos. He would somehow find the most daring adventures for us all to partake in. Everyday Atlas and I would follow Teo blindly, knowing that no real harm would fall upon us as long as Levi's watchful eye was on us. At least that's the memory I hold of the time we spent together.

None of them cared if I was the only girl among them.

They accepted me as their own, and together for an entire month, we were all we had.

But then my mother died, and everything changed.

My father grew weary of their visits and ended them altogether, no longer wanting to play the role of host to his vassals without his Queen at his side.

I was heartbroken with my father's decision. They had been the only friends he allowed me to have, and here he was ripping them away from me when I needed them most.

But as the years passed, memories of them began to fade and their absence from my life no longer hurt as much as it used to. I guess that's a good thing, because if I still held any affection for them, then their current betrayals would have hurt me deeply.

I was a child when I knew them, and now they are all grown men.

Kings.

Kings that have turned as cold as the northern snow that falls on the ground.

But I can be cold too. Calculating and ruthless, even.

I can be terrifying.

Just like them.

I need to show them that the young, innocent girl who used to run after them, laugh at their jokes, and hang on their every word no longer exists.

Salome is right.

Maybe instead of reacting to their villainous ways, I should be causing my own tyranny. Reminding them that I'm their queen, and that if they want to keep their heads, they must bend the knee and be loyal to the one crown that rules them all.

But how can I do that without bloodshed?

Think, Katrina, think.

There must be a way that I can turn the tide in my favor.

There must be.

But what?

It's the knock at my bedroom chamber's door that ends up disrupting my muddled thoughts.

"Enter," I order, knowing that at this early hour, it can only be my room servants and handmaidens ready to prepare me for the day ahead.

As expected, they all rush into my room, Kari and Ebbe hurriedly placing fresh linens on my bed while Inessa and Anya prepare my bath. I fall into the routine of letting them bathe me in rose petal scented water, making sure every inch of me smells sweet and fresh, all the while wishing they could cleanse my troubled thoughts as easily.

When they ask if I had a good night's sleep, all I do is nod. I'm in such an apathetic state, that summoning the will to talk feels like a burden I have no strength for.

Sensing I need a distraction, they begin to gossip around me about their latest conquests and admirers just to fill the silence. They all giggle away at the antics of their men who seem to think they are close to winning their hearts, or in most cases, getting them to slide naked into their beds.

"Men are fools when their little heads are doing their decision-making for them," Anya utters whimsically.

"Aye, but they're even bigger idiots when they are trying to win our hearts," Ebbe offers with a lovestruck blush to her cheeks.

"Ego," Inessa interjects coldly. "That's all it is to them. They don't care if you love them back or not. Not really. All they care about is the conquest. They want to be number one in all things. Even in love. It has nothing to do with winning hearts, but more to do with their own pride," she adds bitterly, dismissing her friends' opinions on the matter.

While they all continue on defending their own points of view on the games of love, they don't realize that unintentionally I'm devouring each morsel of information they offer. Their words begin to seep into my subconsciousness and suddenly, for the first time in months, a smile begins to tug at the corner of my lips.

And as a plan begins to take form, my smile only blooms brighter, so much so it ends up making my handmaidens uncomfortable seeing it on my usually expressionless face.

"Is everything all right, Your Highness?" Inessa asks worriedly, not used to me smiling like this.

"It is more than alright. It's perfect," I singsong excitedly, jumping up from the tub, the water dripping down my naked form. "Hand me my robe, Inessa. There is much to do today."

Inessa swiftly brings me my robe, all four girls drying me as best they can before decorating me with the lavish gown and jewels they had prepared for me last night. Anya brushes my long blonde hair back, letting it fall down my shoulders before tying it into a long braid, its end hitting my waist.

Once I'm fully dressed, I dismiss them and rush to find the one person who I know will put my plan in motion. Five minutes later, I find him in his quarters breaking his fast.

"Your Highness," Uncle Adelid greets, springing up to his feet before bowing to me.

"Good morning, Uncle," I retort, unable to keep the smile on my face hidden.

"Well, look at you, child. You look awfully upbeat, all things considered." He chuckles, sitting back down to continue his meal.

"That's because I am," I reply, stealing a grape from his plate and popping it into my mouth.

"And will you share with me whatever joyous news has put that glorious smile on your face?" He laughs, amused, instead of swatting my hand away when I go for a second grape.

"In due time. First, I'd like you to order another council meeting. I want every lord in my great hall within the next hour."

His broad smile instantly drops from his face with the order.

"Is that wise, niece? After yesterday, I would have thought you'd only ask for another gathering after you've established a solid way of defeating our enemies. Facing the lords without a well-thought-out plan seems unwise."

"Then it's a good thing that I have one. One hour, Adelid," I command cheerfully before walking away to leave him to his duty.

A smidge of guilt rises in my chest that I didn't tell him my plan right there and then, but I want to see the look of surprise on my uncle's face when I announce it to everyone. Yes, the solution to my troubles is a bit controversial, and it will demand sacrifice on my part, but in the end, it's one I'm happy to pay if it will ensure that my people's lives are spared.

The more I think about it, the more the idea grows roots inside my soul. It's perfectly simple but wholly effective. It's the answer to all my problems and it's baffling to me how I never considered it before.

Men are simple creatures with huge egos.

They all want what they cannot have.

So why not let them tear themselves apart and wash my hands of the tedious effort?

They want my crown, then I'll dangle it in front of their faces, and stand back as they destroy each other to have it.

An hour later, as instructed, Adelid has made sure that my great hall is filled to the brim with all the lords that were in attendance yesterday. When I walk in and take my rightful seat at my throne, I feel the weight of their stares on me, all of them perplexed at this unexpected summons.

"My lords," I greet, keeping my excitement hidden from all these vultures. "I have thought long and hard about the tribulations and hardships my kingdom is facing. I know that each one of you believes that King Levi, King Teodoro, and King Atlas have broken faith with us and should be held accountable for their treachery. Some of you have been very vocal that war is our only hope to ensure my sovereignty. I, however, am of a different mindset. Like me, these kings deserve respect, and I fear that the north has been less than kind when it comes to showing this to them, causing this tragic rift to grow between us. This cannot be. Not as long as I am queen, which I intend to be for a very, *very* long time."

All eyes are on me as I square my shoulders, looking impervious to their confused glances.

"As you all know, it has been twenty-three winters since I was born, and if my father were still alive, he'd want me to find someone worthy to stand at my side. Someone to share all my burdens with, and to also ensure that my family's lineage continues. Who better suited for such a privileged endeavor than a king?"

The words have barely left my lips when audible gasps and hollers of excitement split the room in half.

"Adelid," I turn to my uncle, ignoring how his face has grown pale from my decision, "please send letters to all three kings. Tell them that I remember a time when, as young men, they visited my home and were met with nothing but friendship and hospitality for the duration of their stay. Inform them that I expect the same treatment to be bestowed onto me while I visit their lands within the next fortnight. My intention is to spend one month in the east, south, and west, respectively, and reacquaint myself with these treasured friends of my youth."

My uncle nods submissively to the order, keeping his true thoughts to himself.

"Once my visit has been completed, I will then return home and invite all three kings to come to me in the north to pay tribute to their queen. Then, and only then, will I decide which king will be my betrothed. This kingdom's strife will end in celebration of my upcoming nuptials and this kingdom will be unified once again."

I stand up from my throne and leave the parting remark that will set the wheels of retribution in action.

"May the best king win my heart."

For my kingdom will never be theirs.

Chapter 3
Levi

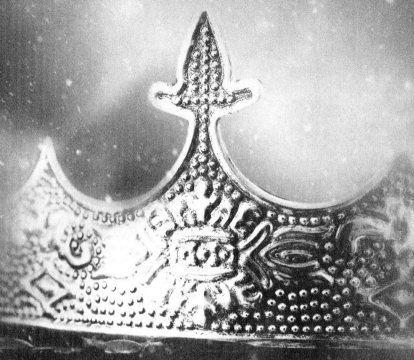

"Clever, clever girl." I smirk after I've reread the royal letter in my hands for the fifth time tonight.

Once I've established that I'm not going to get any more out of it, I throw the wretched piece of paper on my table.

"I don't get it," my general and best friend, Brick, mumbles aggravatedly, picking up the scroll and reading the same words out loud, thinking the sound of his voice will help him decipher its true meaning. "We're right at her doorstep, and instead of locking the bolts to her front door, she's willingly leaving it wide open for us… to propose marriage? The fuck is that about?"

I pour some wine into my goblet and fall to my seat, cracking my neck before taking a sip.

"Levi, will you explain this shit to me, please?" he belts out, frustrated with my silence, slamming the decree back on the table. "Am I getting your soldiers ready to march farther north or am I telling them that we're turning back home because you have to get your dick wet with royal pussy?"

"Brick." I scowl menacingly, not liking the way he's talking about Kat.

We might be on the verge of war, but she's still my queen.

She's still my Kat, even if she's forgotten.

"Fine. I'll hold my tongue against her royal pain in the ass. But can you just tell me what our next move is here? Huh? Because this wedding bullshit is sounding like a trap to me."

"That's because it is," I deadpan before taking another sip of my cherry wine.

"Fuck. I knew it," he grumbles despondently.

"Did you expect the contrary? She had to retaliate somehow." I chuckle. "Although, I have to hand it to her. I never saw this move coming. And I see everything." I grin, running the pad of my finger over the rim of my wine glass.

"This is not the time for games or riddles, Levi. The men won't be happy to wage war on the north if they think you can get the crown without their lives being forfeited," Brick states evenly, going right to the root of my problem.

"Ah," I exclaim, touching the tip of my nose with my finger to point out to my confused friend that he just hit the nail on the head with his statement. "That's exactly why her conniving plan is so clever. Don't you see? That reaction right there is exactly what she's counting on."

"I don't get it," he mutters, his bushy auburn eyebrows pulling together at the center of his forehead, demonstrating how these royal games fly straight over his head.

I stand up from my chair and walk toward him, picking up the jug of wine and an extra goblet on the way. I pour him a glass and hand it to him to drink.

"Will getting me drunk make it easier for me to understand what the fuck is happening?"

"It might." I chuckle, reaching for the scroll and smoothing it out on the table in front of us.

"Read the decree again."

He does as I order and when he finishes, he offers a perplexed shrug, still unable to connect the dots on his own. I sling my arm over his shoulder, and stare at Katrina's blue rose sigil at the bottom of the decree.

"She is offering marriage, yes, but that is all. I'd be her husband in name only, but never the true king of the north, therefore never king to the Kingdom of Aikyam."

"Okay," he mutters, still confused.

"But to Aikyam, that piece of information doesn't matter. The people would still hail us both as king and queen, regardless of the fact that I hold no real power. They would assume I'd have it, and that assumption is all that really matters," I explain, shedding some light to this fucked up situation Kat has put me in. "It's just like you said. Why would my men willingly sacrifice their lives for me to win the north when all I have to do is marry its queen to conquer it? If I fail in winning the throne this way, that failure is on my shoulders, and mine alone. No one in the east would back my claim to the throne after such a debacle since I had unwillingly proven that I am not worthy of it. Don't you see? She checkmated me in two moves."

"Two?" Brick questions, still looking like his head is going to explode with all this information.

"Yes, Brick. Two. Or did you miss the part where I'm not the only one she sent this letter to?" I explain, ripping the goblet from his hand so I can drown myself with another glass of wine.

Well played, Kat.

Well fucking played.

"Shit. Teo," he grunts the name like it's a curse, finally understanding the shitstorm she's put me in.

"Yes, Teo," I repeat, pouring myself another glass. "He's going to do everything in his power to win her over, just to show me that he can. It won't be hard for him. The gods have blessed him with looks and charm, and most women flock to him without him even trying. The Winter Queen won't be an exception."

Memories of a laughing Kat running through the snow, her pale blonde hair flowing in the wind as she chased after Teo around her castle, assaults me.

Yes.

Teo always did know which strings to pull to get his way. And now Katrina has just dangled her crown in his face. There's no way he won't rise to the challenge.

"But wait, wait," Brick interjects, trying to piece together the clues to the puzzle. "Even if Teo wins, won't that mean he's just as powerless as you would have been as king of the north?"

"Don't underestimate Teodoro. He'd find a way to eventually take the crown from Katrina. Even if he had to smother her in her sleep after she's given him a few heirs. Although, I don't think it would come to that. Teo has always had a weak spot for Kat. He'd find a way to manipulate her to get what he wants without drawing blood."

Brick stares at me, and I hate that I see a small flicker of admiration for the lengths Teo would go to ensure his seat on the northern throne. I turn my back to him, not wanting to see such respect for my sworn enemy in my best friend's eyes. Especially after all he's done to me and my kingdom. To my family.

I'm nothing like Teo.

I don't cheat or steal.

I don't conspire or manipulate.

Yes, I'll draw first blood on the battlefield, but that is it. I have my honor. In war, everything goes, but that is as far as I'll take it. Teo, on the other hand, has no honor. A lesson I learned well when we were both still teenagers, and one I will never forget—or forgive.

Unable to remain in my tent where Teo's name has been uttered, I walk outside, the brisk night air hitting my stubbled face and cooling my temper somewhat. Days spent in the arctic north are harsh, but they fail to compare to how vicious the nights can be. The cold sinks into my men's bones in such a way that it makes it hard for them to find any warmth in the campsite, making rest or even logical thought almost an impossibility.

The last time I traveled up these roads, I was barely a man, so was there any wonder I had forgotten how cruel the ice and snow could become? But then again, why would I remember such things when at the time, all my thoughts were of *her*.

Just picturing Katrina's face kept my blood fully heated, my heart filled with a fire… fire that yearned for only her.

But those feelings no longer consume me.

Her father made sure of it.

"Levi," Brick calls out, walking out of the tent to stand shoulder to shoulder with me. "What about Atlas? Do you think—"

"Atlas will remain loyal to me," I interrupt before Brick suggests the contrary. "He's lost as much as I have, if not more. He'll remain true to me and only me."

Brick hangs his head down low, sensing my mood has turned as black as the night sky. But before he decides to leave me to my melancholy, I order him to fetch me my fastest rider, needing to take some form of action. Within five minutes, both men stand in front of me, waiting for my instruction.

"I want you to ride north to our queen and tell her that I will personally escort her to my castle in Arkøya. Tell her that my men will travel east before daybreak, save for a few who will travel with me to ensure the safety of Her Majesty and entourage."

"Anything else, my liege?" the squire asks, eager to have something to do instead of spending another cold night at camp.

"Yes. Tell our queen that I look forward to winning her heart."

And her throne.

North meets East

"I don't want you to go," Elijah weeps on my shoulder, hugging my neck so fiercely that my cold heart begins to splinter in two for him.

"I'll be back before you know it. You won't even miss me," I try to console with a smile.

"Not true," he continues to sob, pulling away from me just far enough so he can wipe his tears.

"It will only be four or five months. I'll be home before you know it," I coo softly, helping him dry his chubby cheeks with the sleeve of my white coat.

"People will be mean to me. They always are when you're not around. Five months will feel like an eternity," he continues to sob.

Rage starts bubbling inside me, as I tilt his chin gently up to gaze at his crestfallen face.

"Which people? Who has been mean to you?" I question, hiding my fury as not to scare him.

He shrugs, biting his quivering bottom lip, and lowering his eyes away from mine just so he doesn't have to give me a name.

Knowing that I would need a lot more time to pry the names of whoever is tormenting my brother—time that I currently don't have—I let him go and stand up straight, while reaching for his hands to hold on to for a little while longer.

"Look at me, Elijah. You are my brother—the queen's *only* brother. If anyone so much as looks at you the wrong way, they will have me to deal with. And everyone knows that forgiveness is not in my nature. Do you understand?" I coldly explain, loud enough for everyone in this court to hear and take the hint that my brother is not to be messed with in my absence or suffer the consequences.

He gives me a shaky nod and then lunges at me again, hugging my waist, his head pressed against my stomach.

"I'm going to miss you," he sobs inconsolably.

"I am too, sweet boy. So much," I whisper for his ears only.

I hug him to me one more time before bending down to kiss the top of his sweet little head.

"Enough of that, Elijah. You'll make the queen late for her travels east," Salome interrupts hurriedly, pulling her son away from my arms and hugging him to her side to keep him in place.

"I wish I could take him," I mumble, staring down at my baby brother, needing to take a mental portrait of him to store safely inside my heart.

"He's too young to be traveling the world, Your Highness. Maybe one day you can take him on an adventure, but not today," Salome retorts, her own eyes starting to water, yet having the fortitude to keep her tone even.

It's the formal way with how she addresses me that reminds me that our teary farewell is being witnessed by most of the high lords in the courtyard. With that reminder, I square my shoulders and hold my head up high, conforming to the arctic behavior that is expected of me.

"Yes, one day. Take care of yourself as well as my brother, Salome."

On cue, she curtsies in front of me, and I hate how I can't hug her goodbye like I want to. It's one thing for me to be affectionate with my brother, it's a whole other matter showing that same affection to a woman who is hired to tend to the castle's gardens. Doing that would make me look weak, and most of my court already believes that I am just based on my gender. No need to give them more ammo to use against me.

Still, it pains me that I have to hide my feelings just for their merit. A king can bed his entire staff, and no one will think less of him, but if a queen even dares to befriend a servant, she's viewed as overly emotional and soft. The double standard is infuriating.

Not wanting for us to part in such a cold way, I hold out my hand for Salome to kiss. When she does, I discreetly squeeze her hand in mine, my own non-verbal way of telling her how much I will miss her company.

My chest tightens when I feel a tear escape Salome and land on my knuckles, but thankfully, when she stands back up, her schooled expression is as serene as ever. She then takes two steps back with Elijah, letting the other lords take center stage, as is their right.

"Is there no way I can change your mind?" my uncle Adelid asks, still not on board with my plan. "This all seems… dangerous to me."

"Don't be such a worrywart, Adelid. I picked Her Majesty's bodyguards personally. They are my best men and will ensure that our queen returns to us safe and sound," Monad interjects, patting my uncle's back, looking proud that he's able to ensure my safety.

"Well, they better, or it will be your head, as well as theirs," Uncle Adelid asserts menacingly, but Monad just shrugs his threat away with a chuckle.

"Safe travels, Your Highness. May the gods look after you," Monad says, all smiles.

"Yes, safe travels, niece. I will count the days for your safe return," my uncle adds, less cheerful.

It's only when both men pay their respects to me by curtseying and bowing their heads that I notice not everyone in my court came out to bid me farewell this morning. Otto's absence in the large crowd immediately raises concern.

"Still no word from King Atlas?" I ask, knowing the rebellious young king must be the reason why my treasurer is locked away in his chambers, crunching numbers, praying that somehow, he can magically come up with enough funds to pay our debts as well as restore our previous contracts.

I bite into my inner cheek when Adelid begins to shake his head in response.

"No word has arrived from the west yet, I'm afraid."

My fists clench at Atlas's stubbornness.

Long gone is the boy who would say yes to anything I asked of him.

"Very well. Send word to me the minute he does," is my clipped reply.

"I'm sure the king of the west will come to his senses soon enough. Gods be good that at least King Teodoro has sent us enough food to last the winter," Monad chimes in, rubbing his pot belly, no longer looking grief-stricken that he won't go off to war on my behalf. "I had the pleasure to check his crates myself and can tell you that he's been very generous. He even sent us strawberries, my liege. Strawberries! I haven't eaten strawberries since I was Your Majesty's age," he adds, licking his lips like he can already taste the sweet fruit in his mouth.

A smile tugs at the corner of my lips with the way my chief of arms' eyes sparkle in glee. If I knew strawberries would make Monad so docile, I would have begged Teo to send them to me years ago.

But queens do not beg.

They rule.

It's time these kings remembered that.

With firm resolve, I end my goodbyes and step into my carriage, anxious to meet the first antagonizing king on my list. By my count, my entourage and I should be over the northern mountains and reach King Levi's camp by the week's end.

I must admit that I was pleasantly surprised that he ordered his troops to return east, but a little ticked off that he didn't go with them. No matter what my council believes, Levi staying back in his campsite just to escort me to his castle himself is anything but chivalrous.

It's a strategic power move.

I can just picture it now. Levi entering his city's gates on horseback, looking majestically draped in his armor, with me trailing behind him in my carriage. He'll make a grand spectacle of it, of that, I'm sure. It will be enough to show his people that even though he didn't go to war, he still won his prize.

He always was smart.

Smarter than Teo, Atlas, and I combined, back in the day. Always picking up on our weaknesses before we ever could. A fact I need to keep in mind and be wary of when I meet him.

Thankfully, I'm no longer that young impressionable girl who was blinded by his mere presence.

Or by his smile.

In the last six months as queen, I've learned that for men to take me seriously, I have to remind them that my father's blood courses through my veins. If Levi wants a show of strength, then I'll give it to him.

Just so happens, I have the perfect performance in mind.

"Your Highness, we should be arriving at the camp within the next ten minutes," one of my riders advises me through the small window of the carriage's doors.

"Thank you. Please ride ahead and alert King Levi to my arrival," I retort, giving him consent to drive off before closing the royal blue-rose printed curtain.

My bones and muscles ache from the ten-hour ride down the last mountain. All I yearn for is a warm bath and a good night's sleep, but unfortunately for me, I still have Levi to deal with tonight.

I bet this was his plan all along.

I'll arrive looking disheveled and worn out from the past seven-day expedition, while he'll look fresh as a daisy.

Any other day I would laugh at the comparison of Levi to such a flower, but my sore body would no doubt protest at the endeavor.

I should have thought this through.

Maybe even have ordered my men to make camp on the mountain overnight and then ride down to Levi's camp in the morning. But deep down I knew that wouldn't have been a wise alternative. The weather up in the mountains has been brutally inconstant. Our winter winds and blizzards don't intimidate me much, but avalanches, on the other hand, are true cause for concern. I couldn't put my neck—as well as the brave men and women accompanying me—on the line for another night, just so I could look well rested for Levi's sake.

No matter.

If this is how I'll meet the treacherous king after seven years of not laying eyes on him, then so be it.

A few minutes pass before the first signs of a campsite come into view through the small crack of my curtain. Even though Levi's soldiers have left my border, there are still traces of their previous stay all around the large forest. Thousands of unlit fires, soot, and ash coloring the white snow on the ground.

Gods.

We would have been outnumbered ten to one.

A cold sweat drips down my spine as I see with my very eyes how close Levi was to dethroning me. With an army of that size at his beck and call, he would have been able to conquer my castle with the bat of an eye. I knew my kingdom was in danger, but I never realized how close to the precipice of losing everything I hold dear I truly was.

Why, Levi?

Why are you so eager to rob me of my birthright?

I thought you were a better man than that.

There was a time I actually considered you to be the best man there was in the whole of the Aikyam kingdom.

So why, old friend, have you turned into my enemy?

If my heart was not as cold as the northern ground he has maliciously stepped on, I would have taken his offense personally. But this has nothing to do with me and everything to do with power. A power that I intend to keep.

When large lit tents come into full view, I close my curtain again, not wishing Levi to think me curious to see him after so many years. He's proven beyond a shadow of a doubt that it's my crown he wishes to set his eyes on—not me.

When my carriage finally comes to a stop, I shut my eyelids and send off a quick prayer to the gods.

Be with me, oh heavenly ones.

Let the cold northern wind seep through my bones and offer me courage.

Let the snow at my feet crunch loudly, a preview of the enemies' skulls I can crush with my heel.

For I am the Winter Queen.

And no winds from the east, south or west could ever defeat me.

I then open my eyes, feeling suddenly refreshed and reborn, ready to meet the first king who has dared to defy me. Levi might have come at me with soldier steel, but I have the gods' true justice in my corner.

It's time he was properly introduced to it.

Chapter 5
Levi

A nxiously, I pace back and forth in my tent, waiting impatiently for Brick to return and announce Katrina's arrival. A formality, since I heard her train of men and horses' gallops into camp over an hour ago, my heart thumping in tandem with the crunching sound of horseshoes digging into the snow.

But it's not the fifty odd soldiers she brought with her that has me so anxious.

My frown deepens as I realize that even after all that has transpired, this whisper of a girl still makes my heart leap into my throat with nerves. My back molars grind at my weakened state as I try to focus on all the damage her family has done to mine to strengthen my resolve.

This reunion should not elate me.

It should anger me.

With one stroke of the pen, she foiled my well-laid-out plans with her prosperous game of a marriage proposal. I could have stolen her crown in the dead of night with my troops, and yet with one single, two-paragraph letter, she was able to outmaneuver me.

Like she premeditated, the minute my men heard the rumor that I could win the north without any of them drawing up their swords, their hardened spirits softened, looking to me to spare their lives as well as redeem my kingdom's pride. Thoughts of waging war on the north were quickly tempered to the ground, thinking their king would achieve what I had promised them just by wooing a simple girl.

But Kat was never simple.

She was always a conundrum to me.

One that I thought with time, I could decipher and maybe… just maybe… make mine.

But those foolish ideas were dreamt up by a young boy whose soft heart sought only her attention. Half a decade has passed since that boy has even existed. Her father made sure to plunge a sword through his bleeding heart and kill him for good. Katrina should count her blessings that I'm not as ruthless. If I were, the minute she stepped into my camp, I would have ordered the remaining soldiers I have on hand to butcher hers on the spot. Her pretty little neck I'd slit myself.

I still might.

"Levi, I did what you asked," Brick states after finally popping his head into my tent. "I told the ice queen you wanted a word with her after she got settled in. But she says there's no need for further delay and wishes to see you now."

"Is that so?" I counter, grabbing a pitcher of wine to fill my goblet, having no intention of jumping to her command.

When all Brick does is nod as he steps beside me, I realize that my general looks somewhat ashen, a far cry from his usual impetuous disposition.

"Has she gotten under your skin already, old friend?" I taunt, wondering why he looks like he'd rather we flee than have me meet our so-called queen.

"Fuck you. Give me one of those." He points to the jug of wine.

Smirking, I pour him a glass and hand it to him.

"Then why the long face?" I ask him, genuinely intrigued as to why my best friend looks like he just saw a ghost.

"It's the only one I got, okay?" he retorts, drinking the goblet in one quick swig, then cleaning the droplets of the cherry wine on his red beard with his sleeve. "I just got a bad feeling, that's all."

"You always have a bad feeling," I taunt, while refreshing his glass.

But my light teasing only seems to trouble him further. He slams his glass on the table, and abruptly steals mine out of my hands before I can taste another drop.

"You're going to need a clear head for this shit, Levi. I don't want you to meet *her* with your head all fuzzy with booze."

My brow arches in increased curiosity.

"Has our dear queen put the fear of the gods in you already, Brick? I'd have thought you were made of stronger steel than that."

"Yeah, well, let's see how well you'll fare," he snarls with a snide grimace.

I chuckle, watching him wipe the cold sweat off his brow.

"She's a child. What could she have possibly done to you in the five minutes you were with her to cause you to act this way?"

"That *woman* out there," he points to the tent's flaps, "is no child. I don't know what type of relationship you had with her when you were a boy, but the woman I just met isn't her. I swear I saw my own death in her eyes as clearly as I'm seeing you right now," he explains with such earnestness, I almost believe that he's serious. "Levi…" he starts worriedly, running his fingers through his auburn hair. "I think we've made a huge mistake. We should have attacked her when we had the chance. Now I'm not sure if any of us are going to come out of this with our necks intact."

My hackles instantly rise at his reaction to meeting Katrina.

Brick is many things, but he's never been a coward. His fear is real, which means that I must be extra cautious.

I should have known.

Here I was, whimsically recalling our tender shared youth, when I should have been strategizing on how best to defeat Kat at her own game. The decree she sent should have been my first clue that the girl I once adored above all, no longer exists. She's gone. And in her place, only Orville's daughter remains.

"Stay here," I snap at my best friend. "You're no use to me tonight."

"Nope." He shakes his head furiously. "No way in hell am I letting you meet her on your own."

I flash him my gritted teeth, my eyes piercing him to the spot.

"Do you have so little faith in your king, soldier?"

The look of shame immediately accosts him, his head hanging down low.

"No, Your Highness, of course not. You are my king. If there is anyone that can conquer that winter witch, it is you. Of that, I'm certain," he retorts evenly, steel back in his voice.

My teeth grate further at his description of Kat, but I don't reprimand him for it. Instead, I turn my back to my closest confidant and walk toward my tent's entrance.

"Where is she now?" I demand.

"I had your men usher her to her tent, Your Majesty."

"Good. This won't take long," I tell him and step outside, the cold wind that strikes my stubbled cheeks the cruel reminder that I'm on her turf and not my own.

That will change, though.

I'll let her rest for the night, but at the crack of dawn, we will ride to Arkøya.

As soon as her feet land on eastern soil, I doubt she'll feel so empowered to strike fear in my men so easily. Let her see with her own eyes all the green meadows and valleys that compile my kingdom, completely untouched by snow and hail. Let's see how strong she is without her high mountains to protect her or her harsh winds to freeze us to the spot.

No.

Katrina will be utterly defenseless in the east, unable to pull strength from her winter elements. Let the melody of spring wrap itself around her frigid heart in a vise grip and smother it once and for all.

With restored determination to meet the ghost of winter past, I walk through camp in the direction to her tent. When I finally reach her door, I grin menacingly at the four guards standing post outside, their fresh faces telling me that they have never witnessed the horrors of battle for even a day.

Not that it surprises me.

For as long as he was alive, King Orville preferred to sacrifice *my* countrymen and call them to arms whenever there was a war to wage. It was only after his so-called reckoning seven years ago, that he kept his own battalions guarding his fortress up north, preferring to solely let my men bleed for his greed.

That was his first mistake.

For men who have never witnessed their compatriots die in front of their very eyes or felt the heat of a sword slice into their skin are not soldiers—just very ineffective bodyguards. A weakness that I am all too happy to exploit.

Take these men before me, for example. I could snap their necks as easily as I could break a twig in half before they even realized what was happening. But to start Katrina's visit with me killing her men sets a bad precedent.

I'll have plenty of time for that afterward.

"Tell your queen that I'm here for an audience with her," I state as amicably as possible, while inside I cringe at the fake pleasantry.

If I had it my way, I wouldn't even have bothered to tell them to step aside and would have just marched right on in. But if I'm to play the role Katrina has cast me with—of her potential suitor instead of her rival—then best keep up the facade for as long as I can stomach it. Something tells me I'll grow tired with the pretense before I reach my home soil, though.

One soldier heeds to my order and rushes to alert his queen of my presence, while the other three try to look imposing by staring me down. My jaw tics in aggravation at their blatant disrespect, but I don't raise a hand against them. I'm here for their queen. She's the only one I truly want to see on her knees.

"Her Highness is ready for you," the soldier says upon his return.

I give him a curt nod and strut right on in, holding in my smirk when I see that in little over an hour, Kat has taken all the liberties she could to make her tent fit for a queen, apparently not content with the humble accommodations I left her. White bearskin rugs are all strategically placed around the floor, accompanied by a vast display of candles, white veils and pillows adorning the tent with a large bed at its center, already made for her royal head to sleep on. Unlike outside, this winter wonderland is warm and inviting.

But none of it holds a candle to the silhouette staring at the open flames of a fire pit in the corner of the tent. Katrina's back remains to me as I take in her feminine features. Diamonds, reminiscent of frozen teardrops, are embedded in her long pale braid. It hangs down low, pointing to the small of her back, making the jeweled lace slash that hugs her slender hips that much more prominent. As I take one step closer, I realize that she's taller than I remembered her to be, looking all grown up in a snowy white dress.

She's winter incarnate.

"Kat," I call out, needing her to turn around and face me, so that I may see if there are any other changes to her that I've missed.

But when she does, my heart stops, freezing in my chest.

Cold, dead gray eyes pierce me to the spot.

"There is no one here by that name, Levi. You will address me as your queen, for that is who I am to you. Nothing more. On your knees."

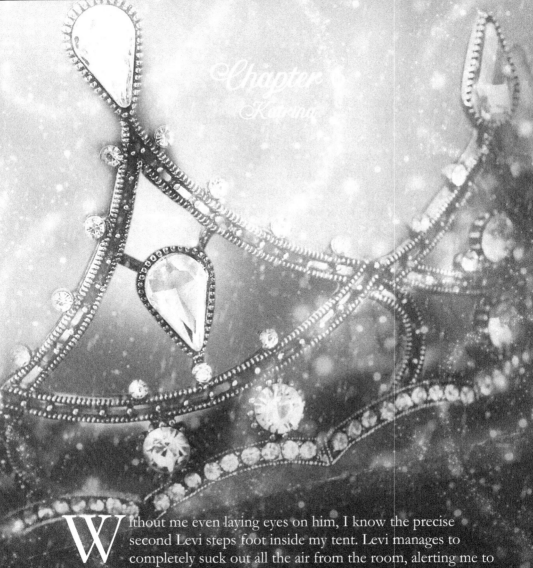

W ithout me even laying eyes on him, I know the precise second Levi steps foot inside my tent. Levi manages to completely suck out all the air from the room, alerting me to the danger I'm in, in more ways than one.

The small hairs on the nape of my neck stand on end as I feel the weight of his stare on my back. My heart jackhammers in my chest as I hear his footsteps slowly approach me from behind. I steady myself to remain remotely still, not wanting to turn around until I'm absolutely certain I have my wits about me.

I need this first meeting between us to go off well, to make it clear in his mind of who exactly is in charge here. But that small girl that once believed this man—this stranger to me now—could do no wrong, has suddenly resurfaced, eager to reunite with her long-lost friend.

But then he calls me by the one name he shouldn't, ruining all those misguided notions.

Kat.

How could he call me by that name?

A name that, once upon a time, was spoken with tenderness and loyal friendship. A name that is still tied to my most joyous childhood memories, which he made sure to tarnish with his betrayal.

How dare he even utter such a lie?

For that is exactly what that name signifies to me now—a beautiful lie once uttered by my would-be usurper.

Just his audacity in using such a nickname brings up all the animosity I have for him. It reminds me that if it weren't for this so-called king of the east, I wouldn't have felt the need to leave the security of my castle to fight for what is entitled to me by birth.

Resentment and loathing fuel all my senses, successfully erasing my nervous state, coaxing me to turn around to face this wretched king at last.

"There is no one here by that name, Levi. You will address me as your queen, for that is who I am to you. Nothing more. On your knees."

Emerald eyes stare back at me, and for a brief second, I almost make myself believe that I see a flash of hurt and longing in their wondrous green meadows. My heart squeezes in my chest as I chastise it for being so naïve in having such a ludicrous thought. And even though I manage to straighten my spine when Levi dutifully lowers his head and takes a knee before me, the vise grip around my heart tightens, making it almost impossible to breathe.

"My queen," he offers, his tone now as cold as the chilled wind blowing outside.

I take a moment to look him over now that his gaze is fixed to the floor. My hands clench into fists with the sudden need to run my fingers through the various black-ink braids on his head. His shoulders are even broader than I remember them to be, two square boulders on an imposing frame.

Even in his submission, he's magnificent.

As magnificent as any weapon forged from steel could be. A weapon that just a few days ago intended to strip me of everything I hold dear.

After the thumping of my loud heartbeat simmers, I take a step back and order him to rise.

"Stand, Levi. What use is it for you to kneel to me when there is no one around to see you do it?" I order, not making any efforts to hide the bitterness in my tone.

60

Levi stands back up straight, and within an instant, I curse myself for the mistake I've unintentionally just committed. I should have kept him on his knees a while longer for my own benefit.

With Levi towering over me now, it takes all of my will power to keep my expression as even keel as his. Because like this, there is no question of who amongst us two is the more intimidating. Even the simple task of looking him dead in the eye, requires me to crane my head back, ensuring I accommodate him and not the other way around.

I don't like it.

And by the glimmer in his jeweled eyes, he not only knows how displeased I am, but is also taking great satisfaction in my aggravation.

"You've grown since we last spoke," he states plainly, with no emotion whatsoever in his voice.

"Most children do. Or would you have preferred I had stayed a child? Gods know it would have made things simpler for you," I reply stoically, mimicking his tone.

And although my neck is starting to hurt keeping eye contact with him, my glower never wavers from his.

"Easier, yes. But not very gratifying," he rebukes with a sardonic grin.

Is he joking?

The gall of him!

"I see the years have treated you kindly, Levi. I don't remember you having a funny bone in your body when we were kids," I retort with the fakest of smiles.

"Are you saying I didn't have a personality?" He arches a brow.

"Not one that was amusing."

When his nostrils flare, my smile turns genuine.

"Well, then. I guess we've both changed. I don't remember you being this cold or contentious either."

My mocking smile immediately falls from my face.

"What did you just say to me?" I seethe, stepping closer to him. "Remember your place, Levi. I am your queen, not some wench you've met in a tavern."

"Believe me, I am well aware of who you are. And don't be so dismissive of tavern wenches. The ones I've met have given me warmer greetings than the one you gave just now."

I'm going to kill this man.

We continue to stare daggers into each other, the air between us tense and suffocating. His eyes scan my face, hatred bleeding from him, but when his gaze falls to my lips, the air around us shifts into something different… something electric.

My heart starts beating a mile a minute, my hands inexplicably clammy. And when he lets out a ragged exhale, his warm breath fans my face, leaving the scent of cherry wine to envelop me in its hold and successfully hazing my thoughts.

"You're drunk," I state as evenly as I can, considering every nerve ending in my body has suddenly sparked awake with life.

"Hardly," he replies with a standoffish smirk.

Damn the gods.

He's always had a beautiful smile, even when he meant it to be fierce.

I remember how as a little girl, I would do the most absurd things just to coax out one of his rare genuine smiles. Each time I managed to get one from him, it made me feel like I had won the most precious thing the east had to offer—its prince's adoration.

And just when the air couldn't get more tense, Levi bridges the small gap between us, until our chests are mere inches apart. He's not even touching me in any way, yet I can feel the heat coming off his body in long, sluggish waves, intent on melting my glacial walls.

"Maybe you're the one who needs a drink. I've found that wine can do wonders to heat up even the coldest of creatures," he taunts brazenly.

"Remember your place, Levi. I won't remind you again."

"And what place is that, my queen? On my knees or right here where I'm standing?" He smirks, knowing full well his intimate proximity is unnerving me.

"Very well. I see that tonight we aren't going to see eye to eye," I state, feeling annoyed. "Maybe we should postpone this meeting until you're feeling more like yourself."

"I'm good."

"Well, I'm not," I reply curtly.

"I really couldn't care less," he deadpans.

Fury returns to me at how antagonizing he's being.

Of course, I never assumed that Levi would welcome me with open arms, but I didn't expect such hostility either. With the promise of marriage to his queen, a smart man would have played his part dutifully right from the get-go. Made sure to show me all his esteemed attributes and maybe even shower me with praise and embellished flattery during our first encounter.

I played out this scenario a million times in my head and none of them resembled anything close to what's happening now.

His aggressiveness is taking me off guard.

I'm not sure what to make of this first interaction between us.

He's just so… infuriating.

Even more so when he refuses to give me back my space. Having his large frame tower over me this way, makes me feel small. Delicate. Fragile.

Everything that I'm not.

Seeing that he's not going to move, I break our staring match and turn away from him, rushing to a nearby table where a pitcher of ice water rests. I take my time filling up the glass with the cool liquid, coming up with a different strategy to defuse this perilous situation before turning to face him once more.

"I have to say, I'm a little disappointed."

"Is that so? And just how did I disappoint you, *my queen*?" he asks, this time, adding a bitter emphasis on my title.

I don't have time to reprimand him for it since I'm too consumed watching him walk over to a nearby cushion to sit down. His large body occupies most of it, his arms stretching over the white fur, dominating the room with his very presence.

It's the oddest thing I've ever seen.

Dressed in all-black gear, he should look out of place amongst my things, and yet he somehow manages to make it his own. Owning each and every thing in here with just his very being.

This is a king.

A king who is used to holding everyone's attention. Ruling and dominating everything in his sight.

However, if he's under the illusion that he can dominate me as easily, he has another thing coming to him.

I lean against the table, running the tip of my finger over the rim of the glass.

"I was half expecting to be wooed. Isn't that what men do to women they want to marry?"

"Who says I want to marry you?" he retorts with a smug grin, making my cheeks heat up in anger.

"If that's the case, then maybe I should travel south to Teodoro in the morning, seeing as you're not interested."

This time it's Levi's arrogant grin that is swiped off his face.

Good.

I struck a nerve.

"Well? Am I wasting my time here? Should I head south and not east as I had planned?" I bait him further.

"You're coming home with me, Kat. That much I can promise you," he replies, stone-faced.

I don't scold him for using my childhood nickname this time, too proud of myself for finding a chink in his armor this soon in the game.

"I need more than promises from you, Levi. I need to know that you are worth my time."

His formidable square jaw tics, his leg bouncing up and down in annoyance.

"Well, Levi? Are you worth my time? Because I'm pretty sure there are other kings who are."

When he springs to his feet, and quickly strides over at me like a predator who has had enough of toying with his prey, my whole body tenses. I place the glass of water back on the table, squaring my shoulders to look just as menacing as he does. My jaw slacks when he has the nerve to grab my chin and pull my face up toward him.

"I'm not going to play this game with you. I know what you're doing and I'm not going to be another pawn in this twisted game you've got going."

"I have no idea what you're talking about."

"Yes, you do. That stupid decree you sent out had only one purpose and it had nothing to do with you trying to find a husband. You want to pit us against each other, but I'm telling you now, your plan isn't going to work. I couldn't give two fucks about Teo or any other king for that matter. Remember, Kat, I could have stolen your throne right from under your nose if I so wished. Me playing along is a courtesy I'm giving you. Consider it my way of honoring the friendship I had for the sweet girl I grew up with. The one I see no longer exists in you."

I slap his hand away from me and dig my finger into his chest.

"I could have you killed for touching me."

His head falls back in a cruel cackle.

"If I'm to be your king, I'll do much more than touch you, Kat."

My cheeks flush crimson at his crudeness.

He wasn't always like this.

The honorable, kind Levi of the past would never speak to me this way.

"What happened to you?" The words are out of my mouth before I can pull them back in.

"I could ask you the same thing," he retorts with sudden sadness in his voice.

I stand still for an agonizing moment, letting his eyes scrutinize my every feature. He then lowers his gaze away from me and takes a healthy step back.

"Rest, Your Highness. It's a long ride east. We leave at dawn."

And with that, he turns his back to me and leaves.

I'm still reeling when my favorite handmaidens, Anya and Inessa, who I had chosen to accompany me on this trip, appear inside my tent.

"Your Highness?" Inessa questions carefully, seeing that I'm not quite myself. "Are you well?"

"I'm not sure. Ask me again in the morning," I reply half-heartedly, still shaken with the whirlwind meeting I just had.

Inessa doesn't press me for more, rushing over to my bed to take down the covers for me.

Anya, though, isn't as subtle.

Once she's managed to walk me to the vanity and sit me down to help me with my hair, she mischievously smiles into the mirror's reflection.

"These men from the east are not what we are used to, are they, Your Highness?"

"No. I'm afraid not."

She nods, pulling the diamonds carefully out of my hair.

"But I guess that's a good thing. Makes things more interesting."

"Hmm," I mumble.

"I mean… they're all so savagely rugged. Handsome, too. And King Levi… well… I can see why he's their king. I doubt the east has a finer specimen of a man."

"Anya," Inessa immediately chides her friend for speaking her mind so freely with me.

"It's true," she quips back unashamedly. "King Levi may look hard and savagely crude, but he's also easy on the eyes. Don't you agree, Your Highness?"

I bite into my cheek as my handmaiden leans into my ear and whispers.

"He's the kind of man that makes a woman wonder if everything about him is that hard."

"I'm not interested in any of that. It's not what I need. What I need is obedience," I retort with a sharp bite.

Anya's expression turns pale as she pulls away, sealing her lips shut, too afraid I might cut out her tongue if she says another word.

I should feel guilty for snapping at her like that, but I don't. I don't want any of my handmaidens talking about Levi in such a way.

You're coming home with me, Kat.

I'm not sure if I should take his words as a threat or not.

They didn't feel like a threat.

They felt like something else. Almost as if there was an underlying promise tied to them. One I can't quite decipher yet.

I guess I'll learn it soon enough since, as of tomorrow, my future lies eastbound.

What happens after, only the gods know.

Chapter 7
Levi

The rumors were true.

Her heart has turned to stone.

I didn't want to believe it, but now that I've seen Katrina in the flesh, there is no questioning the veins that once bled crimson, have turned to ice.

What happened to her?

She had been such a bubbly child, always smiling and laughing at those around her.

And then from the sidelines I had watched how in her teen years she had turned curious in nature, wanting to experience life, in all its forms. It had been intoxicating to watch her discover the world on her own. How she sucked the marrow of it with such passion and vivacity.

But now?

Now she's this cold statue of a thing. Beautiful to uphold but dead on the inside.

When news of King Orville's death arrived in the east, my people ran to the streets to rejoice and cheer his demise. I wasn't as eager to join the celebration. Instead, I stayed in solitude in my castle, troubled that with the news of his death, another accompanied it.

Katrina had been crowned queen mere hours after his passing, and no one in her court so much as saw a single tear being shed for her late father.

Not that I would have wept for the bastard, but all the memories I treasured of his daughter told me she worshiped the ground he walked on. She admired him as much as she loved him, and I couldn't fathom what could have possibly happened for his death not to wring one single tear from her eye.

I told myself that she must have mourned him behind closed doors, not wanting to look weak to her court. But now that I've been in the same room with her, I'm not sure grief is even an emotion she is familiar with. In fact, she appeared as if wearing her father's crown on her head wasn't a burden at all. That it was always hers to claim.

The fuck happened to you, Kat?

Did he ruin you as much as he ruined me and everyone I loved?

What?

Maybe it's best that I don't have these answers.

That I remain clueless of it all.

For if I'm to strip Kat of her power, then what good will it do me if I gain a sliver of sympathy for her?

I know for a fact that Teo won't think twice about her feelings when he takes her throne. And if I'm to get my due on those who wronged me, I need to concentrate on the long game of it all.

Fuck.

I really do need to get my shit together.

Even if that means I must pretend that the girl who once had bewitched me, body and soul, never existed.

Maybe I won't be pretending at all.

Because the person I met last night has no similarities to my childhood love.

None.

Not even those light gray eyes that had always reminded me of pale moonlight hold the same light to them.

There had been a flicker.

When I pressed up against her.

There had been a flicker of life in them then.

"We're ready," Brick calls out, pulling me out of my pensive thoughts.

"Good," I retort gruffly, clearing my throat while putting on my winter coat. "Let's go home. I'm done with the snow."

"You're telling me," he says, rubbing his hands together before blowing hot air onto them. "I've been dreaming of the hot springs for days on end. Can't wait to be back to wash this place off me and bring some much-needed heat to my bones."

"You do know that if all goes well, we'll have to return to the north in a few months. I might even have to live there for the first few years of my marriage."

His eyes light up at the remark.

"So does that mean last night's meeting with the ice queen went well? Is she already aching for your cock?" he teases, but the ill-tempered joke only makes me scowl.

"The meeting went well enough."

It didn't.

It was a fucking fiasco.

Not that I'll ever admit it to Brick.

He might be my closest confidant but give the man a few jugs of ale, and he'll be dishing out my business to anyone with a pair of ears. My men need to think that I have this marriage business under control. There mustn't be any doubt Katrina will pick me and refuse the other kings in play.

But even if that falls through, there is always plan B.

If by chance I can't guarantee my engagement with her, then I always have Atlas to do the dirty work for me. The gods know he's made his way into more women's hearts than most, so it won't be too hard for him to seduce her into his bed and, ultimately, into her heart.

She might be made of ice, but she's still a woman.

And every woman has a weak spot.

Atlas is good at discovering those.

And by the way I left things last night, I doubt I'll be able to.

Not that I'm surprised.

I never had it in me to play a part or fake affection for whatever gain. Maybe Kat and I are more alike in that way than I care to admit. Somewhere along the line, my heart turned to stone, too. Where hers is made of the coldest clear diamond, mine is bred from scorched obsidian rock. Being this impenetrable might have made me a better soldier, but I doubt it has made me a better man. At least not one a woman like her would be interested in.

Her sights have always been on another.
The man I vowed to kill the next time I laid eyes on him.
Teodoro of Derfir.

"Levi," Brick mutters, concerned at my sudden silence. "Are you all right?"

"More than all right," I try to mollify. "We're going home, Brick. There isn't anything that will ruin my spirits today. Not one thing."

"Glad to hear it," Brick replies with a chuckle, obviously appeased with my answer. "Best get moving on then. We've got at least a five-day ride waiting on us until we reach Arkøya's gates. I don't know about you, but I'm ready to stop feeling so goddamn homesick all the time."

To this, I smile and pat his shoulder.

"Me too, old friend. Let's go."

In tandem, we start walking toward the line of soldiers on horseback and carriages waiting on the main road to start the journey home. Against my better judgment, I find myself scanning the perimeter, wondering which carriage Kat is in to make the voyage east.

But just as I tell myself that I shouldn't care, I halt to a dead stop when my gaze lands on the infuriating woman herself.

Looking indisputably like the queen she claims to be, Katrina is mounted on a majestic white horse, looking ready to lead this train all the way to Arkøya all by herself. Not only that, but she's also wearing some kind of skintight white pants underneath her long flowing coat. And with the way the material hugs her legs, leaving very little to the imagination, she might as well be naked as far as my men are concerned.

Her apparel, unconventional as it may be, is not my main concern, though.

It's the possibility that she may be stolen from me before we even have a chance to pass through Arkøya's gates that has me up in arms.

It's blind fury that snaps me out of my trance and has me rushing toward her at lightning speed.

"Just what the hell do you think you're doing?" I blurt out when I reach her, loud enough for everyone on the train to hear.

"What does it look like?" she counters, bored.

"You look like you're about to ride east on horseback."

"Hmm," she hums, tugging softly at the reins in her grip while continuing to look straight ahead. "The gods *have* been good to you, Levi. With the amount of times I would assume a soldier like you was knocked on the head on the battlefield, I wasn't sure you could be so perceptive."

My hands ball into fists at my sides.

"As much as I would love nothing more than to give you a witty comeback to the insinuation that I'm thick in the head, I'm more concerned about your pride, my queen. It will get you killed."

"Really?" she coos, turning that gorgeous arctic face of hers my way. "After last night, I would have bet that my safety was at the bottom of your list of priorities."

"If you're to be my queen as well my lady wife, then your safety will always be my number one priority."

"I *am* your queen," she seethes through a gnashed smile. "Your wife, on the other hand, is still up for debate."

"Kat," I warn through gritted teeth, finally coming to my wits' end. "Get off that fucking horse. Now."

With blatant defiance, she stares me down, white knuckling the horse's reins.

"Mind your place, Your Grace. The only one here entitled to shout out orders, is me. Remember that."

Her glower persists, stubborn to the very end and forcing my hand to consider all my options.

The road home is hard and full of perils, and I'm not sure how experienced a rider she's become since I've last seen her. What I do know is that Kat has never traveled east in her life and therefore has no clue to the dangers the open road holds.

Even the most veteran of us know that this journey isn't without its hazards. Not only does Mother Nature have a way of keeping us on our toes, but so do the wild beasts that freely roam the vast terrain between the northern mountains to the eastern meadows.

There are other monsters who like to hide in the forests, too. Men made of flesh and blood who wait steadily for the perfect mark to reach their sights. These unscrupulous bandits and thieves won't think twice about taking her hostage for a few bags of gold. One glance at her diamond-encrusted coat would be enough for them to know she's of means, and therefore their pick to kidnap. Kat should know better than be this reckless. Especially considering what she went through when she was young.

I'm starting to think that no one is more dangerous to Katrina's safety than herself.

This nagging feeling that she'll end up falling and snapping her pretty little neck just because she is too proud to do as I say, is far too real for my liking. As much as the idea intrigues me, I can't let her die under my protection. The kingdom would split in all directions and war would undoubtedly ensue, all battling for a chance at the throne. And all because I couldn't keep her in one piece long enough to reach Arkøya.

"So are we riding out or not?" the brat has the nerve to taunt.

"Not."

She lets out an exaggerated exhale at my reply.

"Now there's the Levi I remember. Always so boresome in his need for safety."

"Don't make me take you off that horse," I warn, aggravated with how she's chosen to remember me. "Believe me when I tell you that I'll drag you off there if I have to. Don't test me, Kat."

The flash of hatred I see in her eyes anytime I call her by her nickname has my heart in a vise grip, squeezing it to the point of pain.

"No," she quips, turning away from me, eyes back on the road. "I'm riding down east and there is nothing you can say or do that will change my mind."

Gods, she's as stubborn as they come.

"Fine. Stay up on that high horse," I shrug off, conceding to her whim.

"As if I needed your approval." She scoffs.

"Oh, Kat. You might not have my approval, but you will suffer my company."

And before she has time to ask what I mean by that, I step onto the horse's stirrup and swing my leg over to the side, sitting right behind her, my arm flinging around her waist and pulling her back toward me.

My men begin to chuckle at the sight while hers seem at a loss as to what to do.

"What exactly do you think you're doing?" she mumbles under her breath so no one can hear her reprimand.

"If you insist on being a petulant child, then I will treat you as one."

"Get off," she grunts, elbowing me in the gut, thinking that will release my hold on her.

"Not a chance. I need you to reach Arkøya alive, and like hell will I let you steal my victory by getting yourself killed."

"I can ride just fine without you."

"I'm not taking that chance. Now we can either ride on horseback together, where you don't have to look at my face, or we can ride in your carriage, where you will be forced to. Your choice, Your Highness."

I feel her body tense, her rigid form telling me that spending time with me in such close quarters is the last thing she wants.

"Fine," she huffs out. "Let's get on with this, shall we? The faster I get east, the quicker I'll be able to leave it too."

"So eager to be done with me already?" I smirk behind her.

She glances over her shoulder, those piercing gray eyes taking my very breath away.

"You were done with me long before I had a chance to be done with you."

My brow creases at her words, but I don't have time to decipher their meaning since it's at this moment that she raises her hand in the air for all to see and orders the train to ride. My men don't even question the order and do as she commands, the horses and carriages steadily strutting down the snow-covered road. She's only been in their presence a day and already, subconsciously, they have just legitimized her reign by following such a simple order.

Holding her a bit too tightly, I lean down to the side of her face until my lips are at her ear.

"Clever, clever, Kat."

The way she tries to subdue her smile tells me she knows exactly what she just did.

There is a small part of me that is in awe of how strategically calculating she is. But while this is her first battle, it's far from being mine.

She might have just started this war.

But I'm the one who intends to finish it.

I t's been five hours since we left camp and already, my body is breaking down, showing signs of fatigue. I wasn't lying when I told Levi that I was capable of riding on my own, but even I must admit that no matter how good an equestrian I am, nothing could have prepared me for this arduous journey. Every limb in my body aches, screaming for some relief.

You did this to yourself.

I hear Levi's voice taunt me in my head.

But what was the alternative? Me riding comfortably in my carriage, whilst trailing behind him? Not a chance. That would suggest that I'm weak. Although I'm not sure what it says about me to be riding with Levi at my back either.

Throughout the whole ride I've had half a mind to push him off my horse. I would have done too, if I didn't think his men would raise their swords against me. I did get a kick of seeing them following my command to march east, though. Maybe more so since I knew how much it displeased Levi.

Then again, it only serves him right.

It's not as if he's tried to be very accommodating with me.

I knew when I sent the decree offering marriage that not every king would fall on their hands and knees for me, but I at least expected some sort of pretense. I forgot that Levi was never one to fake pleasantries. He was more the brooding, quiet type. The type of boy who was happy just to sit on the sidelines and only talk when he had something meaningful to say.

But alas, the boy I grew up with has turned into a man of even fewer words, leaving his actions to speak for themselves.

As if he has a direct line to my thoughts, Levi's hold on my waist tightens. My body begins to stiffen when he leans down to my ear and whispers into it, making my skin break out in goosebumps.

"We should take a break."

"I don't need it," I reply with a monotonous tone.

"Yeah, well, maybe you should stop thinking about your needs and focus on others' instead. My soldiers are tired and hungry, and I expect so are yours," he scolds, making sure that guilt begins to seep into my veins since I didn't even consider my own entourage's discomfort.

And all because I was too busy trying to prove a point.

Damn it.

I offer him a curt nod in reply and raise my hand for all to see before turning it to a fist. At once, we come to a full stop and I hear an immediate exhale of relief from the train. My lips dip into a frown with how disappointed I am in myself, hating that I didn't even think of taking a break earlier. I was so consumed in showing Levi that I was as strong as he was, that I totally forgot I wasn't the only one suffering because of my pride.

Levi gracefully jumps off my horse, stretching his hand out for me to take. Begrudgingly, I reach for his hand, only to feel my shaky legs give in and begin to fall. Thankfully, Levi's masterful reflexes are on point and he's able to catch me at once, preventing me from making a total fool of myself. His strong hands grip at my waist as he places my feet on solid ground, keeping our chests pressed together.

But then the weirdest thing occurs.

Suddenly, I'm being pulled back into a willfully forgotten past. Memories of the last time his concerned green eyes pierced mine like this. Like they would scorch the earth to keep me safe.

The world around us begins to disappear and in its place resurfaces a time where Levi wasn't my enemy but my knight in shining armor.

My champion.

Fifteen Years Old

"Come on, kitten! Let's see how fast you can run on those paws." Teo laughs, running toward the forest just outside the castle's walls.

"If I'm a kitten then you're a mouse. Only scared mice run away from little girls!" I shout back at Teo, laughing, running as fast as I can, while Atlas lags behind, doing his best to keep up with the pair of us.

Teo continues to chuckle away as he gains speed, and before I can stop it, he's amongst the high foreboding trees.

"Teo! Wait! Stop! Don't go in there," I yell as loud as I can.

"Don't be such a scaredy-cat, kitten! Come find me!" he yells back excitedly, and before I can convince him to not go any farther, the forest's shadows swallow him up and hide him from my view.

Panting, I stop just at the edge of the forest, bending down to hug my stomach while desperately trying to catch my breath. My eyes scan the large snow-covered trees, hating the eerie silence coming from in between them. Momma forbade me to ever go into the forest alone long ago, telling me fantastic tales of woodland creatures that would love nothing more than to sink their teeth into little princesses like me.

I'm sure she was exaggerating. I'm sure all those scary stories were just so she could keep me safe. Because that's what you do when you love someone. You do everything in your power to make sure they don't get hurt. That's why Momma likes it when I stay within the castle's walls, so she can keep an eye on me. She's especially vigilant this time of year when my boys come to visit. She says I'm more unruly when they're around. She's not wrong.

I keep staring at the creepy scenery in front of me, worried that maybe Momma's tall tales hold some truth to them.

Doesn't matter if they do.

Teo will be with me.

He won't let any harm come to me. He loves me. He said as much last night at the ball.

So, what am I afraid of?

Teo is waiting for me. He's waiting.

With that encouraging thought in my head, I muster up all my courage and decide to go in. But just as I'm about to enter the forest, Atlas comes from behind and grabs me by the wrist, halting my step.

"Atlas, let go."

"No." He shakes his head adamantly. "Don't go. Let's turn back," he says, true fear in his light blue eyes.

"But what about Teo?" I ask him with a soft smile. "We can't just leave our friend, Atlas. That's not what friends do."

Atlas frowns at my explanation, seeming not entirely convinced by it.

I try to unlatch his fingers off my wrist, which shouldn't be a hard task for me to accomplish, since Atlas has always been so frail. But somehow, he's garnished whatever strength he has to keep his hold steady on me. So much so that I'm positive he's going to leave a bruise.

"Atlas, you're hurting me."

It's all he needs to hear to unleash his fierce grip. Unfortunately, he takes two steps in front of me to stand in my way, blocking me from my goal.

"Don't go after Teo. You don't know what monsters live amongst the forest."

"That's just an old wives' tale." I smile. "You think my momma didn't tell me the stories about how beasts roam the cold snow and need the blood of the innocent to feast on to keep warm too? She did, but you and I both know it's all nonsense. We're no longer little kids, Atlas. We can't let our parents keep us afraid. We can't let others keep us small."

I chew on my lower lip as I watch Atlas begin to hesitate at my words. I knew before I even said them that they would cause an impression. It's no secret that Atlas is always trying to prove how brave he is, trying to surpass his illness by showing the world that he is just as courageous as the rest of us. But deep down, I know he's a lot like me. Always afraid that people will see that truth. That we are weak because we are vulnerable. Him for his illness and me for being born a girl. Both traits that will do our kingdoms no good in the long run.

That's why he's probably my best friend between the three boys.

He understands what it feels like to be underestimated. Perceived to not hold any actual worth.

My throat begins to run dry when Atlas refuses to back down, the flash of a true king in the making coming out.

"If you go in there, Teo won't protect you," he says with such certainty I almost catch myself believing him.

"You don't know that," I reprimand. "And frankly, you shouldn't say things like that about your friend. It's disloyal."

"Don't talk to me about loyalty," he spews angrily.

What has gotten into him?

Where is my sweet friend who always has my back no matter what?

"I don't know why you are acting this way," I reply, just as infuriated as he seems to be, "but I'm going in, with or without you. Are you coming or not?"

He shakes his head.

"Fine, then step out of my way."

When I see that he won't budge, I use all my strength and make him.

A pang of shame pierces my heart with the way Atlas's clear bright eyes dim, looking saddened that I pushed him. Unable to see such disappointment in his eyes, I head toward the forest like I intended, only to stop when I hear him mumble under his breath behind me.

"Hope his kisses are worth it."

My cheeks instantly flush crimson at his accusation. I turn around to confront him yet again, but Atlas is already gone, rushing back to the safety of my castle's walls.

Damn the gods.

Atlas must have seen Teo kissing me last night. That's the only reason why he would say such a thing. The ugly feeling of guilt starts bubbling in my chest, making it hard for me to intake air. Now I understand why he didn't want me to go after Teo. He's hurt. Our kiss hurt him.

I don't regret the kiss I shared with Teo, but I never meant to hurt Atlas. I adore my blue-eyed boy more than words could say. He's my kindred spirit in all ways. The other half of me.

And I hurt him.

Worse still, I'd do it again if it meant I'd kiss Teo a second time.

There I was telling him friends protect each other, when I made no such effort to protect Atlas's heart.

Then suddenly, another realization comes to me.

Did Atlas tell Levi about our kiss?

Gods, I hope not. It hurts me deeply that I've caused Atlas pain, but I couldn't stomach Levi's disappointment in me. Anything but that.

The cold wind howls behind me, reminding me that I've lost too much time in my own thoughts when I should have been following Teo all along. Who knows where he's gone off to by now.

He must be close.

I bet he's got his eyes on me right now, just waiting for me.

Atlas was right on one account.

The only reason why I'm even considering walking into these woods is because, deep down, I want Teo to kiss me again. Alone, and without eyes on us, I can only imagine how divine this kiss will be. He'll take full advantage of the situation of our solitude by pulling me into his arms and imprinting me with his ardent kiss.

It will be worthy of sonnets. I just know it.

With new resolve, I run into the forest, uncaring of all the ghost tales and horror stories ever told. Amongst these harsh trees hides the boy who has my heart, and I'll be damned if I won't go to him just because of some stupid superstition.

"Teo!" I shout gleefully, my shoes sinking into the snow, its cold bite clawing around my ankles. "Teo! Where are you?!" With a giggle, I continue to run in the direction of the footsteps dug into the snow, knowing Teo must have left them for me. Little breadcrumbs for me to follow.

But all too soon does my excitement begin to fade, leaving trepidation to settle in my head instead. After what feels like a good twenty minutes of running, I start to second-guess myself. Depressingly so, now that the snow is falling down hard from the dark night sky, covering whatever trail Teo left me.

This was more than foolish. This is dangerous.

"Teo!!!" I scream, the panicked sound of my own voice curling my blood.

No matter how many times I call out for him, Teo is nowhere to be found. I'm so deep in this unfamiliar forest, and I have no idea from which way I came or how to return home.

"Easy, Kat. No use in panicking now," I say out loud.

I stare up at the full moon, now high up in the sky, announcing how late it truly is. When I don't make it to dinner, I'm sure my parents will send out a search party for me. Atlas will tell them where he last saw me and soon, men in armor will rescue me from this place. All I have to do is not die from the cold while I wait.

Not wanting to get more lost than I already am, I lean against a tree, hugging my arms toward my chest for warmth. I watch the white cloud of my breath come out of my mouth, my body starting to shiver. All the heat my adrenaline gifted me is long gone, and now only cold resides in me. It seeps through my bones, icicles starting to cling to my hair and eyelashes.

And then a terrifying thought comes to the forefront of my mind.

What if Teo is hurt?

What if the reason why he was unable to hear me was because someone or something has him? Every horror my mind can conjure up comes to life as images of Teo's lifeless body assault me. Tears start streaking down my face, turning to droplets of ice the minute they touch the ground. I'm so consumed with the nightmares playing on a loop in my head that I don't even hear the footsteps closing in on me. It's only when a hand clasps over my mouth that I realize I'm no longer alone.

But it's not my saviors that found me.

It's the monsters my mother always warned me about.

"Looky, looky. What do we have here?" my assailant says, his foul stench making my skin crawl.

"Looks like a good time to me," his friend replies, eyeing me up and down.

"A mighty good time," the man with his hand over my mouth adds ominously, but it's only when he licks the side of my cheek that I understand their meaning.

Safe to say, it's enough to snap me out of my shock. My legs start kicking every which way, my body thrashing in my captor's hold, and when that doesn't work, my teeth sink into his fingers.

"Bitch!" he shouts before throwing me to the ground.

I don't hesitate, not even for a second, hurriedly picking myself up and running as fast as I can. Unfortunately, his friend catches me, swinging me in his embrace to face his injured friend.

My captor walks in a beeline straight toward me with such evil in his eyes, I almost choke on it. He slaps me across the face, only to punch me in the gut afterward. The man that is still holding my arms behind my back laughs like a jackal, enjoying my punishment.

"What do you say? Should we keep her? Mighty lonely up in the mountains," he says, tugging my arms back so forcibly that I'm afraid he might break them off.

"Screw that. I'd rather we fuck every hole in her right here and now. After she's good and used, we take her into town and sell her ass. She'll fetch a pretty little penny at the whore house."

"Don't you dare touch me!" I scream. "My father is King Orville of Bratsk! King of the Kingdom of Aikyam! He will have your heads on spikes if you so much as dare touch me!"

But instead of the fear I would assume the name of my father would inflict on them, their eyes actually widen with elation.

"Oh fuck! We just hit pay dirt! We're about to be rich!"

My muscles begin to relax at my captors' reaction.

Good.

They want money.

My father will promise them all that they want.

And then kill them for laying hands on me before they ever see a dime.

"Don't be an idiot!" the one that is still bleeding from his fingers barks out. "We can't sell her now. If she is who she says, then the king will go to the ends of the earth to track us down and kill us. Nope. We get rid of her."

"What? No!" I plead. "My father will pay you whatever fortune you desire. He has to after I tell him you both saved me when I got lost and that your kindness should be rewarded."

The man holding me nods in agreement, but it's the other who doesn't take the bait.

"She's lying. She'll throw us to the wolves before we even step foot inside the castle. We are as good as dead men if we try to take her back."

"So, what do we do?" his friend retorts, disheartened that he won't be showered in riches.

"I say we kill the bitch. Slice her up to look like some wild animal got to her. No one will be the wiser and come looking for us."

"Fine," his friend retorts despondently.

"Cheer up, Eger. Tell you what? First, we fuck the bitch, then we slice her throat. How's that sound?"

"Yeah?" the man who apparently is named Eger retorts, sounding more upbeat. "Who gets first dibs? Me or you, Dima?"

A cold chill runs down my back that they no longer care to keep their names and identities hidden from me.

"Who says we have to choose? I say she can take us both on at the same time," Dima states. "Pin her down."

I flail in Eger's hold, but it's no use. He flings me to the frozen ground, then falls on top of me, his large body covering all of mine. He goes to his haunches and unzips his pants, grabbing the ugliest-looking member I've ever seen in his hand. I continue to wrestle him off me, but his weight alone is an advantage against me. He then raises my skirt and pulls down my wool stockings with an unyielding yank. Tears sting my eyes as he aims that horrid thing he has for a penis on my stomach. Dima walks over to my head, a sinister smile to his lips, as he holds my wrists above my head.

"Open her mouth for me, Eger. Make sure she doesn't bite my dick off."

"Gonna be a little hard to do that and still fuck her," Eger mumbles, pissed that he has to multitask.

"Figure it out," Dima grunts, releasing his own dick from his pants, holding it in one hand while his other is clutched around a blade to my throat. He stares into my tear-stricken face, unbothered by my weeping.

"If I so much as feel your teeth, then you're as good as dead. Fucking you alive or dead makes no difference to me. Understood?"

I narrow my eyes at him, and spit in his direction.

"She's a firecracker, this one." Eger chuckles.

"Soon she'll be a dead firecracker." Dima scowls, pure hatred dripping from him. "Keep still, bitch, or I will kill you!"

"Do it! I'd rather be dead than suffer looking at your gods-awful faces a second longer!" I shout.

I don't even see him do it, but when Dima's boot hits my mouth, blood splatters onto the snow beside me. My teeth feel like they are about to fall out, my head hurting with unimaginable pain.

He crouches down, his rotten breath fanning my face and corrupting my skin with his stench. Having this upside-down view of him only makes him more monstrous in my eyes.

For the longest time, all he does is look at me, but when a sinister smile begins to crest his lips, I become almost paralyzed with fear.

"No, princess. I see what you're doing. Trying to force my hand to give you a quick death. But you're out of luck. I'm going to keep you alive. I want you to feel every second of what Eger and I are about to do to you. I'm going to make sure that the last hour you spend on this earth will be utter hell."

My nostrils flare in disgust and loathing even as the tears fall down my cheeks. I read the threat in his eyes and know he means every word. They're both going to ruin me, and once they have taken the last bit of dignity from me, they'll kill me.

I either meet my makers as a coward, or as the future queen I was always meant to be.

I chose the latter.

"Do what you will. You're a dead man either way."

Dima pulls at my hair, my scalp burning from his grip.

"By the time we are done with you, you'll be begging for mercy," he spits out, his saliva hitting right in the face, making me want to gag.

But I never let him or his friend, Eger, see how truly terrified I am. I may be a woman, the weaker sex, as my father so loves to point out, but I have northern blood to cool my nerves and offer me the strength to overcome any storm.

"The only thing you'll hear from me is me cursing your very existence."

"Dima," Eger interjects on a grunt, starting to lose his patience. "Are we gonna fuck her or continue to waste precious time chitchatting? Her father's men must be searching for her royal head as we speak. No way she could have walked out here on her own without anyone knowing about it. I say we play with her for a bit and then leave her for the wolves to find."

When Eger's member starts to dig into my tender flesh, vomit begins to rise up my throat.

"You're right. Hold her still, and get that goddamn mouth open for me," Dima replies with a snarl.

But just as Eger widens my jaw open with all his might, a dagger flies through the air and pierces him right between his eyes, his limp body crashing over me.

"THE FUCK?! Dima hollers, turning around, but as he does it, the edge of a sword slices him through, from head to navel.

Blood and guts cover my face as I roll my eyes back and see the avenging dark angel who had vowed to protect me with his life.

"Levi," I breathe out, tears of happiness replacing the fearful ones I had been crying.

Levi jumps off his horse, and quickly kicks Eger off me, pulling me up and into his embrace. He cups my face in his hands and starts kissing my cheeks, my temples, uncaring of the blood on my skin.

"I thought I had lost you," he chokes out, staring down at me, looking just as devastatingly torn as I am.

Levi shouldn't be kissing me like this.

If my father found out he took such liberties with me, he'd be as dead as the two men lying on the ground.

But I can't find it in me to even think about that right now. All I can manage to concentrate on is how my Levi, my protector, looks like he's on the brink of madness. All because of me. All because he thought I'd be lost to him forever.

I don't even question what I do next.

I go to the tips of my toes, and softly place my lips on his. I feel his body go rigid but then quickly soften, giving sway to my kiss. His lips are warm. So warm. Tender yet strong. Just like him. Just like my Levi.

But just as I try to deepen the kiss, Levi growls and pulls away, keeping his hands on my waist.

"Levi," I stammer.

"You're in shock, Kat. We need to get you home. Get you out of these clothes and into the safety of your father's castle." He then turns his attention to the slayed men, their blood polluting the white driven snow. "I was reckless. I should have kept them alive and let your father deal out their punishment. He'll be upset that I took that right from him."

"He won't." I sob, my smile splitting my face in two. "He'll reward your bravery. I'll make sure he does."

"That wasn't bravery, princess. It was vengeance."

The way he says the word should frighten me, but it doesn't. Like a warm winter coat, it envelops around my heart, making the blood coursing through my veins heat up with glee.

"How did you know to come find me?" I ask, not wanting us to go home just yet.

"Atlas." He frowns. "When you refused to listen to his counsel and stubbornly came into this forest all by your lonesome, he found me. I told him to find our fathers and tell them that you were in danger, and rushed to follow you before the snow could cover your tracks. I was close to losing my mind when the snowfall began covering them all. But then I heard you scream out. It was your voice that led me to you," he says affectionately, running his thumb over my lower lip. He then remembers himself and pulls it away, leaving me bereft of his touch. "I'm sure by now your father has a search party covering these woods. Best find them and save any wretched soul that they might find on the way."

I offer him a nod, my palms still holding on to his lapels.

"I'll never be able to repay you for saving me, Levi. Never."

His cheeks turn pink as his gaze falls to my lips once more.

"Maybe one day you can. One day when another man's blood isn't covering your pretty face."

There is this unexplained feeling that takes over my lower belly.

He thinks I'm pretty.

Why that matters, I'm not sure.

I'm not the type of girl who hasn't heard her fair share of praise, but to have it come from Levi?

Means something to me.

I stare into his emerald eyes and lose myself in their safe meadows. The need to kiss him again is overwhelming, but just as I try to steal another from him, we both hear a snap of a twig nearby. Levi raises his sword, pushing me to stand behind him.

"Show your face! Who's there?" Levi shouts out.

It's only the fear that there are more villains ready to pop out the woodwork that has me hiding behind Levi's back. But when my eyes lock on Teo walking toward us, my anger comes forth with the power of a thousand suns, making me step out of Levi's shadow. I'm about to lunge myself at him, scream in his face, wanting to know where the hell he had been hiding when I was about to get raped and killed—and not necessarily in that order—when Levi prevents me from getting in a word edgewise, holding me back from unleashing my fury on our friend.

"See what your selfishness has done?" Levi belts in my stead. "See what the repercussions of your thoughtless actions are? She could have died, Teodoro. She could have fucking died. And for that?! I should kill you where you stand."

Teo, looking grief-stricken, takes another step toward us, as if ready for Levi to do just that.

"Do it," he orders without missing a beat. "Do it, Levi, now that I've given you reason to. You've been dying to use that sword against me since we were knee-high. Do it. Do it! Show Katrina just exactly who you are. Because believe me, I may be flawed and reckless, but you're no better. You want what you will never have. Never, Levi! Might as well cut me down now because that is the only way you'll ever best me."

Even though his words should be a provocation, it's his tone that troubles me.

He's baiting Levi. He wants him to strike him down. And when his pained gaze falls to the men who would have harmed me, I understand why. He thinks he deserves to die for putting me in such perilous danger. It's only with that realization that my angry animosity for him evaporates from my heart.

There has been enough death for one day.

I won't let Levi kill Teo.

If I did, it would be like giving Levi permission to kill a piece of my heart too.

So, I do the only thing I can in this situation. I raise my hand and wrap it around Levi's wrist, ordering him to put down his sword. On cue, he follows my silent command.

"Take me home, Levi. I want to go home."

Levi gives me a curt nod and sheaths his weapon. He then picks me up by the waist and flings me across his horse, pulling himself up by his bootstraps next to take his seat behind me, keeping his arm protectively secure around my waist.

"Are you just going to leave me here?" Teo asks, incredulous that his life should be spared.

I look down at him, love mixed with disappointment spewing inside of me.

"Yes, we are. Walk back, Teo. Consider it a mercy that you'll be able to return with your head still attached to your shoulders," I tell him, and then give Levi the go-ahead to take us home.

As the horse starts trotting through the snow through vast woods, my tears start once again falling down my cheeks. I hurry to wipe them away, but I know Levi hears them regardless.

"Levi," I utter when I'm sure my voice is strong enough. "No one must know it was Teo who lured me into the forest tonight. You must promise me that my father will never find out."

His body promptly turns to stone at my plea.

He knows what I'm trying to convey without making me come right out and say it.

My father doesn't disapprove of me spending time with Levi, Teo, and Atlas, as he believes we are nothing more than close friends. If he so much as thought that brotherly affection was the last thing on my mind in regards to any of them, then he would lock me away, making sure to end our friendship once and for all.

If I'm to be wed one day, my father needs to guarantee that I remain virtuous. Unspoiled and untouched.

Even the kiss I shared with Levi a few minutes ago would be enough to ruin my reputation. And although Levi would never tell a soul, me running after Teo into the woods just to spend some alone time with him would set off alarm bells to my father. He would read the writing on the wall and see that Teo and I are not just merely good friends.

We're so much more than that.

And to my father, that would be a problem.

Whoever my father picks as my future groom will have to benefit the Kingdom of Aikyam. There's no question in my mind that when the time comes to find me a husband, his gaze will go to other kingdoms instead of our own.

"Teo deserves your father's wrath," Levi states as fact.

"That might be true, but Teo won't be the only one on the receiving end of it. I'll suffer too. Please, Levi. Be my savior in this and keep my secret."

Levi grows silent for longer than I would have liked him to think on the matter, but thankfully he shows me mercy and nods, accepting my request. I let out an exhale of relief, thanking the gods that it was Levi who found me and not one of my father's men.

My hands grasp over his hand that is planted protectively on my stomach.

"You are the best man I know, Levi. I mean that."

He frowns.

"I'm not a man yet, Kat. But one day, I will be. And when that day comes, you will have to decide. Him or me."

I gnaw at my bottom lip, not daring to answer that loaded question.

Because deep down, I know I'll never have to. I'll belong to someone else.

And as much as my heart grieves with that stark truth, it also offers some comfort.

If I don't have to choose, then I won't break anyone's heart but my own.

I can live with that.

I stay rooted to my spot, as if frozen by her intense gaze, my arms unable to let Katrina out of their grasp. Her silver eyes continue to expectantly stare up at me in the same way they did that night— on the night evil threatened to ruin and steal her away from me.

I can still recall every little detail of the horrid event.

How my rage took over and the need to kill those men a thousand times over utterly consumed me from within.

I had seventeen springs under my belt, therefore had yet to experience such hate.

Oh, but that night, how I felt it.

A visceral loathing that demanded retribution.

If the gods had been kind, they would have let me breathe life back into those two bastards just so I could drain it out of them again.

Only this time, I would have taken my time.

I would have tortured them until there wasn't a pound of flesh that hadn't suffered my wrath.

I had loved my Kat that much.

I had loved her to the point of madness.

But it's the flash of Teo's stricken face that ends up reminding me that the girl I would have torched the world for was never mine to begin with.

Not that I care anymore.

My Kat is long gone.

This ice queen version of her is all that is left.

It's that reminder that has me finally stepping back and releasing her from my grip. I try not to cringe when she almost stumbles and falls again to the ground with how abrupt I was. Thankfully, like the cat she is, she ends up landing on her feet, brushing off the moment we just shared like it was nothing.

Not wanting to stand here and look at her perfect face for another second, I turn my back to her and walk away, needing to put some much-needed distance between us. I pretend a stroll is just what I need to relieve my aching muscles, when in fact, its purpose is to clear the lovesick haze the old memory conjured up in me.

Truth be told, I could have ridden all day and night and not even felt a pinch of soreness. As a seasoned soldier, I've spent many hours on horseback. Days, even. My men are just as experienced, but I could tell by the way Katrina was starting to shift in her seat that she was in pain. And as much as I hate everything she represents, I'm not a sadist. I don't take pleasure in other people's suffering.

I'll leave that shit to her father.

This is his fault anyway. He turned her into this... cold, heartless thing.

Was it any wonder that she would turn out just like him? Ruthless and void of all emotion?

Not that it surprises me. King Orville is the reason why my whole kingdom is broken, dreaming of the day when vengeance will finally be ours.

Vengeance.

There is that word again.

When I killed her would-be assailants, I honestly believed that the thirst for vengeance could only ever rise from me when it came to protecting anyone who dared hurt a blonde hair on Kat's head.

How wrong I was.

For I will have my revenge, and I won't think twice about who gets hurt in the process—especially her.

My wayward thoughts are interrupted with the sound of a loud horn.

"Rider! Rider!" my men shout.

I turn my attention to the rider fast approaching, holding my sword to my side as I walk back toward the train. As if knowing who I am, the rider halts before me, jumping off his horse and kneeling at my feet.

"Your Highness," he says, holding his hand to his heart while keeping his eyes bowed down from me.

"Rise," I snap, never one to enjoy seeing anyone on their knees, even if it is to show respect.

The man does as he is told, his hand going to his coat. On reflex, my men behind me instantly raise their swords, thinking this stranger was sent to murder me, no doubt. I roll my eyes and take a step toward him, seeing the familiar crest on his ring.

"You bring news from the west?" I ask, to which he nods hesitantly, his gaze still fixed on my men's weapons aimed at him.

"I do, Your Highness. A letter from my lord and liege."

I almost chuckle at his choice of wording, since I know full well that his so-called lord is even less interested in such monarch tradition than I am.

"Well, give it here, man. I don't have all day," I quip impatiently.

He nods and pulls out a scroll from his coat pocket before handing it over.

"My lord requests a fast reply to his correspondence, Your Majesty."

"And you shall have it," I retort, waving him off.

"It's of the utmost importance that you do," he adds anxiously, fidgeting from one foot to the other, his gaze locked on the pointy steel swords that never lower.

"How about I read the damn thing first? Yes? Can't give you an answer if I don't know what the question is, now can I?" I explain, a little annoyed at his persistence. "Wait here."

"Your Highness!" he shouts before I'm able to move too far away from him. "Could you please tell your men to lower their swords while I wait?"

I almost chuckle at his request.

"Tell me, squire, would your lord and liege—as you fondly call him—do the same for any man I send his way with word from me? Or would your king have a knife at my man's throat just to make sure he wasn't some assassin sent to kill him?"

The rider's eyes instantly fall to the snow.

"That's what I thought. Stay here," I repeat more sternly, before turning away from him.

As I start walking down the small hill to find some privacy amongst the trees, I feel Kat's eyes on me. I turn around and smirk when she pretends that she wasn't just staring at me.

The Kat of my past had always been the curious type. She hated secrets. And whenever she thought one was in her midst, she did her very best to reveal them. I guess some habits are hard to break.

Ah, Katrina, has no one ever told you that curiosity killed the cat?

Even though it must eat away at her, Katrina continues to pretend she doesn't care one bit what news I possess in my hands and continues faking that whatever silly chatter she's having with her handmaidens is far more interesting.

Now that I'm certain she won't follow, I walk farther down the small hill until I find a boulder to sit on. After I've swiped the snow off it, I take a seat and stretch my legs, and take a breath before breaking the orange marigold seal to read what's inside.

Dearest brother,

I hope this letter finds you well and at the start of your journey home.

If you are reading these words, then I can take some comfort knowing the bitch of the north hasn't sliced your throat yet.

Be careful, Levi.

I know from experience what it feels like to be pulled into her web of lies and eat them up like they are the sweetest dessert to ever touch your lips.

Don't believe anything she says.

She's the enemy.

She always has been.

We were just too blinded by youth and naivete to have seen it before.

If you have any doubts, then all you need to do is remember this chess match she has us playing.

Offering marriage is her way of manipulating us into servitude.

My people and I will never be slaves to the north again.

Never again, Levi.

Having said that, I admit I'm curious to see the Winter Queen for myself.

I can only imagine what you must have felt seeing her after so many years.

Is she as beautiful as she was then?

Does her smile still make you feel like you are standing on top of one of her white mountains?

Does she still curl the corner of her lips when she doesn't get her way?

Ah, but what I wouldn't give to see that quirk with my own two eyes.

Still, don't be fooled, old friend.

No matter how many similarities she may possess with our childhood love, it's not her.

Mark my words, she's banking on that affection. Praying we begin to reminisce on the past and that the fondness we once stored in our hearts for her still prevails.

For me, it does not.

So much so that I vow you this, brother.

Once you are married and crowned king, I will plunge my dagger into her cold heart on her very bridal bed as my wedding present to you.

I swear it on the blood that was shed in her family's name.

Until then, I will wait.

Patiently.

Like I have done for these past seven years.

For now, all I need are assurances that you are still the beloved brother I would follow over a cliff and beyond.

The same loyal friend who swore to me that revenge would be ours in the end.

That the dead would be avenged, so that their spirits could finally find peace.

Tell it to me true, and I will believe you.

For there is no one in this world who I trust, save for you—the true king of Aikyam.

Your loyal brother in rightful vengeance,

Atlas of Narberth

King of the west

After reading the letter a second time, I raise my heavy head from the inked parchment and safely guard it in my breast pocket.

Atlas needs an answer.

I could read it in his tone how on edge he is now, so close to getting justice—anxiety getting the better of him.

He needs reassurance and I fully intend on giving it to him.

I scan my surroundings, until I find exactly what I'm looking for. Ever so quickly, I march to a nearby fallen tree branch in the ground. After close inspection, I thank the gods that it's not too wet from the snow for what I have in store for it. I break a good chunk of the wood apart with my foot, grabbing the better piece, intent on taking it back with me to the boulder.

But first things first.

With the remains of the branch, I go to my haunches and start a fire. Once the first flame catches on, I remove Atlas's letter from my inner pocket and tilt it to the flame. The instant the fire flicks at it, I drop the letter onto the makeshift pyre, and stand back up to my full height. I wait until every bit of it burns to ash, Atlas's words unable to be read by any other eyes but mine.

Then and only then do I return to my rock and get to work.

Every so often while I carve away, I feel the restlessness of the party up on the road, looking down the hill, waiting impatiently for my return.

She's impatient.

But it's just as Atlas wrote.

We've waited years.

Years!

She can wait a few goddamn hours.

Not that there's much choice. Since I haven't done this in so long, I'm unable to be as fast as I once was, only managing to complete it after a good solid hour of arduous work. When the final cut is made, I sit back and smile that it didn't come out half as bad as I thought it would.

My grin widens when I walk back up the hill and find Atlas's squire dripping in sweat, my soldiers with their swords still raised at him.

"Your Majesty." He bows ecstatically, looking like the gods themselves have appeared before him. "Do you have an answer for my lord and liege?"

"I do," I state, handing him the small wooden-carved boat I just made.

He looks at it as if it's going to jump and bite him in the face.

"Your Highness?" he asks, confused, still perplexed as to why he's bringing his king a child's toy from me.

"He'll know what it means. Now, best be on your way. Your king hates to be kept waiting."

Not needing to be told twice, the squire bids farewell and runs to his horse, all too eager to return to where he came from.

I, on the other hand, am in no rush to return to my journey.

Riding on the same horse as Katrina has been *challenging*.

On my sanity.

My will.

And even my cock.

With the way her ass is always brushing up against it, she's made sure to aim for the full trifecta, guaranteeing that I slowly go insane with each mile we pass.

My people and I will never be slaves to the north again.

Never again, Levi.

It's Atlas's letter that brings me back to my senses. It's almost as if he knew I needed a little dose of reality. A reminder that our cause is so much bigger than us.

Even more important than our need for vengeance.

It's about our freedom.

Our kingdoms as much as our own.

And if the price for that freedom is the Winter Queen's slender neck, then so be it.

I won't shed a tear for her.

She sure as fuck never shed one for me.

And after everything the north has put us through, even if she cried me a river, it wouldn't be enough.

Not even close.

"W hat's taking her so long?" I grumble over to Inessa, whose worried gaze is fixed on my leg that keeps bouncing up and down in irritation.

Aggravated, I force myself to keep still, Inessa's attention falling away from my restless knee and back on me.

"These things take time, Your Highness, but I assure you if there is anyone that can get you the information you require, it will be Anya," she states confidently.

"Hmm, she better," I mutter under my breath, Inessa's self-assured expression slipping away at the silent warning in my tone.

Unfortunately for my handmaiden, I don't have the energy or the will to comfort her. She should know me better by now that I'm not going to do anything to her friend even if she is unsuccessful in her mission.

If the gods be good, then Anya *will* return to me with the intel I crave. But if by chance they are not, and Anya is unable to obtain the information I so desire, then sadly there isn't much I can do about it, save for licking my wounded pride.

Argh.

How dare anyone send a rider to our camp and not have the decency to acknowledge my presence in this train and write to me, their queen?

Maybe I'm being paranoid.

Maybe the letter is nothing to worry about.

Maybe it came from his people in Arkøya, making sure that their king is up to date with what's happening in his kingdom and the preparations that are being done for our arrival.

But what if it's not?

What if its contents prove that Levi is in cahoots with the other kings? Proof of their elaborate plan to dethrone me, written in ink for all to bear witness to?

Even if that were to be the case, what could I do with that piece of information?

Would the people of Aikyam revolt if they had proof that these traitorous kings sought to steal my crown from me, or would they rejoice in the knowledge that my reign was in peril?

All I have are questions, and very little answers.

And one question surpasses them all—why?

What happened for them to hate me so? What did I ever do that was so wrong to make them behave this way? To make them feel that I was unworthy of my title? Not once did I even consider stripping *them* of their birthright. So why is it so easy for these men to plot away my demise?

Questions.

Questions.

Questions.

All these questions do my head in.

I want answers.

I *need* answers.

But today, I'll settle for at least one.

As if sensing my thinning patience, Anya suddenly appears, rushing into my tent, cheeks flushed, brow sweaty, looking somewhat breathless. She throws a mischievous wink to Inessa, who continues to stand beside me, before eating the distance between us and curtseying at my feet.

"So? Were you able to learn who sent the rider?" I belt out frustratedly when she takes too long to talk.

"I have, Your Highness." Anya smiles, pleased as she stands back up.

"Well, are you going to tell me or keep me in this infernal suspense? A name, Anya! Give me a name."

"It was from King Atlas, Your Highness," she rushes to explain.

"Atlas? Are you sure? What proof do you have that it was him?" I interrogate, my hope waning as I watch Anya's cocky grin fall to the floor with each question I throw her way. No longer looking so confident, her gaze falls from me to Inessa, as if her friend could collaborate her story. "Don't look at her, look at me!" I insist. "You aren't sure, are you?"

"I'm as sure as I could possibly be, Your Grace," she insists, holding her chin up high. "King Levi's man swore to me that the squire wore the marigold seal on his person. He swore to it."

"Did he tell you this before or after he bedded you?" I cock a knowing brow.

Her cheeks flush crimson at the insinuation that she let one of Levi's soldiers have his way with her just so she could retrieve this particular crumb of information for me. Although everyone in this room knows that's exactly what Anya did.

I even counted on it.

Anya's seductive skillset is one of the reasons I chose her to accompany me on this trip to begin with. With her hourglass-shaped figure, long flowing red hair reminiscent of an open flame, and gentle submissive facial features, she's every man's wet dream. Hence her appeal to me.

"Anya, Her Majesty has asked you a question," Inessa chimes in, more for her friend's benefit than for mine.

"During, my queen," Anya finally responds.

In other words, the soldier would have said just about anything just so he could rut inside her.

Gods be damned!

"He sounded sincere. I believed him. But if you need me to steal the scroll so that you can see it for yourself, I'll do it. I'll do whatever my queen wishes."

I pinch the bridge of my nose with my fingers, trying to ease the building headache forming there.

"I doubt King Levi will leave the scroll out of his sight," I mutter, disheartened.

"Even a man like him needs to sleep, Your Highness. They usually do… after," she whispers suggestively, alerting me to the fact that most of her lovers are so spent that they have no choice but to give in to their slumber.

My hands ball into fists with the suggestion, and before I know what has come over me, I lean in and grab Anya's chin, sinking my nails into her skin.

"King Levi will share no woman's bed, but my own, if I so wish it. Is that understood, Anya?"

Her eyes widen in horror as I shove her away, making her land on her hands and knees. She bows her head and body to kiss the tapestry immediately, stretching her arms and placing her open palms on the floor.

"I never meant to offend you, my queen. I live to serve you. Serve you and you, alone. Please forgive me. I meant no harm by it."

Damn it.

I know Anya's loyalty is to me.

I may not be able to say that about most people in my court, but where Anya and Inessa are concerned, I know their hearts and loyalty are only mine. But Anya suggesting that she bed Levi struck too much of a nerve inside me. A nerve long forgotten. Just picturing the two together has me fuming with rage.

Gods.

I let out an exaggerated exhale and count to ten in an attempt to simmer my temper since Anya is not at fault for my nonsensical reaction.

"Stand, Anya. I'm not cross with you. Just the situation I find myself in," I explain evenly.

If I wasn't her queen, I would apologize for my brutish ways toward her. However, that is exactly who I am, so to even say the word sorry would be a show of weakness on my part. And as it stands, my enemies have already listed plenty of those against me. I shall not be reminded of how many more they have yet to uncover.

On shaky knees, Anya stands before me, her expression grief-stricken that she's offended me. Sometimes I forget that, unlike me, there are men and women whose hearts are easily mangled. I wish I could feel an ounce of that emotion. It would mean that I'm not made of ice, as people are fond of accusing me of being. But alas, my heart stopped beating long ago, and I fear nothing will ever jumpstart it to life again.

"Tell me what you need, Your Majesty. I'll do it for you. Anything," Anya begs, needing to do whatever it takes to get back in my good graces.

"As much as I would like to see the scroll for myself, I'm pretty sure Levi has probably already destroyed any proof of it. However, I would give my left arm to know for sure if it was Atlas who sent a rider to him. The gods know he hasn't made any such attempt in contacting me," I explain defeatedly.

"There still might be a way," Inessa interjects, pulling my attention away from a demure Anya and onto her.

"If you have a better suggestion than Anya's, please be my guest. I'm all ears."

Inessa hesitates for the briefest of seconds but ends up finding her voice.

"I know it isn't my place, but I watched you ride with the king. Although he tried his best to hide it, I have no doubt that he's fond of you. And fondness has a way of corrupting a soul when it's not nourished. You can use that to your advantage."

"Fond of me?" I let out a loud laugh. "The man had an army at my border threatening to take my throne, Inessa. How could he possibly be fond of me?"

"The heart works in mysterious ways. Sometimes not even we can decipher all its wants and secret desires until they are right within arm's reach," Anya adds softly to her friend's piece of advice.

I school my features, so my handmaidens don't see how their words just sent me into a tailspin.

Could it be possible?

Could Levi still harbor feelings for me, even if he refuses to acknowledge them?

I shake those foolish notions away.

"You're wrong, Inessa. Levi doesn't care for me. In fact, he would have probably celebrated my defeat by putting my severed head on a spike for all to see."

Anya cringes at the turn of phrase, while Inessa remains adamant in her convictions.

"That might be true, Your Highness, but it doesn't make my statement false either. My humble advice is this, my queen, send word to the king that you request his presence for supper. Once he's wined and dined, ask him outright who the messenger was from."

"He'll never willingly offer up such information." I shake my head.

"He will if he believes that he's speaking to his future bride," Inessa insists. "Men are simple creatures, my lady. Give him something he craves, and trust that he will return the favor in kind."

"And what exactly do you believe King Levi craves?"

"Nothing more than your undivided attention," Inessa says with a straight face.

"Seduce him, you mean?" I rebuke, going to the root of her advice.

"Plainly speaking, yes," she confesses.

I think long and hard about her proposal, trying to discover if it holds any merit. My handmaidens have gossiped around me enough through the years to have me believe Inessa might not be all that wrong when it comes to the male sex. Some of them can't help but be prisoners to their urges and desires.

I've heard tales of how devoted duty-bound men were quick to forget whatever vow they swore to their wife and crown, in the hopes that a slender young body would share their company and bed. If that hadn't been the case, then Anya wouldn't have been so successful in her mission with Levi's soldier. Even the most loyal of men have their weakness, their allegiance put to the test just by the way a woman smiles at them with promises of lurid days and even wilder nights.

But this is Levi we are talking about.

Not once in all the time I've known him was he easily enamored by a pretty face or a seductive smile. The man is born of steel, groomed to feel nothing—just like me.

Maybe because we are so similar, I'll be able to find a chink in his armor.

I guess there is only one way to find out and that is to test Inessa's theory.

"Very well, Inessa, send word to the king. Tonight, we dine."

She bows to me before rushing out of my tent to deliver the message.

"Your Majesty, if you would allow me," Anya begs, her tone still apologetic. "Let me get you out of your garments and into something that will leave your king breathless at the mere sight of you."

"He's not my king, Anya. He's my servant," I quip, but let her lift me from my seat and lead me to the other side of the tent where my bed and garments are.

"True, that he is. And if all goes well, he'll be serving you in more ways than one tonight." She giggles, her bubbly personality starting to come through.

I don't have the heart to reprimand her for her choice of words. Especially since I had been so harsh with her before, but even I have to admit the cold blood coursing through my veins is uncharacteristically warm with the idea of Levi serving me in any capacity.

Anya begins to peel my coat off me and then proceeds to pull at the strings of my corset.

"There will be no need for such a constricting thing on you tonight. Most men like easy access to their women," she singsongs. "I've even had a few where their hunger for me had been so severe, they ripped my clothes off my body with ease."

"I doubt King Levi is such a slave to his desires," I mutter, hating how she planted the animalistic image of Levi tearing my clothes off with his teeth in my head. It only serves to cloud my thoughts.

Completely unabashed now, Anya giggles and leans into my ear.

"By the time I get you ready for dinner, he won't be able *not* to."

"Do you have such strong faith in your abilities?" I reprimand, my throat feeling oddly parched.

Her face screws in puzzlement at my statement for a spell, her gaze softening afterward.

"No, Your Highness. It's not in my abilities I have faith in. It's *you*. I have faith in my Winter Queen. Always and forever."

Chapter 12
Levi

"I've heard enough," I grunt, annoyed. "Take two soldiers outside with you and bring him to me. I'll deal with his betrayal myself."

As the young squire quickly retreats out of my tent to do my bidding, I don't miss how Brick stares a hole into the back of his head. My general looks like he'd love nothing more than to kill the messenger of such ill tidings just so he could expel his aggravation now rather than later.

"This isn't good, my king. If she knows…" Brick begins to say once we're alone.

"We have no idea what she knows," I cut in before his pessimistic nature gets the best of him.

"Oh, *we know*." He scoffs with a frown. "There's no way the boy wasn't telling the truth," he adds, referring to the squire who was lucky enough to leave with his head attached after bringing us such news. "I know the girl he was talking about too. You can't miss her when she's walking about the camp. The woman oozes sex," he groans, pouring himself a glass of wine to drown his sorrows.

"Does she now? I hadn't noticed," I reply, playfully stealing his cup out of his hand.

"I'd rather you had," he snaps.

"What's that supposed to mean?" I ask, intrigued.

"Maybe the real question you should be asking yourself is why you haven't noticed that red-haired perfect piece of ass when she is all your men can talk about?"

"Maybe because I have more important issues to worry about than to notice such things, dear friend. You do know that not every male thinks with his dick, right?" I chuckle.

"Bullshit. We all think with our cocks. Especially when there are beautiful women walking about. The real reason why the queen's handmaiden has skipped your attention is because someone else already has it."

"And by someone, you mean…" I bait.

"Don't make me say her name," he mutters, staring about the tent suspiciously.

I can't help but chuckle.

"Do you think that just by saying Kat's name, she will magically appear? She's not a witch."

"She might be," he grumbles.

"You do know that there are no such things as witches? Gods, Brick. I never took you to be so superstitious. She's just a woman. A flesh and blood woman with no magical powers to speak of." I chuckle again.

"It's no laughing matter, Levi. I swear I saw my own death in her eyes," he insists, frantic.

"You saw what she wanted you to see. Kat isn't a witch. She's just a girl with too much power for her own good."

"Can you quit with that shit? It's the second time you've called her Kat. You're not friends. Friends don't let their father butcher their friend's whole fucking family."

My smile instantly drops from my face.

"I'm well aware."

"Are you sure? Because it kind of looks like you need a reminder why we are doing this shit in the first place."

"It wasn't Katrina's hand who raised the sword," I reply factually. "And it wasn't her who gave out the order."

THE FROST TOUCHED QUEEN

"Aye, but she didn't stop it either," Brick states harshly. "She didn't warn you. She didn't prevent it from happening. And she sure as shit wasn't there to pick up the pieces afterward. As far as your people are concerned, her hands are covered in the same east-born blood as her father."

My back molars almost break with how hard I grind them, but I don't give him a response.

He's right.

Katrina made no such effort to spare my family.

None.

A truth that I must keep close to my heart in the days ahead.

Even if all it does is harden it further.

When Brick realizes that his words have turned my mood charcoal black, he becomes subdued.

"I'm sorry. I've spoken out of turn and said too much," he apologizes. "I'm just worried, that's all. Worried that you'll get played by a pretty face with a witch's heart."

"You forget, dear friend. My life is already cursed, as you just so eloquently pointed out. What could she ever do to me that her father hasn't already?"

Brick lets out an exaggerated exhale, before placing a friendly hand on my shoulder.

"Don't underestimate the power of a woman. They tend to know exactly which buttons to push to cripple us. To make us lose our way and leave us a ghost of our former selves. And one such as the Winter Queen must have been taught those types of tricks from the crib."

My knee-jerk reaction is to defend Kat. Or at least the Kat that I had grown up with and explain to him that she wasn't always like this. That when we were young, she wasn't this terrifying thing that Brick sees now.

She was different.

Softer.

Kinder.

But then I remember Atlas's letter as well as Brick's counsel, and they are all I need for any words I may have conjured up in her defense to die a quick death at the tip of my tongue.

Queen Katrina of Bratsk needs no defense from me.

What she needs is reckoning.

And by the gods, I shall be the instrument used to deliver exactly that.

I crack my neck, feeling more like myself than I have in days, and look my friend straight in the eye.

"Settle your mind, General. You need not worry about your king. He is of one mind and one mind only."

"Pray tell?" He arches an unconvinced brow.

"The northern throne."

To this, Brick's face lights up, his lips stretching into a satisfied smile.

"The gods be good." He pats my shoulder down hard in elation.

"Yes, the gods be good," I repeat under my breath. "For I shall not be."

Brick opens his mouth to say something else but is interrupted when one of my soldiers comes into my tent with a message.

"Your Highness, there is a visitor here to see you," he announces.

"Hmm. Must be your men with the asshole who spilled the beans to the Winter Queen's jezebel," Brick mumbles, going back to pouring wine for himself to drink. "Not that I blame him. A woman like that could seduce a priest out of a monastery. Might as well bring the poor fucker in and get this over with."

"No, Your Grace," the soldier interjects. "It's Queen Katrina's handmaiden who would like an audience with the king."

Brick spits out his drink, eyes wide in alarm.

"Shit! Now the witch is sending that sexpot to your tent?! Is she mad?"

My soldier looks confused as to why his general looks like he's about to have a seizure, but I'm in too foul a mood to pay him any mind. But when Brick begins to fix his attire and comb his wild auburn hair back with his fingers, I begin to share in my soldier's baffled sentiment.

"You do know that if the queen sent this red-haired vixen to my tent, it's with the sole purpose of seducing me, not you, right?" I say with as straight a face as I can muster.

"Couldn't pay me enough to care. A girl like that is bound to need to blow off steam after a long day of doing her queen's dirty work for her. Wouldn't mind it one bit if she did it with me." He winks.

Any other day, I would have chastised him for his perversity, but I'm too curious as to what could have passed through Katrina's mind to send her seductress my way.

I guess there is only one way to find out.

"Send her in," I order.

A few seconds later, my curiosity doubles as a no-nonsense raven beauty marches inside my tent, instead of the red-haired seductress Brick had his heart on meeting.

"Your Majesty," she utters impassionedly, curtseying before me.

Brick and I rapidly share a confused glance before she lifts her head back up at me.

"And you are?"

"My name is Inessa of Bjørn, Your Majesty. I am one of Queen Katrina's lady's maids. I've come to deliver a message from our beloved queen," she explains, her tone as expressionless as her face.

They must put something in the water up north, for I swear every woman I meet that's from there is as cold as the driven snow. Like Katrina, Inessa's face alone is something to behold, almost as if sculpted from the fairest clay. But it is the bite of bitterness in her eyes that makes all that beauty look harshly severe instead of pleasing to the eye.

"I see. Tell me, Inessa of Bjørn, what message does the queen have for me that she couldn't deliver herself during the ten-hour journey we just made together?" I cock a brow.

"Apologies, Your Highness. It's not a message, per se, but an invitation that I bring. My queen would very much like to dine with you this evening and will not take no for an answer."

Dinner?

Kat wants to have dinner with me?

She barely spoke two words the whole ride here and now she wants to talk?

Hmm.

I stroke my stubbled chin in deep thought, listing the pros and cons to such an invitation. The only way Katrina would even contemplate breaking bread with me is if she's somehow smuggled poison into it. My safest bet would be to stay clear of her, but then that would defeat the purpose of trying to ascertain that she chooses me to be her lord and groom.

Tricky.

"My lord?" Inessa questions when I take too long to offer a reply.

"Were you expecting me to say something? Did you not just inform me that the queen will not take no for an answer? Tell me the hour and she shall have me there."

"At sunset, Your Highness," she advises.

"At sunset it is, then. Anything else I should be made aware of?"

When Inessa's gaze discreetly scrutinizes the dirty riding clothes I still have on, I almost believe her brave enough to tell me to get a bath before dinner. But alas, Inessa's humble station has taught her to keep her own opinion to herself or suffer the consequences. A maid telling a king he stinks and is in dire need of a bath is a sure-fire way to live out the remainder of your days in some dungeon.

"No, Your Highness," she finally says, taking another bow and rushing off to tell her mistress the news.

It's only when the tent is completely silent that I realize that Brick hasn't said a word or even cracked a joke at my expense.

"Brick?" I call out, when I find my best friend in a daze staring at my tent's entrance.

"Huh?" he stammers, shaking his head in disbelief.

"You look out of sorts. Are you okay?" I ask, starting to worry that my friend might have had a bit too much to drink.

"I don't know," he retorts, confused, still staring at the tent's flap. "I'm not sure that I am."

"Still upset that you didn't get to meet the redhead?" I joke lightheartedly.

"Who?" he counters absentmindedly, while his eyelids blink rapidly as if trying to clear whatever fog has taken over his sight. "Oh, her? The redhead. Right. Yeah. No. It's fine. No matter," he adds, his tone not holding his previous excitement over the woman.

The fuck is wrong with him now?

"My king," a soldier announces as he steps into the tent. "We've got him."

Right.

I almost forgot.

"Bring him to me," I command, walking over to a nearby chair to take a seat.

In no time at all, four of my most loyal soldiers appear with their prisoner. I let out an exhale when I see that the young boy in question must not have seen twenty springs if he's seen a day. Still, loyalty knows no age. He needs to learn his lesson as well as be made an example of.

The boy, now stripped from his soldier uniform, wearing only his undergarments, doesn't even resist being manhandled by his peers as they place him before me. Another telltale sign of his guilt. That and the fact that his head continues to hang low, unable to meet my eyes.

"Do you know why you are here?" I ask outright, but the boy is too ashamed to answer.

That won't do.

I need to know exactly what he told Katrina's handmaiden, down to the very last detail.

"Answer me!" I shout, slamming my fist onto the chair's arm and splintering it. "Do you know why you are here?"

To this he nods, his whole body shaking in fear.

I lean back into my chair until my temper is under control.

The boy made a mistake.

One that many would have made in his shoes.

I can forgive a mistake, but not disloyalty.

"Very well. I'm going to ask you a slew of questions. Bear in mind that your fate depends on the answers you give me. Speak true and you shall have mercy. Speak false, and may the gods have mercy on your soul."

Another nod, this one accompanied by a sob.

"My squire has advised me that you've been seen fraternizing with one of the queen's handmaidens. Is this true?"

This time, whatever courage still resides in him, appears long enough for him to lift his head and look me in the eye.

"It is, my king."

"And while you were conversing with said maid, did she by chance ask you questions about me, your king?"

"She did, my king," he admits sullenly.

"What questions did she ask you?" I ask, my voice calm and collected.

The young soldier swallows dryly, his gaze bouncing off his general and the other men in the room, before it fixes back on me.

"She only seemed interested in one thing, my king."

"That being—"

"The letter you received earlier today," he chokes out. "She wanted me to tell her who it had come from."

"And what did you tell her?" I insist.

"At first, I told her I had no idea. That my job was to keep a sword to the rider's neck while you read the letter. That I didn't even see the parchment, so I had no way of knowing which seal it held," he begins to explain at rapid speed.

"You said at first," I point out. "Which makes me believe you told her something in the end."

"I told her I wasn't sure. I told her it could have been my imagination. But… but…" he stammers, eyes filled with fear as well as remorse for his actions.

"But," I encourage, "you saw something. Didn't you?"

He nods, silent tears streaking down his face.

"The rider had a ring. A ring with a marigold on it," he confesses at last.

Fuck.

If he told her that, then there is no way Katrina doesn't know it was Atlas who sent me the letter.

Fuck!

"I'm so sorry, my king. I'm so sorry," the boy breaks down, my men holding on to his arms the only thing preventing him from falling to the ground.

"Did you fuck her at least?" Brick belts out, sounding more like himself and interrupting the young soldier's wails of regret.

The boy's face flushes, his tear-stricken gaze lowering to his dick.

"I see. She used her mouth to ensure you'd use yours." I groan. "What's your name, boy?"

"It's Sten, my king."

"Before today, have you ever had a woman?" I ask consolingly.

"No, my king." He shakes his head.

"Hmm. How old are you?"

"Nineteen, my king."

Shit, even younger than I gave him credit for.

"And at what age were you forced to serve the crown?"

"Eight springs, my king," he answers somberly.

Fuck.

A baby.

He was ordered to hold arms while still a child. All he's seen has been bloodshed and grief. Is it any wonder a woman was able to entice him with something that he's probably spent his whole life wishing for? Some warmth and affection?

Damn the gods.

"So is it a fair assumption that up until today, you've never been with a woman, nor wise to their ways?" I ask him, even though just by looking at him I already know the answer.

He shakes his head, still looking like he would take it all back if he could.

He would take that one moment of bliss, in a life that had held no joy for him, and reject it, if given a second chance.

"Fair enough. I've heard all I need to. I will spare your life, Sten. I believe you made an error in judgment, one that you will think twice about making again." His bloodshot eyes stare back at me with such gratitude and awe that it almost pains me of what I'm about to do next.

"Still, a price has to be paid for this treachery. I will strive to be a king worthy of your loyalty, Sten. But you will also need to prove to me that you've learned the error in your ways. That you will not betray me again for a pretty face or for the promise of a tender caress."

Sten lets out another wail, this one filled with relief and gratitude.

"I will never forsake you again, my king. Never," he promises.

"For your sake, I sincerely hope not," I tell him. "Brick, you know what to do."

"Aye," Brick retorts. "Hold him down, boys."

The soldiers holding Sten's arms push him to his knees, while keeping a tight hold on him. Confused, Sten looks in every direction, focusing on Brick's looming form as he makes his way to him.

"Now, this is going to hurt like a motherfucker. No use in sugarcoating it, boy," Brick explains, uneasy with the task at hand. "Just remember one thing. You'll leave here with your life. It's a fucking mercy, boy. I wouldn't have been so lenient with you."

Brick then pulls out his dagger and orders my men to strip Sten of his undergarments, leaving him as naked as the day he was born into this earth.

"Here," Brick orders, shoving the boy's undergarments into his mouth. "Bite on that."

Sten does as he's told, eyes wide in alarm at what is in store for him.

"Now, this is the tricky part. I'm going to need you to hold your pecker in your hands. You need steady hands, boy. One wrong move, and you'll end up as a eunuch. I don't want that, and I doubt you do either. So steady hands. You understand?"

Even though he's bound and gagged, Sten has the fortitude of mind to nod.

"Good. This will be over in a second, don't you fret. Just going to slice the tip. Just the tip, so you'll have a good old reminder that no pussy is worth betraying your king."

Sten offers another nod.

"To do this right, I have to look, but there's no shame if you don't want to."

Sten shakes his head and stares at the shriveled member in his hands.

He's brave. Green in the ways of the world, but brave, I'll give him that.

Before Sten's nerves get the better of him, in one smooth blow, Brick slices off his foreskin, making the boy fall over in agony.

"Oh, stop your crying, boy. Babies in the west get the tip of their cock cut off from birth all the time. It will still work. You should count your blessings that the king didn't order me to cut the whole thing off," Brick playfully abolishes. "Now, you four." He points to the other soldiers standing by. "Take the boy back to your tents and tend to his wound. I don't want it on my conscience that this boy here ends up dying in a few days just because you were squeamish in helping him with his cock. I want him looked after and I want daily reports on his health. He's your brother in arms, so I want you to treat him as such."

They heed the warning in Brick's tone and rush to usher Sten out of the tent, but not before the boy turns his watery sights to me.

"Thank you, my king. Thank you."

I offer him a consoling nod, and let my men take him to be looked after.

"Shit, but that boy has steel in his veins. My bladder would have given way with the thought of someone chopping my dick off." Brick laughs, wiping the blood from his blade.

"It's like you said, he's lucky his life was spared. If King Orville were alive, he wouldn't have been."

"Fuck Orville. If we ever do go back up north, I'm going to take a long piss on that bastard's grave." Brick scowls.

"Then I guess I best make sure that we do." I smile. "Call my squire and tell him to fetch me a bucket of warm water and some clean clothes. I'm dining with royalty tonight, so I need to look my best."

"Right, I forgot about that. What are you going to do? She knows the letter was from Atlas. The boy confessed as much."

"Don't you worry about that. I know exactly how to play this."

"And how's that?" He raises an inquisitive brow.

"By doing what she does best—lie."

"**H**e's late," I fume, insulted that Levi thinks it's acceptable to keep me waiting like this.

To keep *his* queen waiting for him.

But just as that thought pops into my head, another one follows. What if I'm being stood up?

What if he rethought my invitation and concluded that spending ten hours with me riding on horseback was all the time he could tolerate being around me?

Argh!

If he dares not to show his face tonight, then I can't be held responsible for my actions.

"Would you like more wine, my queen? Maybe it will relax you," Anya offers hesitantly.

"Are you saying that I don't look relaxed?" I counter, tapping my fingers on the table where two empty plates still lie.

Anya bows her head, not courageous enough to give me an answer. Inessa, on the other hand, isn't as cowardly.

"It's a cold night, Your Highness. A bit of wine will warm the blood," she explains, picking up the jar of cherry wine and filling my cup.

"Blood can't course through iced veins, Inessa. But I'd welcome a glass," Levi says just as he enters my tent.

My handmaidens instantly bow to him, averting their gaze, while I remain perfectly still in my seat, staring indifferently at him, not wanting to let on the turmoil I'm suddenly in.

I was expecting the monosyllable-speaking brute I had been riding with to waltz through my door.

Instead, I got a king.

Wearing all black from the tip of his boots to the fine woven braids of his hair, Levi is a formidable sight to behold. Clean shaven and freshly washed, Levi looks as if he hasn't seen a second of our arduous journey, looking refreshed as one does after a good night's sleep.

With each stride he walks my way, I can't help but let my eyes linger on the differences that the man before me has with the one I left just mere hours ago. He looks majestic in his black bearskin coat and dark assemble, so much so that I'm unable to reprimand him for his tardiness. In fact, if this is the result of me having to wait an extra hour for his arrival, I'd be more than happy to have waited some more just to see what other miracles he is able to perform on his appearance.

Maybe that would have given him time to take out his braids.

What a silly thought to have. He'd never do that.

Not for me at least.

Unlike northern men, you will never find an east-born male with his hair cut short to the nape of his neck or hanging down loose by his shoulders. Eastern custom prevents as much. Levi's kingdom has some very specific practices when it comes to their male population's hair, preferring braids as the look of choice. I would imagine that they keep it this way as not to be a burden to them while on the battlefield, but the mind does travel to see such raven locks free from their bondage.

"My queen," Levi says, kneeling before me.

It's an empty gesture at best, but still I appreciate his diligence in maintaining the honorable decorum.

Levi then lifts his head just a tad and grabs my hand to place a kiss on my royal ring.

"There. You have your witnesses," he whispers with a smug smirk.

"When I said there was no use for you to kneel without any witnesses, my intention wasn't that you do it in front of my loyal servants," I proclaim, snatching my hand away from him.

"I'll try better next time," he taunts, going back to his full height and leaving me even more out of sorts with his imposing form.

It's only when he's finally seated at the table across from me and at a safe distance that I let myself breathe.

"I'll have that wine now, Inessa," he says, and there is something about hearing him order my handmaiden around like she belongs to him that irks me to no end.

"That won't be necessary. Inessa, Anya, you can go back to your tents. I won't be needing your services this evening," I announce, surprising even myself with the off-book decision.

"Yes, Your Highness," Inessa and Anya reply in tandem, curtsying and leaving before I have time to change my mind.

Levi leans back in his chair, placing his arm over the back of it, while I get up from mine and walk toward him. I grab the pitcher of wine and start filling his glass to the rim.

"Interesting," he muses, running his thumb over his lower lip. "Never in a million years did I think this day would come. To have a queen serve me."

"Do you think I am incapable of doing such menial tasks? If that is true then it's no wonder you came with your army to cross my borders, seeing as you think me incompetent in all things."

"That wasn't the reason I came north," he says evenly.

"No?" I arch a brow, placing the pitcher back on the table. "Then what was?"

Levi grabs his chalice and drinks his wine, down to the very last drop.

"Do you mind?" he goads, waving his glass in the air so I can pour some more wine into it, instead of giving me an answer.

A forced smile crests my lips, but I proceed to repeat the task yet again.

"I guess I should get accustomed to it," he mumbles, watching the liquid pour into his cup.

"Accustomed to what?"

"You serving me. As my lady wife, you'll be expected to do much more than satiate my thirst. You'll have to satisfy my hunger, too. Amongst other things," he states, his tone thick with innuendo.

My grip on the pitcher's handle tightens at the audacity of his words. He was never this crude.

Never this mean.

He was… sweet and caring.

Honorable.

He'd never dare speak to me so… so… vulgarly.

After his cup is full, I rest the pitcher back at the center of the table. I don't wait for him to pick it up, preferring to walk back to the safety of my seat.

"I think maybe that glass should be your last, as the first has already gone to your head."

The cruel chuckle he lets out has my cold heart in a vise grip, tightening it to the point of pain.

"I didn't say anything that wasn't true. As my lady wife, you will have to serve me and only me."

"As your queen, I already do serve you."

"Really?" He lets out a sarcastic chuckle. "How so?"

"I serve you by being the reason why you hold your lands and get to call yourself king of the east. I serve you by letting you live and forgive your treachery by offering you the possibility of marriage. I serve you by allowing air to fill your lungs. But make no mistake, that you are not the only one I serve. I'm also a devoted servant to the kings of the south and west."

Levi's beautiful facial features turn harder at the mention of the other two kings.

"Your loyalty to your vassals has no bounds, it seems," he states coldly.

"As is my duty. Otherwise, what kind of queen would I be?"

Levi doesn't offer a reply to my provocation, preferring to drink his alcohol instead. When he suddenly gets up from his seat, I half expect him to fill his glass for a third time, but am pleasantly surprised when he fills his plate with the pheasant carrot stew my cook prepared instead.

"Apologies, Your Highness, but I'm afraid if you invited me to dine with you this evening, expecting to be entertained with mindless conversation, then you will be disappointed. I'm not much for idle chitchat," he explains, vigorously slicing his meat with his knife and fork as if it offended him in some way.

"You never were," I mutter under my breath, but thankfully Levi doesn't pick up on it. "I don't mind dining in silence," I retort a little louder. "I quite prefer it."

"Fine by me," he grumbles, shoving his fork in his mouth.

I, too, go through the motions of filling my plate, although my appetite has waned somewhat.

This was not how I expected this dinner to go. I need confirmation that Levi received a letter from the west and if said letter had been written by Atlas himself. How am I to do that when it's obvious Levi won't say another word to me for the whole duration of the meal?

Why does he have to be so obtuse and hardheaded?

Gods give me patience.

Although he tried his best to hide it, I have no doubt he's fond of you. And fondness has a way of corrupting a soul when it's not nourished. You can use that to your advantage.

Those had been Inessa's exact words to me when trying to convince me that I could get the intel I needed all by myself. At the time, I let myself believe that maybe there was some merit to her observation, but now… I'm not so sure.

Where Inessa saw fondness in Levi's eyes, I only see hate.

He hates me.

I don't even care why he does right now. All I care about is that his hatred is making my life a million times more difficult than it has to be.

I have to find a way to tumble the protective walls he keeps built up around him down, so that I may get the answers I seek.

If Anya were here, her counsel would be to seduce the dark king, but unlike her, I have no real experience in doing such things. I've grown up too sheltered to have acquired such female expertise. And besides, can a man who has sworn to loathe me for his entire life be seduced by the object of his hatred?

Doubtful.

So instead, I give in to my defeat and eat my dinner in total silence, hoping that between now and dessert, I'll come up with a plan that will work in my favor.

Unfortunately for me, Levi has a different idea in mind.

After we're both finished with our meal, he gets up and walks toward me, stretching his hand out for me to take.

"After dinner, I always feel better to take a walk before retiring to bed. Would you like to accompany me?"

I'm so taken aback by his unexpected proposal that all I do is nod.

He takes my hand and pulls me out of my seat before retrieving my long cloak.

"It will be warmer as we get closer to the east, but as it stands, tonight is well below zero degrees. I wouldn't want you to catch a death from the cold."

"Wouldn't you, though?" I arch a suspicious brow.

"If death is in your destiny, I doubt very much it will be caused by a simple chill. Can the queen of winter even freeze as us mere mortals do?"

"I don't mind the cold," I answer honestly, since his tone is less hostile than it was when he came in. "It comforts me. Reminds me of home."

"Are you homesick already?" he teases, a playful glint in his green eyes.

I let him put my coat on me and offer a nonchalant shrug.

"I haven't had time to be homesick."

I've been too busy wondering why you wanted to dethrone me.

Wondering why you hate me.

"Understandable," he says, his voice slicing through my somber thoughts. "It hasn't even been a week, but it's normal that you're not homesick yet. However, as the months trail by, I'm sure you'll end up yearning for the familiarity of home," he adds, grabbing my arm and hooking it with his, leading me out of the tent.

"You sound like you have experience on the matter," I reply, letting him take the lead as we walk amongst the camp.

"I'm a soldier, Kat. I have been for most of my adult life. I've spent more time on distant shores and foreign lands than I have in my own kingdom. So yes, I'm quite the expert when it comes to longing for the place you call home."

"Hmm. So what you're telling me is that it will only get worse from here?"

"So much worse, Kat." He chuckles softly.

My immediate reaction is to demand that he not call me by that name again, but this is the first time I've seen Levi even looking a fraction of his old self. I don't have the will to chastise him for it.

At least, not right now.

"As the days turn into weeks, and weeks turn into months, you'll miss home that much more. But there is something that I must warn you of," he cautions seriously.

"And what is that?"

"When you do finally manage to go home, you'll find that it too has changed. That it isn't how you left it. You'll find it smaller somehow, find certain aspects of it obsolete and outdated. But your home is not at fault as to this new way you're perceiving it. It didn't change. You did."

I find myself hanging on to his every word. The scent of food over open fires and soldiers laughing as they dine around us are nothing but background noise to Levi's cautionary tale. I'm pulled back to a time when we were children and Levi seemed to know all things. Wise beyond his years, he would make it a point to share his learned experiences with us, so that we learned from his mistakes as well as be inspired to go on the same adventures he had.

"Tell me about your home. Tell me what's it like in the east," I hear myself ask.

The small smile he sends my way feels like a dagger is slowly chipping away at my frozen heart.

"You'll see soon enough."

"I know. I just want to be prepared for what awaits me."

There is a sad glimmer in his eyes, but all too soon does it disappear as he begins to tell me about hot springs where you can bathe and open fields where you can ride your horse for days and still only find the vastest of green of meadows. He talks about flowers adorned with an array of colors that bloom all year long. He continues on, describing his home with such passion that my reluctance of stepping foot on eastern soil slowly begins to dissolve.

We must walk for over an hour as he continues to excitedly list all the reasons why he's so happy to return home and how his people will rejoice in the streets with our arrival. I don't miss how he intentionally leaves out the part that me coming with him will also be cause for added celebration. Not only will his people be thrilled for having their rightful king return to them, but they'll also be proud that he was able to make good on his word of conquering the north. At least to an extent, they are right to think as much. His kingdom will see me by his side and think they have won. The politics behind that naïve perception won't be of importance to them.

Until it is.

Then everything will change.

When Levi escorts me back to my tent, I'm almost sad our walk has come to an end.

It's been the only highlight of this whole damn journey, thus far.

But then I remember why I invited him to dine in the first place, and suddenly, all my good disposition flies out the window.

He tricked me.

He kept me entertained with talks of his home so that I lost track of my goal.

I lost sight of the fact that no matter how charming he's able to be for an hour, he's still the same man who brought tens of thousands of soldiers to my doorstep, threatening to overthrow me. He succeeded in making me forget that he's still my enemy. Maybe in the future he can call himself my husband, but that won't change the fact that he is not my friend, but my foe.

Before Levi even has a chance to open his conniving mouth and bid me farewell, I go straight to the cut of it.

"You received a letter earlier today," I state matter-of-factly.

"I did," he retorts in kind.

"Was it Atlas? Did the king of the west send you that letter?"

"Yes."

It takes everything in me to keep my jaw in place and not let it fall to the floor.

"I can't believe you admitted it," I croak out, genuinely gobsmacked with his answer.

"You expected me to lie?" He smirks.

"Yes," I answer truthfully.

He runs his thumb over his lower lip, bringing my attention to it.

"I did consider it… lying to you," he confesses unrepentantly.

"Why didn't you?" I choke out, averting my gaze from his full lips, since they are too distracting to keep my focus where it needs to be.

"Because I remembered the man that I am and the one I wish to remain. I value honor and integrity. What would it make me if I had lied to you, the woman I'm in a race to conquer and marry?" he states with conviction. "No, Kat. I won't lie to you. And I'll never lie *for* you either. This is who I am. You may not like my truths, or how I say them, but that is all you will ever get from me."

I chew on his admission as well as his reasoning behind it.

Unfortunately for me, my puzzlement must be written all over my face, because Levi begins to softly chuckle under his breath.

"Is this amusing to you? Why are you laughing? Do you think it wise to be laughing at your queen? To her face?" I whisper-yell in disgusted aggravation.

"Wise, no. But I'm not laughing at you, Kat. I'm laughing at that." He points to the way the corner of my lips curls up in disgust.

"I don't understand, but in all honesty, I don't care to, either. Tell me why Atlas wrote to you. Or better yet, give me the letter and I'll read it myself," I command, holding out my open palm for him.

"I can't do that," he replies, no longer sounding amused.

"And why not? I'm ordering you to give me that letter."

"You can order me all you want. Until you are as blue in the face as a northern rose. I can't give you what I don't have."

"What do you mean you don't have it? What did you do with it?" I ask frustratedly.

"I burned it," he admits without missing a beat.

I'm all but fuming now.

"And why, pray tell, did you do that?"

"Because my personal correspondence is exactly that. Personal— mine to do with as I see fit."

Even with me staring daggers at him, Levi doesn't so much as break a sweat.

"And if I was to ask you what that letter's contents were, would you be as forthcoming as you were when you confessed who wrote it?"

"You can ask but then you will force me to remind you of our earlier conversation. An honorable man does not lie, nor does he betray those who are near and dear to them," he baits, and I can see it in his eyes he won't tell me a goddamn thing, his loyalty bound to Atlas. "Is there anything more that you desire, my queen?" he adds smugly, knowing that I have lost this battle.

"No. I think I've heard all I need for one night. It's been enlightening."

"Glad to be of assistance," he says before bowing his head. "Good night, Your Highness."

I don't even bother replying to his farewell, rushing into my tent just so I don't have to look at his smug face for another minute.

Levi bested me tonight.

He pulled me in without me even realizing it, making me lose sight of this chess match we're in. And while in a game of chess, the king might be the most important piece at play, but in terms of raw power, it's the queen who rules the chessboard.

Before this journey is over and done with, I will make sure that Levi learns that lesson by hcart.

Chapter 14
Levi

I'm not one bit surprised that Katrina has gone back to not speaking to me, the following day. Throughout our journey east, she doesn't say a word, limiting our only contact to letting me aid her in getting off her horse, and nothing more.

I wish I could say her indifference to me didn't sting.

I wish I could say a myriad of things to the contrary, that I prefer her silence to the sound of her voice.

I wish I could say that…

But then I would be a liar.

Last night, as we walked amongst the camp, her attentiveness to all that I had to say brought back memories of a young girl who thirsted for any knowledge or new experience I was able to share. For a fraction of a second, she was that same bright-eyed girl who hungered for my attention and approval. Who thought I hung the stars and moon only for her, and at the time, I would have if given the chance.

I forgot how addictive it was to have that type of power over someone.

To be able to wield it like the wind bends light, and either captivate your audience with its sparkling shine or trap them into its shadow.

Last night, she gift wrapped that power back to me, and let me believe...

Let me believe that *my* Kat lived.

That she was still inside this ice sculpture of a woman.

All she needed was to be set free.

It took me a minute for my feet to find their way back to solid ground, for reality to slap me in the face, but damn was it the sweetest minute I've tasted in the longest time.

Still, all good things must come to an end, and before the night was over, we were back to our defined warring corners, the haze of youthful memories no longer clouding our senses and judgment.

And all of that would be good and well, if it wasn't for this unexpected visit that stands before me now.

"With me? Your queen wishes to dine with me? Again? Tonight?" I rush out to ask, since I'm at a complete loss as to why Katrina's handmaiden, Inessa, is once again in my tent extending such an invitation.

"Yes, Your Highness. Queen Katrina insists on it."

The hell is she up to?

Bewildered at this unexpected change of events, I look to Brick to see what his thoughts are on the matter, but the fucker doesn't even look my way, too focused on the stern-faced beauty in our midst.

"Brick? Would you mind escorting the queen's handmaiden out for a few minutes while I consider her invitation?"

By the way his eyes light up, my general looks like he's just hit pay dirt in receiving such a command.

"My king—" Inessa interjects, not happy that I have to think on her mistress's proposal, but I cut in before she has time to give me her objections.

"It will only take but a minute, I assure you. Brick, please escort Inessa out."

"Of course, my king," he says, all smiles, but as he rushes to escort her out, I call out to him again.

"Brick, let one of the guards watch over our guest and return to me at once."

His ecstatic expression falls flat to the floor with that.

"As you wish, my king," he replies, deflated.

I watch the unlikely pair walk out of my tent before I attempt to move a muscle. It's only when Brick returns that I jump out of my seat and crook my finger to him, commanding him to me. Begrudgingly he eats the distance between us, already having a fair idea of what I'm about to say.

"These are the times that I need someone to give me counsel, Brick. Someone who can keep a cool head about him when I cannot. I need my general, not some lovestruck fool," I admonish, placing both my hands on his shoulders as his cheeks turn even redder than his hair. "Now, are you the man that I need, or not?"

"I am, my king," he grunts, nostrils flaring. "I'm no fool."

"I said lovestruck fool," I instigate.

"Not one of those either. I got my head in the game. I do," he promises, giving me his meanest glower.

"Good. Glad to hear it. Now, General, when at war, do we invite our enemies to dine with us?"

"No, my king. The only dining we do is when we feast on their bones after defeating them on the battlefield."

"As it should be. So tell me what you make of our so-called queen inviting me to supper a second time in as many nights?"

"She's springing a trap. That is the only reason she would be doing such a thing."

"Aye, but what kind of trap?" I venture, looking up at the ceilings as if the gods will answer that question for me.

It's Brick's scoff, though, that ends up being my reply.

"Do you have something to add?" I cock a brow. "If so, say it, man, and stop wasting what precious little time we have."

My general fades, and in his place, my best friend, Brick, arises.

"You're not going to like it, Levi. Safer for me not to say anything or risk you giving me a black eye for my honesty."

"And when have I ever done that?" I laugh.

"Never, but when it comes to *her*, I always feel like I'm on thin ice with you, no pun intended."

I let go of his shoulders and take a step back to stare at my friend.

"Say what you have to, Brick. That's an order," I demand forcibly.

I swear I think I hear him call me fucker under his breath.

"Fine. But if you're going to hit me, do it here." He points to his chest. "I kind of need my pretty face to stay as it is, if you don't mind."

"If you think the woman outside will be tempted by a pretty face, you have another thing coming to you. That woman out there, the one that you are unabashedly lusting over, is made of the same ice as her queen. Your fiery hair and beard will not melt such glaciers," I provoke with a mocking grin.

It's all the incentive Brick needs to charge at me and push me back a step.

"Okay, Mr. Know It All. You want a reality check, here's one for size. Last night when you returned from dining with her, *you* were the one who looked like a lovestruck fool. It's the northern stars in your eyes that blinds you from seeing the truth. You're besotted with her. Don't try to deny it."

My smile dies on my lips at his accusation.

"Not only are you seeing things, old friend, but you're also projecting. It's your own infatuation for Inessa that makes you see things that aren't there."

"Bullshit!" he shouts. "I saw what I saw, and so did every soldier here with a pair of working eyeballs. She's playing you for a sucker and you are letting her. Go and dine with the northern bitch. See what good it does you!"

I don't even realize I've done it until it's too late. My closed fist lands right across Brick's mouth and jaw, splitting his lower lip in two.

"Fuck the gods!" he growls, wiping the blood off his lip. "I knew you were going to hit me! I fucking knew it! Gods be damned!"

Both of us breathe heavily as we glower at each other for a charged pause, only for it to be interrupted by our sudden burst of laughter. I walk over to him and squeeze his shoulder again, while inspecting the damage I've done to his face.

"I'm sorry, old friend. I don't know what came over me," I confess, rattled that I let my temper go there.

"Oh, I know exactly why. I should have known better than to speak my mind. Live and learn, I guess." He laughs, already over the sucker punch.

"No, Brick. You are one of the few people I trust in the world to tell it to me like it is. I refuse to have it any other way."

"Yeah, well, I don't think my face is in agreement. It's not looking so pretty right now. My lip is going to swell like a motherfucker."

Guilt accosts me that he's right. It will blow up to the size of a melon by tomorrow. He won't be able to eat for days without hurting.

Damn it. Why did I have to punch him?

"Again, I'm sorry."

"No need to apologize. I know what I did was wrong," he mumbles sullenly as he wipes the blood with his sleeve.

"All you did was give me your opinion on last night."

"No, Levi. I did more than that. I insulted *your* queen by calling her a bitch." On reflex, my fists instantly close into two fists, Brick's gaze going immediately to them. "See? You can't help it. It's ingrained in you. This incessant need to defend her. Even if only subconsciously." He sighs. "You need to let go of that shit, Levi. The sooner you realize the girl you used to be friends with is now your enemy, the better. Otherwise, she'll use that dormant affection to her benefit. That's what these dinners are for. To prey on your one weakness—her."

I let his words sink in, knowing there is an ounce of truth to what he's saying. The thought that Kat would use my misguided feelings for her in our youth did cross my mind. As did Atlas's, or he wouldn't have written to me with that same warning.

"Let her believe what she wants. If this is her only strategy, then I don't see why I shouldn't use it against her and to my own advantage. Remember, Brick, for all intents and purposes, I'm supposed to be wooing my way to the northern throne. I won't be able to guarantee she picks me to wed if her animosity for me grows. Which it will, if all she gets from me is my cold shoulder."

"I would think the Winter Queen would be used to the cold. That she even prefers it," he tries to joke to lighten the tension in the room.

"Be that as it may, her preferences are no concern of mine. Only my people are," I rebuke, knowing what sacrifices I must make for the betterment of my kingdom.

Once my mind is made up, I ask him to call Inessa back in.

"Shall I tell the queen that you have accepted her offer?" Inessa is quick to ask when she returns.

"Aye, you may. Tell your queen that I'll be there at sunset," I announce, throwing a glance over at Brick. "But before that, I have a favor to ask of you." Even though she keeps her expression even, I can tell she's taken aback by this unexpected request. "As you can see, my general is injured and would benefit greatly to some tending to. Could I ask you to mend his wound? I'd be forever grateful if you paid him this kindness."

Inessa looks over at Brick, his split lip still bleeding all over his shirt. Her brows pull together in deep thought, but in the end she relents.

"Of course, Your Highness. It would be an honor to assist you. I only ask that I relay my message to my queen first and then tend to your man."

"As you should. Brick will accompany you."

Inessa curtseys and leaves, while Brick holds back a little while longer.

"Remind me to let you punch me more often," he teases, throwing me a conspiring wink before rushing after Inessa with a new spring to his step.

Once I'm left to my own devices, my wayward thoughts begin to resurface.

I tell myself it's only curiosity that has me accepting Katrina's invitation.

I'm curious to see how far she's willing to go to play this game of hers.

I tell myself a great many things, but in the end, I know the real reason why I said yes to her request. There's a part of me that still hangs on to hope. Hope that somehow, my Kat isn't lost to me.

This never grows old.

Seeing her like this.

In her element, oozing confidence and regal power.

At first, it put me off since it only served as a reminder of how different she's become.

Now, I must admit I'm a little awestruck by it.

How she commands a room without uttering a word.

The hem of her white gown grazes the floor as she walks toward me, pitcher in hand. My gaze lands on the white fur at the end of her sleeves, wrapped around a slender tilted wrist, as she pours wine into my empty cup. Her pale blonde hair looks luminous by candlelight, the diamond studs embedded in it, making each lock sparkle as if she'd somehow managed to pluck the stars from the sky to weave into her hair.

The woman is a true treasure amongst men.

A winter jewel.

And when Katrina is close enough to me that her rose-scented perfume begins to invade my senses, my hand impulsively wraps itself around her fair wrist, stopping her in her tracks.

"That's enough," I groan.

She arches an inquisitive brow, her gaze bouncing off my face and onto where my fingers have latched onto.

As if burned with the feel of her skin to mine, I snatch my hand away from her wrist and clear my throat.

"I'm sorry. I didn't mean to startle you. I'm just not in the mood for wine tonight."

I need to keep my head clear when I'm around you, Kat.

Or gods know what I'll do.

"You didn't startle me," she assures with a hint of curiosity to her voice. "Would you prefer I fetch you some water instead?"

"No. One glass of wine won't kill me." I force a smile.

She nods and turns to return back to her seat.

With her back turned to me, I swallow dryly and pick up my glass to empty its contents in one fell swoop to quench my parched throat.

Thankfully, when Katrina sits back down, she doesn't instigate conversation, happy for us to dine in complete silence. I peacefully enjoy the rest of the meal this way, unease only creeping up my spine every so often when I feel her gaze lift up from her plate to look at me. I pretend her discreet glances go unnoticed, preferring to concentrate on my food than wonder what she's thinking.

When we finish our meal, Katrina surprises me yet again, by getting out of her seat and grabbing her long coat.

"It's a nice night for a walk, don't you think?" she asks as slips her coat on.

"Hmm," I mumble, not entirely sure how to respond.

Seems like Kat is full of surprises tonight.

I wasn't expecting to dine with her this evening, and I sure wasn't expecting her to want to walk with me afterward like we did last night.

Why go out of your way to be so hospitable to someone who wants your crown?

To say the Winter Queen is a complex conundrum is an understatement.

"Shall we?" she asks when she sees I haven't moved an inch from my seat.

"If you wish," I finally declare, standing and walking toward her.

I offer her my arm, to which she takes, steadily hanging on to it as we step in unison out of her tent. We walk throughout the camp for a few minutes in total silence, just taking in the scenery before us.

Compared to the soldiers I brought with me up north, this camp almost looks like a joke. Between her entourage and the few soldiers I kept behind to accompany her down east, this camp is as tame as they come. Eighty souls, at best, have pitched their tents on these grounds, whilst before, it had been close to twenty thousand. If Katrina had seen my original party, I doubt she'd be clinging to my arm so fiercely as she is now.

We trudge on, words failing on what to say since I wasn't expecting this.

I wasn't expecting any of it.

But unlike last night, it's Katrina who breaks the ice first.

"You laugh."

"Pardon? Did you just say I laugh?" I repeat, confused.

"Yes. You laugh. You didn't use to… before. At least I don't remember you doing it very often. But now… I hear you laugh all the time."

My forehead wrinkles at such a peculiar observation.

"When have you heard me laugh?" I ask, intrigued with her remark.

"With your men," she explains, looking just as mystified as I feel. "Every time we stop for a break on the road, you immediately go to them to see how they are faring. And then you laugh. You joke and play with them. I've never seen anything quite like it before."

"Care to elaborate? What part of me checking on my men and having a laugh with them confuses you? Because that's exactly how you sound. Confused."

She throws quick glances at my soldiers, all in front of their tents and open fires, eating and drinking the night away.

"Maybe because I am," she admits, her attention on some nearby soldiers playing cards, who interrupt their gambling long enough to throw me an acknowledging nod. "They look up to you," she adds, still staring at them. "Most importantly, they respect you. They're loyal to you. Even when you show your humanity so unabashedly. Even when you show them that you can laugh like they can. There's this shared sense of camaraderie between you. Almost as if you were one of them and I'm not quite sure what to make of it," she ends on a pensive note.

"But that's just it, Kat. I *am* one of them."

She shakes her head and turns to face me head-on.

"No, you're not. You're their king."

"I'm a soldier, Kat," I cut in with a bit more bite than I expected. "Before I was their king, I was their peer. A soldier in the trenches with them. I bled when they bled. I starved when they starved. I tended to their cuts and bruises, and they tended to mine," I explain, feeling more collected now. "It's easy to play and joke with men who have seen you at your worst. Who have watched you steal the life of some poor devil who probably had no idea why he was on the battlefield to begin with. They are me and I am them. We are one and the same." When her gaze looks even more baffled, I let out an exaggerated exhale before continuing on with my rant. "So yes, my men respect me even if I crack a joke here and there with them. And yes, their loyalty to me is without question but not because of a crown that was placed on my head, but because they know, without a shred of doubt, that I would die for them if need be. It's not a crown that wins people's hearts, Kat. And it's not a title that inspires people either. It's sacrifice."

Katrina goes awfully still, her lips a thin line across her face, making me wonder if anything that I'm saying is getting through to her.

Of course, I didn't tell her all I needed to. I was cautious to leave a few things out.

How I've only started to laugh after knowing her bastard of a father was buried ten feet under. How his death was the real motivator in lifting my spirits. I doubt Katrina would have liked to hear such honesty coming out of my lips.

"I forgot," she suddenly says.

"What?" I choke out. "What did you forget?"

"How passionate you are."

My chest tightens at her words, my throat feeling as if she's wrapped a rope around it, gently pulling at it for her pleasure.

"Passionate? Me?" I let out a self-deprecating chuckle. "The night we first met you led me to believe you thought me a bore."

She shakes her head.

"I never thought that. Never."

"So you lied?" I try to play off, hoping it's enough to lighten the tense atmosphere between us.

"I might have stretched the truth," she admits, a ghost of a coy smile reaching her lips. One that sends an arrow straight to my heart, and pierces it right through the middle, leaving a hollow gap.

"I'd rather you were always honest with me," I whisper, caught in her light gray gaze.

"As you are with me?" She arches her brow.

"I've told you before, Kat. I'm a man of honor. Lies have no room in my life."

"But keeping secrets does?" she asks, going to the root of it.

"A casualty of being king, I'm afraid."

"Heavy is the head," she mumbles under her breath despondently with my reply.

"Yes. It can be. If you let it," I caution wholeheartedly. "Its weight depends solely on you, Kat. You alone are judge and jury in that regard. No one else can help you there."

"What a lonely thought," she whispers again, her gaze fixed on mine.

A gentle breeze passes us by, the wind leaving an errant strand glued to her cheek. The urge to gently pull it back to its rightful place behind the crook of her ear is overwhelming, and yet I force myself to resist the temptation.

But even though I succeed in ignoring that compulsion, another one arises when she asks me her next question.

"Are you lonely, Levi?" she asks, her voice dropping an octave. "Being the beacon of your people, does it ever get… lonely?"

"Why are you asking me that?" I question back, feeling the rope she's latched around my neck starting to pull and suffocate me.

"Why are you evading the question?"

"I—" I open my mouth to reply, but the words never come out. *Am I lonely?*

Is that what she sees when she looks at me?

Loneliness?

"Doesn't matter," she says when I take too long to reply, and shrugs, looking done with the moment of vulnerability that just transpired between us.

My shoulders sag as I step beside her once more and proceed to lead her through the campsite.

For the rest of our walk, we don't say much. And whatever we do manage to converse about, I make sure to keep it as far away from anything that feels like a trap to my sanity. Anything that might pull us back to that spot at the center of the camp where we let our masks slide off, even if only for a second. I then escort her back to her tent, a little disappointed the night has come to its end.

"Thank you. I've learned a lot tonight," she says, her expression back to its blank form.

I don't ask her what she means by that, fearing I won't like the answer.

"Glad to be of service," I say instead.

I half expect her to rush inside to the safety of her tent and call it a night, but she takes a minute just to scan my face.

"You always were a dutiful teacher. I forgot that, too."

She then bridges the gap between us and places a chaste kiss on my cheek, leaving me in a complete daze.

The following morning when Katrina struts over to her horse, with not so much as a good morning for me, I don't take offense.

If she needs to keep her thoughts to herself as we ride east, then so be it. If she uses that time to plot against me, then that's a risk I knowingly take.

All because I know that Inessa will come to my tent later that night and invite me to dine with her queen once more.

I'll take her silence during the day if it means I have her attention in the evening.

It may be a gamble on my part, but it's one for her also.

This can all be a strategy in her game, a ruse to get my guard down and keep it there.

But I was never one to back down from a challenge.

Let's play this game to the end, Kat.

And let the better of the two win.

With each passing day we ride east, and the closer we are to reaching the gates of its capital city, Arkøya, the more unsettled about it I become.

I need more time.

My plan to wine and dine Levi into gaining his trust can't be accomplished in a mere few days. If I want him to tell me why he and the other kings in my kingdom all have suddenly decided to conspire against me, I need more time than what's been afforded to me.

I also need to be vigilant in how I go about it.

Levi is far too intelligent to fall for my ploy on the first day. I can sense his resistance. How his strategic mind—the same one that has done wonders for him on the battlefield—urges him not to fully buy into my act. But it's the hopelessly optimistic side of him, the one that dares him to see the best in people, that I play into.

He always did have that endearing quality about him.

Or at least when I was younger, I considered it a quality.

Now? Not so much.

It's a weakness I intend to exploit for all its worth.

Levi might have grown into this formidable man who has turned against me, but some things never change. His belief that people are generally good, if given the chance, is his downfall.

How could I ever show that side of me to a man who threatened to invade my home with an army that was sure to kill us all?

No.

Levi's made his decision.

He's my enemy through and through.

But if I have to play the fool and pretend that he's not, for my own aspirations, then so be it.

Although pretending to care for Levi isn't without its challenges.

Sometimes when we go out on our nightly walks and we lose ourselves in conversation, it takes me a minute to remind myself that this king is my enemy and not my friend. The way he talks about his experiences and the way he knows the world has me in a trance, completely captivated with all he has to say. Every night as we eat, I can't help but be impatient, needing to be done with the meal, just so we can go outside, and he can recount all his adventures while imparting the wisdom he gained from them. I feel like a young schoolgirl anxious to start her lessons, completely smitten by her teacher.

There are other feelings that arise too.

Ones that I dare not dissect.

I catch myself looking at his strong, square jaw and wonder how it would feel to caress it with the pad of my finger. Or if his stubbled cheek would prick mine if I just grazed it against his.

Or if his lips taste as decadent as they appear.

His voice alone sends shivers down my spine, making my lower belly quiver with every word he speaks.

And all these feelings serve to do just one thing—split my focus and lose track of my mission.

Maybe that's his plan all along.

While I connive in breaking his walls, maybe he's found a subtle way of doing the same to me.

It also doesn't help that he's insisted on riding with me on the same horse the whole way east. His protective hand and arm can always be found on my body, be it on my hip, or wrapped around my middle, palm flat on my stomach. With each gallop we make, I can feel his rock-hard chest against my back. So much so, the two have morphed into one, syncing our breathing. Even the air he pulls into his lungs and then sets free does something to me, as it trickles down the nape of my neck, sending delicious chills to course through my entire body.

I make it a point not to talk to him on these rides, mostly because by the end of the day, I'm a rattled mess and need a few hours before dinner to regain my cool composure.

Fear of him seeing what he subconsciously does to my body is the real reason for my silence. To offer up such knowledge to him would be giving him power, and I dread that he has too much of that already.

My pensive thoughts are abruptly interrupted by the rumbustious cheers coming from the front of our train.

"What is it?" I ask, wondering what all of the commotion is about.

Levi leans down, his lips so close to my ear, I have to bite down my inner cheek just to keep myself still.

"How about we go and see for ourselves?" he says, a playful hint to his voice.

All I can summon the will to do is nod.

With a smile to his lips, Levi softly kicks the horse with his heel so he can break from our position and ride on in front of everyone.

I let out a relieved breath when the cool wind brushes up against my warm cheeks, successfully cooling the heat simmering in my veins. But just as we get closer to the head of the train, my blood freezes over. Levi halts our horse to a dead stop, just so I can stare at the scenery before me, northern snow-white covered ground meeting the green earthy tones of the east.

"There," Levi says, pointing to the invisible line between our kingdoms. "There it is, my queen. Home."

'That's not my home' is what I want to respond, but the words never come out, preferring to stay locked away in a place that Levi can't hear or see.

"We'll camp here for tonight, and in the morning, cross over to the east. If all goes well, before day's end, we will reach the gates of Arkøya."

I know his enthusiasm to go home is genuine and has nothing to do with me.

So why does it all feel like an ill-begotten threat?

Again, all I do is nod, so he can't hear the trepidation in my voice.

Tomorrow, we will reach the gates of Arkøya.

Gods be with me.

"Inessa," I call out. "Please tell King Levi that I've changed my mind. Tonight, I dine alone," I tell her while grabbing my coat.

"Is that wise, my queen? He might be on his way here as we speak," Inessa ventures, concerned.

"Then best be on your way then to stop him. Go, Inessa!"

She bows in obedience, but I can see it in her dark eyes how she doesn't agree with my decision.

"Shall I set the table for one, then?" Anya asks, not one bit concerned that I've diverted from my initial plot.

"No, Anya. Thank you." I shake my head. "I'm in no mood to eat. But a walk and fresh air will do me good."

"As you wish, Your Highness," she says just as she reaches for her own winter coat.

"Actually, Anya, I'd rather walk alone," I announce, stopping her in her tracks.

My handmaiden's eyes instantly sadden at the rejection, undoubtedly thinking I'm still cross with her. Since the day Atlas sent that wretched letter, Anya hasn't been her usual bubbly self. Nor has she spoken her mind so freely as she once did, thinking it displeases me. It's gotten so bad that even Inessa has become more prickly than usual, not liking that her friend is suffering so.

"Anya, come here," I order calmly.

She does as she's commanded, but she hangs her head down low, unable to meet my eyes.

"Look at me, Anya."

She lifts her head and is unable to mask the tears in her eyes.

"Why are you crying?"

"Because I have failed you and now you want nothing to do with me. I'm not even good enough to accompany you on a mere walk," she stammers.

I let out a sigh, hating that my coldness has put such thoughts in her mind.

"That isn't true. I do enjoy your company. Very much, Anya. If I didn't, I would have chosen someone else to accompany me on this trip. I chose you, and I'm glad I made such a decision."

Her brow furrows, unable to believe a word I tell her.

How can I convince her that all is good? That I bear her no ill will whatsoever?

I am them and they are me.

Those had been Levi's exact words when explaining his close relationship with his soldiers.

Aren't my handmaidens my own personal army?

Don't they share in my joys and misfortunes?

Doing everything in their power to see me prevail?

With Levi's words swimming in my head, I try a different approach with Anya—a more honest and vulnerable one.

"A queen is not supposed to have friends," I say after a pregnant pause, gaining Anya's full attention. "A queen is to be admired from afar and worshiped by her people. Such a royal being has no room in her life for friendships since there is a good chance that they are fabricated for political gain. But you and Inessa…" I pause to let out a sigh. "You've been the closest confidants I've had since my mother passed away. Without you two, I wouldn't have survived my grief. And when my father died, you were the ones who kept me steady. Who kept me from breaking down so that I could fulfill my duty as Queen." I lift her chin with my forefinger, her tears now falling for a different reason. "Friends fight, Anya. And not everything you say or do will be to my satisfaction, but the same can be said for me. So, no, sweet friend. I am not cross with you, nor is the reason I want to go for a walk alone because I don't wish to have your company. It's fine company. The best a queen could hope for."

I wipe away her tears, her expression looking somewhat in shock at my words. But when she finally snaps out of it, she jumps at me and wraps her arms so fiercely around me, I almost forget to breathe.

"I thought you hated me." She sobs on my shoulder.

"Never."

A sense of peace and relief envelops me like a warm blanket when Anya's little wails of grief turn into giggles of happiness. When she finally remembers herself, that a woman of her station should not be hugging a queen, she begins to apologize and pulls away.

"I'm sorry. I just… I wasn't expecting it, that's all."

Neither was I.

I didn't even know I felt this way about my handmaidens until the words stumbled out of my mouth, each one more honest than the next.

Hmm.

I must admit that the night Levi explained the reason behind why his soldiers loved him the way they did, I had my misgivings. My father didn't rule that way and he was the best king the kingdom of Aikyam has ever seen. Hence why I may have been skeptical in the ways Levi chose to govern his people.

But I can't deny the warm feeling I got when I opened myself up to Anya in such a way. When I spoke my truth without fear of judgment or that she would respect me any less from showing such vulnerability.

Maybe there is more than one way to lead.

More than one way to rule.

Maybe I don't have to keep an arctic distance from my subordinates as I have done in the past, or rely on force and fear, as my father had done before me.

Maybe Levi's way of governing isn't without its merits.

Maybe.

Now looking more like her old self, Anya quickly rushes to grab my gloves and hurries to put them on me.

"Even though the east wind is within reach, the weather still favors the north chill. Wear these, Your Highness, while you go for your walk."

"Thank you. I shouldn't be long," I advise her and pull my coat's hood over my head.

As I strut out of my tent, I tell the guards that there will be no need for them to accompany me either. If I didn't want Anya's company, then I can also do without my protective shadows. The campsite is filled with enough soldiers to guarantee my protection.

Unlike the other nights I strolled the campsite with Levi, the scenery around me doesn't fill me with the same sense of tranquility. In fact, it does the opposite. As I watch Levi's soldiers celebrate the fact that by tomorrow they will be once again with their loved ones, an uneasiness creeps up my spine.

Tomorrow I will be surrounded by strangers who all raised glasses to their king and his quest to steal the kingdom that is so rightfully mine away from me. I'll be completely outnumbered by these men who plotted, conspired, and almost succeeded in taking my throne.

How will I ever have a moment of peace in such a hostile environment?

I'll have to be on guard, twenty-four seven.

And even though I tried my best to gain Levi's trust, I know I haven't accomplished such a hefty goal yet. Nor will I do so in the small time I have until we reach Arkøya.

He will not lift a finger to protect me against his people or his men when we arrive.

If one so devoted to the east should conspire to try and assassinate me to clear the path to the northern throne for his king, then who's to stop him.

Levi? The man who led such a battalion to my borders?

I think not.

Monad's bodyguards?

The same men who haven't once raised their swords in battle or slain more than a pigeon for their stew?

Also doubtful.

My handmaidens?

Sensitive Anya would be too crippled with fear to be able to protect her queen from harm.

Inessa, though, wouldn't think twice in charging at the villain, but not having had the proper military training, I doubt she would impose much of a threat.

Me?

I'd thrash and spit, curse and kick, but like Inessa, I'd be no match against a professional hired assassin.

No.

I'd die on foreign soil, my crown no longer a concern.

I'm so in my thoughts that I don't even realize that my feet have led me away from the campsite and farther into the woods. Owls hoot their hellos, as other small creatures rush to hide in their homes, unsettled with my presence. The cool wind brushes each leaf of the tall oak trees I'm surrounded by, creating an ominous melody that brings ill-gotten memories to the forefront of my mind. My shoes crunch the fallen snow, now more brown than white, as I turn around to see just how far from the campsite I am.

All I see are trees.

No trace of the camp whatsoever.

Damn the gods for me being so in my head that I lost track of where I was going.

The whole purpose of my walk was so I could enjoy the last time I'd be protected by the northern soil and its elements, but now that I've lost my way, I fear protection is too far away from me to call upon it.

I take a minute to breathe, knowing that panic would do me no good in this situation.

I push all thoughts away from the last time I got lost, and square my shoulders, my spine now ramrod straight.

"It's fine, Kat. Just follow your footprints. That's how Levi found you last time," I tell myself encouragingly.

My eyes scan the perimeter and thankfully, I find shoe prints on the ground, the puddles of mud making them more visible than the snow. I begin to follow my own tracks, hoping I didn't stray too far from camp.

How long had I been walking?

Half an hour?

An hour?

Couldn't have been that long.

Could it?

I shake my head, hating that I have no correct answer to those questions. I was so preoccupied in painting the worst possible outcome of my stay in the east, that my own feet brought me to such a perilous situation.

Thoughts of thieves and kidnappers, and worse, consume me as I quicken my step, needing the comforts and safety of my tent more than I would have ever realized possible.

But then I hear it.

A growl.

A growl so menacing that I freeze in place.

I close my eyelids and swallow dryly, my breathing becoming halted as the growl grows nearer to me. Terror has my skin breaking out in goosebumps as the growl is now accompanied by another, and then another. It's only when my ears deafen with a piercing howl that I open my eyes and see the pack of gray wolves circling me. When I slowly take a step back, they bare their fangs at me, their sinister amber eyes locked on their prey, telling me to stay exactly where I stand or suffer the consequences.

Damn the gods, what should I do?

I just can't stand here, for they'll make a meal out of me if I do.

I don't have any weapons on me to fight them off and they are far too fast for me to outrun.

My mind is spiraling with all the scenarios I conjure up, each one having only one end—me being wolves' meat.

They continue to slowly march in my direction, their intent as clear as the full moon above me.

I let out a disparaging giggle, thinking how ironic it is that on my walk to clarity, in trying to come up with a plan to ensure my survival in the east, I personally hand my enemies what they crave for—my death and demise.

But just as I am coming to terms with my somber fate, the sound of hooves pulls my attention off the wolves and onto the man on horseback, riding like the devil himself toward us.

Levi jumps off his horse, the same one that cuts through the wolves' formation and breaks them apart. In their disorientation, they disperse from the pack, Levi using it to his advantage as he slaughters them one by one. I am left rooted to my spot, watching his sword slice through their flesh, killing them in an instant. Sliced, cut-up balls of gray fur fall dead on the ground, while others flee from the bloody scene, preferring to spare their lives than help their fallen pack members. Once all is said and done, Levi wipes his blood-soaked sword, panting heavily as he makes sure that the threat has been fully defeated.

After he's caught his breath, he then turns his sights on my shaky frame and lunges at me.

At first I think he's going to console me after the fright I just had, but all too soon do I realize by the disdain in his glower how wrong I am. He pulls my hood down and wraps his hand around my neck, pushing me toward a nearby tree. My back slams onto the bark as Levi's face comes within inches of mine.

"You stupid, stupid girl!" he shouts, looking even more menacing than the wolves had been not a minute ago.

"I'm not a girl. I'm your queen. Remember your place, Levi," I snap back with all the fortitude I can muster, given I'm still in a shock.

"You were about to be a dead queen."

"Like that would trouble you."

"You think I want wolves to kill you? If I wanted you dead, I would have done it myself already."

"Ha! There he is! That's the Levi I was waiting for! I knew you were playing me!" I shout, angry that I let myself believe my ploy was working.

"And you haven't been playing me?" He scoffs. "Maybe I should have let the wolves have at you. It would have solved all my problems. You're more trouble than you're worth," he barks out with so much hatred, I can almost taste the venom on my lips.

"And you're not? For a king, you sure are a brute! I've never once met a man so unsophisticated and crude."

"And for a queen, you sure are a pain in my ass!"

My eyes widen at his audacity.

"I should have you killed for talking to me like that."

"Yeah?" He smirks cruelly. "Dead queens can't shell out orders," he says, making sure I hear the underlying threat to his words.

149

But instead of backing down like he expects me to, I provoke him further.

"Do it then. We're alone. There isn't a soul around for miles. Do it, Levi. Kill me," I taunt with gritted teeth.

His hand tightens around my neck, the wood at my back pricking my skin. But instead of the fear that I should feel, there is something else that blooms inside me—a thrill like no other I've ever experienced.

"I could snap your neck right here," he grunts, scanning my face with his eyes before they fall to my lips.

"You won't kill me," I breathe out with a certainty I didn't have before.

"No?" He arches a mocking brow.

I shake my head and lick my suddenly dry lips.

"How can you be so certain?" he asks, his tone as thick as the air between us.

"Because," I choke out breathlessly, "you want to win my crown fair and square. You're a man of honor. Like you keep reminding me."

"I don't feel so honorable right now." He groans, his eyes trailing the way my tongue swipes at my bottom lip. My chest heaves when Levi takes one more step toward me, eating all the space between us. "There's something I want more than your crown right now."

"What could you possibly want more than that?" I ask on bated breath.

"This," he whispers before crushing his lips to mine.

I ce melts to me, burning me with her kiss.
Lips, the softest I have ever tasted, mold themselves to mine as she breathes life into me.

Her flower perfume intoxicates all my senses as Kat's lips ensure I go mad with just one kiss.

"Levi," she moans, coaxing me to tighten my hold on her neck and rub my aching cock against her stomach.

Her eyes glaze over with want as I deepen our kiss, desperate to steal the very oxygen in her lungs.

This woman...

This ice queen of a woman...

Will be the death of me.

And the worst part is, I'd welcome death as a long-lost friend if it meant I could keep kissing her like this.

Her hands grip my forearms and slide up to my neck, until she begins to toy with the ends of my braids, threading her fingers through my hair. She sinks her nails into my scalp when my teeth bite into her lower lip, a lust-filled cry leaving her lips.

I should stop this.

I *need* to stop this.

But for the life of me, I have no will to do so.

All of me wants her.

And if the way her breasts keep rubbing themselves against my chest is any indication, then Kat wants me just as bad.

I pull away just a tad, Kat instantly tightening her grip on me.

"No," she orders, panting. "More. I want more."

"How much more will satisfy my queen's hunger?" I ask, releasing my grasp on her neck, just so I can kiss the small bruise my fingers have made.

"I don't know," she says breathlessly, her eyes half-mast as she stares down at me.

"This much?" I taunt, kissing the slope of her neck down to her chest.

She shakes her head and closes her eyelids before gently slamming her head back against the tree.

"This much then?" I tease further, as my kisses go to the swell of her breasts.

"Oh the gods," she whimpers as I nibble on the soft piece of flesh.

"Hmm, not enough, I see," I grunt, getting as worked up as she is.

My gaze fixes on her small, diamond-shaped nipples and how they look like they might punch a hole through her gown just so I can feast my eyes on them. Mouthwatering, I go to one and sink my teeth around it, sucking her nipple through the fabric. Kat sobs beautifully at the sensation, arching her back just so that her hot core ends up meeting my throbbing cock, coaxing me to curse under my breath. I let go of her nipple to show its counterpart the same attention, while my hand cups her swollen breast, wishing I could rip her dress off her to give it the proper treatment it deserves.

"Levi," she wails again, completely lost to the myriad of sensations her body is being put under.

"So hungry, Your Highness. It leads a man to believe you've never been touched before."

When her cheeks flush with a pretty shade of pink, my cock swells even further, precum leaking from its crown. I stand back up straight, gripping her delicate chin with my hand so that I may lift it up to me.

"Have you never been touched, my queen?" I ask, breathing hard through my nose, my last thread of restraint threatening to break if her response is yes.

But instead of answering, she lowers her eyes away from me. My gaze darts hurriedly all over her face, trying to find the lie to her silent answer and being utterly shocked by what I find. Needing her to say the words, I gently tighten my hold on her chin and crane her neck all the way back.

"Tell it to me true, Kat," I command with a gentle tone. "Has no man ever touched you the way that I am now?"

She lifts her eyelids up, uncovering a vulnerable glint in her eyes that has me second-guessing all my assumptions about her.

"Who would dare touch a hollow statue made of ice when the end result would be his certain death?"

"A man who has faced death more than once and bested it. That's who, my queen."

Her eyes soften to reveal the loveliest shade of gray. She begins to fiddle with my locks again, pulling me even closer to her lips.

"Is such a man here with me now?" she asks in anticipation, her tongue peeking out to lick her lips.

"He is. Steel doesn't fear death. Or ice," I retort, my sight locked on hers.

"And are you made of such steel, King Levi?" she taunts, batting those gorgeous eyelashes at me.

"You tell me," I groan, flexing my hips so that my cock stabs at her belly.

"I'd rather you show me instead," she pants. "Show me how steel can conquer the most frozen of glaciers. Cut me down into tiny pieces until you can find something that resembles a beating heart. Destroy this frozen cage it has been possessed by with each diligent incision you make. If you are who you say you are, then I dare you to do your worst and slice at the very heart of me," she pleads, her throaty voice so desperate that it ignites a fire inside me.

"I would rather watch you burn," I threaten, grabbing the nape of her neck and finding purchase on her lips once more.

This time our kiss isn't one of awestruck wonder or self-discovery. It's fire and ice colliding and warring with each other. Our tongues battle it out in this game of dominance, refusing to submit to the other. Lips, teeth, and tongues clash together, uncaring to stop even if it means breathing air becomes the rarest of commodities. Kat's ravenous fingers begin to forcibly pull at my braids, causing a delicious sting of pain to shudder through me. My fingers dig into her tender flesh at her nape, while my other hand begins to pull up her dress, roaming its way up her inner thigh, until it meets her hot, wet cunt.

The gods.

I've only kissed her and yet she's dripping for me.

"Look at me," I growl, officially out of my mind with lust.

She does as I command, pulling her head back to stare into my eyes.

"I want you to look into my eyes as you melt for me."

I watch her swallow hard as I slither my hand up to her mound, the pad of my thumb finding its hidden treasure instantly. I bend down just so my lips are only a hairsbreadth away from hers, while my digit begins to toy with her sensitive folds until it reaches her clit again, this time adding a little pressure to it. Kat's eyes go wide in alarm, or it's an instant reaction for me to pull my hand away.

I cluck my tongue disapprovingly, shaking my head.

"None of that, Kat. This is what you begged for. Now take it like the good girl you pretend to be."

Kat whines in protest as my thumb keeps to its slow, teasing tempo, until I'm sure she can handle some more. Beads of sweat begin to cover her forehead, my heart rate picking up with proof of how I have the Winter Queen thawing at my fingertips. And when she begins to rock against my digit, as if her body knows that the ache inside her pussy can only be satiated one way, I insert a finger in her tight cunt while vigorously rubbing at her clit.

"Levi!" she shouts, completely out of her element of control.

"Your king, sweet Kat. Call me by the name you despise, for he is the cause of the pleasure you're enjoying."

Her eyes slice to me in defiance, but all too soon do they widen with an urgency that even she cannot explain. When her legs begin to tremble, Kat clings to my shoulders to keep herself steady. My smirk dies a quick death, though, when she arches her left leg and cradles it on my hip. Her dress now raised up high, it gives me the perfect view of her long, creamy white legs. And either on impulse or depravity, I roughly pull the hem of her dress to her lips.

"Bite on this, my queen," I gruffly order, too impatient to see her soaked pussy with my own two eyes.

Instead of the words of insubordination I expect to hear come out of her mouth, I'm stunned still when Kat does exactly as I say, biting the fabric with her teeth to keep it in place. The urge to kiss her is so strong with this one show of obedience, that I steal it out of her clenched jaw and lay my lips on hers. Unlike the ones before, this kiss is sweet in its passion—my own way of thanking her for her gift of trusting me. When we part, our eyes linger on each other's for a moment, as if that kiss held more truth and raw vulnerability than its predecessors.

"I want to see you," I explain in a gruff tone, my hunger for her coming out in waves. "I need to see that pretty pussy you've been hiding under this dress."

She gives me an anxious nod, unaware of how difficult it will be for me to restrain myself once I've had a peek. Ever so gently, I pull the hem close to her mouth, Kat snatching it up with her teeth, showing that she's as impatient as I am.

The cool wind that brushes up against her bare legs doesn't do a thing to simmer the heat she's under. My hands, now on her outer thighs, scorch as they make their way down as I go to my haunches.

But the minute my gaze is at eye level with her pussy, I curse the gods for letting me do such an ill-minded mistake. For right in front of me is the prettiest pink pussy I've ever seen. Clean shaven and glistening with her juices, the damn thing begs to be kissed.

As I see it, I have two options.

Ask for permission first or beg for forgiveness later.

It is honor that prevents me from doing the latter.

My knees fall to the brown slush of snow, while my hands grip around Kat's ankles. I tilt my head back and see that her eyes never left me.

"I've kissed your lips tonight, Kat. And now I'm going to kiss these ones right here," I explain, brushing her folds with my knuckles. "Nod if you understand."

With heavy lids, she nods, sending a lightning bolt of excitement coursing through my veins.

"One kiss," I tell her, not sure if I can keep that promise.

My heartbeat drums in my ears as I lean in so close that her scent engulfs me in utter euphoria. My hands travel back up her thighs as my head gets lost in between them. When I feel like I am close to losing my mind, my tongue gives her pussy a dutiful slow lap, one that ensures I'll have her taste dance on its buds.

Fuck the gods.

But has there ever been anything sweeter than this?

Crazed and hungry, my mouth latches onto her pussy, needing to drink every drop of her essence. My fingers dig into her thighs as I feast on her cunt like a man who has been starved of food all his life. I hear a loud wail come up from above, Kat's dress falling over me.

Even though she can no longer see me, and I her, we still feel what we do to the other. There is this fire that spurs us to be so reckless and give in to our animalistic wants and desires.

I've never been weak.

I've never been one to be manipulated into doing anything I didn't want to.

The gods have mercy on my soul, for all it took was this fucking pussy to turn me into one too.

My strong, able tongue continues to lap at her, until that no longer satisfies this hollow need inside of me. My teeth graze her sensitive clit before my mouth begins to suck at its little bud, coaxing her delectable nectar to drip down her thighs. I lick her thighs clean of her juices, giving one a large bite before my mouth returns to its home.

As for Kat, she sings like a mockingbird, the wind carrying her song east for all to hear. Her hands grab at my head over her dress, keeping me exactly where she wants me. Her arousal is thick on my tongue, my cock desperate to be free of its restraints. When her legs start to quiver again, I can even taste how all it would take is a little spark for her to leap off into the abyss. My tongue continues to toy at her clit, as I pull one hand off her thigh and slowly insert a finger inside her entrance. She's so fucking tight and prime that all it takes is the tip for her to scream out her orgasm to the high heavens.

Fuck!

Fuck!

Fuck!

I continue to tease her sweet bud while drinking up her release, until the shivers of ecstasy that rack through her body die down. I'm pissed as hell when I pull the dress off my head and stand back on my feet.

Kat just had her first orgasm, and like the greedy fool that I am, I missed it.

Looking properly fucked, Kat almost purrs when I grab her by the throat and turn her, pressing her flushed cheek to the cool oak bark.

"You came without my say so," I growl in her ear, my cock pressed against the crook of her ass.

"You never said I needed permission, my king," she teases, knowing damn well what that does to me.

"Aye, next time I won't be so careless. When you come, I want to see you do it. Understand?"

Her ass presses against my cock, and for a woman who claims to have never been touched, she sure knows how to provoke a man.

My nose rubs at the sliver of flesh behind her ear, my eyelids closed, still savoring her taste on my tongue.

"Your pussy tasted so fucking good, Kat. I bet it will feel even better wrapped around my cock."

Her chest begins to heave up and down, her frightened yet curious gaze darting to mine.

"Does that scare you? How much I'd love nothing more than to stretch you out, and have you beg me for more?"

Her jaw goes lax, eyes wide as she struggles to form a reply.

Not that whatever she says will dismay me. Either I fuck her against this tree tonight, or later in our bridal bed.

'Once you are married and crowned king, I will plunge my dagger into her cold heart on her very bridal bed as my wedding present to you. I swear it on the blood that was shed in her family's name.'

It's the memory of Atlas's words that douses my libido in ice water.

And to my chagrin, Kat immediately picks up on my shifting mood.

This time when she opens her mouth, I know exactly what her question will be.

But then, as if the gods have personally come to my aid, I hear my men calling out for me.

"Over here!" I bellow, releasing Kat from her imprisonment.

Her inquisitive brows are still scrunched together on her forehead as she silently watches me fix her wrinkled dress and ruffled hair as best I can.

When five of my most trusted soldiers on horseback appear, I grab hold of Kat's forearm and push her toward them.

"Please take the queen back to her tent, and tell her guards that if they ever lose track of her and fail to protect her again, they'll have me to account to."

Kat pulls her arm from my grip, her facial features back to their original cold, arctic front. The deathly stare she gives me over her shoulder as she walks toward my men chills me to the bone.

A part of me wants to pull her back into my arms, while another wants her as far away from me as possible.

Brick's right.

She *is* fucking with my head.

And worst of all, she's starting to fuck with my heart, too.

Which is very inconvenient, since she's put a plan in motion where she could end up belonging to someone else instead of me.

Teo instantly comes to the forefront of my mind, his smug smile taunting me.

But after what just happened here in these woods…

After I tasted her sweetness, and felt her body melt to mine…

Like hell I'll ever let him have her now.

The minute we step inside the camp, I order Levi's guard dog to halt his horse so that I may walk the rest of the way. To my fury, the young soldier has the audacity to look over at Levi riding beside us to get his consent.

Fury blinds me to turn around and pull at his lapel.

"Listen here, soldier. You obey my orders, not his! Do you understand me?!" I shout.

"Let her go, Sten," Levi belts out. "I've seen firsthand how mean she can get when she doesn't get her way. I've even got the claw marks on my shoulders to prove it."

My gaze cuts to Levi, wishing I could slice him up into tiny pieces just as easily. My anger only grows when the other men in his rescue party begin to chuckle under their breaths, understanding the insinuation loud and clear.

"Stop. This. Horse." I seethe through gritted teeth.

Petrified that I might hurt him, Sten reins his horse in, stopping smack in the middle of camp. Since I'm riding sideways on the saddle due to wearing a dress and not my usual riding gear, I don't wait for him to help me down, and jump off, my feet hitting the ground with a loud thud.

Still furious that, after all that had transpired between Levi and I back in the woods, he should treat me so callously, I storm off in the direction of my tent.

"Good night, my queen. Sweet dreams," Levi shouts, laughing with his men.

I'm so upset that the devil himself must take over my body, because I raise my hand and flip him off with my middle finger.

Now it's the whole camp that chuckles at my ridicule, Levi's laughter ringing the loudest. I hurry my steps, needing to get to my tent or risk going back to Levi just so I can give him a good piece of my mind. However, when I finally get within a few feet of my tent, Anya pops her head out of its flaps and starts running toward me at rapid speed. So much so that when she reaches me, she's unable to stop fast enough for her chest not to hit mine, making me almost tumble over. Thankfully, her hug keeps me from making a fool of myself twice in one night.

"I was so worried! You were gone for hours. We didn't know what to do," she explains, the trace of the panic she must have felt still lingering in her voice.

"I'm fine, Anya." I smile, thankful to have such a friend who worries over me so.

"Anya!" Inessa calls out in reprimand, a man with wild red hair and hazel eyes at her heel. "Anya, remember yourself, girl," Inessa berates, pulling Anya's arms off of me.

"It's quite alright, Inessa. Actually, it comforts me that at least there is one person in this camp who is glad to see me."

I can tell by Inessa's cold stare that, although relieved to have me back, she's more disgruntled that I went on a walk all by myself to begin with.

"I am glad that you have returned to us safe and sound," she says, bowing her head at me.

"Why do I feel there is a but in that remark?" I smile.

"If it's all the same to you, my queen, I would rather I give you my opinion on the matter when we are in more intimate surroundings."

It's here when she glances over at the man standing tall beside her that he grabs my attention.

"And you are?"

"This is Brick, my queen," Anya cheerfully responds in his stead. "King Levi asked that the general here keep us company until your safe return." Anya winks suggestively at an annoyed Inessa.

"Did he now?" I scrutinize the general from the tip of his unpolished boots to his auburn hair. Unlike most of the men here, his hair is parted into two sides, his left wild and free, while his right constrained into three long braids. It's the way he wears his hair that reminds me how we met.

"Your face is familiar to me. You're the one that greeted us on the road up north instead of your king. Isn't that correct?"

"It is," he replies, and I don't miss how he refused to call me by my royal title.

Thankfully, Inessa doesn't let that slide.

"It is, *Your Highness*," she corrects him. "Queen Katrina of Bratsk is the ruler of the kingdom of Aikyam, therefore it is your honor to be in her presence. Show some decorum as well as the respect that is entitled to her by birth."

Brick's cheeks turn almost as red as his hair, as if her reprimand gained human form and slapped him across the face.

I thin my lips, praying that I don't burst out laughing, while I pretend to wait for Brick to follow Inessa's not-so-subtle demand.

"It is, *Your Highness*," he repeats, looking like he just took a bite out of a sour lemon.

It's too funny a scene not to lift my spirits.

"Thank you, Brick, for taking such good care of my handmaidens. Both are near and dear to me."

Inessa's arctic gaze softens at that, while Brick hears the warning in my words.

Hurt Inessa in any way, and I'll cut out your heart and feed it to the dogs myself.

My threatening smile only widens when he bows his head and bids us farewell.

The girls rush to pull me inside my tent, which I'm thankful for, since every limb in my body screams for a hot bath and my bed.

I'm not sure if it was the long walk in the woods, Levi's clever tongue, the horseback ride back to camp, or all of them combined that depleted all my energy.

Levi.

He's the culprit behind everything.

"Come," Anya beckons, hurrying to sit me on my chair. "Let us take these clothes off you and wash the dirt away from your walk."

Inessa keeps her mouth shut as she boils some water for the tub. My eyes never leave her as Anya continues on with her task.

"Did you fall, my queen? You have chips of wood all entwined in your hair," Anya asks curiously as she plucks said chips out.

"Hmm." I offer a noncommittal nod, while my eyes trail every move Inessa makes.

Her silence is starting to become unnerving.

"Oh, just come out and say it, Inessa," I finally order, since it's apparent she won't do it willingly.

"It's not my place, my queen."

"When has that ever stopped her?" Anya whispers with a giggle.

I feel my lips tilt into a smile, but I know that doing so would only infuriate Inessa further. I let out an exaggerated exhale and stand up, bridging the gap between me and my friend. I pull her hands to mine, surprising her with the tenderness that she hasn't been accustomed to. Not by me, her queen, and not by others either.

"I know," I chuckle. "I'm new to this too. But maybe the old ways of doing things no longer serve us as they once had."

Even though Inessa maintains the perfect blank expression on her face, it's her dark brown eyes that betray her. There's a smidge of hope in them, one that no matter how hard she tries to extinguish, is always there, right beneath her cold exterior.

"Go ahead. Speak your mind."

"It was foolish," she replies, stunning even herself that the words fell out of her mouth.

When she realizes I won't retaliate, she continues.

"It was foolish and reckless. Walking anywhere in this camp without a chaperon is just asking for the worst to happen. We don't know these men, my queen. To them, we are the enemy. As they are ours. Do not think that one of them wouldn't do you harm if they thought their king would be grateful for it. You cannot be so reckless with yourself, my queen. It's not only your neck that should concern you, but that of your people. What if something happened to you? What would become of the north?"

"Don't hold back," Anya mumbles across the room. "Geez."

Shame that my own handmaiden is thinking more clearly than I am accosts me.

"You're right," I confess with a sigh. "You're absolutely right. I should have known better. I should have taken precautions to ensure my safety. And for that, I apologize."

Inessa takes a step back, unable to mask her shock.

"Queens don't apologize. Ever."

"No, they don't. But friends do," I tell her, giving a soft squeeze to her hands. I watch her fury and anger toward my recklessness dissipate right in front of my eyes.

"Now that we covered that issue, I want to discuss another. Is this Brick character someone I should be concerned about?" I ask her outright, releasing my hold on her.

"No." She shakes her head. "He's no one of importance. I'll deal with him."

"Aw." Anya pouts. "I like Brick."

"You like everybody, Anya." Inessa rolls her eyes.

"No, I meant I like Brick for *you*," Anya teases, poking her tongue out at her friend.

Inessa's eyes turn pitch black as she stares daggers at her friend.

"Enough of that talk," she reprimands. "And now that we're at it, enough of hugging our queen willy-nilly whenever the inkling strikes you. She is not some stuffed animal for you to hug. She is your queen!"

Anya just shrugs, not one bit troubled.

"Kat didn't mind," she mutters under her breath.

"Kat?!" Inessa bellows, looking like she might have a stroke by Anya treating me so informally. "I swear to the gods, Anya, you are thinning my patience. Help Her Majesty with her clothes while I fix her bath," she orders.

This time Anya does as she's told, pulling me back into my chair so she can continue to pick out the leaves and wood splinters that made their way through it.

But Anya wouldn't be Anya if she didn't mischievously whisper in my ear, always needing to have the last word.

"You know what she needs? A good tumbling. I bet Brick would be all too happy to put a smile on her face."

My cheeks heat up as I recall Levi whispering in my ear, saying something far too similar.

Your pussy tasted so fucking good, Kat.

I bet it will feel even better wrapped around my cock.

Does that scare you?

How much I'd love nothing more than to stretch you out, and have you beg me for more?"

"My queen?" Inessa calls out, rushing over to me. "You look flushed. Are you feeling ill? Quick, Anya. Let's get Kat out of these filthy clothes and into a bath. Quickly, Anya. Quickly."

I must be in a state for Inessa to call me Kat and not realize her slip of the tongue. I let them wash me and put me into bed, unable to offer them words of comfort since my mind is back in those woods where Levi got the best of me.

After they believe me to have fallen asleep and go to their respective tents, I just limit myself to lie in bed, recalling every detail of our encounter. I trace my fingers over my lips, remembering Levi's brutish kiss. The way he tasted on the tip of my tongue. The way he forced my body to sing for him with his forbidden kiss.

I never knew this side of him could exist. Never even knew it could even be a possibility. Growing up, Levi had been so different. Tonight, it felt like he wanted to devour me, a predator ready to sink his teeth into his prey.

But back then...

He was the boy that kept the monsters at bay.

Back then, the only music he was interested in was the one we could dance to.

And oh...

How we danced.

Chapter 13

Katrina

Fifteen Years Old

"Where are we going?" I giggle as Teo leads me by the hand away from the main hall where everyone is celebrating my father's birthday.

My father, the king, always invites his vassals to come up north to Tarnow and spend a month in our castle to celebrate his upcoming winters. It's the happiest time of the year for me, because I get to see my friends again.

How I miss them when they are not here.

Atlas with his shy smiles and sympathetic ear.

Levi with his imparting wisdom and grand aura.

And Teo, the boy who always seems to plant butterflies in my stomach whenever he's near.

All of them so different, and yet still the same, since they all belong to me.

"Move those feet, kitten. I have a surprise for you," Teo chuckles as he maneuvers his way through my castle's walls.

"I'm trying. It's not easy to run in heels, you know," I laugh, hurrying up my pace.

"No, I don't know, 'cause I've never worn heels," he jokes.

"Lucky you. Remind me to make you one day, then you'll see what I'm talking about."

Teo stops abruptly, almost causing me to run into him.

"Give them here," he asks, stretching his hand to me.

"Give you what?"

"Your shoes, kitten. Your shoes." He laughs, going to his haunches so that he can take my heels off my feet.

I hold on to his shoulders to keep steady, confused as to why he wants my shoes. Once he has them in his hands, he turns his back to me and looks over his shoulder.

"Don't just stand there staring at me. Jump on." He chuckles, patting his back to drive the point home.

Giddy, I do as he says and jump on his back, Teo holding on to me as best he can with my heels in his hands.

"Hold tight, kitten," he warns before taking off.

I giggle excitedly as Teo runs as fast as he can with me on his back through the maze that is Tarnow Castle. I have no idea where he's taking me, but knowing Teo, it will undoubtedly be the best of adventures.

It's only when he takes a right turn on the ground floor that I realize where he's leading me to—my favorite place in the world—Momma's winter garden. I hold on to him even tighter, my heart feeling like it may jump out of me in anticipation with whatever plan he's got up his sleeve. When we reach outside, I breathe in the cold night air mixed with the scent of our traditional blue rose. Teo continues to carry me through the vast garden until we reach the white gazebo that's located right at its center.

My mouth opens when my eyes land on countless blue petals all spread out on the floor, strategically placed to look like a heart.

Teo gently plants my feet on solid ground, though I still feel like I'm flying.

"What's this?" I stammer, still awestruck at such a sweet gesture.

"What does it look like?" he asks, his voice no longer holding that mischievous playful quality he's known for.

I bite my bottom lip, unsure of what to say, so I end up saying the obvious.

"It looks like a heart," I blurt out nervously.

"It does, doesn't it?" he retorts with a light chuckle, even though his golden eyes still look serious.

My heart beats a mile a minute as I lose myself in his amber abyss.

"Come here, kitten. I need to tell you something. Something that I've been trying to tell you since the day we met."

"When we were in diapers?" I try to joke to lighten the mood.

When Teo lets out a laugh that comes from his gut, I relax a little, comforted in the knowledge that even though he's trying to be serious, my carefree Teo still lives inside him.

"Okay, maybe not since then, but it's been a long time coming."

When my feet refuse to move, Teo pulls me to him, placing his palm on my lower back.

"Teo," I whisper. "This is dangerous. If anyone sees us here… together… alone—"

"No one will see. Everyone's upstairs enjoying the ball. They are too busy eating and drinking to notice our absence. It's the perfect opportunity for us to be alone together."

He planned this to a T.

Whatever it is, for whatever reason he brought me here, Teo made sure to cover all his bases so as to not get caught.

Teo pulls me even closer and runs his knuckles up and down my cheek.

"You're so fucking beautiful," he whispers, causing my throat to dry. "There is no girl quite like you, kitten. Claws and all."

My lips curve into a smile, but I'm too on edge to say anything back.

"Shit." He laughs nervously. "I'm more nervous than I thought I would be."

I smack my dry lips, and tentatively raise my arms to wrap around his neck.

"It's just you and me here, Teo. Nothing to be nervous about," I reply with a shy smile.

His amber eyes turn soft.

"There isn't, is there?" He grins, his smile lighting up his face. "Because you're my girl. And I don't have to be nervous around my girl."

My breath hitches at his words.

Teo has never claimed me in that way. I always felt that I was his, but never once did he confirm it. I beam excitedly and nod, before nestling my head into his chest. He plants a kiss on the top of my head, and just holds me for a minute to bask in his essence.

Teo then pulls back a little so I can look at his glorious face.

"We're fifteen now, love. Which means that in less than three summers' time, your father will start to search for a worthy prospect to have your hand in marriage."

I gulp at where Teo is going with this. He looks so determined that I don't have the heart to cut into his train of thought.

"I have already talked with my father and told him of my intentions. The instant word breaks out that the king is looking to marry you off, my father will offer me to be your wedded husband. Then the entire world will know that you're mine."

My heart begins to rattle in its cage, both because Teo just announced his intention to marry me, and because I know he never will.

As I stare into his loving eyes, I let him continue to believe that it's a possibility.

How I wish it was.

"Well, kitten? Aren't you going to say something?" he asks, sounding even more anxious.

Unable to break his heart, I end up telling him the only truth I can that won't do any damage.

"I'd love nothing more than to be your wife, Teo."

It's not a lie.

If I could, I'd marry Teo this very night.

But that is a dream for another princess to have. Not me.

He cups my face in his hands, pulling it so close to his that his breath fans my cheeks.

"I love you, Katrina of Bratsk. I will spend my whole life loving you. This, I vow."

Tears begin to sting my eyes.

"Shh, love," he whispers, cleaning the errant tear that falls down my cheek. "Soon we'll be together in the south, where we can bathe in the ocean and feel the warm sun on our cheeks. You'll leave this winter wonderland and enjoy the spoils of summer. We are going to be so happy, kitten, that the gods will be envious."

"I don't doubt they would be," I whisper on a soft sob.

Even I am jealous of the woman who will end up having such a life.

I bury that wretched thought deep until even I can't find it, and focus on what is right in front of me—Teo.

I haven't lost him yet.

He's still here with me.

Loving me.

I still have this and right now, it's more than enough.

"Do you love me, kitten?" he asks.

I nod, unable to form the words.

It's all Teo needs to see for him to softly press his lips against mine.

My eyes widen at the unexpected kiss, since he's never kissed me before.

In fact, I haven't kissed anyone until tonight.

I close my eyelids and let myself be taken by the moment. Butterflies fly in my lower belly as his lips mold to mine so perfectly it's almost as if the gods themselves created them just for me. My racing heartbeat is dangerously close to leaping out of my chest with each second that passes by.

But just as I try to deepen our kiss, Teo pulls away and curses.

"Shit. I have to go," he utters, pissed, looking over my shoulder.

I turn around but don't see anything or anyone there.

Teo lets me go from his embrace and starts to rush out of the gazebo.

"Wait! Teo!" I shout, confused.

"I'll be back, kitten!" he shouts back. "Just stay here and wait for me."

Without even waiting for my reply, he rushes off to only the gods know where.

My shoulders slump as I walk over to the nearby bench where Teo had placed my heels and I begin to put them back on my bare feet. I stare at the blue roses on the floor while counting down the minutes to his arrival.

It had been sweet how he chose to declare his love for me.

It really had been.

If it wasn't for the fact that, after our kiss, he ran out on me as fast as his feet could carry him.

And every minute I stay sitting here, waiting for him to come back to me, the more foolish I feel.

After what feels like a full twenty minutes of just waiting for Teo's return, I get up from my seat and give up.

If he really wanted to be with me, he would have stayed.

Maybe I'm the world's worst kisser.

Argh!

Having had enough of this sitting around, I get up and return to my father's feast before someone realizes that I've left. I walk amongst jubilant courtiers, drunk-off-their-rockers lords, and their wandering-eye ladies. Everyone is having a grand old time, while I'm sadly perusing the grand hall, feeling sorry for myself. I stand in a corner and just watch the pairs dancing in tune with one another, staring into their partners' eyes as if they were the only two people on earth. The makeshift dance floor oozes intimacy as well as seduction. Two things I'm a complete novice at and, by the looks of it, won't be an expert in anytime soon.

It's the gentle nudge on my shoulder that breaks through my pity party.

"You look awfully sad for such a grand occasion," Levi says, with a drink in hand.

"I guess I'm not in the celebratory mood."

"Hmm. Not like you. You always love these things."

I furrow my brow and crane my neck back to look at him. Levi has always been the tallest of all of us, which is understandable since he's also the oldest. But over these past few years, he's kept growing, like a tree who is adamant in touching the sky with its branches. Thankfully, I'm wearing heels tonight, so I don't have to strain my neck too far.

"Why would you say that?" I ask, intrigued with his observation of me.

"Because," he shrugs, "you love any excuse to dance."

A small smile starts to tug at the corners of my lips.

He's right.

I do love to dance.

Usually, I can count on Atlas or Teo to swing me around the dance floor, but tonight they both seem to be off doing their own thing without me. It occurs to me that in all the feasts and balls my father has thrown over the years, I've never danced with Levi, though. Which has me wondering—why?

"How come you don't dance?" I ask curiously.

"Because no one has ever asked me to."

"That can't be true." I shake my head, my smile fully on my lips now.

Levi is the best man I know in all of Aikyam. At least, in my eyes he is. Not only is he wise beyond his years, but he also doesn't make you feel less than for your lack of experience. Patient to a fault, with an enormous need to protect those who need it most. Never have I heard him say a mean word or cruel joke just because he could. Levi, to me, is what every man should aspire to be. And he's only seen seventeen winters, which means the best of him is yet to come.

A girl would be a fool not to want to spend every waking second in his presence, much less refuse to dance with him.

"Aye, but it is." He sheepishly grins, and in that one smile, my heart pitter-patters.

That's another reason why Levi is so special.

He rarely smiles, but when he does, it's like the sun has just broken through the cloudiest of days, shining its light on you.

It's so breathtaking it takes me a minute to gather my thoughts.

"I… um… I…"

"Yes?" He cocks a confused brow at my sudden stammering.

I clear my throat and plant a smile, hoping he doesn't realize how his smile always takes the wind out of me.

"What I was going to say, or ask, I should say, is why you never danced with me?"

I know what he's going to say.

That he thinks of me as his little sister and that I should dance with boys closer to my age, but Levi surprises me when he bends down, his lips so close to my ear that I feel a small shiver run down my back.

"For the same reason," he whispers. "You never asked me."

It's only when he pulls away that I'm able to breathe again.

"Well, that's a silly reason," I laugh off, praying to all the gods that he thinks my heated cheeks are due to the warm hall and not his nearness.

"Is it?" he counters.

"Of course, it is. I'd be honored to dance with you."

His green eyes sparkle at my answer.

"You want to dance? With me?" he asks suspiciously, his gaze scanning the room for something or someone.

It occurs to me that maybe he's looking for my usual dancing partners, but tonight I don't want either one of them—I want Levi.

I jump in front of him and go to the tip of my toes, pulling his chin to me. I try to pretend that I don't see the flame in his emerald gaze flicker away, since it would only put unrealistic ideas in my head.

"I said it would be my absolute honor, Levi." I then pull away and curtsey in front of him. "Prince Levi of Thezmaer, will you do your humble servant the honor of a dance?"

I don't have to wait too long for an answer, since Levi grabs my hand and almost flies me to the middle of the dance floor. I giggle with glee at his eagerness, but the laugh dies a quick death when Levi plants his strong hands on my waist. I swallow hard, doing my best to control my beating heart. But by the way my chest is heaving up and down, even Levi notices it, his gaze falling to the swell of my breasts.

I wish he wouldn't have done that, though, because now I'm at risk of hyperventilating.

"Kat," he says, my nickname on his lips always sounding like it's a prayer. "We have to move our feet if we're supposed to be dancing."

Right.

Feet.

Move, feet! Move! I order subconsciously, and thankfully they end up hearing my silent command, to which Levi begins to lead me around the dance floor.

As big and tall as he is, you would think he'd have lead for feet, but Levi is the very definition of graceful. I guess you have to have some kind of agility to be a soldier. My heart sank when my father had informed me a few years back that Levi was now a part of the Aikyam army. I never quite understood why he was subjecting himself to that kind of life. He's a royal prince. One day he'll be king of the east. Why risk being slaughtered in the battlefield when he could have stayed safe and sound in his castle back at Arkøya?

I had even asked my father as much, not wishing to insult Levi with my questions. All my father said was that Levi was doing his duty and that was the end of it.

Still, I wish he hadn't enlisted.

The only comfort I have is that my father insists on having all his vassals present on his birthday month. Which means, near or far, Levi must have departed from whichever foreign land so he could be here.

With me.

"That's quite a necklace," he says, his gaze still lingering on my chest.

But that's when I remember what I have on.

"Oh, this," I pull my hand away from his forearms to trace the heart-shaped diamond necklace. "It's my mother's. She let me wear it tonight."

"Hmm," he hums noncommittedly.

"Don't you like it?" I ask, placing my hand once more on his tree trunk of a forearm.

"Did I infer that I didn't?"

"No." I frown. "But you didn't say that you did either. You think it's ostentatious, don't you?"

He opens his mouth but then shuts it.

I knew it.

He does think it's grandiose and pretentious.

The other kingdoms always do when we flaunt our diamonds. The thing is, our people would be just as proud to wear sandstone or coquina or even the darkest obsidian if it represented the north. Where others see a disparity of wealth, we see it as a symbol of our northern pride. Our diamonds, as well as our blue roses, are as much a part of us as steel and green meadows are to the east.

"I'll have you know that this necklace was passed down from generations from mother to daughter. It's as old as Aikyam itself. And one day my mother will pass it on to me. This is not just a diamond, Levi. It's a token of love. That's why it's shaped like a heart. So that even when a daughter marries into another family, she knows she will always be loved by the ones who brought her into this world."

I'm about to continue on my rant, when Levi presses his finger right at the center of my lips, stunning me silent.

"I like the diamond just fine, Kat. That's not why I didn't say anything."

"Oh?" I manage to croak out after he's pulled his finger off my lips.

"It's just that…"

"That what?" I wait with bated breath.

"It's just that you look absolutely transcendent tonight."

My heart melts into a puddle at our feet.

"I do?"

"Like the finest star the gods could ever make. Exceptional."

My eyelids grow heavy at his words, while the rest of my body feels like it might burst into flames.

"Oh."

"Yeah. Oh," he repeats, that same shy smile of his cresting his lips.

Left at a loss for words, I just let Levi take the lead.

We dance and dance until my feet beg for me to sit down.

But I don't want to.

I'll dance the whole night away as long as I get to do it with Levi.

Because if I'm a star for him, then Levi is the sun.

While one boy vowed that he loved me with mere words, the other showed me how much he cared for me with his actions.

Who am I to believe?

Who is my heart to trust?

Not that it matters.

I'll never get the opportunity to choose.

That night we danced until there was no one left on the dance floor. It had been my late mother who had eventually pulled me away from Levi's embrace, later whispering in my ear that if I wanted to keep receiving him and his family each year, that I shouldn't be so transparent with my affection for him.

At the time, I had brushed it off, but now...

Now I wonder if Levi had my heart all along.

Such a troubling thought when my purpose is to conquer his affection instead of the other way around. Still, I can't deny how he has slowly gotten under my skin. And after that brief intimate moment we shared in the woods, I doubt I'll ever be able to rid myself of the memory of his touch.

His kiss.

His scent.

The way he ignited my body to the point that it no longer belonged to me but was his completely to do with as he saw fit.

It's enough to drive a sane woman mad.

And then when his men arrived, the dark king returned—ever the pompous ass.

I still can't believe I let him treat me that way.

I'm his queen, not some harlot he can use and abuse and then discard.

Rage like no other begins to course through my veins, making me spring out of my bed and put on my coat. Levi, like everyone else at camp, is probably asleep at this late hour, but I don't care.

He's going to get a piece of my mind.

I run toward the tent's entrance, only to take a huge step back when I come face to face with the man I was intent on waking up. The menacing expression on his face has me calling out to my guards, only to find them all lying in the dirt.

Fearing he's come to kill me or worse, I turn around and grab the first weapon I see, a dinner knife on top of the dining table Levi and I shared our meals at. When I turn around to face him, he's already on me, disarming me with ease and putting the knife to my neck.

"Is this why you're here? To kill me?" I scold with all the venom I can conjure.

"No."

"Liar! Did you kill my guards?" I spit out.

"No."

"Another lie! I saw them on the ground!"

"They'll wake up with a mean migraine, but assure you, they'll live," he explains with that smirk of his that is both aggravating as it is sexy as hell.

"So if you're not here to kill me, then what do you want?"

"What I've always wanted. You."

And then to my shock, Levi takes the knife to my nightgown and shreds it down the middle, leaving me completely bare to him.

"Much better." He licks his lips.

I slap his cheek as hard as I can, but I doubt he even feels it. I, on the other hand, feel like my palm is on fire.

"Tsk. Tsk, Kat. Haven't you ever heard that you should only pick on people your own size?" he teases, and then he grabs my wrist, only to place a tender kiss at the center of my palm.

His emerald gaze is set on fire when he begins to trail it over my entire body.

"Levi—" I start, my whole body beginning to tremble with the same need I see in his eyes.

It's his name on my lips that brings his attention back to my face.

"Whatever you're thinking of doing, don't."

"And what exactly do you think I'm about to do?" He smirks, running the knife between my breasts, the cold steel sending shivers through my body.

"You're going to finish what you started… back in the woods," I state, doing everything in my power to keep my voice strong.

"Are you saying you don't want me to?" he counters, his brow raised high on his forehead.

Am I saying that?

"Are you saying that you haven't spent every little second since we returned wondering what could have happened if my men had arrived just an hour later?"

I swallow hard, my breathing becoming shallow.

"Are you saying that the thought of me not touching you hasn't kept you up all night?"

I bite my lower lip and nod.

"Now who's the liar?" he taunts with a wolfish grin.

He eats up the space between us, and bends down just enough for his lips to graze my ear.

"Tell me, sweet Kat," he whispers gruffly, "if your pussy isn't dripping for me."

I lie and shake my head.

"Such a bad little liar," he taunts, and when I feel him lowering his knife past my breasts, down my belly and toward my core, I close my eyes and pray to the gods to save me from what's about to happen.

I whimper in relief when I feel the wooden handle of the knife instead of its blade gently slide across my folds. Levi then lifts the blade, and with the pad of his tongue he licks the hilt clean. My belly quivers at the sight, my nipples hardening.

"Like I said, you're drenched, *my queen*."

This time, before I'm able to slap him once more, he grabs both of my wrists and tugs them away behind my back, imprisoning me.

"Let me go, Levi, or I swear—" I say with gritted teeth.

"You'll what, my queen?" he taunts. "Scream for help? The guards posted outside your tent are knocked out, while the rest are snoring away, too drunk on cherry wine to even hear you. So tell me just exactly what you will do."

"I'll have your head for this," I threaten, but both he and I know that we're in his territory now. Even if I commanded that the east seek retribution for what their king is doing to me, they would deny me. If they didn't stop him from marching north to invade my kingdom, then they won't bat an eye at him invading my bedroom.

"You can have my head, my queen. This head," he says, releasing one of my hands to forcibly cup his crotch.

My eyes widen in alarm at his girth.

Curse the gods but does all of him have to be so intimidating?

He's huge.

I had felt it back in the woods, pressing up against me, but now that I feel the weight of it in my hand, it seems so much bigger.

"Cat got your tongue, my queen?" He chuckles playfully.

He's messing with me.

The infuriating man is messing with me.

Playing on my inexperience and predilections.

Fine.

Two can play this game.

"Oh, you mean this head?" I ask, giving it a good squeeze.

Levi's expression morphs from taunting to downright heady.

"Kat—"

"Hmm, with your pants on, I can't really tell if it is worth the trouble. Best check to find out."

With only one hand, I manage to pull at the strings of his trousers, just enough for me to be able to slide my hand in.

His breath hitches when my hand fully cups his cock, the feel of smooth velvet tickling my fingers.

I just wanted to mock him as he was taunting me, but now I'm not so sure we're playing the same game as before. I begin to stroke his cock, ever so leisurely, completely captivated by how it seems to swell with every stroke.

Levi lets go of my other wrist, preferring to wrap his hand around my neck, but he doesn't tighten his hold. He then bends down just enough for his temple to kiss mine, our eyes locked on each other's.

"What are you doing, Kat?"

"I don't know," I answer truthfully, no longer committed to our game of hate and distrust. "Do you want me to stop?"

"Fuck no," he grunts, pulling hard at the strings of his pants to give me more room.

My mouth dries at the feel of his warm skin on my fingers. I want to see his cock for myself, but I'm in too much of a trance with the way his eyes shine on mine.

"Why are you really here, Levi?" I ask, feeling if there is ever an opportunity where he will be honest with me, this is it.

"I needed to see you," he pants, as my thumb brushes over his balls.

"Why?" I question, my breathing just as hard as his.

"Because I couldn't wait until tomorrow," he groans, this time using his free hand to play with my breasts.

My eyes begin to roll back inside my head when he toys with my nipples until they are two sharp peaks.

"Why?" I manage to say again on a loud wail.

"Fuck, Kat…" he groans, softly brushing his thumb over the outside of my throat. "Because when I went back to my tent, your smell still lingered in the air around me. On my clothes. On my fingers. I could fucking taste you, Kat. I just needed…"

"What? What? What did you need?" I question on bated breath.

Levi pulls his temple away from mine just a smidge to fully stare down at me.

"You. I needed you. Any way I could have you."

My cold heart thaws at his words, and for a moment, I forget that he's my sworn enemy. Right now, he's that boy who danced the night away with me.

I tilt my head back and close my eyes, my silent invitation for him to kiss me. Levi doesn't hesitate and crashes his lips to mine. This kiss is punishing in its brutality, and yet it's exactly what I needed. His strong lips and tongue conquer mine with the greatest of ease. Any other time I would resist his dominance, but I find myself aching for his guidance, submitting to him willingly. His kiss must frazzle me, because Levi pulls his hand off my neck just to grab onto my wrist.

"If you continue to stroke it like that, I'll end up coming all over your hand. And that just won't do," he teases as he pulls my hand off his member, but there is no malice in his tone, only endearment.

The memory of him down on his knees back in the woods comes to the forefront of my mind. A lurid idea also springs forth, and before I can second-guess myself, I plant my palms on his chest and push him just far enough to give me some room.

Levi doesn't resist, taking two steps back.

It's only when I fall to my knees in front of him does he say a word.

"What are you doing?"

I pull the sleeves of my winter coat and ruined nightgown off me before I turn my attention to him.

"I don't know," I answer, and again I'm being as honest as I can be.

I have no idea what I'm doing. I only know that it feels right.

Nothing in my life has felt right for years, but here… now… all of this feels… right.

Levi's Adam's apple bobs as I diligently take off each of his boots, before I turn to his pants to pull at its strings. The black fabric falls to the floor, Levi kicking them far from us. I close my eyes and take a deep breath before opening them up to stare at the hard-as-steel cock bobbing away just inches from my face.

Oh, how the gods have favored him.

First, I play with the sack underneath his long, thick member, knowing how sensitive it is. I watch in wonder as Levi's head falls back over his shoulder with my delicate touch. Encouraging me that I'm on the right path, I slide my hand around the base of his cock and trail it up, only to stroke it back down again.

Levi's breathing becomes even more ragged, fueling my own desire to multiply. There's a certain power in this. How even on my knees, I'm the one who is making him undone. I lick my parched lips, and the little air I let out must brush against his length, because he then weaves his fingers through my hair and pulls it back with a sharp pull.

"That's enough, Kat," he growls, his green eyes two shades darker.

"But I haven't even started."

"For fuck's sake, Kat, I know that. Don't you think I know that?" he almost shouts, pulling on the ends of his own braids.

"A kiss. You owe me a kiss," I try to negotiate. "You gave one to me. It's only fair I get to give you one too."

His long black lashes beat a mile a minute, as if he's not recognizing this creature on her knees before him. If I'm being honest with myself, his guess is as good as mine, since I have no idea who I'm becoming.

"One!" He raises his finger at me to drive his message across. "One, Kat, or I swear I will beat your hide red with this very hand."

My pussy clenches at his words, and for a moment, the idea of Levi spanking me drowns out all the illicit ideas I could have ever come up with on my own. My depravity more than my curiosity has me doubling down on the kiss Levi expects from me.

With my eyes fixed on his, I innocently bat my eyelashes at him and use my full tongue to lap at him, from the base of his cock right to its crown. Once my lips are at the head, I wrap them around it and slowly take him inside the cavern of my mouth. There is an instant sting to my scalp, Levi pulling at my hair, trying to prevent me from going any further.

He should know me by now.

I don't quit in the face of a challenge.

I knew from the start it would be difficult to swallow Levi's cock all the way, but my father always said that just because a task is difficult doesn't mean they are impossible to overcome. Breathing hard through my nose, I relax my throat as much as I can and take him in a little at a time. Tears begin to sting my eyes with the effort, making me pull back up just to push back down again. It's only when I am fully at the hilt that I celebrate, uncaring of the tears that streak down my cheeks. Encouraged by my newfound proficiency, I hollow my cheeks and start sucking like the end of days is right around the corner. Every moan he lets out, every pull of hair, only inspires me to do my very worst, or in Levi's case, my best.

"Fuck! Fuck! Stop!"

I don't pay him any mind since this is as much for me as it is for him. The power I feel over him is too deliciously intoxicating for me to stop now. He swells deeper in my throat, his curses music to my ears. My usually cold skin feels like it was doused in kerosene, and Levi set the match, intent on watching me burn.

And there's something else that is happening.

There's this emptiness inside.

Too hollow to be ignored and begs to be filled.

Yearns and prays for it.

Suddenly Levi isn't the only one that's moaning. Whiny moans leave me as my legs rub together, needing to relieve the ache in between them.

"Fuck! No more!" Levi shouts, and this time he shoves his hands under my shoulders and pulls me up. On wobbly knees I stand up straight, while Levi grabs at my chin, pulling me right to his face.

"One kiss, my ass. If your intention was for me to come in that pretty mouth of yours, you're in for a world of disappointment. When I come, it will be here," he warns, shoving his hand in between my aching thighs.

I let out a loud wail, rubbing myself on his hand just to take the pain away.

"Are you hurting, my queen?"

I nod vigorously, my eyelids too heavy to keep open.

"Look at me," he orders.

With much effort, I do as he commands.

"Do you want to marry me as a virgin, Kat? If so, tell me now so we can stop all of this while we still have the chance."

"Who says I'm going to marry you at all?" I defy breathlessly, ashamedly rubbing my pussy on his fingers.

"Wrong fucking answer."

Before I can stop him, his hands go to my waist and he lifts me off the floor, only to plant me on his shoulder.

"Remind me never to trust you again," he says, slapping my ass cheeks. "One kiss! You have no idea how you were two seconds away from drinking up all my cum. And I would have made you, too. Drink every last drop of it. I'd even make you beg me. Misbehave like that, and I will."

Another slap.

Hmph.

The throbbing ache in my pussy increases with every slap, the sting making me weep from it. I thank the gods for small mercies when Levi flings me onto the bed, unable to prolong the never-ending suffering his so-called punishment was affecting on me.

Standing tall at the end of my bed, he slaps each one of my ankles, forcing them to spread apart and expose myself for him. I bite down hard on my lip as he begins to take off his coat and pull his shirt over his head, throwing them behind his shoulders.

My eyes eat up every hard inch of him as he snakes his way onto the bed, positioning himself in between my thighs. When he finally reaches my face, his anger with me is long gone, and in its place, the same urgent need resides.

"You will choose me, Kat," he forewarns, plucking my lower lip from my teeth's grip. "You will. Because you won't be able to forget that I'm the man who tasted every inch of you. That stole your innocence and made you come with his tongue and his cock. I will haunt you forever. You won't be able to choose anyone else, because they will all be lacking in your eyes."

It should feel like a threat.

A vile threat only an enemy would make.

Yet each word feels like a kiss to my skin—a heartfelt promise.

On instinct, I wrap my legs around his waist and cling my arms around his broad shoulders.

"You don't scare me, Levi. Remember, I'm the only one here who is truly terrifying."

His eyes scan my face, reading the truth in my words.

"Terrifyingly beautiful," he whispers under his breath, gently stroking my cheek with his knuckles.

My bravado dwindles with his sweet endearment, and once again, I'm pulled back into the past, where the man towering over me now would prefer to die an excruciating death than cause me an ounce of pain.

"Transcendent," I whisper back, a flash of recognition in his eyes.

It's all the motivation he needs to press his lips against mine in an arduous kiss. His tongue forces itself inside me, just to battle it out with his counterpart. My nails sink into his shoulders as he deepens the kiss in such a way, I'm not sure where Levi ends and I begin.

It's all too much, I think to myself, but I should have known that this was only the beginning for what Levi had in store for me. I feel his crown edge at my center, the empty ache inside of me begging it to breach its doors. But Levi is so consumed with our kiss, that he's in no hurry to satiate my hunger.

Unable to hold out for another second, my nails pierce his flesh, creating crescent moons on his shoulders, while I use it as leverage to pull myself down his engorged length. My back arches off the bed and my sight turns black as the pain of being split wide open is too much for me to take.

"Fuck, Kat! Why the fuck did you do that?" he grunts, sweat beading on his forehead. "I wanted to take my time with you. The first time is always the hardest. But you're always so impatient. So fucking impatient," he continues to reprimand while leaving butterfly kisses all over my face, thinking that will ease my suffering.

I breathe through my nose until my sight returns to me. I had no idea how painful this could be. By Anya's accounts, a good tumbling is all about pleasure. Never once did she warn me that it could be the opposite.

"Breathe, Kat. Soon, all of this will feel good. I promise."

I try to believe him, but in my current affliction, it's very hard to.

Levi, sensing the immeasurable pain I'm in, begins to kiss me. I focus on his kiss and soon, as he said, I feel my body mold itself to his. I pout when Levi breaks our kiss, but then smile when he starts kissing the slope of my neck, all the way down my chest until his lips latch onto my nipples. His teeth gently bite into my sensitive flesh, creating that all-too-familiar sting that ignites my lower belly. Suddenly, Levi moves inside me, and this time there is no pain to speak of—only pleasure.

Pleasure that I've never once tasted before.

It's like the purest light trapped in a bottle and once let loose, it blinds you with its explosion.

My throat becomes hoarse with all the high-pitched cries that spill out of me.

Levi whispers words of praise as his thrusts increase in speed.

"You look so fucking beautiful right now. Taking my cock like the fucking queen you are. That's it, my queen. Take it. Take it all."

With each pounding thrust, I lose control over my body, and when it starts to convulse, the fire inside me threatening to melt my very being, my sight leaves me once more. Only this time, I'm not welcomed by the dark, but by blinding light. A white-hot warmth shrouds over me, leaving me breathless in its wake. I'm still panting for air when Levi pounds into me two more times before having his own celestial experience. He drops on top of me, his weight almost crushing me to the bed. I wiggle a bit to the side, but keep his head placed in between my breasts.

It takes us a while to even our breathing, but the shared silence between us feels comfortable.

Familiar.

Right.

"Can I ask you something?" Levi asks after a while.

"Hmm," I hum, my fingertips playing with his braids.

"Why did you cancel our dinner tonight?"

"Do you want the truth?"

Levi raises his head and plants his chin in between my breasts.

"If I said yes, would you lie to me anyway?"

"I might," I tease.

His expression saddens, and before he's reminded of the fact that he doesn't necessarily like me very much, I opt to tell him the truth.

"I was too worried to be a good hostess tonight," I admit, still playing with his hair.

"What were you worried about?"

"If I tell you, then you might be the one forced to lie to me."

"Try me," he smiles, that all-consuming Sun-God smile of his.

It's enough to have me relenting.

"Tomorrow, my true test begins. When we pass your city's gate, who knows what is there to greet me. I'm sure there are many in your court with hefty purses who might be inclined to gain favor with their king by murdering me."

"He'd have to kill me first," Levi utters with conviction.

"Even if he's doing it for you?"

"Killing you isn't something I want. I don't think I ever really did."
His brow furrows in thought. "I don't want you to be afraid in Arkøya.
I'll protect you. No one will dare lay a finger on you."

He says it with such passion, that even if logic tells me not to, I trust
him.

"No one will touch me?" I tease, biting the corner of my lip as my
finger trails over his lush bottom one.

"I'm the only one that can. And I'll be doing lots of it," he jokes,
pulling me up to his chest.

My palms lay flat on his firm six-pack, while my eyes linger on his
beautiful face.

"How much touching are we talking about?" I cock a teasing brow,
rubbing my pussy on him.

"I'm a man of action, Kat. How about I show you?"

"Please do." I giggle, as he flings me once again to my back,
towering over me with his huge frame.

"You'll be sore as fuck tomorrow," Levi warns, his cock at full-
mast.

"That's a problem for the queen tomorrow. Tonight, I'm just Kat."

"I thought you hated that name," he taunts while slowly caressing
my arms.

"It's growing on me." I wink at him.

"Something's growing all right, my queen. Don't come complaining
to me in the morning."

"I wouldn't dream of it." I laugh.

But like he's prone to do, Levi makes sure to halt my laughter to a
dead stop, ensuring that for the rest of the night, the only sound he
hears is me screaming out his name.

Chapter 20
Katrina

Everything is different the next day.
The beautiful truce our bodies made the previous night long
forgotten.
Levi's different today.
Distant.

When I awoke this morning to find my bed empty, a part of me
already knew that the day ahead would be a sullen one. And now that
we have officially passed through Arkøya's wide arched gates, I fear the
worst is yet to come.

We gallop through his city, with our train trailing behind so that the
person they see first is their king. People wave at the parade of soldiers,
all welcoming them home, thankful that no harm has come to them.
The crowd cheers in utter jubilation as Levi struts down the
cobblestone path that leads to his castle up the hill.

Every so often, Levi waves to the large mass, his lips in a thin line. I don't wave, since the mob of people are here for him, not me. I'm just the prize he's brought from the north. While his people welcome him with open arms, there is a definite disdain and loathing toward me. Some of them are even brave enough to hurl out their curses and spit on the ground as I pass by.

I knew they hated me.

They must if they were able to convince their king to try and overthrow me.

But why?

What did I ever do to deserve such contempt?

I've been queen for barely half a year. What wrong could I have done that was so unforgivable in that time span?

The only thing that causes me to hope is that anytime a curse rings out attached to my name, I feel Levi go rigid behind me, the hand on my waist fisting the fabric of my gown. We may have returned to our default ways, adamant to be on different sides of this silent war that we're waging with the other, but one thing I'm certain of—Levi doesn't like it when his queen is being mistreated.

I guess he prefers to be the only one who has such a privilege.

I try not to let it affect me, his people's condescension, or Levi's sudden apathy toward me, since I was half expecting it already. When I put this plan in place, I knew there would be unpleasantries I needed to endure. I'd be a damned fool if I were clueless as to what I was getting myself into.

There would be no parade for me.

I knew I wouldn't be celebrated or welcomed.

I may be the queen of all of Aikyam, but to them, I symbolize a foreign invasion—a queen out of touch with her kingdom.

And to a point, they're not wrong.

Haven't I favored the north, my birthplace, over the rest of my kingdom?

Didn't I give room for their resentment to fester?

In all my twenty-three winters, this is the first time I have ever left my home to visit the other lands I reign. And that was under duress. If that hadn't been the case, it would have never even crossed my mind to visit such lands.

And that right there was my first mistake as queen.

For the north might love me, but the rest of Aikyam does not.

Like a flower, love and loyalty needs to be nourished, and you can't do that if you deprive it of sunlight. My kingdom has been deprived of their true ruler for years on end, never even having laid eyes on me until now. Even the gods have statues of themselves in their houses of worship so that their faithful disciples can look on and pray to them.

How can I expect blind loyalty when they don't even know who they are being loyal to?

But the east knows Levi.

And it's not too far a stretch to think that the south recognizes Teodoro and the west, Atlas.

To them, those are their true sovereigns.

I thought when I started this game of chess that the end goal was to conquer these defiant kings, but now I see the rot goes so much deeper than that. I need to win the love of the people, cradle them into my bosom, and demonstrate that I'll never desert them again, if I'm ever able to be as beloved.

The mask that I had perfected so well will not serve me here.

Yes, I need to show strength, but not at the cost of their love.

Ice cannot melt hearts.

And though I felt a part of mine thaw last night, deep down I know it's still rock solid. As hard as it always was. Too much has happened for me to be able to soften its hard edges with the snap of my fingers.

I'm too much like my father in that way. He too had a block of ice where a heart should lie. The only person I ever saw that could smooth off his rough glacier edges was my mother. After her death, though, his heart, like mine, turned into the coldest diamond rock.

Losing someone you love does that to a person.

I should know, since I lost everyone I cared about at the same time.

How is a heart even supposed to beat when there is no one to beat for?

Ice is the only true friend I have.

It never abandoned me.

It never died on me.

It always prevailed.

So yes… ice cannot melt hearts, but neither can it can't break them.

It has only made mine stronger.

And with that thought in mind, I keep my chin up and school my facial features to their usual arctic form, uncaring of anything that is thrown my way.

When we reach the castle, we quickly dismount from our horse, Levi looking like he'd rather be anywhere than here.

"Levi?" I call out when he looks like he's about to make a quick exit.

"I have matters to attend to," he cuts me off, and then points at his general who is helping Inessa and Anya out of their carriage. "Brick will show you to your quarters."

"Levi, don't…" But words fail me.

What can I tell him that will change his mind as well as his somber state?

So instead of telling him not to leave me, that I don't want to walk through his castle's halls without him, I say nothing at all.

Levi stares at me for a tense-filled pause and then scowls before bowing his head.

When he lifts himself back up, he leans into me, to whisper his last humiliating taunt.

"Make sure your handmaidens prepare a bath for you to soak in. You're bound to need it after such a thorough riding."

And with that, he turns his back to me and walks away.

Chapter 21
Levi

For the rest of the day, everywhere I go, I'm consistently congratulated for something I have yet to achieve—conquering the north.

But to my kingdom, it's as good as won and they have their king to thank for such a glorious achievement. With every uttered praise I receive from the high lords in my court, they are always followed by a derogatory slur, cursing the very queen they wish me to marry. It's a wonder I'm able to keep the stern expression in place on my face when inside, considering I'm a mass of utter chaos. I feel my blood boil with every clink of a glass and every pat on the back.

Fearing I'll end up locking every last soul in my court that dares speak against Kat, I use the excuse of being weary after such a long journey home as my way out of the situation and lock myself in my chambers.

But I'm the furthest thing from being tired.

I'm far too troubled for that.

Memories of lying in Kat's bed last night consume all my thoughts.

The way she tasted on my lips.

The way she moaned out my name.

The way her virgin pussy hugged my cock and milked it for all its worth.

Yes.

While my people celebrate my hollow victory over the queen of Aikyam, I fear my dawning defeat. My mind is riddled with too many doubts and even more uncertainties.

Last night, as she laughed and joked and played with my hair, it was almost as if a window to the past had opened its shutters just to give me a glimpse of the girl I loved. My Kat was right there, so close that I could almost touch her, bathe in her very essence.

But with this Katrina, I can never be too certain. Could it have been just another one of her ploys, another strategy to break my defenses? Was it all an act? Tricking me into believing that last night was real for the both of us and not just smoke and mirrors, obscuring my sight from the truth. That her body is just another tool in her armory to vanquish me once and for all.

And fuck did I ever let her destroy me last night.

The way her lower lip trembled as I slid inside her still has me hard.

It might all have been a lie, but one thing for sure wasn't—how her pussy bled around my cock with each punishing thrust.

I know Kat would do just about anything to keep her crown, but offering up her virginity to a man she has sworn to hate doesn't seem likely.

Or am I fooling myself?

Could she be that conniving and calculating? That cold and unfeeling?

Just how far is Katrina really willing to go to keep her seat on the throne?

These thoughts haunt me as the day passes and by nightfall, I'm all but done.

So much so that when Brick waltzes into my chambers, I don't even acknowledge his presence, preferring to pretend that I'm preoccupied with all the correspondence and ledgers on my desk.

"Your silence is awfully loud, dear friend," Brick says when he's fed up with waiting for me to lift my head up from my work.

"Hmm," I mumble non committedly, eyes glued to the same scroll I've been staring at for the past hour.

Brick lets out a loud exhale before venturing closer to me.

"I'm not sure if what I have to say will be an improvement," he adds, leaning over my desk and planting his palms flat down on its edge.

"And what do you have to say?" I ask absentmindedly, still trying to ignore him.

"That she's winning."

My tongue rolls over my upper teeth, and I throw the scroll on the table so that I can lean back in my seat and stare at him.

"Is she now?" I question, crossing my arms over my chest. "And how have you come to such a conclusion?"

He mimics my form and crosses his own arms.

"Because you didn't sleep in your bed last night. Don't try to deny it either. A few soldiers saw you leaving her tent in the early hours of the morning before we broke camp to head home."

I keep my expression even keel, refusing to confirm his accusation.

When he sees he's not going to get anything from me, Brick shakes his head before running his fingers frustratedly over his hair.

"You know what soldiers do when they're not off to war and fighting? They gossip like old fucking maids. If you wanted to keep your indiscretions a secret, then you're shit out of luck. Word is out now. All of the men are too elated that their king is going to bed his way to the throne to keep their mouths shut. I give it a week before all of Aikyam knows. Two at best."

Good.

Let it spread that I claimed what others could only dream of.

The flash of Teo's disgruntled face instantly lifts my spirits.

"The problem being?" I interject with a cocky grin.

Brick's hazel eyes widen at my response.

"If you weren't my king and best friend, I'd have half a mind to punch your face in. Maybe it would knock some sense into you," he grumbles. "The problem being that it will not only be your enemies that get wind of such news. Your allies will too."

"Atlas," I mutter under my breath.

"Finally, a shred of sense has made its way through that thick head of yours!" he scolds. "Yes… Atlas. How do you think he will take such news? That you've bedded the very woman we agreed to join forces and ruin?"

"He'll take it as our men did. He'll think it's a strategy."

"A strategy?!" He chokes in outrage. "Do you think Atlas is so credulous? He knows you, Levi!" Brick shouts in indignation, pointing an accusing finger my way. "Like I know you. You would never result to such underhanded manipulation. Honor prevents you. If you laid with her, it was because you wanted to. Atlas will know it. And so do I."

My back molars grind together as my general stares me dead in the eye.

"This is not how the game should be played. You're falling into her trap, just like she calculated you would."

"I don't fall for traps, I make them!" I shout, springing to my feet and slamming my closed fist on my desk so hard that its legs shake.

"Not when it comes to her, you don't," he replies, defiance clear in his tone.

Brick has never once spoken to me like this.

Not as my general.

Not even as my friend.

"It seems we will not reach a consensus tonight and I'm too tired to argue with you," I state, needing him out of my sight before I end up punching him again.

Only this time, I wouldn't call for his precious Inessa to tend to him.

He'd have to do it all by his goddamn self.

"And will you be sleeping in your bed or hers?" he provokes, gaining an evil glare from me. "Yeah. That's what I thought. Careful, my king. Your fight is for her crown. Not her heart."

He turns his back to me and walks out the door, leaving me to deal with my fury on my own.

Although his words irked me to no end, I know they come from a place of loyalty.

Brick doesn't want his king to be blindsided.

And the fucked-up thing is, I'm not sure I'll be able to prevent it.

Anya and Inessa are busy untangling the crystal diamonds from out of my hair when Levi barges into my room.

"Leave," he commands brutishly, making both girls jump and sprint rapidly out.

The cowards.

"Remind me again, when did I ever give you the authorization to order my handmaidens around?"

But Levi doesn't rise to the provocation, preferring to walk to where I'm seated and finish what they started. Stunned silent, I limit myself to watching his reflection through the vanity's mirror as he delicately plucks every diamond out and then begins to free my hair from its braid.

There is a ghost of a smile threatening to appear on his lips as he rids each knot.

I'm not prone to wearing braids, but I thought if I had one on when reaching Arkøya, it would demonstrate to the east how I respect their traditions. A small peace offering that only Levi seemed to notice.

I swallow dryly when Levi picks up a brush and begins to use it on my now loose hair, the tenderness in his actions leaving me both confused and completely enamored.

"I used to spend hours just staring at this hair," he whispers softly. So softly that I have to lean back in my chair just so I don't miss a word he says. "How it looked as pale as snow sometimes. But when the sun was out and it hit your locks just right, they looked like spun gold. I used to daydream about the day I could touch it. Run my fingers through it. Brush it against my cheek."

I turn to my side and crane my neck back to look at him.

"You did?" I ask, my question just above a whisper, my lower belly tightening.

"Hmm," he mumbles, no smile to his face. "For years this hair has haunted me. It would appear in my dreams and in my fantasies."

Throat parched and heart thumping loudly, I gently take the brush out of his hand and place it on the vanity. I turn around and lift my hair off my nape so it can drape over the chair. Levi accepts my silent invitation and begins to thread his fingers through each lock. Gently at first, as if mesmerized by it. But then all too quickly is the spell broken, Levi brutishly wrapping my hair around his wrist and then pulling it all the way back, until my neck is craned as far as it can go. My eyes find his haunted—just like he said.

Levi then leans down and whispers in my ear, his warm breath fanning my skin, leaving a trail of goosebumps behind.

"I bet if I wanted, I could beat my cock with this hair and you'd let me."

He watches as my throat swallows down his words and heats up my cheeks.

"Is there nothing you won't do to get what you want?" he accuses, his tone hard like eastern steel.

I shake my head as far as he allows me and lick my lips.

"I thought as much." He scowls. "So tell me? What reward do you want in exchange for me defiling this hair with my cock and cum?"

His words are crude and vulgar, with just enough of a pinch of cruelty to have my heart doing backflips and my pussy slick with desire.

A reward.

If I let him use and abuse me, I get a reward.

And I know just the one that I want.

"Your braids, king. That's the reward I want. I want to feel your hair run through my fingertips like you've done with mine."

Shock expels whatever animosity he was holding on to.

"My braids?" he parrots, unbelievingly.

"Yes. Those are my terms. My hair for your braids."

He stares disbelievingly into my gray pools as if grasping for an answer to a question he refuses to ask out loud.

My neck starts to hurt with the way it's inclined in such an awkward angle. Levi must see the agony I'm in and decides to show me mercy, releasing my hair from his grip. I don't wait for instruction, and quickly get out of my seat, patting it so he takes the hint.

A tight-lipped Levi sits in my chair, while never taking his eyes off me. The way they move when I move makes me think that Levi believes our roles have somehow reversed, making me the predator and him, my prey.

I'd laugh if I didn't consider myself one.

Prey are victims and I'm no victim for any man.

I take what I want, when I want it, and right now, the thought of seeing Levi's raven hair all wild and out of its usual prison is too much of a temptation to pass up on.

Seven braids.

All tightly bound to his head, his nape clean shaven up close to the middle of his head.

Seven gorgeous obsidian braids, ready to be freed by my hand.

The excitement is more than I can stand.

"Are you smiling, Kat?" he asks, his tone less lethal as he watches me through the mirror.

I catch a glimpse of my reflection and see that, in fact, my smile is close to splitting my face in two.

I don't answer him since I'm too eager to start my task. Ever so gently, I start on the bottom of one and make my way to the top. Lush black locks fall to Levi's shoulder, the mere sight of it urging me on to do the same with the others. My fingers work double time to disentangle every last one of them, and before I know it, there isn't a braid left.

My greedy eyes drink up the sight. My fingers thread through his silky mane like it's the most exquisite thing they have ever touched. Tears of joy sting at the corners of my eyes as I take one small step back to appreciate my handiwork. It's only then that my eyes draw over to Levi's in the mirror, him looking like a wild god amongst men.

"You're beautiful," I say, the words out of my mouth before I realize I've even said them.

"Fuck, Kat," he grunts in pain. "You're going to ruin me."

He then turns in his chair just enough to stretch out his arms to pull me onto his lap. His lips are on mine in an instant, tasting like cherry wine and the sweetest temptation, all rolled up into one. My arms wrap themselves around his neck while my hands never leave his hair.

Levi, on the other hand, is too consumed into being reacquainted with my body to care how hard I pull on it. He lets out a visceral groan when I start rubbing my ass cheeks on his cock. I eat up all his animalistic grunts and swallow them whole. My breasts begin to ache with just one kiss, my pussy getting so slick I feel its juices starting to run down my thigh.

Levi then breaks the kiss by wrapping my hair around his wrist again and pulling me away from his mouth.

"How sore are you? Did you soak in a bath like I told you to?"

"I did," I pant, closing my eyes as I rub myself unashamedly on him, needing the friction to relieve the suffering I'm under.

"Did it help? Can I fuck you like I want to or are you in too much pain?"

"I'm never in too much pain. Pain and I are paramours. I like inflicting it as much as I like receiving it. Didn't you know?" I tease, feeling his cock swell beneath me.

"Believe me, I'm starting to get an inkling," he grunts, letting go of my hair so that he can grab my hips and help me stroke his cock over his clothes.

He then surprises me by rapidly shifting us on the chair so that we are both facing the mirror, my arms pulling away from his neck and onto his outer thighs to keep me steady.

"Look at what you've become. A queen so hungry for my cock, she can't even think straight."

I stare at the image in front of me and realize that he's not wrong. My cheeks are flushed, a crimson blush making its way from my chest all the way up to my face. Beads of sweat start to accumulate on my forehead as I pant for breath.

This woman, this wanton of a woman, would do just about anything for a release. It coils in my lower belly, begging to be set free and shatter me into a million little pieces. Levi can give that to me. That euphoria of being struck by lightning. He can give it to me and so much more.

I turn my head so that we are just a hairsbreadth apart.

"Are you saying that you don't want me just as badly?"

Levi scans every inch of my face.

"I want you more."

"Then I don't see a problem, do you?"

I watch his Adam's apple relentlessly bob and take my tongue to it, licking the slope of his neck until my lips reach his.

"Take what you want, my king."

"Fuck!"

He quickly lifts me up from his lap so that he can pull the strings of his pants, releasing the monstrosity that is his dick. I lick my lips, hungry to taste it, but Levi isn't up for taking requests. He seats my ass back on his lap and then lifts each one of my legs, planting each of my feet on his knees. He spreads his legs apart, forcing me to do the same, all the while staring at our lurid reflection in the mirror.

Like this, I feel more exposed than I have ever been in my entire life. There's something to be said about that. How, in this minute, I'm as vulnerable as a woman ever can be, and yet, I still feel in control. Even if that control is dwindling down with each second Levi takes to own me completely.

He must be in tune with my thoughts because he then pulls at the middle of my nightgown and shreds it until it becomes no more than a rag. With one hand, Levi holds me up by my hip, while his other hand gives two long strokes to his cock before aiming it at my dripping center.

"This is going to be dirty and fast, my queen. Remember that I gave you an out and you didn't take it," he warns, his green meadows ablaze.

"The only thing I want is you inside me," I breathe out.

"Then your wish is my command."

He sinks me down to the hilt of his cock, a shroud of blackness once again paying me its visit. I curse myself for not paying my sore limbs any mind, thinking myself capable of withstanding such pain.

"Greedy, greedy girl. You're your own worst enemy," he whispers in my ear, biting its lobe.

Levi continues to nibble on it while I get accustomed to his size.

"Look at yourself, Kat. Just look," he encourages, and I force my heavy eyelids to open and do as he says.

A little moan falls from my lips at the image of our connecting bodies. Him, all clothed in his usual black pants and shirt, and me, glistening porcelain, impaled on his hard cock.

A rare diamond being pierced by the finest steel.

North and east unified as one.

My core begins to clench around his stiffness, the image of us united, doing its trick to relax my limbs. My nails sink into his thighs as I push myself up and then slowly back down on him. Levi's mumbled curses are all the praise I need to continue. Up and down. Up and down. Slowly at first, until I find my rhythm and pick up to a pace that will satiate my hunger.

His hands are all over me by then, grabbing my breast and then pinching my nipples to the point of pain. I arch my back, but his palm on my stomach forces me to slam onto his cock, over and over again. Sweat pours down my temples and chest, as his wicked fingers travel south to my apex, landing on my clit. He shows me no mercy, rubbing and pinching at it all while his cock thrusts deeply into my womb. His teeth bite into the crook of my neck, his tongue licking the tiny specks of blood he induced. He sucks, and plays, and toys with my body in a way that has me drawing nearer to that almighty precipice.

All the while, we never take our eyes off each other in the mirror. Him needing to watch me come undone just as much as I need to watch him.

It's all so decadent. So obscene and erotic.

So perfect.

Right.

Again, I'm astounded by how every little thing Levi takes from my body feels like it was predestined. That it was always supposed to be this way. Proof to that effect is how his touch sets me on fire when before, I was just a discarded block of ice. Every inch of me burns alive, and I welcome the flames that flicker along my skin.

"Kat," he groans, pulling my attention back to him, his expression pained.

"I need you to come, Kat. Fuck, I really need you to come."

"Then make me, King."

He lets go of my breast and shoves his hand in my hair, pushing me to him. His lips latch onto mine, the desperation and need of his kiss the spark I need to have me tumbling down over the ledge, falling... falling... falling into a ball of blinding white light.

"Levi!" I shout at the top of my lungs, him eating my wails with his kiss.

He prolongs my earth-shattering orgasm by flicking my clit and biting into my lower lip. My calves burn trying to keep to my tempo, needing to ride this out to its end. Liquid ecstasy courses through my body, leaving a warm feeling of contentment once it leaves my system.

Still in a post-orgasmic daze, it takes me a minute to realize that Levi is calling out my name. In fact, I only do when he gives my hair another brutish tug.

"I've paid your price. Now I want my reward," he threatens huskily, lust thick in his voice. "On your knees, my queen."

When he pulls out, I all but pout at how deprived I feel. Levi doesn't give in and shoves me on my knees in front of him. I barely have enough time to blink, before my hair is trapped around his favorite wrist, while his other hand forces my mouth open to take his cock into my mouth.

"Can you taste yourself, my queen? Can you taste how you came so beautifully on my cock?" he says while thrusting inside my mouth, his mushroom head almost passing my throat.

My gag reflexes gasp for air trying to push him out, but Levi isn't having it.

And neither am I.

I hold on to his waist and relax my throat, intent on owning him completely. I feel his grip on my hair lax, making me lift my reprimanding gaze to him. Levi quickly recovers from his mistake, giving my hair another agonizing tug, its sting making my heated skin sing. Breathing hard from my nose, I hollow my cheeks and suck him all the way down, using my tongue to lick his salty essence on the way up. I feel his thighs tense up with each stroke of my tongue, emboldening me even more. I grip his cock at his base with my hand, stroking it as my tongue licks at the head, sucking it every so often into my mouth.

The mix has Levi howling, pulling my mouth off his cock so that he can stroke it. Three hard tugs later, spurts of cum splash all over my face and hair. I lick it off my lips, my fingers bringing it to my tongue to suck. Levi's eyes are like two dark pools as he uses his fingers to massage my scalp, making sure each strand of my hair soaks up his cum.

It's dirty.

And filthy.

And right.

Once he's made sure that he's left his mark on me, his expression looks finally at peace, serene even. Levi gently picks me up from the floor, cradling me in his lap, before landing the sweetest of kisses on my lips.

A kiss so opposite to what we just did.

A kiss that promises more than lewd, salacious encounters.

A kiss with purpose and meaning.

A kiss that turns my world upside down and rattles me to my very core.

He breaks the kiss and hugs me tightly to his chest, as if afraid I'll cease to exist.

"I want to hate you," he says after a long pause. "But my heart refuses to. Why?" he asks, gently stroking his knuckles on my cheek.

I stare into his eyes, mimicking his caresses by running the tips of my fingers over his stubbled cheek.

"If you ever know the answer to that question, please tell me. I'm having a hard time figuring it out too."

He lets out a defeated chuckle, one that I recognize all too well.

"You're not what I expected," he adds in a whisper.

"Who did you expect?"

"Your father's daughter."

Chapter 23

I don't let the lingering stares we get as I give Kat a tour of my castle affect me.

I'm in too good a mood for that.

With Kat hanging on my arm, we peruse my castle so that I may give her a little taste of what life is like here in the east. Kat eats up my words as I explain the traditions of my people, eager to learn all of it.

It feels like we crossed an invisible line last night.

One that had been traced between us, intent on dividing us.

There's this sense of a new beginning for us, one I'm all too willing to explore.

Still, there is this nagging little voice in my ear that whispers this can all be part of her game. A way to unarm me so that I may lose focus on the end goal.

But I brush it to the side.

My end goal has never been clearer.

I will be crowned King of Aikyam, and Kat will be my wife. Not because her own decree demands it, but because she wants to be. Because this feeling that is kindling between us, if nourished and protected, can be just the thing that ends up saving us both.

"I wish Inessa and Anya came with us. Especially Anya. She would have loved this," Kat remarks when we reach the highest tower of my castle. The scenic view of Arkøya surrounded by lush green meadows looks like something out of a storybook. Spring rules my land, making the flowers and all its greenery rich in color.

But the sight is lost to me, since I only have eyes for the woman standing beside me.

With my knuckles, I lift her chin and tilt it toward me.

"Is my company so bad that you need chaperones to distract you?"

The sly grin that tugs at her lips grips my heart into a vise.

"That's not why I wanted them here."

"No?" I tease, running the pad of my thumb over her chin.

She shakes her head.

"No. It's only that I know they would have loved to see this view. Feels almost sacrilegious not to share this view. It's breathtaking."

Not as breathtaking as you, Kat.

Not nearly enough.

"Although I do prefer it when it's just the two of us."

"Do you, now?" I ask, running my thumb over the seam of her lower lip, her tongue peeking out to lick its tip.

I let out a groan, pulling my finger away from her tempting mouth and gripping her waist to slam her against me.

"Do that again, and I'll fuck you right here where the world can see."

Her eyes light up at the threat, my insatiable Kat liking that idea very much.

But as much as I would like to accommodate her ravenous desire for jumping on my cock, there is still too much I want to show her. We have the whole month to quench our most twisted desires. We can make do with losing a couple of hours to sightsee.

A month.

The thought throws rocks at my stomach.

In a month's time, she'll leave me to travel south—*to him.*

"Levi?" she calls out my name with concern.

"All is good, Kat. I just remembered something."

"What?"

"To tell Brick that he has my leave to show your handmaidens around the castle as well as Arkøya."

Kat's worried expression quickly turns annoyed, as she slaps my chest and pulls away from me.

"You will do no such thing. Inessa is already tired of him always sniffing around her. And frankly, so am I."

"Has my general offended you?" I interrogate, steel in my tone.

I swear, if Brick has insulted Kat in any way…

"His mere presence offends me. Inessa deserves better than that brute."

"Hmm. There was a time you thought the same of me," I taunt.

"Who says I still don't?" She bats her eyelashes at me.

I pull her to my chest again, this time unwilling to let her go, and tug at her long hair to crane her head back so I can have a perfect view of her glorious face.

"But you like this brute. He's getting under your skin, isn't he?"

She swallows hard, her lids becoming heavy.

"I'm not sure I know what you're talking about," she sasses, the swell of her breasts lifting up and down and pulling my eyes toward them.

"You know exactly what I'm talking about," I groan, bending down low enough so I can lick the bead of sweat in between her breasts.

The little sob she lets out as she presses further against me has me rethinking this whole tour.

"You're a man of many contradictions. Your words say one thing, while your actions say another," she says, her breathing becoming a shallow mess of want and need.

"And what exactly do my actions say?" I counter, licking my way up her neck and to her ear until my teeth sink into her earlobe.

"That you would rather take me to your chambers and have your way with me than show me your great city."

I chuckle, only to moan two seconds later when her hand slithers in between our bodies until it finds its way to my already stiff cock.

"I must admit, I am of two minds about it."

"Is there anything I can do to give it clarity?" she taunts, knowing exactly what wicked spell she's put on me.

I look around the tower; the watch guards who are usually on post are nowhere in sight. Which means their shift must have ended and their replacements are soon to arrive. There's not much time, but I have always fantasized about fucking someone while looking at this view.

Not someone.

Her.

With no time to lose, I flip her around and place her hands on the wall's edge. Kat leans her head on my chest and giggles while I struggle to pull at the strings of my pants. When I finally get my dick free, I lift the skirt of her dress and press my hand on her back so that she bends down until her porcelain ass is lifted up high.

"Let's see how much you laugh with my cock inside you, my queen," I threaten with a smirk.

But like it always is with her, our laughter dies the minute we connect and become one.

Fuck.

But a pussy shouldn't feel so good on a man.

I swear it was put on this earth to madden the strongest of all of us.

As I slide back and forth into her pussy, I'm astounded at how it always seems so ready for me. Wet, hot, and inviting. Kat doesn't need poetry or song to stimulate her desire. All she needs is me whispering the filthiest things I can come up in her ear for her body to come alive with want.

And I'm all too happy to oblige.

My hand snakes around her until it feels the little swollen nub aching to be toyed with. I play with her clit as my thrusts pound into her sweet, hot cavern. Kat moans out loud, gripping the gray cemented edge for balance. Her head hangs down, unable to keep it up with all the sensations wrecking her body.

With my free hand, I wrap her braid around my wrist and give it a good tug, so that she has no choice but to look at the land in front of her.

"That, my queen, is Arkøya," I grunt in her ear as I continue to pound at her. "That is who you're fucking. Who your pussy is clenching around, just begging to milk it dry. For Arkøya is me. And right now, Winter Queen, Arkøya owns you—body and soul."

Her silver gaze falls to the sweeping landscape in front of her, her breathing coming out in spurts. Her cheeks a beautiful shade of pink, her brow damp from excursion.

"Do you concede, my queen? Will you allow yourself to be conquered?"

Her gaze darts to me, a salacious smile to her lips.

"Never."

With that response, I have no choice but to thrust so deep inside her that her eyes roll to the back of her head.

"Do you concede, my queen?" I repeat, my own breathing erratic.

I'm so fucking close to coming, but it's her defiance that spurs me on.

She shakes her head again, and again I bury my cock so deep inside her that she screams out my name.

"Levi!"

Sweat blurs my vision and stings my eyes. I either tolerate the pain or wipe the sweat off my eyes, forcing me to have to choose between releasing her hair or taking my fingers off her needy cunt.

Fuck that shit.

I'm keeping them exactly where they are.

I've suffered through worse.

"Do you concede?" I growl, flicking her clit and adding more pressure to it.

But Kat is too far away to hear my demand.

Her mind is gone into another world, one where only pleasure resides.

"You're full of contradictions too, sweet Kat. Your mind might not want to concede, but your body already has. It's mine for the taking. To do with as I wish. And right now, I want it to come all over my cock."

I drive mercilessly into her, the head of my cock banging at her walls, hitting just the right area to have Kat seeing the gods themselves. She yells out for salvation, her body damned to crave mine for eternity. I take her to the very brink, and like fine crystal, she shatters, looking delicate and fragile in my unworthy hands. It doesn't take much coercion after that for me to follow her, needing that sweet feel of release, knowing my cum will fill her to the hilt and drip down her thighs.

Depleted and satiated, I turn her in my arms so I can kiss her lips, the doors to my redemption.

It's always like this.

After abusing and desecrating her body, there's this unbridled need in me to be gentle afterward, even if I can only show her such tenderness in a kiss.

And every time I do, it always feels far more intimate than the exchange of our bodies.

It's almost as if in this one kiss, we are committing to so much more than a good tumbling.

That we are committing our very souls to each other.

A silent promise that neither one of us dare say out loud.

The rest of our day goes remarkably how it began.

Me trying to show Katrina the ways of the land by taking her into the city, only for her to grow impatient and pull me into some back alley or hide us behind some tree or bush just so we can fuck the hunger out of us.

But instead of simmering down our lust with each stolen kiss or manic fuck, we only seem to crave each other more. But it's those precious, fleeting moments we share, when we're all spent and our masks slip off that really do a number on me.

It almost has me believing that falling in…

All too soon, when those words start to bloom in my heart and threaten to take root, I am reminded why Katrina of Bratsk represents everything I hate.

"Oh, the gods!" She gasps, letting go of my hand to run to the fountain statue in front of us.

After we've had our fill of the cobblestone streets of my city, Kat was adamant that she needed to see my garden, as if that was the most important place a castle could have.

I wasn't as excited to come here.

Exactly for the reason that lies tall in the middle of my spring garden, a statue dedicated to the memory of my father and mother.

Kat tilts her head to the side, her gray eyes drinking in every little inch of the marble. Her gaze wanders over the statue, marveled by how the artist was able to grasp my father's likeness in such a way that feels like he'll move. How my mother looks serene sitting in her favorite chair, her fingers entwining with my father's on her shoulder. It is the way my mother lovingly looks up at him, that shared glance between them that makes me miss them that much more.

Katrina's awe quickly morphs into grief. She then turns to face me with that same look in her eyes that my mother once held, reminding me what a beautiful liar she's become.

"I always felt guilty that they died," she has the gall to say. "They were always so lovely with me. Your mother always had a kind word for me, and your father treated me with the same respect he would a boy. Not many in court did. I loved them dearly. And I'm sorry."

"Are you now?" I spit out, my nostrils flaring.

She nods sheepishly, her gaze falling back to the two people I loved most in the entire world until her kind stole them from me.

"I am." She sighs. "Sometimes I replay the last day you and your family came to visit us. How your mother wouldn't leave until she said goodbye to mine. My father gave explicit instructions that no one go into my mother's chambers, but they were such close friends, I didn't have the heart to refuse her."

I grab her forearm and spin her around to look at me.

"What the fuck are you talking about?" I snap, my hold on her arm a little tighter than she's used to.

Her gaze looks confused as she stares up at me. But not more confused than I am at this present state.

"The ailment, Levi. The sickness that took my mother from me was the same that killed your parents. I thought you knew this," she explains, shame and guilt written all over her face. "It was me, Levi. I'm the reason why they died. Your mother must have caught the same disease mine had been infected with. And when you left, she must have unknowingly spread the disease to Teo's mother and Atlas's too. Don't you see? If I had been strong and held my father's order, they would all be alive. It was because of me."

I cringe at each word that falls through her lying lips. And when she lifts her hand to cup my cheek, I flinch away.

"You'll never forgive me, will you?"

I say nothing.

Not when she continues to play this game with me.

This cruel, grotesque game.

"I know that apologizing for my actions will never bring them back. I know that. But I was young. I had no idea the risk I was taking. I thought I was doing your mother and mine a kindness. I swear to you."

I turn around and close my eyes, not even being able to look at her.

After all we've done today, for her to come up with such a fabricated lie, a lie that I'm sure has been told a thousand times for all of the north to believe, taints every perfect moment we shared.

"I've upset you," she whispers behind me. "I've upset you by calling up such a wound. One that hasn't probably healed fully."

"Do you believe yourself to be so in tune with me already?" I hear myself say.

"I know you enough to know when you're upset."

White-hot fury blinds me, coaxing me to turn around and raise my hand to go right to her throat.

"Yes, Katrina. I'm very fucking upset. Does my pain satisfy you? Does it feed your cruel heart?"

"Let me go, Levi. You're hurting me."

"I'm hurting you?! I'm hurting you?! Hear this, Katrina. I haven't begun to hurt you."

I expect villainous anger to coat her silver gaze, but all I'm met is with sadness. My fingers dig themselves deeper, yet she refuses to fight me. To defend herself.

It's almost as if her guilt is genuine.

A lie, Levi! Just another lie!

Disgusted with her pretense, I pull my hand off her. Kat immediately starts coughing for air. My chest tightens when I see my finger marks on her pale skin. Not an hour ago I was worshiping her body, making her feel more alive than she had ever been before.

And now?

I was close to killing her with my bare hands.

The very woman who I was falling for.

"Go away, Winter Queen. Go. Run while you still can, for I cannot be trusted around you right now," I plead, turning my back to her just so I don't see the bruises I inflicted on her.

But to my bitter disappointment, she doesn't so much as move.

"There's more to the story, isn't there?" she says, committed to her performance.

I scoff.

"Don't pretend you don't already know. Don't pretend you have no idea what really happened to my parents. Don't stand there and lie to me like that. It would fucking hurt less if you killed me."

"Levi?" she starts, and when I feel her hand on my back, it cinches through the fabric of my coat, forcing me to step away from her.

"Don't. I'm tired of your games, Kat. I'm so fucking tired of them."

"What games?" she suddenly shouts, throwing her arms in the air to show her frustration.

I turn around and slice my eyes to her.

"Stop, Katrina. Just… stop.

"Not until you tell me why you're being like this. We were having such a lovely day and then we started talking about your parents—" I flinch at the mere mention of them.

"There!" She points at my face. "That is real. That pain I know all too well. It's suffocating and it drives us to be people that we are not. I know that pain. I feel it every day. I have done, for the past seven years. It's more than grief. It's the wound of an unforgivable betrayal. Of being hurt by the ones you trusted."

My blinding hate of her is momentarily subdued with curiosity of who she is referring to—me or her.

"It's because of them," she adds, baffled. "Your anger has to do with your parents. But why? What could cause such fury to be born if the cause of their death was natural?" she asks, as if trying to piece together all the clues she has at her reach.

If I didn't know better, I would swear her reaction is genuine.

"Tell me," she orders, her puzzlement turning into obsession. "Tell me what happened to your parents and what part I played in it other than letting an old friend say farewell to another."

"Kat—"

"Tell me!" she shouts with such passion and conviction, it takes me aback.

"You really don't know?" I whisper, astonished that maybe she's genuinely clueless to it all.

She shakes her head.

"I really don't, but I want to. So please, don't leave me in the dark and tell me what happened."

"Come here," I command, pulling her to my chest and tilting her chin up. I stare into her eyes, trying desperately to see the deception in them, but when I come out empty-handed, I realize that Kat has been lied to all this time. Kept in the dark to what was happening in her kingdom, all because Orville so wished her to be.

He really was a cunt.

I place a kiss on her temple and weave my fingers with hers, pulling her to sit on the grass in front of my parents' statue. Once I have her on my lap, I pepper butterfly kisses on the red marks on her slender throat. "I should be flogged for this and then put in a dungeon, without food or sunlight for the rest of my years."

She cups my face to hers and presses a chaste kiss to my lips.

"Do you think me so fragile, my king? Need I remind you what I'm made of? Your steel cannot hurt me, Levi. Even if it did leave its mark."

"Doesn't decrease my shame, nor sorrow, any less. I'll never be able to make this right."

"You will, Levi. Help me understand what happened to make you so blinded by hate that you put your hands on me in such a way. Explain why that same hate was what brought you to charge north with the intention of stealing my crown, for I believe the two are one and the same."

I offer her a defeated nod and then I tell her. I tell her everything.

"There was only ever one disease that cursed the kingdom of Aikyam. And that was your father."

"*There was only ever one disease that cursed the kingdom of Aikyam. And that was your father.*"

Immediately, my defenses go up at the mention of my father.

"My father was the greatest ruler to ever reign over Aikyam," I protest, confused as to why Levi believes such a lie.

"No, Kat. He wasn't. He was the villain that terrorized us as well as his people. He was the monster that kept the east, south, and west in bondage for decades."

With my hands on his chest, I try to shift off his lap, but Levi only tightens his hold.

"You want the truth or not, Kat? Because what I'm about to tell you isn't pretty. It will change the way you think, feel, and remember him. But on my honor, everything that I'm about to tell you is the gods' truth."

I stare into his eyes and see such conviction, such certainty in his belief, that I force myself to relax on his lap.

"Tell me. Tell me what you believe to be true."

"It's not a belief, Kat. It's a fact. Your father was the worst thing that could have ever happened to Aikyam."

"How?"

His expression turns pensive, as if trying to find the right words to make me understand.

"When we visited my city earlier today, did anything stand out to you?"

"Aside from your people looking down at me in distaste?" I counter coldly.

"They were only being that way because they don't trust you or your motive."

"I got the message loud and clear," I interject.

"You can't blame them for their animosity toward you. They are only reacting to years of distrust from anything pertaining to the north. But I don't want you to focus on that. I want you to think really hard about what you saw today. What conspicuous peculiarity grabbed your attention?"

My brows pinch together at the middle of my forehead as I try to recall the many places we went to earlier and if anything felt unusual or off about it. It's a difficult task to do, since my mind wanders not only to the ugly looks I got, but also to the stolen intimate moments Levi and I shared.

"Kat, please, think. This is important," Levi encourages when I take too long to answer.

But then it comes to me.

As we walked through his cobblestone street filled with shops of merchants and swordsmiths, I was surprised to see that most of them were run by women. In fact, there were very few men amongst the shoppers too. Even the children that playfully ran in the streets were mostly girls.

"Men," I finally state. "There weren't many men."

"No, there were not," Levi agrees sullenly. "For every east-born male, there exists at least five women to him in comparison. Can you venture a guess as to why that is?"

I want to say that the same plague that took my mother was responsible, but sickness is not prejudice nor selective in the lives that it takes. Then I recall the camp I found Levi in after I left my home. There was ample evidence of the tens of thousands of men that had been there, ready to invade Tarnow Castle before they were ordered to return east.

"War. War is the only reason I can think of that could cause such a gap in percentage."

When Levi lets out an exhale, his tense muscles relaxing instantly, I know I got the right answer.

But then a new one arises.

"No." I shake my head, still confused. "War can't be the only denominating factor for such a large, disproportioned difference. For it to be so, it would mean that every living male had to be enlisted in the great army of Aikyam."

"That's right. It does mean that. From the tender age of six, every east-born man must pledge his life to defending Aikyam at all costs. Babes are taken from their mothers to become soldiers when they haven't even had time to be children. The only exception to this law passed by your father is for those of noble birth, and even they must answer the call after their fifteenth spring has been reached."

"No," I belt out in denial. "I would have heard of such a law."

"Would you?" he counters patiently, stroking my cheek with his knuckles. "You weren't even born yet when your father passed such a law, one that only affected the east. The northern mountains that you so adore, the ones that make sure to keep Tarnow safe from their enemies, also ensures that they keep you clueless to what life is for the rest of us who had the misfortune of not being born in the north. Each of our kingdoms, be it east, south, or west, pays the price of servitude in their own way. A hefty price at that. The king of the north demanded it so. And for decades we obliged, knowing that to defy him would be treason to the kingdom we so loved."

The sense of dread consumes me as I feel this conversation is about to get ten times worse—the burning question lodged in my throat terrified to come out.

"What really happened to your parents, Levi? For I fear the plague that stole my mother didn't steal yours."

"No, it did not," he retorts, that sharp edge of steel back into his tone.

He hears it too.

Levi takes a fortifying breath, calming himself before he utters another word.

"After news broke of your mother's untimely death, all the kingdoms mourned the loss. While King Orville had been a tyrant, it was well known that Queen Alisa did not support her husband's methods or views. Yes, she may have stood by his side as his wife and queen, but she tried to ease our suffering by offering her own counsel. I can only speak of her kindness when it comes to the east. Especially, because she had used my own mother to deploy most of her messages to my kingdom. Where Orville demanded that all men be enslaved to the crown by going off to fight his wars on foreign lands, Alisa made it evidently clear that the children not bear arms and serve in our troops in lower-level capacities. Be it mending our armor, securing our weaponry, or cooking our meals. The law had been clear, and yet she found a loophole where she could save our younglings from seeing bloodshed for as long as we could keep it that way."

Having Levi talk so fondly of my mother, brings back memories of her to the forefront of my mind.

He's right.

She had been born from winter, yet she still managed to have a warmth about her. A diamond heart that wasn't hardened but shone brightly for all the world to see.

"But while we mourned, your father plotted," he continues, his nostrils flaring. "For all his faults, your father loved your mother. She was his conscience. Or at least as much as she could have been to a man whose ruthlessness and greed knows no bounds. The minute she left this mortal plane, your father became the thing we always feared he was—a monster."

My heart begins to drum, recalling how in fact my father changed when my mother died.

Before he would talk to me. Even if only to ask me how my day had gone. He was never gentle or kind, nor did he ever pretend to be that kind of man, but at least he tried to show some sort of fatherly affection toward me. A gentle hug every now and again. A little praise here and there. A kiss goodnight. He tried. And because he did so, I loved him even more for it.

It's easy to love someone who showers you with love and affection because it is in their nature to do so. But when it's not, and that person tries with all their might to show you they care, even when it goes against the very fabric of their being—that to me is an even greater show of love.

Or for a while, I thought it was.

After her death, though, my father no longer saw me as a daughter, but the next in line to his succession. He rarely spoke to me but when he did, it was always to educate me in the ways of politics and dealing with our court. He would easily get frustrated with me, saying my womanhood made me soft and that if I were to rule, I had to be made of much harder ice than the one I possessed. There was hardly ever a time where I said or did the right thing in his eyes.

Still, for years I tried to mold myself to become the daughter he wanted me to be. But nothing ever felt like enough. He was the only parent I had, and I loved him dearly, yet somehow to him, I never quite measured up to his expectations. Knowing my father had died disappointed in me was a cut that I have yet to heal from.

But all of that didn't make him a tyrant in my eyes.

Just a man with high expectations.

A man who knew his daughter would be queen someday and needed her to be prepared.

To me, that had been his new way of showing me that he loved me.

And that had been enough.

So to hear Levi call him a monster sets my teeth on edge.

"You're still loyal to him?" Levi scoffs. "He's rotting away in the dirt, but you remain loyal."

"He was my father."

"He was a cunt."

I try to break free from his hold but Levi isn't having it.

"No!" he shouts while I keep trying to wrestle free. "You wanted to know what happened and by the gods, you'll hear me tell it to you," he yells, holding the nape of my neck forcibly, only to ease his grip a second later when his gaze lands on his fingermark around my throat.

"I'm sorry," he whispers sullenly, taking the wind out of my sails. "Please, Kat. Just… listen."

I try to calm myself down as best I can, considering that I'm also invested in what Levi has to tell me. It might hold the answer as to why he took his army north.

Once he's sure I have cooled down, he continues with his story.

"As I was saying." He lets out an exaggerated exhale. "After your mother died, Orville needed something or someone to lash out at. And when the idea was whispered in his ear that maybe the late queen didn't die of natural causes, but from poison, that was all the excuse he needed to seek out his revenge on us."

"Poison?" I parrot, incredulous. "My mother wasn't poisoned. The healers said it was some kind of influenza that got into her lungs and made them stop working."

"Aye, I'm well aware. But there are some herbs that are found in the earth that can make the healthiest of persons allergic to its substance. Allergic enough to contaminate a person's airway and close it shut."

I tilt my head to the side to stare into his eyes.

"There is no such herb or flower in the north," I tell him.

In fact, there isn't much that does grow in my kingdom, save for our northern blue roses. They are the only things that seem to bloom in such a harsh environment, making them one of our most treasured emblems.

"No," Levi begins to say, "but there is one that is known to bloom outside of the north. A fact that your father knew all too well. He used that knowledge against us, and ordered us to turn against each other to find out the culprit behind his wife's death. When neither kingdom was able to oblige him, he turned on us all."

"How?" I ask hesitantly, sensing I'm not going to like his answer.

"If the north lost a queen, then so should the other kingdoms under his rule."

My throat begins to clog at his words.

"You mean—"

"I mean he demanded that all three kingdoms hand over their queens to him, or suffer the penalty of death."

My gaze flits away from Levi and onto the statue in front of us of King Krystiyan and Queen Daryna of Thezmaer.

I'm accosted by a myriad of memories of them laughing together, whispering in each other's ears, while they got lost in each other's eyes. The way they would hold each other's hands anywhere they went.

"Your father would have never given up your mother. Not even to the king himself," I state knowingly.

"You're right. He wouldn't. Neither would any righteous man who loved his wife," Levi says assuredly. "The north may think differently when it comes to their women, but us? Here in the east? Women are not bargaining chips, nor are they something to be traded off. Not even if that trade guarantees your life. For what is a life without your heart? That is who my mother was. Not only to my father, but to his kingdom. There was no possible way he or the east could depart from their queen."

I swallow dryly and turn to face Levi once more, his gaze never having left me.

"So what did your father do in response?" I ask, knowing that whatever it was wasn't enough if both of them are now dead because of it.

"The only thing he could do. If King Orville had obviously gone mad, then he was no longer worthy of the throne. So my father rallied his troops and called on his allies to help him rid the world of such oppressing force."

"Save his wife while gaining a crown. Doesn't seem all that romantic to me when you put it like that," I interject, angry that diplomacy wasn't even on their scope of alternatives.

"Romantic?" Levi chokes out the word like it's a curse. "What room is there for romance when lives are involved? No. My father did not want the crown for himself, only that it no longer belonged to yours. Once my father was able to bring down Orville from his high seat, the kingdoms would have to come to a consensus as to who would be his successor. My father had even made his feelings known that if it were up to him, the north should still rule."

"You mean—" I stutter, flabbergasted, not expecting Levi to insinuate such a thing.

"Yes." He nods. "As far as he was concerned, you were to keep your birthright. His war wasn't with you or the north, per se. It was with your king."

"So what happened?" I ask hurriedly, fully invested in his tale of woe and sorrow.

"What always happens when power is at play—betrayal," Levi explains, hatred once again tainting the gorgeous hue in his eyes. "My father trusted the wrong people. People that he considered not only allies, but friends. He wasn't the only one," he growls, his teeth grinding so hard I can hear them clatter. "They came to our home under the guise of forming a plan with my father that would ensure our victory, only to butcher us in the dead of night. They murdered my mother first and then killed my father next. They did it in that order because your father insisted mine see his love die before his very eyes. It was sadistically cruel how they waited and held my father back by his arms as he suffered for his loss. Unable to touch her. Unable to kiss her goodbye. They waited. And laughed. And joked. And desecrated her body in front of him before cutting off his head. That was what they did! That was what your father ordered them to do!"

My eyes begin to water at the imagery of such a scene.

"If…" I stammer, emotion getting the better of me. "If this is all true, and my father was such a villain, then that must mean that he is responsible for Teodoro's and Atlas's parents' death also."

I don't miss how Levi's nostrils flare in utter contempt at the mention of the southern king.

"What your father did or did not do to them, is not my story to tell. But hear this now and hear me true. If Orville has blood on his hands, then Teo is soaked in it."

My brow furrows at that ominous remark. I open my mouth to ask what he means by it, but Levi shakes his head, closing the door on that conversation.

"I've said more than enough for one day. Having to go back to that place brings out the worst in me. And I've treated you too poorly as it is."

Levi begins to lightly caress my neck, his sullen emerald eyes losing its shine with each tender touch. I hate that he believes his anger hurt me. It didn't. Not when it was the catalyst I needed for him to confess the reason behind his loathing of me and the north.

And then it suddenly occurs to me.

In his recounting of events, both he and his father were reacting to what my father had done to them. I was never viewed as a threat or a danger. So why have I gained that same hatred toward me?

"Why did you march north?" I ask outright. "Your quarrel was with my father. If your intention was to seek revenge, then why not do it when he was still living? Why aim your thirst for vengeance on me?"

Levi doesn't so much as bat an eye at my accusation.

"Because through it all, you didn't lift a finger to help us."

"I didn't know. Any of it. I didn't know any of it. If I had, I would have done something. Anything to prevent it."

His gaze digs into mine as if trying to decipher if I'm telling him the truth or not.

I am.

If I had a whisper of an inkling to what the east had to endure under my father's rule, I would have done something. What, I'm not sure. But I was never given the chance to either.

His now stern expression never wavers, but neither do the small caresses his thumb makes on the side of my neck.

"Once my parents were gone," he begins to explain, "your father made sure to keep his spies spread throughout my kingdom. I never knew who to trust. I never knew if I could trust you. But through the years, I kept a list. A list of everyone I believed to be loyal to the north and its king. When news arrived that the king was dead, my first order was to gather up all my suspects and drag a sword through their wretched hearts. I would not be betrayed again," he says with a chilling snarl. "And then I waited. I waited for your coronation to see what type of queen you would be. And when no decree was sent abolishing the law that sent infants to the battlefield, I had my answer."

"You could have abolished such a thing from continuing to happen. You didn't!"

"It's still Aikyam law! How could I expect my people to follow a king who would defy the crown in that way? My honor would be questioned from there on out."

"And yet, you still marched north," I accuse him.

"Aye, I did. But once the throne was mine, no one would even question how I went about changing a law that should have never been born in the first place. With Orville alive and well, and all his spies circling in the shadows around me, I couldn't risk sending my men to the slaughter. His personal army might not have posed a problem to mine, but your father had friends in other kingdoms besides our own. Rich friends that owed him enough favors that they would have left their homes just to aid him and defend his rule. Now the Winter Queen, a girl who would prefer to hide in her castle than acknowledge anything beyond its walls, was a different story. I could easily have stolen the throne from such a girl."

"I'm that girl!" I point to my chest. "I'm that girl, Levi, whose only sin was that of ignorance."

Levi lets out another exhale and runs his hand through his freshly done braids.

"I didn't know that at the time. And it's still hard to believe that you could have been so clueless to all of this. To everything that has been done in your family's name."

"You think I'm lying?" I question, insulted at the accusation.

"Have you given me reason to believe otherwise?" He cocks a brow.

My lips curl at the side, knowing he's got me there.

I've done my share of lying since we've met.

But not about this.

I'm not lying about this.

My hands cup his face and pull it as close to mine as I can without us touching.

"Yes. I have lied. I have done all I can do to break your defenses." When he starts to pull away, I use all the strength I have to keep him still. "I had to. I needed to know the reason behind your actions. At least understand why you tried to conspire against me."

"Not tried, Your Highness. I still am conspiring against you."

His words feel like a slap to the cheek.

Levi brushes my hands away and places his own hands on my face.

"Like I told you before, my queen. I will never lie to you. The truth may be a hard pill to swallow, but that is always what you will get from me. The truth. So as long as there is a law that sends children to their slaughter, I will keep conspiring until you change it."

I pull his hands away from my cheek and reach for the dagger at his waistbelt. Levi instantly tenses, eyeing my every move. After I've unsheathe the dagger, I draw it in a straight line across my palm.

"Kat, the fuck are you—" Levi begins to shout, but quickly silences when I rest my blood-soaked hand on my heart.

"I vow you this, Levi of Thezmaer, king of the east, defender of Arkøya and all of the eastern borders of the great kingdom of Aikyam, such a law will no longer exist under my rule. I abolish it, here and now, and in your presence, so that you are witness to my decree. For that is my wish and my wish is word, as queen of the north and all of Aikyam."

Levi blinks once, twice, three times before he's able to process what I've just done.

Within a blink of an eye, he pushes me to the grass and towers over me.

"Just like that? You'll abolish it just like that?" he utters both in awe and incredulousness.

"Give me parchment, pen, and ink and I'll make it known throughout the entire kingdom."

Levi just stares at me.

And then that genuine smile of his, the same one that casts out all the dark clouds in the sky just so the sun can shine its rays of light upon us, appears on his lips.

He runs his thumb on my lower lip, his gaze scanning my face.

"You're making this so fucking hard for me," he mutters under his breath, confusing me with the remark.

"I just saved us and our people from being at war with each other by giving you what you wanted on a silver platter. I think I'm making it quite easy for you," I try to joke but it comes out too breathless to be amusing.

It's that familiar look in his green eyes that has me struggling for breath, needing something to tether me to the ground or risk me flying off into the cloudless sky.

"No, that's not what I meant," he explains, his own voice deep and husky.

"What did you mean then?" I lick my lips, the small ache of my cut palm not even registering with how wildly my heart is beating with the way he's looking at me. "Levi? What did you mean?"

"That you're making it hard for me not to fall in love with you again."

My eyes go wide at his confession.

"Again?" I croak out.

"You must have known," he whispers, drawing circles on the swell of my breasts while his gaze pierces mine. "We were just kids, but even then, I knew. I knew no one else would have my heart. Only you. Forever you. My Winter Queen."

"I... I... didn't know."

"You do now. So what are you going to do about it, my queen?" He raises one eyebrow with a playful smirk.

What am I going to do?

The only thing that I can do.

The only thing that feels *right*.

I kiss him.

Seated at the head of the great hall in Arkøya's castle, I pick up my drink and sip on the wine, hoping its alcohol will cool my nerves. Levi sits next to me, talking to one of his high lords that approached our table. He was one of the very few people who were brave enough to venture coming so close to us. I doubt his fear had anything to do with his lord and king and more to do with the woman seated at his side.

This grand affair is supposed to be my introduction to the east—a feast for a queen.

But all I see are enemies, ones that wouldn't think twice about poisoning my cup and laughing as I dropped over dead.

Just the mere thought of such a thing has me placing my glass back on the table, my enjoyment of wine long forgotten.

But am I to blame them?

If everything Levi told me earlier this afternoon was true, then don't these people have a right to distrust me? To hate me, even?

I would, if in their shoes.

Why, Father? Why do this? Why send little boys off to war? And why only the east, for no such law was passed in the west or south. And what other laws have you passed that have oppressed my kingdom so? What will I find when I go south in a month? Or when I travel west in the month after that? Will I be forever persecuted by your sins?

All these thoughts banging in my mind have me light-headed one minute and suffering from a migraine the next.

Was it grief, Father?

Was it your broken heart that made you demand the wives of those who swore to serve you?

Did it hurt that much for you to want... no, *need* to hurt whoever had a sliver of happiness and love in their lives?

One thing is for sure, I will not be that type of ruler.

I will not let my own heartache ever make a monster out of me.

Because if Levi's accounts of the night his parents died are true, then that was what my father was. A monster.

So why do I still love him?

Why do I feel like I'm betraying his memory by undoing all he's done?

By falling...

On reflex, I tilt my head toward Levi, who is still in high spirits after this afternoon. He must sense my eyes on him since he turns his head over his shoulder to gift me one of his smiles.

My lower belly quivers when he stops the conversation he was having to whisper in my ear.

"Look at me like that again, my queen, and I will cut this feast short just so I can fuck you on this table."

I keep my expression perfectly blank, but inside, I'm a raging volcano of need.

This man can't open his mouth without having me weak in the knees.

It's highly inconvenient, especially when I'm supposed to have my wits about me.

"What? No witty comeback, Your Highness?" he teases.

I turn my cheek to his other side, so no one can read the words that are about to come out of my mouth.

"I would have thought you'd have had your fill of me by now, Your Grace."

He licks his lips, his wolfish stare going right to the swell of my breasts.

"It will take me a lifetime for that, but I'm up for the challenge if you are." He wiggles his eyebrows suggestively, placing a tender kiss to my cheek.

He then goes back to the conversation he was having with his man, the same one that currently has a puzzled look to his face. If only he knew that before this social affair started, I had his king on his hands and knees, his head in between my thighs as I wrote my new law that would abolish that grotesque excuse for a decree my father had created decades ago. When they say a woman is skilled in multitasking, they aren't lying. I moaned in ecstasy while still being able to sign my name on the dotted line on the bill that would ensure no more young boys need to die so callously. And before that, Levi and I had made love on the grass and watched the sunset while discussing all the things I could do to help the east regain its lost pride.

I doubt there has ever been a king capable of doing so much in one day.

Maybe one.

Again, my eyes find Levi's face, and I curse myself for being so weak.

Ever since he said that he was falling in love with me, I can't seem to stop staring at him. As if believing that if I stare at him long enough, his mask will fall, and I'll see the deception written on his face.

How could this man love me?

He doesn't know me.

He knew the younger version of me. The naïve girl who believed that good would always prevail. The girl who believed that her friends would always be in her life, no matter what. The girl whose mother still lived and whose father still tried to love her.

I'm not that girl anymore.

I'm this broken, cold thing who pretends she still has a beating heart.

But it did beat. It beat for Levi. I heard it. And so did you.

I shake the voice in my head away, and pull my eyes from Levi to scan his hall filled to the brim with east-born lords and ladies. There is one particular auburn-haired man that grabs my attention. Especially since he has Inessa trapped between him and one of the large pillars in the room. I'm not sure what he's saying to her, but I know it can't be good by the way Inessa's expression morphs from annoyed to deadly.

I sit back in my seat and try to contain the smile on my lips when Inessa slams her heel on Brick's toes. He begins to jump up and down in pain, while Inessa uses his distraction to her advantage and makes her escape.

"Ah, Brick. You're going to have to be much more clever than that," I whisper under my breath with a little giggle.

My sights then look for Anya in the crowd, hoping she's faring better than Inessa. When I see her surrounded by a slew of high lords who look completely enamored and under her spell, I know she's doing just fine. There's nothing Anya loves more than the attention of the male gaze on her person. While Inessa may prefer to hang onto her shrew ways, Anya is more of a romantic, thinking that she is one good tumbling away from finding her Prince Charming.

But both my girls need love in their lives. True love. Not the kind that goes away once they've taken what they wanted—their virtue—or in Anya's case, her innocence. For all her expertise in the bedroom, she's still very innocent when it comes to the matters of the heart. Too many times have I caught her weeping in the shadows because some asshole broke her heart after he's had his way with her. Inessa would never fall for such a trap. And that's because she refuses to give anyone the chance. While Anya is able to mend her broken heart and try again, Inessa prefers hers to be kept under lock and key.

What type of woman am I?

Am I like my red-haired beauty, who sees love for all its glorious possibility, or am I like Inessa, who deems it too dangerous a thing to touch?

These are the thoughts that rummage through my mind, when the very man who is the culprit for raising those same questions calls out my name. That's when I see that Levi is now standing up from his seat, the hall completely quiet, waiting for him to speak.

With a bright smile still on his face, he stretches his hand for me to take. I plant my hand in his and stand from my seat, schooling my expression to show nothing.

"I have invited you all here tonight for this celebratory feast as my own way of welcoming Queen Katrina of Bratsk, queen of the north and all the kingdom of Aikyam. I wanted her to feel as at home in the east as she does in the north," Levi announces, his eyes never leaving mine. From my peripheral vision, I can see that not everyone shares in his sentiment of being so welcoming, but then again, why would they be? I'm the sole daughter of the man who killed their beloved king and queen. Their animosity is warranted, but I am thankful that at least here, in this hall and in this castle, they keep their opinions to themselves.

"You all know the reason why our queen has ventured to our home. She wishes to unify our kingdoms by offering her hand in marriage. I know many of you wish that she would look to Arkøya to find her king, not because you want to unify the land as she does, but because we need to heal. We need to heal a wound that has been festering for decades. One that still hurts us every day when we send our children to the battlefronts. We want our men to stay home and tend to their families, instead of going to war and returning to us in caskets. Yes, that is the only reason why we east-borns even tolerate this queen's presence in our court."

My cheeks turn hot at Levi's speech, while everyone in the room looks either uncomfortable to be here watching such a scene or counting their lucky stars they aren't missing it. I try to pull my hand away from Levi's, but he keeps it locked with his. My gaze slices to his, but he still looks at me like he did back in his garden—with stars in his eyes.

I'm confused as well as hurt when Levi turns to his people and continues on with his speech.

"Well, let me assure you all of one thing. Hear me now and hear me true. If Queen Katrina ever decides that her fate should lie with the east, and that I be her king, I will accept her offer, not because I want her crown to free us from our suffering but because my heart has been bound to hers since my infancy."

Gasps and hollers split the crowd. I slam my jaw shut for fear that it might drop to the floor.

"You all see a snake in our midst, while I see our deliverance. As I was reminded earlier today, our queen is not her father, nor should she be judged for his sins. As proof to her love for the east, she has abolished the law where children from the age of six onward serve her by enlisting in our forces. But not only that, in the new law she has passed, only those men who feel the need to serve in this way should volunteer themselves to our troops. No longer will the sick and feeble be ordered to abandon their homes to raise their swords against an enemy that was never truly theirs. No longer will mothers cry when their babies are ripped from their arms. She has freed us from the bondage that has terrorized our land. She has given us this gift. What is my heart in comparison?"

The hall suddenly explodes in glee, shouts and laughter all ring loudly and bounce off its halls. Tears of utter joy run down lords' faces, and their ladies' alike. An explosion of such happiness the world has ever seen.

Levi pulls my hand up to his lips and places a tender kiss to it, lifting his head just a sliver for me to catch his eyes. His, too, look watery, as if I have rewritten all the wrongs that have been done to him.

"What is a heart, Kat, when you've given me freedom?" he whispers.

Too out of words to even conjure up a single one, I limit myself to offering him a simple nod. He throws me a wink, and turns his attention to his people, the ones that are still out of their minds with happiness. I watch them all celebrate the news, while my insides are being pulled in every direction.

All I did was write on a piece of parchment and sign my name.

I'm not worthy of this.

The same people that gave me the side-eye and cursed my name a second ago are staring at me like the gods themselves have come down from the heavens just to bless them.

The urge to flee is so strong, I think I might throw up.

"Kat?" I hear Levi whisper, concerned. "What's wrong?"

"This… this… it's too much."

He raises my chin up with the pad of his forefinger and gazes into my eyes.

"This… is because of you. You have liberated us from decades of oppression, Kat."

"All I did was sign a piece of paper." I swallow the tears that threaten to leave me.

"Words hold power, Kat. Your father held that power in his hand and wielded it to enslave us. And it was yours that set us free."

Levi then bends down and gives me a chaste kiss. The kind of kiss that promises he'll find a way of setting me free from my bindings too. The cheers only grow louder, and when I open my eyes, I understand why.

With this kiss, Levi has all but presented me as his future bride, even though I haven't chosen him yet.

And though I'm not yet sure of what will happen to us in the long run, in the end, I achieved what I set out to do.

Levi's loyalty is now mine.

That's what I wanted. All I ever wanted.

So why does it feel like Levi has taken my heart for ransom in exchange?

What is a heart in comparison to freedom?

I guess I'm about to find out.

One Month Later

"Oh gods!" I yell out loud, uncaring of who hears me, even though I know there isn't anyone for miles.

Levi bites down hard on my bare shoulder as he ruthlessly pounds into me, almost as if he has this urgent need to mark my body in any way he can. Bite marks and bruises are his love language. My body needs to show it's been claimed since it's impossible to carve out my heart from my chest to show the whole world his name is engraved on it.

The warm water from the hot springs splashes erratically with each of his thrusts, creating a delicious current to flick against my clit. My arms are pinned up high by the wrists with just one of his hands, the cool rock wall behind me leaving their scratch marks while I continue to bounce up and down on Levi's cock. My legs keep their hold around his waist, as Levi teases my nipple and ruins my pussy.

It's always like this with Levi.

Passionate and merciless.

My body completely yields to his dominance, craving his punishment and loving caresses.

But Levi's seduction doesn't end there.

With his words of praise, my arousal amplifies tenfold.

"So fucking beautiful, Kat. The way your pussy begs to be fucked. Fucking made for me. Take it all, my queen. Take everything. It's fucking yours."

Another moan rings loud in the air between us, and I'm so close to coming undone and shattering in his arms, that I fear the gods themselves couldn't put me back together again.

"Levi! Levi!" I scream when the head of his cock hits that soft spot inside my walls just right.

My king, now all too familiar with the ways of my body, keeps hitting my pressure point, knowing that it will mean my downfall. I cry out his name again, a familiar black veil covering my sight until an explosion of light pierces it and sends lightning bolts to rack all throughout my body.

Every inch of me feels electrified as Levi pulls on my chin so that he can kiss my lips.

This is also his preferred way of falling over the edge—needing my lips to be on his as he finds his own nirvana. Once he's come inside me, his kiss morphs from downright salacious to something far more tender. After he's abused my body so deliciously, Levi always ends it with a kiss that holds a promise—a promise that his heart as well as his body is mine.

He breaks our kiss and releases his hold on my wrists, and begins to pepper me with kisses on every bruise he can find on my body.

"You deserve a better man than me. One that is gentle with you," he whispers, kissing the scratch marks on my arm and elbow.

I cup his cheek with my hand, my gaze still half-mast with both the earth-shattering orgasm he gave me, as well as his words.

"You are the best man I know, Levi of Thezmaer. You are plenty gentle with me."

"Your body might think differently. It always looks like it's gone to war after we've made love."

I pull in the teasing smile that wants to come out, knowing this isn't the time for jokes since he's showing me his vulnerable underbelly.

Levi fucks my brains out anytime he puts his hands on me, saying the most obscene things that would make even the gods blush, but afterward, he always calls it making love. Anya would call it the world's best tumbling and I would be inclined to agree with her, but in a way, I agree with Levi too. This is our own way of loving one another. Yes, it's not sweet, or tender, like most women would prefer, but I'm not most women. I was born from ice, and Levi from steel. Two such people were bound to be different from the fold.

So yes, we fuck.

Hard and brutal.

But it doesn't make it any less beautiful in my eyes—it's all love.

Levi, unfortunately, believes that I should be treated like the finest porcelain, that his unworthy hands shouldn't even touch such a fragile thing, much less manhandle me so brutishly.

"Levi, look at me," I call out, pulling his attention off my scratches and bruises and into my loving gaze. "If my body looks like it's been to war, then I'll wear my battle scars with pride."

His eyes turn the softest shade of green, succeeding in melting my glacier heart. With his gaze still locked on mine, he presses his hand on my belly under the water.

"I wonder if you're with child," he rasps softly. "The gods know it hasn't been from a lack of trying."

My shoulders slump at his words.

Unable to lie to him, I pull his hand from my belly and lift his open palm to my lips to give it a kiss.

"Anya gives me one of her special remedy teas every morning, Levi. We won't be expecting a child anytime soon."

"Oh," he mutters, disappointed, lowering his eyes from mine.

Damn the gods.

"Levi," I call out and patiently wait for him to look at me again. "As much as the thought of having your baby brings me joy, having a bastard does not." His brows pinch together at my words. "Because that's what would happen if I were to conceive now. All of Aikyam would know that the babe was born out of wedlock. I've seen firsthand what a terrible burden that is on a child. I already have a brother who suffers the mark of being a bastard son of a king, I will not let my firstborn have the same fate."

"Of course," Levi is quick to say, logic and sense finally clearing his romantic notions. "You're right. Of course, you're right. I guess I just let my own dreams of a life with you get the best of me. I didn't mean to make you uncomfortable. We have time," he says before planting one of his trademark chaste kisses to my lips.

Time.

Time is what we don't have.

In less than a week, I must travel north and leave my king behind for another.

I never thought it would be harder to leave the east than it was leaving the north. Here I have found more happiness in a month than in my entire life.

And it's all because of him.

As much as I tried to keep my frozen heart away from his grasp, Levi chipped at it with his steel endurance, never quitting until it was fully his. Now, having fallen in love with such a man, the idea of seeking another and proposing marriage feels blasphemous.

Levi is my king.

My love.

My very heart.

No one will ever be able to measure up to the honorable man before me.

No one.

Yet, I still made a promise. One that I cannot break, as my promise is my word, and my word is law. How I wish it wasn't so. How I wish we could stay here in Arkøya for the rest of my years.

But my home needs its queen, as does the kingdom.

I knew right from the start of this whole affair that sacrifices needed to be made. I still need to travel south and be sure that its king won't misplace his food supplies to the north again. I then need to march west and meet the rebel king who refuses to acknowledge my very existence, save for announcing that all our merchant deals are now null and void. As much as I would like nothing more than to stay in my lover's arms, I am not afforded such a luxury.

I'm queen.

And queens must rule over their reign.

The only thing a queen must abide by is her duty—not her heart.

"I know that look," Levi says, pulling my attention back on his majestic face.

"And which look is that, my king?" I tease playfully, hoping I haven't given him access to my thoughts as well as my heart.

But when his facial expression looks as torn as I feel, I realize Levi is more in tune with my mind than I gave him credit for.

"We have less than a few days left before you part for Braaka." He utters the name of the cursed city I'm abandoning Arkøya for.

"We do," is all I muster to reply.

"It will be a hard journey south. A fifteen-day journey by my count," he continues to say.

"Hmm." I nod.

"A queen shouldn't make such a journey south without the proper protection," he adds, his thumb brushing against my collarbone.

"Are you saying my men are unequipped to protect me?"

"I took four of them down before they even saw me coming. I'm not just saying that they are incompetent, I'm stating a fact."

"Are you offering me your men?" I arch a brow.

"No, I'm offering yours," he states evenly. "My army serves its queen in any capacity she desires."

"I rejoice in the sentiment behind such an offer, but how would it look to both Teodoro and Atlas if I show up with soldiers that wear the green hydrangea seal on their vests?"

"Fuck Teodoro. I couldn't give two fucks what he thinks."

My forehead creases at the venom in his tone.

I know Levi and Teo never saw eye to eye, but why does Levi hate him so much? Anytime his name is uttered, Levi goes mad with rage. Much like he is about to now.

"Fine, forget Teodoro. What of Atlas, then? Will he not be insulted when he realizes that you do not trust him? For that is what I'll be saying if I bring our men with me. And though you have refused to tell me what type of relationship you have with the rebel king, I know you care for him and the last thing you want to do is give him cause to mistrust your affection."

"Fuck," he mumbles under his breath. "I hate it when you're right."

"I'm always right, my king. That's why I am queen." I wink.

Levi's foul mood lifts as he sways me in the water, left to right, creating little waves to tickle my skin.

"Fine. Don't take any of my men. Brick will be pissed with me, though. I kind of already promised he'd accompany you south."

I let out a laugh.

"Inessa would have had a fit if that happened. He's enough of a nuisance as it is here. One can only imagine how bad he would get down south."

"You're saying to have a man's love is bothersome?" Levi taunts, nibbling my earlobe.

I slap his back and pull away laughing.

"Are you saying that Brick is in love with Inessa? After all the rejection he's gotten from her?" I continue to laugh.

"Yes, that's what I'm telling you," Levi confirms, quickly sobering me up.

"Wait... Brick is in love with Inessa?"

Levi nods with a smile.

"He doesn't just want a good tumbling?"

Levi shakes his head.

" *Love* love?" I continue to interrogate, not believing what I'm hearing. "The true kind. Like what we have?"

The minute the words leave my mouth, Levi's eyes turn two shades darker.

"You love me, Kat?" he asks, as if it's the most astounding thing he's ever heard.

My throat begins to clog, and my skin begins to feel like it's too tight on my body.

We haven't said those exact words to one another, although we have said them numerous times with our bodies and with our souls.

Do I love Levi?

If what I'm feeling isn't love then I shudder to think what is.

Since what has taken over me since I first laid eyes on him is all-consuming. It's exciting and frightening all in the same breath. It's all I ever wanted, and yet I stay awake at night, fearing its sudden disappearance.

Do I love Levi?

With all of my frozen heart.

I open my mouth to tell him as much, when he places his forefinger on my lips, silencing me.

"Don't say it," he pleads on a strangled choke. "If you say it, then I won't be able to let you leave. I couldn't bear it."

"I don't see how you'd be able to prevent it. Would you lock me up in one of your towers if I said what you long to hear?" I bite my lower lip.

His hand goes right to my throat, my core clenching with how easy it is to provoke the beast that lives inside of him.

"I'd do much worse than that. I'd lock you up in my chambers, tie you to my bed, and fuck a baby inside of you. I'd even have a priest marry us as I did it. He'd have to ask the gods to cleanse his soul from all the wicked thoughts he had while watching me savagely take my wife in our marital bed."

Gulp.

Feeling all sorts of flushed, I pull my hands away from him just so I can splash some water on my face. The hot spring water does very little to cool my libido after such a declaration.

There's a little smirk to his lips, as if he knows damn well what his lewd words do to me.

Who am I kidding?

He knows exactly what he's done.

I plant my hands on his shoulders and jump on top of him so he's forced to go underwater. When he comes back up, he's laughing his heart out.

"You do not play fair, my king. And I thought you more honorable than that," I accuse him with a smirk of my own.

"I am honorable, my queen. Just not when it comes to my intentions with you," he teases, pulling me by the waist until my legs are once again firm on his hips, my core just inches away from his cock. "Nothing I want to do with this body is honorable. Not one damn fucking thing."

"Spoken like a true poet," I tease, laughing.

"Fuck, I'm going to miss that. You laughing is the sweetest sound on earth."

His expression goes somber, as does mine.

"I haven't had much reason to laugh for the longest time. With you, it just comes naturally," I confess, running my fingers through his braids.

If I can't tell him I love him, then I can admit to that much.

"I'm taking you to Teo," he suddenly blurts out.

"What? Levi—" I start to protest.

"It's a fifteen-day journey, Kat," he cuts me off. "If I can't have my men guard you while you're with that snake, then at least give me two more weeks to be with you. Give me that."

Before I'm able to give him a reply, I ask a question of my own.

"Why do you hate Teo so much?

"He's not someone to be trusted, Kat, let's leave it at that."

"That isn't an answer. When we were younger, I knew you both had your ups and downs, but in the end, you loved each other anyway. What changed?"

But still Levi refuses to answer me, preferring silence instead.

If Orville has blood on his hands, then Teo is soaked in it.

Those were the words he chose to use when discussing his parents' death. Somehow, Teo had a part in their untimely demise.

"Levi, if you continue to keep secrets from me, then we won't work," I caution, needing to get to the bottom of this.

"Do you want us to?" he asks, suddenly unconvinced.

"Yes."

"Then stay. Choose me and forget this silly little game you're playing," he says, knocking the wind out of me with how aggressive his tone is.

"This silly little game, as you called it, saved my kingdom from warfare. Or do you think I forgot how your army was about to butcher my people?" I bite back.

Levi instantly cringes, making me instantly regret my lashing out at him. I count to three and breathe before I try again.

"This game, as you so put it, gave your people back their freedom. I can only wonder what I will find has been done in my family's name in the south and west." When his shoulders slack, I see that reason is finally getting through to him. "I gave my word, Levi. You're a man of honor, so you know what it means for a queen to give her word."

"I do. Doesn't mean I like it."

I tighten my arms around his neck and lay my head on his shoulders.

"Please, let's not fight. Not when we have so precious little time left."

"Does that mean you will let me accompany you south?"

"If it means I get a fortnight with you, then I'd be a fool to say no," I tell him honestly.

I feel his body relax now that he knows we have more time. His fingers run up and down my naked back, as my chest molds itself to his.

"Will you miss me, Kat?" he whispers in my ear.

I tilt my head back just a little so I can stare into his emerald eyes. In an instant, I feel a pang to my heart as if someone is driving a dagger through it.

Will I miss him?

I doubt my life will ever hold the same meaning to it with him not in it.

So I answer him the only way I can, without saying those three little words that we both long to hear.

"What is a heart without its reason for beating?"

North meets South

"**I**s that letter from her? From your queen?" Cleo whispers seductively, while running her nails up and down my chest. I slap her claws away and reread my kitten's handwriting, trying to see if there is a hidden message in her words.

"Read it to me. I'm bored." She pouts, throwing herself on my bed and lying on my chest.

I push her away and slide to my side, Katrina's letter safe in my hands.

"You know you've been a real bore since *your queen* sent that decree admitting that she's too ugly to find a husband on her own, so she has to order one of you lot to marry her," she says mockingly, adding emphasis on the word queen in a sarcastic tone.

I turn over again on the bed, placing my arm under my head while my other hand grips Cleo's chin. Hard.

"First of all, *my queen* is the most beautiful one to ever exist. We should consider us lucky that she has limited her pool of endless choices to only the three kings in her kingdom. And second, if I'm a bore, then you should seek company elsewhere and leave me be."

Even though I'm hurting her—my fingers are bound to leave a mark—Cleo doesn't so much as flinch. Not that it surprises me. I've hurt her enough over the years for this to be just foreplay for her.

We both have.

But not anymore.

When I release my grip on her chin, her pout only deepens.

"Go, Cleo. Go find yourself something else to play with. I'm busy," I order as I turn my back to her again.

It takes but two seconds for me to feel her long nails scratch my back to the point of making me bleed. This time, when I turn around, I go for her throat, her eyes glazing over as if this was what she was after all along. I lean in so close to her face, my lips almost brush hers.

"I said go. Leave," I growl menacingly.

Cleo's lust quickly morphs to alarm.

She knows me well enough to know the difference between our little sex games and when I'm pissed beyond measure. This time when I let her go, she quickly scampers to the edge of my bed, gaining a good amount of distance between us. But to my chagrin, she doesn't leave.

"Cleo—" I start, having had enough of her tantrums.

"You're my only friend, Teodoro. Where am I supposed to go?"

My chest tightens at her words, knowing how true they are.

Like me, Cleo is the black sheep of her family. Where most of her brothers and sisters work the fields from sunrise to sunset with her parents, Cleo preferred to earn her way in this world very differently—on her back.

"My parents worked arduously, night and day, without a penny to show for it and two dead children that died from starvation because of it. I swore that I would never have that life. I would never starve again while tending to crops for the rich to feast on," she told me the first night we met.

It all feels like years ago.

One day when I was feeling even more sorry for myself than usual, I decided to take a stroll through the rougher part of my city. I didn't even bother putting much effort into my disguise. I think in a way, I wanted to get caught. Wanted someone to know that I was the crown prince and to either kidnap me for ransom and then kill me or just mug me and then kill me. Whatever they decided to do, I wanted the last

244

part to be the sweet kiss of death. Anything to get me out of the miserable existence I had been living.

But then I stumbled upon one of the most sought-out brothels in all of Nas Laed. I must have stood outside its doors for over an hour, trying to gain the courage to walk inside it. Seventeen summers in and I had only ever kissed one girl, my kitten.

But she was gone to me now.

Her father made sure to isolate her up in Tarnow Castle and keep her locked away from all who loved her. Not that it mattered much to me anymore. By then she would have learnt of what I had done to her precious Levi. She would have never forgiven me for such a betrayal.

I was a walking corpse that no one had the decency to bury.

Loneliness more than curiosity was what drove me to go inside, and there, I met Cleo.

Right from the get-go, I had never met a spirit so free of judgment and guilt. She had everything I ever wanted and desired, yet she was the whore, and I was the next in line to be king.

After that night, Cleo would become my teacher, then my lover, and ultimately, my only friend and confidant. We never promised each other love; that wasn't what our relationship was about.

But we did vow our eternal friendship to one another.

And I'm the one who is breaking that vow.

She never changed who she was. I did.

When the girl I had been in love with all my life sent her decree saying that she was looking to marry one of the three ruling kings of her kingdom, I dared to hope. For the first time in seven years, I had hope in my heart that Katrina was not dead to me as I would have thought.

And in that distraction, I have ignored the one friend who has been by my side throughout my misery.

"Come here, Cleo," I order, making room on the bed for her.

"Is this a trap?" she asks, naturally suspicious.

"No, sweetheart. It's a peace offering. Come. I'll show you the letter."

That's all Cleo has to hear for her to jump from where she is and slide right next to me.

"Show me, show me!" she shrieks in excitement.

"Read for yourself," I tell her, to which she immediately frowns. "Come on, Cleo. I've taught you your letters. At least try to read it. For me."

"I can't. Her handwriting is too damn curly for me to make any sense of it. I'm used to your handwriting. Not hers."

"Fair enough." I let out a sigh, knowing exactly when to push her and when not to. "Okay, this paragraph here is to tell me that she's already heading south and should arrive within a fortnight."

"Hmm. Does that mean we have to leave and head over to Braaka to wait for Her Majesty?" Cleo asks, this time putting less sarcasm to the royal title.

"We do. It's the closest city to the border that they are traveling to."

"They?" Cleo questions, immediately picking up on the slip.

I nod.

"Levi is coming with her." I point to the paragraph on Katrina's letter that informs me that he is escorting her all the way down south.

Cleo goes to her knees and crosses her arms around her chest.

"Will he be a problem?"

"Not one I can't handle." I wink.

"Don't," she interjects. "Don't act like this isn't a big deal. He said he would kill you the next time he saw you."

"Levi says a lot of things." I shrug, unperturbed. "Doesn't mean I should take any of it seriously."

"Teo…" she mumbles worriedly. "I don't like this. I don't like this one bit."

I lift off my bed and place my hands on her bare shoulders.

"He won't kill me."

"How can you be so sure?"

"Because he wants to be king. And he can't be if word gets out that he killed his competition. It wouldn't be the honorable thing to do. He wants to win, fair and square."

"Win? Win what? The crown? But you don't care about any of that shit," she says.

"You're right. I don't. Doesn't mean that I don't want to win," I explain with a cocky smirk. "The end prize is so much bigger than a crown. So much more priceless than being able to call yourself the king of all of Aikyam. This prize is something I have been waiting for, for all my life."

"Her. The prize is her," Cleo says, finally putting it all together.

"She's all I ever wanted, and, in a fortnight, I'll have her."

"But only for a month," Cleo adds, trying to caution my enthusiasm with pesky facts. "Then she'll have to head west."

"Atlas is no rival of mine. Only Levi."

Cleo begins to crack a knowing smile before wrapping her arms around my neck.

"Then I guess you have exactly one month to make her forget he even exists. Are you up for such a challenge?"

"I was born for it."

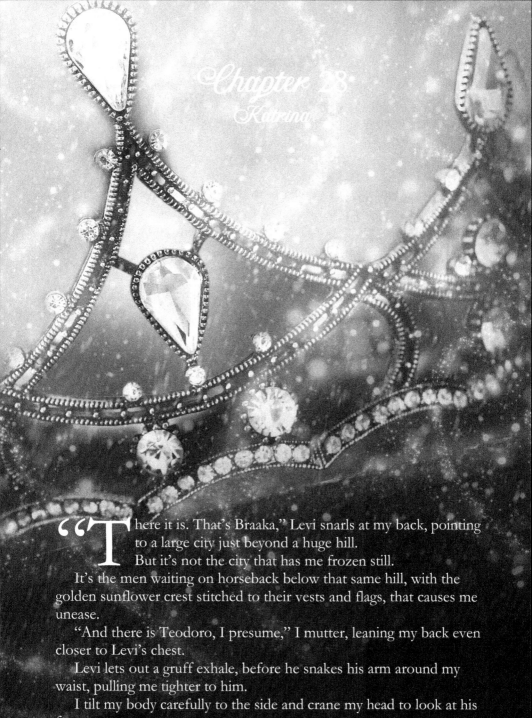

"There it is. That's Braaka," Levi snarls at my back, pointing to a large city just beyond a huge hill.

But it's not the city that has me frozen still.

It's the men waiting on horseback below that same hill, with the golden sunflower crest stitched to their vests and flags, that causes me unease.

"And there is Teodoro, I presume," I mutter, leaning my back even closer to Levi's chest.

Levi lets out a gruff exhale, before he snakes his arm around my waist, pulling me tighter to him.

I tilt my body carefully to the side and crane my head to look at his face.

Everything I ever wanted to tell him feels like it's trapped in my throat, suffocating me if I don't let it out.

"Fuck, Kat," Levi groans, his eyes closing for the briefest of seconds. "Stop looking at me like that, or the only place you're going is back home with me. Fuck whatever word you gave to that bastard."

A small smile plays on my lips, but I'm too sad for it even to come out.

"Home? Is the east my home now?" I ask, running the tips of my fingers over his stubbled square jaw.

"Your home is where you want it to be. Just know that wherever that is, I'll be right there at your side."

"Promise?" I choke, starting to feel too many emotions at once to keep myself collected.

Levi growls like he's about to kill something, but instead of murder, he kisses his temple to mine and breathes me in.

"The gods, woman, but you have ruined me."

"And you've ruined me," I confess on a soft sob.

"Please don't cry, Kat. My heart is breaking as it is. I won't survive if you cry," he whispers huskily, running the pad of his thumb across my cheek and wiping the tear that escaped dry. He then sucks it into his mouth and leans in to kiss me.

I wrap my arms around his neck and give in to his kiss willingly, uncaring if Teo sees it or not. This kiss tells him everything I can't. How much I love him. How he's given new meaning to my life. How before he entered it, my life had been a cold, hollow existence. And in turn, with his kiss, he shows me how I have his heart. How it will refuse to beat until I return to him.

I let out another sob when he breaks our kiss, not ready to face what lies ahead.

Levi looks as if he's in agony, as he presses another tender kiss to my forehead.

Before he has a chance to change his mind, he sits up straight, tightens his hold on my waist, and pulls at the reins, giving our horse the silent command to trot toward the borderline where east meets south.

With each gallop, my sorrow for leaving Levi is just as fierce as my apprehension in reuniting with Teo. I repeat in a loop all the reasons why I have to go through with this when it's blatantly obvious that if I have to marry someone, it will be Levi. Then suddenly, another thought crosses my mind. If Teo did see me kiss Levi just now, then he might retaliate and *misplace* his shipments to the north again. This plan I concocted was so that these kings would be too preoccupied in fighting for my hand to try to plot against me. If they realize that the prize has already been given to another, then they might go back to their initial plans of rebellion.

Stupid, stupid, Kat.

No matter.

I'll think of something.

However, I prefer the truth than any fabricated lie I might be able to summon up.

Or at least a watered-down version of it.

I'll tell both Teo and Atlas, that as it stands, my affections lie with the east and its king. It is up to them to show me that they are more worthy of a contender. At the end of the day, I'll only propose marriage to the best man worthy of the title of King of Aikyam.

And there is no better man I know than Levi.

Feeling more confident in myself and this new plan, I straighten my back and let Levi's scent envelop around me like a warm blanket for as long as I'm able to. Not that a blanket will do me any good in the south. I would have to cover up most of my skin or risk the blazing sun scorching it right through.

But I'd rather die of heat exhaustion than pull away from Levi's strong frame.

Unfortunately, that small moment of comfort is stolen from me far too quickly than I would have liked. Our horse begins to slow his gallops as it draws closer to the king of the south.

My breath hitches as my eyes finally land on Teodoro after so many years.

To my chagrin, he's still the most handsome man in all the kingdoms. With his brown wavy hair and light amber eyes, he was able to maintain that youthful mischievous quality he had as a boy. With his drawn Cupid's bow lips and high cheekbones, he puts most high ladies to shame.

But there are some differences about him.

Differences he made sure to expose by using a white cut-sleeved shirt and unbuttoning it halfway to his waist. He flexes his hard-toned abs while flaunting his tanned muscular forearms by pulling the reins of his horse and strutting toward us.

Vanity had always been his preferred sin.

Mine was pride.

I school my expression to look like a blank canvas, completely devoid of emotion, as his horse stops right beside ours, so that we are facing each other.

"My queen. It has been far too long," Teo says, bowing his head.

"Has it?" I ask coldly.

"Seven years by my count," he retorts with a wink.

The gods.

I forgot how forward he was.

If he doesn't behave, Levi will kill him here and now.

"I must admit, I don't recall the last time we saw each other, King Teodoro. One might say you didn't leave much of an impression if my memory is that hazy."

Teo smiles widely as his tongue licks the tops of his teeth.

"So glad you still have your claws, kitten. It would have been a pity if you lost those." He winks again, this time looking far too pleased with himself.

"This motherfucker," Levi grumbles under his breath with an almighty snarl, ready to cause chaos.

"Oh, where are my manners?" Teo blurts out, slapping his thigh. "I totally forgot you brought a chaperone with you. Maybe my memory is foggy too."

"Teodoro," Levi greets, the name spilling out like a curse from his lips.

"Levi." Teo smiles even wider.

They both stare at each other, neither one wishing to be the first to waver.

But alas, it's Teo who breaks the staring match, cackling like a madman.

"Ah, Levi, nice to see that some things never change."

With my breath halted in my lungs, I watch how Levi leans closer to Teo, white-knuckling his reins.

"If you hurt even a hair on her head—"

"Spare me your threats, Levi. No harm will come to Katrina."

"I would ask for your word, but I know how worthless it is." Levi scowls.

"Oh, you and your word. Doesn't it get boring being so self-righteous all the time, Levi? 'Cause it sure bores the fuck out of me."

Teo pretends to yawn before his smug smile, the same one I used to find so endearing, tugs at his lips again.

"Best we part ways here, before one of you says something he can't take back," I state, hoping the disdain in my voice is enough to cool these two down.

But just as I say it, Levi tightens his hold on me, as if unwilling to let me go. Teo sees it too, his eyes fixing on the way Levi's palm is planted on my stomach.

"I agree, Your Majesty. Soon it will be noon and the southern sun is unforgiving at that time."

I give him a curt nod and begin to shift on the saddle, but Levi refuses to let me budge. I turn to my side, my sorrow visiting me once more with the taint of misery in his eyes. Ignoring the king that awaits me, I press my palm to Levi's chest and lean into his ear, opposite Teo.

"What is a heart…" I whisper, and instantly he covers my hand with his, and pulls it to his lips to offer it a parting kiss.

When I lean back in my seat, Levi gets down from his horse in order to help me do the same so that I can ride in my carriage to Braaka.

Teo, unfortunately, seems to have other ideas.

"None of that, kitten," he tsks while shaking his finger at me, making my eyes go wide with hate. He then pats the empty space on his saddle behind him and grins. "You can sit right here. We'll ride together and catch up. Won't that be fun?"

I bite into my cheek, wishing I could tell him to screw himself with his offer. But since he saw me riding with Levi, it would be an insult to him and the south for me to decline. Levi helps me down with a thunderous expression on his beautiful face. I wait for him to put his hands on my waist, before I put my foot into the stirrup, needing any excuse to keep him close to me a little while longer. Teo must grow impatient, though, because he grabs my hand and basically swings me to sit behind him. With his hand still gripping mine, he wraps it around his waist, making sure Levi sees it.

"Hold tight, kitten. You know how fast I always like to ride," he taunts. "Although if nice and slow is your thing, I might make an exception." He then looks down at Levi with that same smug smile I'm itching to slap off his face. "Is that how she likes it, Levi? Nice and slow? Or is she able to take a good pounding? You have ridden her before, correct? Oops, I meant rode with her."

My cheeks heat up at his audacious insinuation and provocation, and to my discontent, Levi takes the bait.

"When all this is done and over with, I vow that I will have your beating heart in my hands," Levi promises.

"Funny." Teo shrugs, unfazed. "I was under the assumption I already had yours in mine."

And I don't miss the glance Teo throws my way before he smiles maniacally at Levi.

"This has been fun, Levi, but I have a queen to entertain. And believe you me, by the time the south is done with her, she will be thoroughly satisfied with her time spent here."

And before Levi can even utter a word or a curse, Teo kicks his heel, coaxing his horse to take off at lightning speed. I hold on to Teo with both hands, just so I'm able to look back at the man left in our dust.

Tears begin to streak down my cheeks as his frame gets farther and farther away from us, until my love completely disappears from my view.

"I love you," I whisper, emboldened to say the words out loud now that he isn't near to hear them.

If I kept them locked away in my hollow chest for another second, I was sure to not survive their weight.

The south may have my body now, but it will never have my heart.

For it lies dormant in the east, for its king to protect, until my return.

Chapter 29
Teodora

The minute I step into my bedroom chambers, my cocky grin slips off my face as I slam the door behind me.

"It went that well, huh?" Cleo mutters while laminating her nails.

I stand in the middle of the room, breathing hard, trying to keep my shit together.

"So, where is this queen of hearts?" Cleo asks, putting down her nail file to look up at me from her seat.

"In her room. She said she was too tired to get a tour of the castle," I explain through gritted teeth.

"She could be telling the truth." Cleo defends with a shrug. "I mean, she has been traveling for over two weeks now. She's bound to be tired and needs to rest. I wouldn't worry too much about it. You'll see her at dinner and woo her then."

I shake my head, fisting my hands at my sides.

"Katrina says she won't be able to eat dinner tonight with me either. Said she'll probably sleep until morning."

"Okay…" Cleo retorts, not understanding why I'm so furious. "So, you'll see her tomorrow. Or the next day. You have a month, Teodoro. You can sweet-talk her into your bed in a month."

"I don't want to just fuck her, Cleo! I want to marry her!" I shout in outrage.

Cleo stares at me like I've officially lost the plot.

"You do know that you can do both, right?" she jokes, and it is her nonchalance that tips me over the edge.

I let out an ear-piercing curse and start throwing everything I can find to the floor. Vases with flowers on the mantle, family portraits on the walls, anything I can get my hands on crashes to the floor.

"TEO!" Cleo yells, rushing toward me to stop my manic tantrum.

Angry tears stream down my cheeks as I continue to destroy everything in sight. Cleo begins to cry at my pain, putting herself in harm's way when she jumps toward me and grabs me by the waist.

"Teo, stop. Please stop. You're scaring me."

"I'm fucking scaring myself too." I tell her, wrapping my arms around her to weep on her shoulder.

Cleo keeps me steady as I break apart in her arms.

"Tell me what happened? What could have possibly happened to get you so upset like this?"

With the weight of the world on my shoulders, I manage to lift my head and cup her face in my hands. I lean my forehead on hers just to keep me from falling to my knees.

"She loves him," I whisper, unable to say the words louder than the barest of whispers.

"Who? The queen? Who does she love?" Cleo asks maniacally.

"Him. Levi," I choke out the name.

Cleo's expression softens, her sullen gaze looking too close to pity for me to be able to keep eye contact with her.

"It's the gods' cruel joke on me. Their way of evening things out. I took someone he loves away from him, and now he's doing the same to me. Fitting, isn't it? That the one person I have harbored such guilt over betraying finds the perfect penance for my sin."

"You're talking nonsense, Teo. The gods don't punish us like that. They are far too busy enjoying the heavens to even care to."

"A heathen and a murderer. What a pair we make," I mutter, disheartened.

"Aye, I might be a heathen, but you are no murderer, so stop saying that you are," Cleo reprimands, slapping my chest a few times to drive the point home.

I hold her wrists and shake my head.

"We both know that isn't true," I reply sullenly.

"No. I don't believe that. What you did wasn't murder. It was vengeance. Justice for those fallen souls." She lets out a sigh. "And your queen falling in love with the same man that would bathe in your blood if he could is not a death sentence given by the gods either. We mortals fall in and out of love all the time. So don't give in to your sorrow just yet. We both know nothing good will come out of it, if you do."

A little smile tugs at the corners of my lips at her hollow optimism.

I pull away from our embrace, pick up a jug of wine that miraculously managed to survive my rampage, and sit on the edge of my bed. I pour the wine down my throat while Cleo just stands in the middle of all my chaos with her arms crossed over her chest.

"How do you know she loves him?" she asks suspiciously after a long pause.

"If you're going to ask me those types of questions, then best fetch me more wine, because this jug won't do."

"Fine, I'll get you your wine, but first, answer my question. How do you know your queen loves your nemesis."

"He's not my nemesis," I reply on reflex.

"He's not your friend either." She raises her brows, calling bullshit on that remark.

"True, but he wasn't *always* my nemesis. There was a time in my life that he was… my brother. An older brother I looked up to and wanted to impress. We all did." I laugh, disheartened. "We all wanted Levi's approval. Fucking craved it like our southern crops crave the rain and sunlight to grow. As I grew older, I pretended that I didn't. Too vain and cocky to show how much his opinion of me mattered. But fuck did it ever. He was always the compass of morality. What was deemed good and honorable and what was not," I explain, hanging my head down with the weight of such a memory.

Cleo inches closer and drops to her knees before me, so that she can see my face.

"You loved him."

It's not a question, just a fact she lays out.

I nod, unable to lie to her.

"Fucked-up thing is, I think a part of me always will. Isn't that a fucking joke?" I retort with a self-deprecating tone.

"Teo," she calls out softly while rubbing my knees with her hands. "You will never win his love back. Too much has been done for that to be a possibility."

I let out a scoff, before grabbing Cleo by the chin.

"Do you think I don't know that?! Do you think I even care?! HE STOLE MY GIRL!" I shout in her face. "And for that, hate is all he'll ever get from me from this day on."

Cleo doesn't so much as flinch at my rage.

My breathing becomes hard once again, my chest heaving up and down.

It's only when my rage simmers that Cleo opens her mouth to speak again.

"You've said that. That the king in the east has stolen your love. But do you have proof of that or are you just conjuring up your worst fears, hoping to manifest them into reality?"

"I know what I saw," I seethe. "And I know what I heard."

"Which was?"

I release my grip from her chin and go back to getting drunk.

"Which was?" she insists again. "What did you see and what did you hear?"

"I saw a man whose heart was broken by handing his one true love to his sworn enemy. And I heard her tears as I rode her away from him. Then, of course, there was the kiss they shared before meeting me."

"I see," Cleo replies, now grasping the full shit show I'm in.

"Yeah, well, I wish I didn't. I wish I was a blind fool who didn't see a goddamn thing. Ignorance is a fool's best friend, after all," I retort, drinking the rest of my wine, and throwing the jug across the room once I've drunk the last drop. "Get me some wine, Cleo. I've answered your questions, now give me my prize," I command, falling to my back on the bed.

Cleo gets up from her knees and walks toward the door to do as I ordered. But before she leaves, she turns to face me once more.

"You have a month, Teo. If he was able to make her fall in love with him in that short amount of time, then what prevents you from doing the same? Remember... she loved you first. As I see it, you have all the advantages he did not. Don't let this bitter disappointment get in your way. Use it to fuel your drive and win your queen back."

I let out a dispirited laugh after Cleo leaves the room.

If it were only that easy.

When I read her decree, I honestly thought this was my chance at redemption. That the gods had forgiven me for what I had done and were offering me the one thing I always wanted—her.

Shame on me for having forgotten that she was always what Levi wanted too.

Chapter 30
Teodora

Fifteen Years Old

With my lips pressed against hers, I feel like heaven itself is shining down on me.

I have wanted to kiss Princess Katrina of Bratsk since before I even knew what kisses were for.

My heart thumps rapidly in my chest just having her in my arms, but it's her kiss that really pushes me over the edge. My body responds to her innocent touch, sending it aflame with a need I've never experienced before. I groan at the way she presses her chest to mine, how her sweet flower scent invades my senses.

It's too much for me to take.

All too soon do lurid images of laying her down on the gazebo floor and taking more from her than just a simple kiss slither their way inside my head. But if she is to be my wedded wife, then I must treat her like the precious northern rose she is.

Begrudgingly, I break our kiss, and when I open my eyes, it's not Katrina's face I find, but Atlas staring at us.

"Shit. I have to go," I curse out when Atlas bolts from the garden. I take off running after the little fucker.

"Wait! Teo!" Katrina shouts from behind me.

"I'll be back, kitten! Just stay here and wait for me," I yell back, even more pissed with the tinge of confusion and hurt I heard in her voice when she called out my name.

Today is the day that I'm going to wring Atlas's little neck!

I run as fast as I can out of the garden and through the castle halls, praying he's not gotten too far. Thankfully, the gods show me mercy and two minutes later, I'm on his heel.

"Atlas! Atlas!" I shout from behind him, but the little prick raises his middle finger at me and keeps on running.

Curse the gods.

"Damn it, Atlas! Will you stop already? You weren't supposed to see that back there," I rush to explain as I continue to run after him.

"Well, I did, asshole," he yells back before taking a corner and disappearing from my sight.

Fuck.

My legs are starting to burn, yet I keep on him.

"By the gods, Atlas, when did you get to be faster than me?" I joke when my eyes land on him again, thinking that maybe if I inflate his fragile ego a bit, it will make him forgive and forget.

"Fuck off, Teo!" he shouts, never losing speed.

This fucker.

For a sick little dipshit, he sure is fast when he wants to be.

I guess rage can do that to a person, give them the adrenaline they need to overcome any obstacle. But by the gods, he will not get the best of me.

"What are you going to do, Atlas? Don't do something stupid," I demand, worried that in his fury, Atlas will do something we'll both regret.

"What do you think I'm going to do?" he yells with a snarl. "I'm going to tell her father!"

"Didn't I just tell him *not* to do something stupid?" I mumble to myself before I shout at him again. "Will you stop being such a fucking pussy and let me talk to you, man to man?"

"I'm not a pussy!" he howls, thankfully stopping in his tracks.

Thank the gods.

"Then don't act like one." I smirk when he's within arm's reach.

"I'm not!" he insists, his expression filled with loathing.

"Prove it then. Let's go somewhere and talk this shit out. Let's be men about this and come to a resolution."

"You want to talk? We can talk. Won't change my mind about telling King Orville that you kissed his daughter," he seethes.

Now why did he have to say that shit?

Just makes my decision for me. And what I'm about to do is sure to get a whole lot messier.

"So are we going to talk or not?"

"Fine. Talk, asshole," he snaps, crossing his arms over his chest.

"You know, if I didn't love you like my kid brother, I might take offense to such words," I tease.

"I'm not a kid. So don't patronize me by treating me like one."

Fourteen summers this little shit has and already he thinks he can talk like a man. If he wasn't so sick all the time, I wouldn't think twice about slapping him across the head a few times to keep him humble. But just by the way he's wheezing, gasping for air from the sprint we've just done, I know that roughing him up won't be the solution.

"My mistake." I press my palm to my heart. "Come, let's go and talk."

"We can talk right here," he states adamantly.

"And risk someone hearing us?" I shake my head with a tsk. "No. I know the perfect place we can go to talk more privately. Follow me."

I turn around and head in the direction of a door that will lead me to where I need to go. I let out an exhale in relief with the sound of Atlas's soft footsteps following me. I don't dare say a word as we climb down a flight of stairs leading us beneath the castle.

"The dungeons? That's where you're taking us?" he asks behind me.

"Can you think of a better place for us to hash things out where no one will see us?" I say lightheartedly. "The castle is crawling with people for the king's birthday feast. And you know as well as I do that on his birthday, he always shows lenience to whatever prisoners are being held down here. It's King Orville's way of showing benevolence," I joke sarcastically, since we all know the northern king is anything but benevolent.

When Atlas doesn't answer me back, I know I got him.

I step into the dungeon and walk to the closest open cage I can find. Atlas suspiciously walks my way, preferring to keep a small distance between us.

"Okay, you got me here. Now what?" he asks belligerently.

I place my hands on his small shoulders and shrug.

"And now this," I say before shoving him inside an empty cell and clicking its door shut, trapping him inside.

"The fuck are you doing?" he shouts at me with rage.

"What I need to. You want out? Then calm the fuck down. Once you start thinking right, past your damn jealousy, then we can talk. Not before."

"Who says I'm jealous?!"

"I do. You've been pining over Katrina since before your balls dropped. Don't say you haven't. I've got eyes. Following her like a little puppy. Fucking pathetic." I laugh, but Atlas doesn't find me one bit amusing.

"Mark my words, Teodoro, one day I'll kill you dead."

"Yeah, yeah, and you'll steal my girl away from me and marry her yourself. You can have all the wishful thinking you want, it still doesn't make it fact. Just dreams thought up by a boy with too much anger inside him."

"I'm not angry!" he says, banging at the iron bars.

"Could have fooled me."

"Let me out of here, Teo!!!"

"You know the rules. Calm the fuck down and I will."

"ARGH! You smug bastard! I'm going to kill you!"

"Words spoken from the same kid who refuses to see he has anger problems."

Atlas keeps banging at the bars, throwing out all the curses he knows at me, but it's for his own good. He's so angry he can't even see straight, much less think clearly. If I let him out now, then he'll run his mouth to the king about how I kissed his daughter. King Orville would have my head, but then he would lock his daughter away to ensure her virtue and make sure that neither one of us would be able to get close to her ever again. My pretty head would be decorating one of Tarnow Castle's many spikes, while Atlas and Levi would be shipped back to their kingdoms, never to see our Katrina again.

Atlas might not see that now through his rage, but he'll thank me later once common sense pays him a visit.

Unfortunately for me, I underestimated his hatred toward me. Atlas fumes and shouts for hours, never running out of fuel. I limit myself to sitting on the floor, leaning against the opposite wall in front of him, watching him have his meltdown.

He hates me for kissing Katrina.

And right now, Atlas isn't my favorite person either.

I could be upstairs in her garden just basking in her love, but instead I'm spending the rest of my night in this musky, dank dungeon enduring my little brother's abuse.

I must doze off in between rants, only to wake up when I feel something hitting me.

"Do you mind? I'm trying to sleep over here," I say, closing my eyelids again after I realize it's Atlas throwing little pebbles at my head to grab my attention.

"I won't tell her father," he mumbles.

One eyelid opens followed by another.

"Go on."

He lets out an exaggerated exhale.

"I won't say a word to anyone," he promises, his expression filled with defeat.

"And how do I know you'll keep your word?"

"You don't. You'll just have to trust me." He shrugs.

"Not good enough."

"Fine." He throws his arms in the air. "What can I say that will make you believe me?"

I get off the ground and inch closer to the bars.

"I want you to swear on it," I demand.

"Fine. I swear on all the gods that my word is true. I will not tell a living soul what I saw tonight. Not even about how you locked me up in this dungeon."

I tsk, shaking my finger at him.

"Nope. Don't swear to me on the gods. Swear on something that actually means something to you. Something sacred."

"And what could be more sacred than the gods?" he counters with a laugh.

"Her."

Atlas's face turns to stone, just as I predicted it would.

"Swear on Katrina's life, on the love you bear for her, and then I'll let you out. Those are my terms."

His light blue eyes turn into two deep black pools as I watch his hands ball into fists, little drops of blood falling down to the floor with how hard his nails pierce his flesh.

"Go on then," I tell him, doing him the mercy of turning my back to him so that he doesn't have an attentive audience to his defeat. "I can stay here all night, Atlas. Your choice."

Minutes pass in awkward silence but then I hear it… Atlas finally confessing what I knew all along.

"On my heart, the one that beats only for the princess of the north, I so swear that the events of this night shall never be spoken of by me. On penalty of death, on my own soul's torment, this I vow to you."

I spin around, my mischievous grin plastered to my face.

"Now was that so hard?"

"Fuck you, Teodoro. Today you've won, but one day…"

"Yeah, yeah, yeah. I get it." I wave him off before searching for the keys to his dungeon cell. Luckily, I find them quickly hanging by a nail at the entrance of the dungeon. I return back to his cell and unlock the door. Atlas is quick to rush out, hitting me in the process.

"Hey, I know you're mad at me now, but soon you'll understand that I had to do this."

"Whatever," he bites back before running out of there.

My shoulders slump at how pissed he still is at me, but it was the only way I could think of to ensure his silence. But by now, Atlas isn't the only one who is angry at me. Katrina must be pissed too with how fast I bolted out of the gazebo after our first kiss. Not exactly the romantic setting I was going for. When I return to her garden and see that she's not there, a little part of me dies that she didn't wait for me like I asked her to.

I shake my head and reprimand myself for having such a selfish thought.

No.

What I need to do is find her and apologize. I won't be able to tell her the truth, though. She loves Atlas, and if she knew that I just made him spend his whole night locked up in a cage, Katrina would be sure to have my balls.

I have to think of another excuse to give her.

What, I'm not sure yet.

I walk in the direction of the great hall, praying to every god in the heavens that by some miracle she's there. But just as I pass the great arch entrance of the hall, I see that everyone is either sleeping off their wine or gone home for the night.

Everyone has had their fill of the festivities.

Everyone, that is, but the two people who somehow still hear music playing, enough to continue dancing, even though the band is long gone.

I stand rooted to my spot as I watch Levi twirl my girl around and then hold her in his arms. She laughs as he spins her again, before resting her head on his chest, and letting out a dreamy sigh.

My chest feels like a boulder is pressing down on it, as I watch Levi lean to her ear and whisper something that has my girl smiling like there is no tomorrow.

I'm so entrapped by this living nightmare in front of me that I don't even register Queen Alisa suddenly appearing, until she is pulling my girl aside, putting a merciful stop to her dance with Levi.

Katrina curtsies to Levi and thanks him for the dance, letting her mother pull her off the dance floor. It's when she turns her head over her shoulder to smile and wave at him, her silver gaze only holding room for him, that my heart cracks down the middle.

And when Levi continues to stand in the middle of the room, staring lovingly in the direction she went, my sorrow morphs into something else.

Suddenly, the rage Atlas had been consumed by makes more sense to me.

Because right now, I'm fucking blinded by it.

When Levi begins to retreat, I step onto the dance floor and begin to clap.

He turns around, that lovesick haze disappearing from his face.

"Damn. That was quite a show you two gave. I'm almost sad that I didn't catch it from the beginning."

With a stoic expression stitched to his face, Levi crosses his arms over his chest, a tactic he likes to use to intimidate.

But it's all lost on me.

"Are you drunk?" he asks, with a chastising hint to his tone.

"Haven't had a drop of wine all night." I throw him my best cocky smirk.

"You sound off," he rebukes, his forehead creasing as he scrutinizes me from head to toe.

"Maybe it's because I'm still trying to understand why I just caught you dancing with my girl."

"Your girl?" He laughs.

"Yes, my girl." I stab my chest with my finger, looking dead serious.

"We'll see about that," he scoffs, passing me and purposely hitting my shoulder with his.

"Yes, we will," I mutter under my breath as I watch his bulky frame leave from my sight.

Okay, so yes, Levi is bigger and maybe even stronger than me.

Taller, too, the big fucking mammoth.

And yes, he might even be considered more intelligent when it comes to the ways of the world since he's seen his fair share of it.

And amongst all those lists of qualities, he also has one more that I lack.

Honor.

And that shit is bound to get in his way and fuck him up.

Me?

I have no honor.

I'll lie, cheat, and steal to get what I want.

And it just so happens that what I want, Levi wants too.

I can handle Atlas and his schoolboy crush. Atlas doesn't scare me.

But Levi?

He's a threat.

A threat that has only been made evident to me now.

Better late than never, I always say.

Because now that I know what his true intentions are, it will be so much easier for me to crush them.

It's a new foreign world I find myself in.
One that holds no light to it even if the blazing sun reigns in the clear, blue sky.

I cried myself to sleep last night, something I hadn't done since my mother died. I cried so hard that Anya and Inessa could hear me in the next room, preventing either one of them from getting a good night's sleep. When both friends sneaked into my room, each one laying down beside me in my bed, I couldn't help but cry even harder.

They whispered words of solace, even if in the moment, I couldn't find any. They whispered words of hope and courage, knowing full well my heart had grown deaf to such sentiments. They tried their utmost best to rein in my suffering, and it was for them that I got out of bed this morning, willing to try.

Or at least pretend.

Teo sent his man, asking me to accompany him to break his morning fast.

I refused.

He then sent him again around mid-morning, asking if I cared for brunch.

I declined again.

Then noon came along, and with it another invitation, this time to lunch.

I just shook my head, unwilling to even make up an excuse.

So when the orange pink hues of sunset began to color the sky, I was already expecting the knock on the door. Only this time, instead of his man, Teo came to me himself.

"Are you well, Your Highness? Do you feel ill at all? I can call my best physicians to come to you if you're feeling unwell," he says, concerned, as he scans every inch of my face to find what ails me so.

Unless there is some remedy that can mend an aching heart, I doubt any physicians would be of use to me.

"I'm fine, King Teodoro. As I've said, I'm weary from my travels and need a few days to restore my strength. But don't be distressed. You shall have ample time to entertain your queen," I reply coldly, before going to close the door.

To my chagrin, Teo presses his hand on it to avoid me shutting it on his face.

"If sore bones are all that is at fault, then I must insist that my servants take you to our baths. There you will be able to soak those weary bones, while they massage your body with the sweetest smelling southern oils. I assure you, after a few days, you will be as good as rain."

"I'll think about your offer, King Teodoro."

"Fuck, kitten." He starts to chuckle, his amber eyes sparkling at me. "When did you start being so damn formal? It's me. Teo. Remember?"

I'm about to put him in his place. Tell him that the only thing I remember is that even a king should not talk to me in this manner. Should not use such an intimate nickname when addressing me. But then my memory flies back to the past, when I cursed Levi for doing the same the first time he entered my tent.

All words fail me, turning my back to Teo so that he doesn't witness the agony I'm in.

He lets out an exhale as I walk over to one of the many open windows in my room. Now that the sun is saying its farewells, there's a light breeze fluttering through the large room. Still, it's a poor imitation of my northern winds that I miss so much.

"You must eat, Katrina," Teo says sternly after a pregnant pause. "You must eat. You can stay in your room for however long you wish, but at least eat."

"I'm not hungry."

"I don't fucking care. You're going to eat and that's the end of it," he orders with a bite to his demand.

I spin to face this king who thinks he can order me around.

"I may be a guest in your home and kingdom, but, Teo, don't confuse things. I am still your sovereign and queen. You don't order me; I order you."

"That! That right there. I need to see more of that queen, because she has been the one who I have missed all these years. The one who believes herself to be equal to a man." He smiles so widely that it splits his face.

"I never claimed to be your equal and that's because I'm not. I'm more," I rebuke with a coldness I haven't felt in weeks.

Teo bites his lower lip as if my reply pleases him too damn much.

"Truer words have never been spoken. You are definitely *more*."

His giddy reaction is oddly confusing.

And then I remember who I'm dealing with.

This must be a game.

With Teo, everything is.

Not wanting to play into whatever game he's playing, I turn my back to him again, and wave him off.

"As I've said, I'm tired. Please leave."

"Yeah, well, I'm not leaving this room until you've eaten. So…"

Argh! Damn the gods and his arrogance!

"Hmm, then we find ourselves at an impasse," I retort.

"That we do. What are we to do?" he jokes, as if he's getting a kick out of our whole hostile interaction.

I pick up a peach from the fruit bowl on top of one of the various tables in the room and turn around. Staring him dead in the eye, I take a huge bite into it, the peach's juices dripping down my neck, slipping to my chest. But I don't care. I continue to take bite after bite, trying not to moan out with how delicious the ripe fruit actually is. I guess after a whole day of fasting, anything would taste good. After I've eaten the whole damn thing, leaving only the pit, I throw it at him.

Teo catches it easily enough in his hands.

"There? I've eaten. Satisfied?"

Teo licks his lips, his gaze drawn to the indent of my breasts where the peach's juices are slowly traveling to.

"Satisfaction is not the right word I would use, but I am pleased, just the same."

"Good. Then we're done here? You can go," I command, my spine ramrod straight.

He bites the corner of his lips again and starts eating the space between us. I take a step back but stop when my ass hits the table behind me. His hungry gaze lingers on my chest before it meets my eyes.

"Tomorrow, you break your fast with me. If not," he rasps, his finger brushing ever so lightly on my chest, enough to wipe away a drop of the sweet nectar I'm covered in. "I'll come back here and force you to put in your mouth whatever tasty treat I've prepared for you." He then steps away, sucking on his finger before taking it out of his mouth with a loud pop. "Do we understand ourselves, Your Majesty?"

Fury prevents me from uttering a word.

"Good. Sweet dreams, kitten." He winks, then proceeds to prance out of the room with that damn smirk on his face.

"Before I leave the south, I'm going to smack that smug smile off your face," I warn him.

He turns around and gives me an exaggerated bow.

"How I look forward to it, my queen."

The next day, sadness isn't the only thing that occupies my thoughts.

Hate plays a big part on them as well.

With Anya and Inessa walking behind me, I let Teo's servant lead us outside to where I've been blackmailed to break my fast. Teo is already there waiting for me.

Again, he's wearing all white, his sleeveless shirt mostly unbuttoned, showing off his toned physique.

"There you are. I was having doubts that you wouldn't show up like I asked. I don't know if I should be happy or disappointed," he says, all smiles.

"Your mood is of no concern to me. Be happy. Be disappointed. It's all the same to me."

"Now, now, kitten. Put your claws away for when they'll be of better use," he retorts, pulling a chair out for me.

But I remain frozen to my spot.

"There are only two chairs at this table."

Teo's forehead creases as his gaze bounces from said table back to me.

"I don't follow."

"I said there are only two chairs at this table, and as you can see, we are four people in total. Are my handmaidens forced to suffer the humiliation of sitting on the ground as they eat like some pet, or will you show them the respect they deserve by offering a place they can sit?"

Teo's tanned complexion pales, and it takes all of me not to laugh at his discomfort.

Serves him right.

He looks back at the small table that is only big enough for two.

"Is the dining hall fit to break fast for us, Samir?"

"Yes, my king. We made preparations for Mistress Cleo," Samir explains, his head hanging low.

"So be it. Please usher the queen and her ladies there and ask someone to clear this table. It's of no use to me anymore."

"Of course, my king."

As instructed, Samir leads the way back inside, while Teo hangs back just to take one final look at his unreciprocated gesture. There is a sliver of guilt that creeps its way inside me. When Samir told us that we were to eat outside, I knew exactly where Teo had planned our meal—in his garden.

In my battle to fight off the mix of emotions I have been inflicted with since arriving at Braaka, I forgot how well Teo knows me. In my youth, I shared most of my secrets with him, almost every thought. The only person to beat him in that regard was Atlas. And that was mostly because I truly believed that Atlas and I were the same person, separated in the womb. But while Atlas had my confidence, Teo had something else. My utter devotion.

I'm not sure if I should be cross with him by setting up such a stunt, aimed to manipulate my feelings, or saddened that I'm unable to see his sweet gesture as anything but emotional blackmail. Whatever his intentions, his plan fell flat.

"Kind of feel sad for him," Anya whispers behind me.

"Sad? The man had more food on display in that little table than most back home have to eat for a week. Pity those poor hungry souls. Not King Teodoro of Derfir," Inessa snaps, always telling it like it is.

"Listen to our friend, Anya. She knows what she says."

"Yes, Kat. OUCH! Damn you, Inessa! That's going to leave a bruise," Anya belts out, rubbing at her arm where Inessa must have pinched her.

"Oh, don't widen your eyes at me, my queen. You're the one who gave her leave to be so informal," Inessa bites back, shaking her head in dismay. "What if her tongue slips and calls you by that name when others can hear? You'll have to send her to the dungeons just to save face and she'll end up being the pun of every joke. I will not have it."

Thank the gods I have my handmaidens—my sisters—to distract me.

"See, Anya? Even when Inessa is being mean, it's out of love for us." I raise a teasing brow.

"Yeah, well, she sure has a funny way of showing it," Anya mutters, still rubbing at her arm.

"Your Majesty?" Samir calls out a few yards away from us, waving us into a room.

"Come, ladies. Our meal awaits," I tell them, walking toward Teo's man, my friends right at my heel.

The dining hall is large and spacious, a long dining table right at its center that can seat about twenty. I sit on the chair at the head of the table, knowing Teo will be forced to sit opposite me—very far away. My ladies take their respective seats to each of my sides, ensuring those places are filled.

This I can live with.

Not the intimate garden setting Teo had planned for me.

Samir says that he'll be back with our food when Teo graces us with his presence, no longer looking as sullen as he did when we left him. But to my dismay, instead of sitting at the far end of the table, he grabs a chair and plants it at my side.

I'm about to tell him to move, when one of the most exotic women I have ever seen walks into the room.

No.

That's not the right word for what she does.

Her graceful, silent steps almost make you believe that her feet never touch the floor as she glides over to where we are seated.

"Well, this is a pleasant surprise. I was sure I was going to dine alone. Again."

I don't miss how she adds emphasis to the word again as her black eyes go straight to me.

"Change of plans, I'm afraid. I didn't account for the queen's... entourage," Teo explains, flicking imaginary lint off his white pants.

"Entourage, you say." Her gaze flits from me to Inessa and then onto Anya. "And what an exquisite pair they are," she all but purrs, her eyes lingering a little too long on the red-haired woman at my side.

With attentive eyes, I watch this woman sway her slender hips toward Anya, taking a seat at her side. The way she scans every inch of my friend from top to bottom is unnerving. Anya must feel it too because her cheeks start to blush profusely.

"Aren't you a pretty little thing?" she rasps, licking her lips. "Your skin looks like the sweetest cream. I've never seen such flawless skin on a woman."

Anya swallows hard, blinking rapidly.

"You're too kind," Anya retorts nervously, her own eyes going to the smooth, immaculate dark skin of the woman sitting next to her.

Anya can't take her eyes off her. And I'm having a hard time not staring too.

The blood-red low-cut dress favors the woman's rich, dark skin immensely, making it look even more tantalizing to touch. But it's the way she wears her sleek black hair just above her shoulders that really does wonders for elongating her neck and bringing anyone's eyes to the sunflower medallion sitting pretty at the hollow of her throat. I have no doubt that this stranger in our midst must be the goddess of fire personified, with the sole goal to increase the temperature in any room with her mere presence alone.

Strong, beautiful, and fearless.

Those are the words that immediately come to mind to describe such a force of nature.

"Oh, no," she says dramatically, her strategic gaze falling to the little red mark on Anya's forearm. "You're hurt."

"Oh, this? It's nothing," Anya is quick to shrug off, throwing a side-eye to Inessa sitting across from her.

"I know how to make it better," she retorts, batting her long, beautiful eyelashes at my friend, before leaning down and planting a kiss to the small bruise.

"Hmm." She licks her lips, lifting her head just to lean ever so close to Anya's shocked face. "You even taste as sweet as you look," the woman proclaims loudly as if no one else is in the room witnessing their interaction. "I wonder if all of you is as sweet."

"Cleo, behave," Teo interjects with a laugh. "It's time to eat. Not play with our food."

"Like I said before, you can always do both." She winks at him, making him laugh even harder.

Anya is still too stunned to say anything, while I, on the other hand, have plenty to say.

"Teo? Who is this woman and why does she insist on perturbing my handmaiden?" I scowl, throwing daggers at the woman that is making my friend shift in her seat and look all but flushed.

"Oh, there I go again. Forgetting my manners," Teo jokes with a shrug, still not answering my question.

"It's hard to forget something you never had." I throw him my best fake grin.

"Fair enough. This is Cleo. She's my right hand."

"And his left, when he's in the mood for it," Cleo interjects, winking at Anya, who looks like she's about to faint if she doesn't breathe soon.

"Teo, mind telling your *right hand* that she won't enjoy it if I use *my left* across her face if she doesn't stop harassing Anya?"

Cleo immediately pulls away from my friend, giving her enough breathing room, just to stare daggers at me.

"This is our queen? I would have thought her prettier," she insults.

My hand goes to the knife set on the table, itching to show Cleo what we northerners do to people who dare insult us to our face, when Teo grabs hold of my wrist and shakes the knife out of my grasp.

"Be nice, Cleo, or you will eat alone. Today and every other day while the queen visits.

She eyes Anya's beet-red face again and falls back in her chair.

"My apologies, Your Highness. We don't get many guests, so my manners are a little bit rusty. I didn't mean to be rude."

"Yes, you did," I accuse.

Her smug smile affirms it too.

Thankfully, Samir and his colleagues enter the hall, all carrying trays upon trays of food. My frown only deepens at the extravagant display.

"We are but five people, yet there is enough food here to feed a small army," I reprimand, although by the way Teo keeps smiling at me, I don't think he understands that I'm chastising him.

"Tell me, if there is this much food in the south, then why have my last few ordered shipments never met their destination?"

Teo's winning grin falls flat to the floor.

"As I told you, Your Majesty, I sent your shipments, as per usual. My men guaranteed me that they found their way north. If the food never made it to your table, I cannot be held responsible."

"You're the supplier! Who else should I hold responsible?"

"Your men, my queen. The ones who we delivered everything to. Ask them where the food went," he counters, looking dead serious.

"My men?" I blurt out, completely offended.

"Yes, your men. I don't know how I can say it more clearly. I have always fulfilled my obligations to the crown, even when that meant going against my values, and everything I believed in. So to have you sitting here, suggesting the opposite, is not only a slight to me, but to all of the south!" he shouts, slamming his hand on the table.

"Teo," Cleo pleads in warning, sounding uncharacteristically contrite.

"No, it's fine, Cleo. I'm fine," he mumbles, pulling his seat back to stand up. "Ladies, enjoy your meal. Suddenly, I've lost my appetite."

And just like that, he walks out of the room, leaving me completely confused at his reaction.

"What did he mean by that? When he said that serving the crown sometimes went against his values?" I hear Anya ask, but when I look at her, I see the question wasn't directed at me, but at Cleo.

"That, my little cherry pie, is a question your queen should be asking herself."

Cleo then gives a small peck to Anya's cheek before standing up to follow Teo.

"What do you think he meant by that remark?" a previous silent Inessa asks, this time looking at me for answers.

"I don't know," I tell her truthfully, staring at the door from where he stormed off to. "I really don't know."

Inessa pops a grape into her mouth.

"Then use this time in the south wisely, my queen, and find out."

Oh, I intend to.

Chapter 32
Teodoro

Five days.

Five fucking days.

That's how long Katrina has been staying with me in Braaka and she's still acting like I'm a total stranger to her. Time slips through my fingers, and for the life of me, I have no idea how to stop it.

"You have to come up with a better plan than just forcing her to eat all her meals with you," Cleo says, plucking out one petal at a time from the daisy in her hands while whispering something.

"I know," I mutter, kicking the air at my feet as we stroll through the garden.

It may not be as beautiful as the one I have back home, but I was excited for her to see all the exotic flowers that bloom in the south. But she never gave me a chance.

Fuck.

All she does is stay locked in her room writing letters to Elijah—her little brother that she hasn't even informed me she has yet—and of course, to *him*. She's written him letters upon letters in only five days, while to me, she barely says hello. I had the misfortune of reading just one of those letters, a mistake I don't intend to ever make again.

With a little help from Cleo, I was able to distract her rider long enough to steal one from his bag and read her letter to Levi in its entirety. Sure, he would see that the seal was broken and that I must have been the one to read it, but in the moment I didn't care.

After having read it, though, I didn't have the courage to put it back in the rider's purse. It would have been far more humiliating having Levi know I read each line where Katrina all but confesses her love for him, how her days are empty without his love, and how she counts each of them down until they are reunited again.

Yeah, fuck Levi and his fucking letters.

"You also didn't help by trying to seduce her friend," I quip back, needing to lash my anger out at someone.

"What can I tell you? When I see something I want, I do everything in my power to get it. You used to be like that too," Cleo counters, not one bit fazed with my furious outburst as she continues to mumble some kind of gibberish under her breath.

"Yeah, and how is that going for you?" I retort sarcastically.

"Better than I could have hoped." She smiles, her black eyes beaming with light.

And that's when I realize what she's been mumbling under her breath all this time while strolling through the garden, murdering one daisy, one after the other.

"She loves me... she loves me not. She loves me... she loves me not. She loves me..."

I stop moving just to let out a loud, demoralized cackle.

"Great. That's just great. Here I am struggling to win back the love of my life in a month, while you end up falling in love with her handmaiden in less than a week! Just fucking fantastic!"

"Hey, don't take your frustrations out on me! It's not my fault your precious queen is in love with someone else," she yells, scorned, making sure I feel the same with her reminder.

"Fuck you, Cleo."

"No, fuck you, Teo!" she shouts, before pointing a finger at me and storming off.

Damn it!

Fuck!

"Wait, wait!" I yell, running after her, grabbing her wrist and pulling her to me.

"I'm sorry, Cleo. Fuck. I'm so fucking sorry. I was being an asshole."

"You're always an asshole," she mutters, but thankfully spins around and places her palms on my chest. "You're just lucky that I have a soft spot for assholes."

I chuckle softly.

"Yeah, I am lucky. You're my best friend. If I don't have you in my corner, then I'm as good as done for," I admit.

She lets out a little sigh, her black eyes going soft.

"I'll always be in your corner. Always."

I lean in and press a kiss to her temple, my own little way of showing her how remorseful I am for the way I've been treating her lately. I've been so stressed that I've been using my one and only friend as my own personal punching bag. She's never complained, taking every punch like a trooper.

But the minute I started to insult whatever fling she's having with Katrina's handmaiden, she lost it.

Which means she's falling hard for the redhead.

"Anya, is it?" I smile, tugging a loose lock of her hair and putting it behind her earlobe.

"Yeah," Cleo says, her dark eyes sparkling again just with the mention of the girl.

"And does she feel the same?"

"It's complicated," she retorts, pulling her hand off me to bite her thumb.

"Ah, I see. So when you say complicated, what you really mean is—"

"She's never been with a woman before," she admits finally. "She's curious, though. Very curious. But her track record isn't the best, so she's being cautious. All she's known is a bunch of dipshits that say all the right words to get her into bed, and then after they've had their fun, they're out the door. I can't come to her with pretty words. I have to show her that with me, things would be different."

"Hmm. Men are idiots, Cleo. They wouldn't know a good thing if it bit them in the ass. You, however, dear friend, are no idiot. Which means if you care for her, then she's worth fighting for. Make her feel safe, respected—loved. I promise if she gets those things from you, then your situation will get a whole lot less complicated."

Cleo takes my words to heart, and I can see she's already thinking of what she can do more to win her girl.

Meanwhile, I'm still stumped on how to win mine.

"We have kissed, though. Among other things," Cleo adds, to which I smile.

Another sign of being in love, is that when someone gives you an opening to talk about the person who holds your affection, you run with it. Any excuse just to say her name out loud is a good one.

"Come, let's go sit down inside where it's cooler, and you can tell me all about it." I wrap my arm around my friend as she starts telling me everything she's been up to these past few days while I've just been locked in my room, licking my wounds.

"Oh! I just got an idea!" she shouts excitedly, jumping up in front of me.

"Yeah? For your girl or mine?" I chuckle.

"For yours!" She smiles widely.

My heartbeat kicks in as I wait for her to tell me what she's come up with. "Well, go on! Tell me!"

"Okay, so cherry pie—"

"Cherry pie? Really? That's the pet name you gave her? A little on the nose, don't you think?" I tease with a playful smirk.

"Oh, like kitten is so very fucking original." She rolls her eyes.

"Touché. Okay, go on. You were saying?"

" *Anya,*" she over pronounces the word just to taunt me, "says that she hates this place. That everything about it only reminds her of Levi. She says that the queen sits by her windowsill just staring at the hill where they were separated from one another."

"Shit!" I curse.

"I think you're right. Men are fucking idiots. Because a woman would have made sure not to give her a room with such a view." She wiggles her brows.

"Okay, fine. I fucked up. What's your plan?"

"My plan was for us to take the queen home. To Nas Laed. A person would have to have a heart of stone not to fall in love with that place."

"Not stone—ice," I whisper under my breath.

"Huh?"

"Nothing." I shake my head. "But you might be onto something. Nas Laed is one of the most beautiful cities in the kingdom. The queen should visit it."

"And you'd be able to put a lot more miles away from the last place she saw the eastern king. You know what they say—the heart can't feel what it can't see," Cleo singsongs the old southern proverb.

I don't have the heart to tell her that the proverb was made up by cheating men who betrayed their wives with girls like her. Nevertheless, she makes a solid point. If Katrina is taken out of this place and into one as exotic as Nas Laed, then I might still have a shot.

"There's only one downside to this plan, though," Cleo adds, concerned.

"Yeah? And what's that?"

"It's a five-day journey home," she reminds me with a warning tone.

"I know."

"That leaves you with twenty days, Teo. Just twenty days."

"I know," I repeat, liking this idea more and more.

"I don't know, Teo. You would be taking a big gamble. You might not be able to get her to fall in love with you in such a short time."

I smile at that.

"But that's just it, Cleo. I don't need her to fall in love with me. I just need her to *remember* how she's never stopped."

He's taking me to his palace in Nas Laed.

He thinks he can fool me, but I'm no fool.

I know exactly why Teo suddenly needed to return to his home, and it had nothing to do with not being able to afford to stay outside his capital for the full month of my visit.

He thinks that a change in scenery will make me forget eastern meadows and piercing green eyes that haunt me. He thinks that traveling so far south, and adding even more distance between me and Levi, that somehow my heart will forget its true affections.

If that could ever be possible.

But I didn't put up a fight when he gave me the news five days ago. In fact, I rejoiced in it.

Because it meant that I had something to occupy my mind with, distracting me from my sorrow, while eating away at the days that I still had to endure the south and its vain king.

I must have been a foolish child in my youth to ever consider Teo as my soulmate. But I guess my eyes were too distracted by his amber gaze and sly smile to look deeper underneath such an exquisite exterior. Teo is as hollow and shallow as they come, no real substance to him at all.

So let him think his little game is working.

Let him believe that my heart will grow cold toward the east as we travel deeper into the scorching heat of the south.

Let him believe whatever he wants and live in his little fantasy that he could ever steal my heart from its rightful owner.

Although, five days into this voyage, I must admit it is far more arduous than the one I made with Levi east. I knew the south was known for its warm summer days and nights, yet nothing could have prepared me for its reality.

Long gone are the use of my winter gowns, as they serve no purpose here under such high temperatures. Just the weight of them on me had me gasping for breath.

Although I'm still suspicious of Teo's so-called right hand, Cleo was the one that saved me and my handmaidens from heat exhaustion on the first day of our travels, gifting us light, breezy clothing so we didn't pass out in our stuffy carriage. It was, though, the particular gift of sandals that gave me pause, as I couldn't wrap my head around its purpose.

Safe to say after three days in, I understood perfectly.

The large vegetation fields gave way to a horizon of yellow sand as far as the eye could see. We crossed dune upon dune until it felt like I had just stepped into another world, one ruled by the sand and sun. Even the light dresses we wore felt too heavy on our skin, the appetite for food gone, replaced by a thirst that felt like it could never be quenched. Each day that we continue on this voyage feels like Teo's plan was not to win my heart but to kill it.

It's with this certainty rummaging away in my head that I start to hear loud cheers of celebration.

"Please tell me they are shouting because we're finally there," Inessa begs, her arm covering her eyes. "My head can't take any more of this. It feels like someone is bludgeoning it with a hammer."

Anya and I have withstood the heat's afflictions, Inessa not so much.

"Aw, Inessa," Anya coos, pressing a kiss on our friend's clammy cheek. "I hate to see you in so much pain. Is there anything I can do to make it easier on you?"

Inessa moves her arm just a sliver from her eyes and offers her a soft smile.

"You've done enough, sweet friend. More than enough," she replies, since Anya has barely left her side once Inessa started to complain about her migraines.

Anya smiles back, but still is unconvinced.

She takes out her water flask and pours it over a handkerchief. She then slowly removes Inessa's arms and begins to dab the moist cloth on her pale forehead.

"She needs a physician, Kat. She doesn't look well at all," Anya pleads, seriously worried over our friend.

"What I need is some shade and a cool breeze. That's all," Inessa replies on my behalf, but like Anya, I'm just as concerned for my raven-haired friend's well-being.

She spent most of the past few days vomiting, unable to keep anything in her stomach. We've had to change her clothing three times already, each one drenched in sweat. There are large, dark pools under her eyes from not being able to sleep with the heat either. Her gaunt frame, a testament to the hardship of this wretched journey.

If Teo is leading me to my death, then by the gods, I will not let him lead my friends to it, too.

"Enough of this madness. We're going home," I grumble, hating myself for not having made this decision sooner.

"We are?"

"We are?" both girls ask me in tandem.

"Yes, we are. I'm starting to believe that Nas Laed is just a myth and not a real place. A lie Teo has led us to believe with the sole purpose of leading me to my death, so that he may take my throne. No. We are going home at once."

I lift the curtain hanging over the small window in my carriage and call out to the nearest rider.

"Your Highness," he asks, waiting for my command.

"Tell His Majesty, the king, that I need to speak with him immediately. We are to return home at once."

His nose scrunches in confusion.

"Should I ask an audience with King Teodoro now or after we pass Nas Laed's gates?" he asks, his gaze tuning forward.

"What do you mean?" I ask, pulling the curtain fully away so that I can see for myself what has his attention.

I instantly gasp at the sight.

Just a few miles away from us lies the largest oasis known to mankind.

Nas Laed.

It's just as beautiful as he proclaimed when we were children— paradise right here on earth.

Even from far away, I can see that the city at its center is filled with palm trees and exotic birds, waterfalls to the left and a gigantic palace to its right. It's like nothing I have ever seen before or could ever imagine on my own. It's beautiful.

"Your Majesty?" the rider asks after I've gone suddenly mute. "Do you still want me to ask King Teodoro for an audience?"

Still too astounded with the sight before me, all I manage to do is shake my head.

He offers me a curt nod and I close the curtain, falling back in my seat.

"What? What is it?" Anya asks, hurriedly going to the window. "OH THE GODS!"

As Anya shrieks in excitement, I lean forward and place my hand on Inessa's knee.

"We're not going home, are we?" Inessa asks, so in tune with my inner thoughts.

"No, dear friend, we're not."

Her shoulders slump as she lets out an exhale.

"This place better be worth it," she says, covering my hand with hers.

"Believe me, Inessa. It is."

As we enter the palace, I'm still in a daze, soaking in all the beautiful scenery around me.

Everything is exotic here.

From the people down to the food that is served on silver platters. To Inessa's delight, it's also much cooler, with its marble floors and high ceilings allowing the soft breeze to enter from the various large open floor-to-ceiling arch windows. There are also innumerous servants using what I can only assume are peacock feathered fans, all sprawled around the various divisions of the palace, to ensure the heat is kept at bay. Everything is pristine and immaculately clean, white being the preferred color on the walls, floors, and linens to contrast all the other vibrant ones.

I'm surprised that Teo hasn't bragged to me about the slice of paradise he calls home. In fact, he doesn't seem to be paying me any mind whatsoever, his sure steps leading him away from me and down a large open hallway.

Curiosity urges me to follow to see what could possibly be more important than giving me a tour to his palace's grounds. Teo all but runs outside to a garden filled with a myriad of hibiscus and orchids of every color imaginable. But he doesn't stop there and proceeds forward, leaving me little time to appreciate their beauty. It's when the garden gives way to a man-made pond, and a little girl with her nurse feeding the swans that swim in its center.

"Look who's home!" Teo shouts, falling to his knees, his arms wide open.

The little girl shrieks with glee and runs to him. The instant she slams her tiny body to his, he wraps his arms around her and showers her with butterfly kisses. She laughs happily, and when he stops his kisses to start tickling her, she laughs even harder as she tries to wiggle away from his embrace.

It's her laugh that is unmistakable, bringing with it all sorts of memories from our misspent youth.

Teo has a child.

A little girl.

"Has my Zara been a good girl while I was away?" he asks her nurse, while never taking his eyes off his beautiful daughter.

"She has, Your Majesty. Missed you terribly, my king," the nurse replies as she curtsies.

"Is that so? Did you miss me, Zara?" he asks, rubbing the tip of his nose with hers.

"Hmm. Maybe this much," she teases him, holding her forefinger and thumb to show just a little space in between them.

"Just that, huh?" He pretends to frown.

"Okay, maybe this much." She laughs when she stretches her arms wide.

"Now, that's more like it." He chuckles, rubbing his face in the crook of her neck to tickle her. "Because I missed my little princess to the moon and back."

The whole sight has me taken aback.

Not because Teo fathered a bastard and legitimized her existence as his and bestowed her a title, but with how doting a father he is to her, showing me a whole other side to him that I never knew could exist. He must have had her quite young since she looks to be around the same age as Elijah. Maybe a year or two older.

And then I remember myself.

I've just intruded on a very intimate moment—one that belongs only to the father and daughter. I begin to retrace my steps back in retreat, but my sandals must make a noise, because Zara's gaze bounces away from her father and onto me.

"Is that her? Is that the Winter Queen?"

Teo turns his head over his shoulder and sees me. He then places Zara's feet back on the ground and stands up straight, giving her his hand to hold.

"Yes, Zara. It is. Would you like to meet her?"

Zara nods as my throat begins to clog.

When they finally reach me, I plant a sweet smile to my lips and go to my haunches.

"It's so very nice to meet you, Zara. My name is Katrina."

The little girl scans my face, hers looking a little confused and disappointed.

"You said she wore a crown made of diamonds and ice," she says, looking to Teo for answers.

"I do, Zara. However, I left such a treasured keepsake at home, in the north where it belongs," I explain with a nervous laugh, fixing the more modest crown I have on my head.

"That's okay. That one is pretty too. Can I touch it?"

"I... huh... sure," I stutter, handing it to her.

Zara takes my crown and begins to fiddle with it, inspecting the smaller diamonds to see if they are real. When she can't decide, she sprints into a run to her nurse, trusting her judgment over her father's.

Teo lets out a sigh beside me as he watches his daughter.

"Sorry about that. She's obsessed with anything that sparkles."

"Most children are," I retort, observing all the similarities little Zara inherited from Teo. "She's the spitting image of you when you were her age."

"Yeah? You think so?" he asks shyly, obliviously happy to receive such a compliment.

I nod with a smile, while inside my mind wanders to what Zara's mother must look like and if she is as permanent a fixture in Teo's life as Zara seems to be.

"Is her mother around? I'd love to see if Zara bears some of her likeness."

Teo turns to me with the oddest, confused expression on his face. "She passed away in childbirth. I thought you knew that."

I shake my head.

Why would I know if Zara's mother had passed away? I didn't even know of Zara's existence. Not that I don't understand why I was kept in the dark. If I learned anything from my father, it is that kings tend not to like talking about their bastard children and prefer them to be out of sight and out of mind.

Although, it does please me that Teo doesn't seem to share in my father's sentiment.

Then Teo surprises me further with his next remark.

"Would you mind terribly if tonight I was absent from dinner? I know it's only been a few weeks since I left home, but I would really like to spend some quality time with Zara today. Cleo can show you and your handmaidens around so that you are familiar with the palace's grounds."

"Of course. And if it will make life easier on you, Zara can attend all our meals while I'm here," I offer, thinking Zara to be the perfect buffer to keep Teo entertained and not focused on me.

But if I was expecting him to be disappointed with such an offer, then I am sorely mistaken. Teo's amber eyes turn to liquid gold as he lifts my hand up to his lips and presses a tender kiss to it.

"I would really love that. Thank you."

When he turns his back to me to rush over to play with his child, my brows pinch together in utter bewilderment. I start to head back inside, not having the heart to ask Zara for my crown back, when I turn around just to take another glance at them both.

Teo places my crown on little Zara's head and curtsies to her like a lord would a queen. Her giggles are contagious, springing my own smile to crest my face.

And as I soak in this sincere moment of love, a faint memory similar to it emerges in my mind.

Twelve Years Old

"Is it done yet?" Atlas asks impatiently as he jumps up and down behind Levi's back to take a peek over his shoulder.

"All good things come to those who wait." Levi winks at him with a smile.

"I hate waiting," Atlas pouts.

"Come here, Attie. Grab some hay and come sit with me. We can wait together," I singsong, patting the ground next to me.

With his head hung low, Atlas kicks some of the stable's hay in his path, picking it up and placing it right next to me. He takes his seat and lays his head on my shoulder, while hooking my arm around his.

"I hate it here," he mumbles, the sound of strangled tears in his voice. "The ocean is just too far away. I don't hear it calling to me when I'm here."

"I know." I sigh, giving him a little squeeze.

It saddens me how homesick Atlas gets sometimes. Usually, it doesn't hit him this hard, as we keep him busy enough for him not to even remember his home. But when it does hit him… he's inconsolable. Today has been such a day, making my heart hurt for my best friend.

"If you hate it so much, then why do you always come?" Teo asks from opposite me, lying on the hay just watching the clouds float in the sky from the small hole in the ceiling of the stable's roof.

"Because," Atlas stammers while drying the few tears that made their way onto his cheeks. "Kat's here," he says, looking up at my face with a tender smile. "And when I'm home, I miss her more than I miss the ocean."

I don't have to look at him to feel Teo rolling his eyes at him. I kick his foot with mine for being so insensitive with Atlas, especially when he's down. Unfortunately, Teo only chuckles, not one bit sorry that his friend is hurting.

"Cut it out," I order him, hating it when he acts like an insensitive jerk.

"Sorry, princess." He winks at me.

"No, you're not," Levi mumbles, hearing every word we're saying, even with his back turned to us, and focused on the task in his hands.

"Once again, Levi. You're right. You're always right. I'm not sorry. You don't see me crying because I miss my home, and Nas Laed is the most beautiful place on earth."

"Liar," Atlas blurts out.

"You think I'm lying?" Teo lifts himself halfway off the ground with his elbows just to look over at Atlas.

"You're always lying," Atlas defends.

"Not about this I'm not. Don't believe me? Ask anyone who has traveled Aikyam and seen the four kingdoms. They'll tell you. Nas Laed is like paradise on earth, placed by the gods themselves."

"Does it have an ocean?" Atlas questions, still suspicious of Teo's claim.

"No—"

"Then it can't be the best place in all of Aikyam," Atlas quickly cuts in. "If it doesn't have an ocean, then it sucks balls."

"Attie!" I chide at his poor use of words, while I hear Levi chuckle under his breath.

"It's okay, kitten. Let Atlas think whatever he wants. I know the truth."

"Fine then. Tell me one thing Nas Laed has that is better than where we come from?" Atlas insists. "It doesn't have an ocean like we do back in Huwen, so the west is already better than the south in that department. It also doesn't have mountains that almost reach the sky like here in Tarnow. And there is no way your home has caves upon caves of every different colored diamond and jewel you can imagine like the north does either." Atlas continues to defend his case with such passion that all his previous homesick tears have vanished from his face. "Does the south have green meadows as far as the eye can see like the east does? No. It doesn't. All the south is known for is its harvest fields and little else. We grow food too, you know? But unlike the south, we refuse to make every single person abduct their own lands just to make them work the fields for spoiled princes like you to get fat and lazy."

"Attie!"

"Atlas!" Levi and I scold in tandem.

But just like Teo, Atlas just smirks at the reprimand.

And to my surprise, so does Teo.

"Atta go, Atlas. Love seeing you with some backbone, kid." He winks at him.

I shake my head, giving up on trying to understand these two together.

Instead, I turn to Teo and ask him to tell us why Nas Laed to him is the best city in the land.

Teo gets up from the floor, making sure that all eyes are on him.

"First of all, you have to be from the south to even know where it's located."

"So it's a secret?" I ask, sincerely intrigued.

"Why keep it a secret?" Atlas curiously asks beside me.

"For protection." Teo shrugs. "Enemies can't invade a city if they don't know where it is."

"But we don't have enemies," I state, with a confused expression plastered on my face.

"Today we might not, but who knows what tomorrow may bring." Teo wiggles his brows.

"Stop showing off and tell them what they want to know already," Levi interjects, annoyed at Teo's dramatics.

"I was getting to it," Teo replies, giving Levi a roll of the eye. "Anyway, my home may not have an ocean like Atlas accused, but it has a waterfall so high it almost touches the stars. Birds of every feather are free to fly through a sky so bright that you have to put your hand over your eyes to see it. Every cat known to man, be it a black panther or a wild-mane lion, roams around the city like stray dogs roam yours. And our gardens hold more colors in their flowers than rainbows even possess," Teo explains, transporting us all to this wondrous land.

"You're making this up," Atlas mumbles skeptically.

"I'm not. I swear that I'm telling you the truth."

"He is," Levi confirms, his head hanging low as he continues to carve away. "When my grandfather was alive, he went to Nas Laed once on crown business, and when he returned, he wouldn't stop talking about it. He would spend nights telling me these fantastical tales like Teo is telling you. He's not lying. It exists just as he says."

"Now do you believe me?" Teo throws his arms in the air, frustrated.

"Wow!" Atlas exclaims, his eyes almost coming out of their sockets, while mine are filled with all these fantastical images Teo planted in my head.

"Figures. When I say something, no one believes me, but when Levi says the same damn thing, everyone does," Teo grumbles. "One day you're going to have to teach me that neat trick."

Levi turns around and stands up, keeping his arms behind his back.

"It's not a trick, Teo. If you always tell the truth, then no one will doubt your word," Levi explains.

"Sounds boring." Teo scoffs.

"Sounds honorable," Levi rebukes.

"Is there a difference?" Teo taunts by raising a cocky brow.

But I don't have time to get in between them and simmer down their hotheaded temperaments since Atlas is already jumping up to his feet and racing toward Levi. I, of course, get up and follow him too.

"Is it done?" he asks, wide-eyed.

"You tell me?"

Levi then brings his hands to his front and places a wooden toy boat into his palms.

Atlas stares at it like it's the best gift he's ever gotten.

"Do you like it?" Levi asks when Atlas takes too long to say anything.

I must be imagining it, but I sense a bit of insecurity in Levi's voice as he waits patiently for our friend to give his word of approval.

Atlas cranes his head back, his light blue eyes watering for a whole different reason.

"It's… it's… extraordinary," he stutters, holding the boat in his hands like it's his most treasured possession.

"I'm glad you like it," Levi smiles widely, ruffling Atlas's dark golden locks.

"Levi? Do you think… do you think one day I'll be able to sail on one? To actually see what is beyond the seven seas?"

Levi goes to his haunches so that he's eye to eye with Atlas.

"Can you see yourself sailing such a boat?"

Atlas swallows hard, thinks on it for a pregnant pause, but eventually nods.

"Then that's your answer."

Atlas smiles widely and throws himself onto Levi, giving him a huge hug.

"You encourage him too much," Teo chastises, shaking his head at the tender sight.

"And you don't encourage him enough," Levi is quick to snap at him after Atlas breaks the hug to stare at his gift.

"That's because I'm looking out for the kid. He's a crowned prince that one day will be king. To put such foolish notions in his head that he can just sail the seven seas, like he's some merchant or sailor, will do him more harm than good," Teo defends his logic.

"No, what you want is for me to steal his dream away and I refuse to. A man is nothing without his dreams, Teo."

"Is that so? Okay then, now what?" Teo jokes, crossing his arms over his chest. "You have a boat, Atlas, but nothing to put it in. If you haven't paid attention, this is the north. Everything is frozen here. Every lake. Every river. Every fucking pond."

"Watch your fucking language, Teo," Levi scolds, never one to like Teo using such colorful language around me or Atlas, even though he just did it himself.

"Watch yours, you big oaf." Teo laughs before he takes the small wooden boat from out of Atlas's hands. "This is useless. As is any toy for a prince."

Levi snatches the boat away from Teo's hands and frowns.

"Come here, Atlas," he orders with as soft a tone he can muster considering he's giving Teo the evil eye. "Let's show the cocky jerk that he doesn't know what he's talking about."

We all follow Levi, wondering how he'll prove Teo wrong.

I'm curious too.

Teo is, after all, right. At least to me he is. Everything in the north *is* frozen solid. Levi's gesture was a nice one, but in the end, not very practical or logical. Atlas will never be able to play with it. Not in Tarnow, at least. So Levi's gift, no matter how sweet, will only give way for more disappointment.

For more of Atlas's heartache.

And when Atlas hurts, I hurt too.

But just as I think that thought, my heart begins to thump with utter glee.

"It's not the vast wide ocean that you're used to, but at least it's big enough for your boat to float on," Levi explains as he places the boat right in the middle of the horses' watering trough.

"It's perfect!" Atlas exclaims, genuinely excited by the alternative.

Levi then turns to a frowning Teo.

"You think you know it all, Teo, but you still have a lot to learn. My father has this saying. That if you want something bad enough, you'll find a way to get it."

"Yeah, well, my father has a saying too," Teo retorts. "There are fools being born every minute. Make sure you're not one of them." He then throws Atlas a glance, his eyes saddening at how happy our friend is.

Seeing that Atlas is otherwise preoccupied playing with his new toy, Teo uses his distraction to his advantage and bridges the distance between himself and Levi and leans into his ear.

"Atlas is a sick, frail little kid. You may not like the way I look out for him, but between the two of us, I'm the one he should be listening to. Atlas wouldn't survive a week on a boat, much less see the world in it, and yet you just filled his head with a bunch of nonsense that it's something he'll actually be able to achieve. That toy you made him might as well have been a noose, because it's going to get him killed. Tell me, Levi, who is his real friend here?" Teo then looks over his shoulder once more at Atlas, his sad smile tainting his beautiful face. "Have fun, kid. And may the gods protect you, since it's obvious no one here will."

And with that parting remark, he walks away.

Chapter 35
Teodoro

It's working.

My plan is fucking working.

Ever since I made the decision to bring Katrina to Nas Laed, she's been a different person. No longer a recluse to her room, gone is the woman who preferred her solitude to my company. No more riders head out east with love letters to Levi either. Katrina has been so fascinated with my place of birth, that she wakes up early just so she can experience everything my city has to offer.

And me?

Well, I've made sure to be the perfect guide and satisfy her every craving.

"Oh, the gods! I can't!" she giggles, eyeing the panther on my lap.

"Yes, you can. He's as docile as they come," I insist, patting the silky fur of the big cat when what I really want to do is run my hands all over the creamy skin of the kitten sitting at my side.

Katrina bites at her bottom lip as she nervously extends her hand to the predator lying lazily on my lap and hesitantly places it on his back.

"Gently, gently," I warn as she begins patting it.

"I can't believe I'm actually doing this," she stammers, her gaze shining with excitement as she keeps running her fingers through the panther's fur.

"Believe it, kitten." I grin widely when her face doesn't screw up like it always does when I call her by the nickname. In fact, all of her beams with happiness, making my chest tighten with how long I've longed for the day that I could see such joy on her beautiful face.

It reminds me of my youth spent up north when I used every excuse to make her laugh and smile.

Back then, I lived to make her happy.

And as far as I can tell, I still do.

The sparkle in her gray eyes as her gaze bounces from the domesticated cat on my lap to me, is too much for my aching heart to take all at once. So instead of looking at her, I stare ahead at where little Zara, her nurse, and Katrina's handmaiden, Inessa, splash around in the waterfall, having the best time.

"You sure you don't want to join them?" I ask when even a stern-looking Inessa is smiling like she's a little kid again.

Katrina shakes her head and continues gently patting her new favorite pet.

"No. I'd have to put on swimming attire and there are too many people here. It wouldn't be appropriate."

"Appropriate?" I arch a curious brow, staring at the crowd of people in the water, most of them naked as the day they were born. "I don't know if you can tell, but Nas Laed doesn't really care for such decorum. We are free people here. We live by our own rules."

"I can see that." She smiles shyly. "Now I understand why you are how you are. You've never felt burdened with the weight of your crown. You have no restrictions here. No rules."

"Liberating, isn't it?" I wink flirtatiously at her.

"Yes, but terribly frightening too."

"Frightening? How can living free to do what you want, when you want it, be scary to you?"

"Because when there are no rules, then there also are no limits either. What if someone's idea of freedom comes at the expense of another's?"

Well, fuck, she's got me there.

None of this would be possible if there weren't sacrifices being made just for my city to live so extravagantly.

There is a whisper in my head that maybe now is the right time to talk to Katrina about the hardships the south faces every day. About how most of my kingdom is a slave to their labor just so they have enough food to put on the table. How they work hard on the fields from dawn to sunset just to make sure they have produced enough to fulfill the north's demands.

"I've said something to upset you," Katrina utters beside me, attentive to my declining mood.

"I always get upset when my mind travels to the politics of Aikyam. You, however, could never upset me." I force a smile.

Her forehead scrunches in confusion.

"Politics?"

"Never you mind, kitten. It's too glorious a day to speak about such things," I state, not wanting to get into how fucked up my kingdom really is and that not everyone is afforded all the luxuries that Nas Laed offers.

Her brows draw together in both confusion and curiosity, but thankfully she doesn't ask me any more questions.

This is a time to woo. Not to confess that her reign and her father's before her has debilitated my kingdom in such a way that most of its people go to bed hungry every night.

No.

I'll try to talk to her about my people's plight after I've won her heart. Maybe then she'll be more inclined to hear me out and help me. As it stands, it could go either way if I broach the subject now.

To ensure her mind isn't focused on what I just said, I discreetly nudge my feline friend, to which he understands that it's time for him to move. Katrina pulls her hand away immediately, scared that he might attack her, but is pleasantly surprised when all he does is stand up, stretch his paws, and walk over to her to lay his head on her lap.

"He likes you. Not that I'm surprised. You're easy to like."

Easy to love, too, but I keep that thought to myself.

"I have a confession to make," she says as she runs the tips of her fingers over the panther's head.

"Oh, are we sharing secrets now? You know I'm a sucker for those." I wink, nudging her shoulder with mine.

"No," she giggles, making my heart soar to the heavens with the sound. "It's not a secret. Just a confession. Remember when we were kids and you told us about how life was here? I have to admit there was a part of me that didn't believe you."

"No shit." I laugh. "Atlas didn't believe me either."

Not until the great honorable Levi confirmed it, but again, I keep that nugget under lock and key, since I refuse to mention his name in front of Katrina and remind her of him.

"We were wrong to not trust you. I see that now. This place… it's a dream."

It's the whimsical way she says dream that has me in a daze.

Fuck, but I love her so fucking much.

Please, kitten. Please. Remember that you love me too.

I clear my throat and shake the lovesick fog from my eyes, hoping she didn't catch it.

"There is still so much for you to see, kitten. So much. This dream is only getting started. Trust me."

Her eyes glaze over and for the briefest of seconds, I almost see that young girl who fell in love with me.

Stay with me, kitten. Stay with me.

When she shakes her head and pulls her eyes off me, my heart drops to the pit of my stomach.

"I… uh…" she starts. "I think you did leave out some parts, though."

"Yeah, what parts?"

"Well, you told Atlas that you didn't have an ocean, which was a lie. To come to Nas Laed, we crossed dunes and suffered more than one sandstorm. And from the books I've read, where there is sand, there is a beach. And where there is a beach, there is an ocean. You lied." She smirks as if proud she's caught me in one of my lies.

"You think you're clever, do you, Your Highness?" I goad lightheartedly. "But your memory must be hazy because I didn't lie. When we had that conversation, I was merely talking about Nas Laed, not the south. And when Atlas went on his rant and didn't give me the opportunity to add that tidbit of truth, I simply chose to leave it out."

"Why though?" she asks curiously, hanging on to my every word.

"Atlas was so proud in his assumption that his kingdom was the only one that faced the ocean, I didn't have the heart to contradict him. Of course, he was only a kid then. I'm sure by now in his many sailing expeditions, he's learned his way around a map and knows the truth."

Katrina nods pensively, and then says something that has my heart melting at her words.

"You were always a good friend to Atlas. Even when it didn't seem like you were."

"Yeah, well, he never saw that," I mumble, pulling out the grass at my side by its roots and flinging it in the air.

"Does that mean you two haven't kept in touch?"

"Have you?" I raise a knowing brow.

"No." She shakes her head, a sullen expression to her face. "After my mother died, our friendship seemed to deteriorate, too. All of our friendships."

You can thank your bastard of a father for that one.
Mine too.

"We grew apart," I lie, instead of telling her the truth since it is obvious she has no idea what happened after her mother passed away. "It happens sometimes."

"Does it?" she counters with that same somber tone to her voice. "I thought what we had was stronger than that. That our friendship meant something."

"Hey," I interject, placing my hand on her cheek. "It did mean something. We were a family, kitten. One that fought as hard as it loved. And we did love each other. We did."

I still do.

I swallow dryly when she covers my hand with hers on her cheek. "We were a family, weren't we?"

"The best fucking dysfunctional family of all of Aikyam, kitten."

She lets out a dispirited giggle but plants a smile on her lips nonetheless. Her gentle gaze continues on mine as she pulls my hand off her face.

"I would like to see it someday. Your ocean."

My smile is as sullen as hers.

"Maybe one day, my queen. Maybe one day."

If I could, I would take her this very minute, but it's a three-week voyage and the clock is ticking on me as it is.

"However, if a swim is what you want, I can make that happen."

Katrina looks at the swarm of people all happily swimming in front of us, enjoying the beauty of the waterfall above them, and frowns.

"I told you. I can't go swimming here. I'm still the queen of Aikyam."

In other words, she can't get buck naked and rule with her virtue and dignity intact. Not only is the north cold and uninviting, but its lords are a stern bunch, sticklers to their archaic rule that no woman should show her bare skin to anyone save her wedded husband. Not even a queen.

But this is the south.

We do things differently here.

And it's time Katrina had a little taste of freedom.

"If my kitten wants to go swimming, then by the gods, she will." I stand up and give a little pat on the behind of the sleeping panther on her lap. He opens his eyes, throwing me a pissed-off growl, but walks away just the same.

"What are you doing?" she asks when I pull her by the hands to get her to her feet.

"We, kitten, are going back to the palace where it is nice and private for you to go for a swim in one of the pools."

"I don't know," she retorts, but I can hear how tempted she is with the idea.

"I'll tell Zara that she can stay here a little while longer with her new friend." I tilt my head toward Zara and Inessa who seem to enjoy each other's company. "And then we will both retreat to the palace and satisfy the itch that you are denying yourself. This is my home, kitten. And here we do whatever the fuck we want."

It's the promise of such unbridled freedom that has her nodding and accepting my offer.

If she only knew that inside my head, I'm ticking off another part of my plan to get her alone.

Now the real fun begins.

"Here, put this on," Teo demands as he hands me two flimsy pieces of fabric.

"What's this?" I suspiciously ask, staring at the two pieces of flimsy, triangle-shaped cloth being held together by a tiny bit of string.

"That is called a bathing suit. It is what the most modest people in the south wear when they want to go swimming."

I hold up the two separated pieces of cream fabric in each hand and dangle it in his face.

"This is modest?"

Teo only smirks.

"Best I can do for you, kitten. You can either use that or nothing at all. Your choice."

I scowl furiously at him while he just grins like the heathen he is.

He's loving this.

Loving my discomfort and awkwardness.

Not wanting to keep staring at his cocky smirk for a minute longer, I furiously slam my bedroom chamber door in his face and roll my eyes when the door is not thick enough to keep his cackles from being heard.

"I'll wait right here, kitten!" he yells from the hallway.

Great.

I walk to my bed and place the bathing suit, as he called it, on top of my bed. I cross my arms and curl the corner of my lips as I stare at the damn thing, wishing it came with some kind of instructions.

How am I supposed to know how to even put it on?

What goes where?

I mean, what is it supposed to cover, since it looks like it won't cover a damn thing?

Argh!

"The one with the two triangles is for you to cover your chest with and the smaller triangle is to cover the modesty you keep between your thighs. I can't be any more respectful than that," Teo calls out from the other side of the door, as if he can hear the actual panic I'm in.

"Okay. The two triangles are for my chest. So, I can only assume each one is purposely made to cover up each of my breasts. Okay, that makes sense," I mutter to myself as I pick it up with my thumb and forefinger.

To my shame and complete ignorance, it takes me a while to understand that the strings are to tie around my neck and back. But once I do, the second part of the swimsuit isn't so hard to figure out. Once I've made sure that everything is covered, I walk over to the mirror and almost faint at my reflection.

This is modest???

I'm good as naked.

If Uncle Adelid saw me now, he'd have a stroke.

Not that I'm his favorite person right now.

After I sent him a disparaging letter as to why I was never told about what was happening in the east and then added by sending him the new decree that abolished such a law, he hasn't so much as written me, his ego too bruised to send his flesh and blood a letter of apology.

I'll deal with Adelid when I get home.

Right now, there is too much I want to experience in the south.

I'm completely enamored with how carefree and liberated everyone here is. Not only is the city paradise, but its inhabitants don't seem to be burdened with anything. All they seem to care about is living life to its fullest extent with no real care for tomorrow.

They live free, while I was put on this earth to serve.

If I can just taste a little tiny bit of what it feels like to be born in the south, to be that free-spirited, then I will treasure the experience for years to come. That's all I wish to take from here. Memories to keep me warm on those cold northern nights where obligation and duty is my only calling.

"Are you almost done, or do you need me to come in and help?" Teo asks, banging on the door.

"In a minute," I retort, rushing to look around the room for something to wear over this poor excuse of a modest swimsuit.

Where is Anya when you need her?

She would know exactly what I should wear for such an occasion.

When my eyes catch one of Cleo's white spaghetti summer dresses lying on a chair, I rush to it and pull it over my head. It's one thing to wear such skimpy clothing to a pool where the only person there is Teo. It's a whole other matter walking about the palace's halls where servants can see you. Things might be different here in the south, but servant gossip occurs in every palace and castle, no matter its location. And the last thing I want is for idle gossip like me walking around Teo's palace almost buck naked to reach the wrong pair of ears.

Levi would never understand.

And the last thing I want is to cause him more suffering than what he's already going through.

It's Teo's insistence on banging on my door that takes my mind off the man I love.

"Kitten, oh kitten…"

Bang. Bang. Bang.

I swing the door open and give him my fiercest scowl.

"I've never met a person that can go from charmingly sweet to downright annoying as fast as you can, Teodoro."

"So you think I'm charming, huh?" He wiggles his brows.

"That's all you heard? You're incorrigible." I laugh at the angel-like face he's putting on.

"And you, my fair queen, are the loveliest woman I've ever seen," he says, lifting my hand to plant a chaste kiss on my knuckle.

My throat goes tight at the sincerity in his voice.

"I think I prefer you when you're annoying me," I stammer, feeling the heat of his innocent kiss rise up to my cheekbones.

"We both know that you love me both ways." He winks, back to his cocky self.

"Just show me the way to the damn pool already," I state coldly, trying desperately to keep my wits about me when he's acting like this.

"As you wish, my queen," he says, giving me his arm to hold on to.

Instead of doing so, I start walking ahead of him, head held high. I hear him snicker behind me before he rushes to catch up to lead me to where I want to go.

Ever since we arrived here, things have been different between us than they were in Braaka. I'm not sure how our dynamics changed so much either. Whether it was seeing him in his element here in this city or if it was witnessing the way he dotes on his precious little girl. Whatever the reason, I find myself not detesting him as I once did. And a part of me, the part that still dreams of green eyes, hot springs, and open fields, wishes I could have held on to my hatred a little longer.

My thoughts and feelings are so at war with each other that I don't even realize when we step outside into one of the various gardens that surround the palace.

"This way," Teo says, crooking his finger at me.

I slap it away and bypass him, figuring that the white pebbled path on the ground will lead me to the pool. But when I get there, I freeze, stunned at what I find.

"Well, look at what we have here?" Teo whispers behind me. "Looks like my Cleo is throwing herself a little party in our absence. What's that saying again? When the cat's away, the mouse will play." He chuckles.

"Will you shut up and hide?" I order, hiding behind one of the many veils and curtains that surround the various pools of water. When I'm sure no one can see us, my gaze goes back to the unsettling sight taking place right in front of us.

On one of the many white poolside beds lying around, is Cleo. But it's not her presence that has me wide-eyed in shock. It's what she is currently doing and who she is with that has me gobsmacked.

In all her naked glory, Cleo is laid upward on top of a man who is currently moaning out in pleasure as he thrusts deeply inside her ass, while another has his knees placed on each side of her on the bed as he pounds into her pussy, while leaning forward to kiss and suck at the breasts of another woman.

Like Cleo, this second woman is also preoccupied with two lovers. She uses her mouth on one of them, sucking at his impressive-sized cock, as he pulls at her red hair with his fist to plunge his shaft as deeply into her throat as she's able to manage. The other man standing on the opposite side, uses her hand to leisurely stroke his cock to give him the pleasure he seeks.

But as the two women take and give from their male counterparts, they also give the same pleasure to each other. The red-haired goddess is seated on Cleo's face, unashamedly rubbing her pussy on her lips, while using her free hand to play and pinch Cleo's breast and nipple.

It's only when the red-haired woman releases the cock in her mouth long enough to let out a loud moan that I get a clear view of her face. My eyes widen even further when I realize that the second woman is Anya—*my Anya.*

It would be awkward enough walking in on anyone having sex, but for it to happen with one of my dearest friends… well… embarrassment seems too tame a word to describe what I'm feeling.

This… isn't sex—it's a damn orgy.

What else would you call it when there are six people involved?

Unfortunately, even though my mind says that I should feel distaste or even disgust by the event taking place, my body isn't in agreement. The sounds and scent of sex reach us even from where we are hiding, making me swallow dryly as my skin begins to itch when my eyes refuse to look away.

The two women moan, elated, anytime one of the men shouts out obscenities at them. It's almost as if they get off on the verbal abuse as much as they do with the carnal pleasures their bodies are offering.

My heart beats so loudly, I fear it might carve a hole out of my chest.

My lower belly flutters with an energy that's all-consuming.

But instead of running away like I should and leaving them to their private moment, I just stand there, completely captivated by the erotic scene.

I hold my breath when the handsome stranger Anya had been pleasuring with her mouth releases his cock from her hold with a loud pop. Without missing a beat, as if they all had this previously choreographed, Anya redirects her attention and mouth to her left on the man she had been fondling with her hand. The loud ringing noises in my eardrums increase as my eyes are glued on the stranger whose cock keeps hitting away at his stomach with each step he takes, strolling to where his other two friends are connected so intimately with Cleo.

It's only when I realize what he's about to do that I react.

"Oh, the gods! Stop him, Teo! He's going to rip her apart!" I whisper-yell frantically.

But instead of helping me, Teo covers my mouth with his hand and pins my arms behind my back. I wrestle to get free but he's just too strong, preventing me from rescuing Cleo like I want to.

"Shh, kitten. Watch and learn," he rasps seductively, sending an unsolicited shiver down my spine.

Unable to move, I'm forced to watch this horror show unveil.

Since we're too far away, I'm unable to hear what the man says to Cleo as he aims his mushroom head to her center where she is already being penetrated by another. Ever so slowly, he uses her juices to slide into her pussy. And as she stretches to accommodate both girths simultaneously, he takes advantage of learning his friend's tempo to alternate with. All the while, the faceless stranger who is fucking her ass never lets up once.

Oh, the gods.

She must be in so much pain.

I can't watch.

Cleo lets go of a loud wail when all men are in sync with her own rhythm and then surprises me when she belts out and orders for the three of them to fuck her even harder. They do as she commands, sweat glistening over their tanned skin, as the three men give her their all just like she expects of them.

"My Cleo always did like a good spit roasting," Teo whispers in my ear, the tip of his nose rubbing against the sensitive sliver of skin behind my ear.

"They're hurting her," I mumble through his fingers.

"Does she look like she's hurting, kitten?" he asks, his breath on my skin doing very little to cool it down.

Again, I swallow, unable to give him a response.

It's all so lewd.

Obscene and dirty.

I didn't even know a woman's body could satisfy that many lovers, let alone take pleasure in doing so.

With each cry and loud moan Cleo lets out, the more confused and hotter I become. It takes inhuman effort on my part not to rub my thighs together or lean my ass toward what I'm sure is Teo's own arousal behind me.

When Cleo comes on an ear-piercing wail, it's almost a mercy for me.

Yet, Teo keeps me gagged and bound so I don't miss a second of this hell.

Cleo's body shivers with the orgasm that just ripped her into pieces, her lovers quickly following her over the precipice. Anya lets go of the cock she has been sucking all this time to let out a deafening cry of ecstasy, Cleo having tipped her over the edge with just her tongue. Spurts of cum land on Anya's face from the man standing beside her, stroking his cock to achieve his own release.

Cleo then pushes the men who have been pinning her to the bed and gets up on shaky knees to walk over to Anya. She cups Anya's face in her hands, cleaning the cum on her eyes, cheeks, and forehead with her tongue. After she's made sure there isn't a drop left on Anya's pretty face, Cleo kisses her so passionately that Anya's own knees start to buckle. After they break the long kiss, Cleo lets go of Anya's cheeks and the two just stare into each other's eyes as if they are the only two people in existence.

And then… they start laughing.

A laugh filled with joy and wonder.

A laugh that says proudly that what they just did, was for them and them alone.

They continue to giggle away while their loving gaze never wavers from the other.

"She loves her," Teo says from behind me, his heavy breath no longer touching my fevered skin.

It's only now that I realize that in my distraction of watching the girls together, he must have released my mouth and arms from his hold.

"Who does?" I ask after I've spun around to face him.

"My Cleo," he explains, pointing to his chest, "loves your Anya," he ends, pointing a finger to mine.

"You're seeing things," I quip, slapping his hand away.

Anya would have told me.

Wouldn't she?

I turn my attention back to the scene of the crime, only to see the four men starting to get dressed, completely ignored by the two women who continue to kiss and grope each other, almost as if the men were no longer there, having served their purpose.

"Let's go, kitten," Teo suggests, placing his hand on the small of my back. "When Cleo gets this worked up, it can take hours before she's had her fill."

"I never thought something like that could even be possible," I whisper honestly, astounded by what I just witnessed as Teo ushers me along and leads me away from the pool area.

"What? Cleo having sex with five people? That was nothing. I once saw her with double that amount." He laughs like this is an everyday experience for him.

"And you're okay with that?" I question, baffled at his nonchalance.

"Why wouldn't I be?" he retorts puzzled.

"Well... I thought you and her... had an understanding."

Teo halts to a dead stop and turns to me.

"And what type of understanding were you under the assumption we had?"

Oh, the gods!

Is he really going to make me say it?

"Don't be shy with your words when we just watched a bunch of strangers fuck our best friends," he accuses mockingly. "Because that is the only understanding Cleo and I have. We are friends. She is the only true friend I have."

I bite down hard on my inner cheek with how furious he's staring at me right now.

"Don't. Don't do that," he orders, grabbing my chin. "There is no room for shame here."

I relax my jaw and he immediately pulls his hand away from me

"I see you still don't understand us." He shakes his head disappointingly. "Shame is not a word we use in Nas Laed. It's too fucking constricting. Shame is a made-up word created by men who fear women's true power," he begins to explain with the same hard edge to his voice. "And Cleo is a perfect example of a free southern woman who knows her power. Which means she owns her sexuality and uses it any way she sees fit. She doesn't need a man to tell her what feels good or what is appropriate for her to enjoy. She takes her pleasure whenever, and however she wants. So even if Cleo and I had some form of arrangement, as you so put it, Cleo would still be Cleo. A free woman to make her own choices and decisions when it comes to her body, or her life in general. I would have no say on the matter as a lover or as a friend. We don't judge the people we love here. Nor do we warden them." He then takes a beat to catch his breath while still staring me down. "You still don't know what it means to be genuinely free, do you?" he questions, irked, even after delivering such a passionate rant.

"I thought I did. Now, I'm not so sure," I answer truthfully.

Maybe I've always been trapped in an ice-sculpted cage of my own making, that freedom like the one he just described so ardently, feels like an impossibility to me.

Too out of my reach to grasp.

"Well, if you ever really want to find out, come find me. Until then, keep your small-minded judgments and assumptions to yourself. They are of no use here."

And just like that, he turns his back to me and walks away.

Chapter 37
Teodoro

There is a soft knock on my door, but I don't lift my head to see who it is.

Such manners can only come from one person.

"I'm busy," I announce as I try to concentrate on the numbers of this month's harvest.

"You didn't come to break your fast with us this morning so I thought you might be hungry and brought you some fruit," Katrina says, invading my safe space with her presence.

"Like I said, I'm busy. Food can wait," I retort, head still bowed down over my ledgers.

"Hmm, I see," she says, placing the bowl of food at the corner of my desk.

But instead of leaving, she just stands there watching over me. The weight of her stare makes it impossible to concentrate.

I push the scrolls of endless numbers away and lean back in my chair.

"It seems the north has trouble in understanding simple terms like I'm busy too. Please say what's on your mind so that I can get back to work."

"You're still cross with me," she mutters, while nervously shifting her weight from one foot to another.

"Whatever gave you that idea?" I ask sarcastically while maintaining my cold demeanor intact.

The queen of the north isn't the only one who knows how to decrease the temperature in a room.

"You are still mad at me." She thins her lips despondently.

I cross my arms over my chest and sneer.

"You're the queen. What reason could I, a mere vassal, ever have to be upset with his queen?"

"Stop it, Teo. I know that you're angry, and with good reason. I insulted you and your friend. You don't have to be a jerk about it."

"If this is your way of apologizing, then I don't accept. Now please, Your Highness, I have much work to do and little time to console your frail ego."

Her eyes widen in outrage at my response, but I don't really give a fuck.

It still stings the way she just assumed that me and Cleo were involved when I have spent the last couple of weeks doing everything in my power to win her over. For her to think that I was in a relationship with someone and would still pursue her is fucking insulting.

She's bound to Levi and that doesn't stop you.

My nostrils flare at the thought but I quickly push it away.

Her thinking Cleo and I were together isn't the only reason why I'm upset.

Katrina has been in Nas Laed long enough to see that we don't play by the same rules as the other kingdoms do. I thought she understood that. I thought she accepted it.

But it looks like I was wrong.

And if she's unable to accept my people's beliefs and ways of being, then how could I ever expect her to accept me?

There is a long silence between us before I pull my gaze off hers and back to my ledgers.

Unfortunately for me, Katrina can't seem to take the hint, and proceeds to walk over to where I'm sitting.

"You were right," she announces, leaning against my desk.

"I'm right about a great number of things, Your Highness. You're going to have to be more precise than that."

She lets out a soft giggle, making my insides turn to mush.

"You were right about Cleo and Anya. There is something there between them."

"I would have assumed you watching them fuck would have been sufficient for you to realize that."

"Do you have to be so crude?" she balks.

"Do you have to be such a prude?" I snap back, lifting my head just enough to look at her face.

The corner of her lips curl in aggravation, but she doesn't offer one of her witty replies.

But since she's not moving an inch to leave either, I cross my arms over my chest and lean back in my seat.

"Okay, I'll bite. How do you know the girls are together, aside from the obvious."

"I did what any normal person does when they have doubts. I went directly to Anya last night and asked her."

"And her response?"

Katrina's nose scrunches.

"To be fair, I'm not sure she even knows what is really happening between them. But the way her eyes sparkled at the mere mention of Cleo, tells me she's smitten."

"Smitten and in love are two very different things," I mutter, starting to get worried for my friend. Cleo isn't just smitten. She's head over heels in love with the red-haired vixen. This doesn't bode well for Cleo if the only feeling Anya has for her is infatuation.

"They've just met each other, Teo. It's perfectly normal for Anya to have her reservations. Especially because… well, you know."

"Because Cleo is a woman," I finish her sentence for her.

"Yes." She nods. "Falling in love with a person of the same sex isn't something that happens where we are from."

I scoff at that.

"It happens plenty. The only difference is that the north does things behind closed doors where no one can judge them for it. We express our true feelings out in the open. As it should be."

"Yes. I'm starting to see that," she retorts on a long-winded sigh. "Our two kingdoms could not be more opposite to one another if they tried. It has me a bit confused as to who is right and who is wrong."

"Why does there have to be right or wrong?" I ask, my tone losing its hard edge from when she walked in the room. "Haven't you figured that out yet? There is nothing wrong with following your heart. No matter where it might lead you."

She stares at me for the longest time, and now I'm the one who is shifting uncomfortably in my seat.

"What?" I blurt out. "Why are you looking at me like that?"

"Because." She smiles. "When I look at you, I can still see the trace of the boy who was one of my dearest friends. And yet, he's grown to be this exceptional man, and I missed it."

"Friends? Is that what we were?" I smirk, licking my lips when her cheeks turn pink. "If my memory is correct, then we were much more than just friends. Friends aren't each other's first kiss."

Friends don't propose at the age of fifteen.

Friends don't obsess over the other every waking moment of their lives.

"We were friends, Teo. All four of us were," she rebukes, leaning away from my desk to walk over to one of the open windows in the room. She stares into the distance, and I wonder if she's also reminiscing about the night we shared our first kiss.

"Fine. You want to pretend that's all we were, then I will oblige you with that delusion. Just so you know, my memory is crystal clear."

There is a ghost of a smile playing on her lips that has my heart daring to hope again.

"You've made new friends, though. Cleo being one of them. You never mentioned her when you came to Tarnow to visit," she says, her way of steering the conversation to safer territories.

"That's because I hadn't met her yet," I reply, turning my chair to the side so that I have a perfect view of her silhouette.

"How did you meet?" she asks, intrigued.

"After yesterday, I'm not sure you're ready to know."

She turns to her side to face me, resolve stitched to her stunning features.

"I want to know."

"Do you?" I laugh. "If that's true, then take a seat. I don't want to overwhelm your sensitivities to the point you faint on me."

"I think I can handle whatever you tell me," she rebukes with a no-nonsense tone.

"Are you sure about that? Okay. Then I'll tell you. At seventeen, I met Cleo when she was working at a pleasure house."

I try not to laugh when her gray gaze turns to two wide liquid pools of silver.

"You mean a brothel?"

I nod.

"I... uh... was she the owner's daughter?"

"No. Guess again."

"A servant?"

"Oh, my Cleo loved to serve, but no, she wasn't the help. Her talents lead... elsewhere."

"Oh." Katrina swallows hard. "I see."

"Shall I proceed with the tale, or have you had enough?"

Her gaze slices to me, and I can't help but snicker.

"Very well. So, as I was saying," I start, before getting up from my seat, so I can lean at the corner edge of my desk just so I don't miss even one of her expressions. "At the time, I was going through something."

"Going through what?" she interrupts curiously.

"Let's just say that I had a lapse of judgment that made me spiral into someone unrecognizable even to myself. I was inflicted by all those pesky emotions you northerners love so much. Shame, guilt, remorse, all of it weighed on my soul, but it was the feeling of heartbreak and utter loneliness that really did a number on me. I saw all the best physicians in the kingdom and none of them could erase the torment I was under. None of them knew how to help me. It took a whore in a whorehouse to show me the way to my salvation."

"Cleo," she mutters under her breath.

"Yes, Cleo. From the moment I saw her, I knew she was special. I just never realized what a significant role she would play in my life. However, it took that one encounter for me to seek her out again the next day, curiosity being the ruling force behind my decision."

Katrina chews on her bottom lip, walking over to me so she can lean against the desk beside me.

"So she was your lover," she says, no judgment to her tone at all.

"Not at first." I shake my head. "At first all I did was watch. Watch her as she commanded her lovers to do her bidding. And every night I went back, the more entranced I became with the power she ruled over them. I saw grown men weep in euphoria. Women laugh after being unshackled from their personal demons. What Cleo offered wasn't just sex. It was catharsis. Something I unknowingly had been searching for and desperately needed. So one night, I asked her if she would be willing to quit her position at the pleasure house and move into my palace. I needed to have her sole focus on me to cast away all the ghosts that tormented me so, and for that to happen, I had to be her only client."

"So she took you on?" Katrina asks, completely wrapped up in the story.

"Have you met Cleo?" I chuckle. "Not only did she laugh in my face, but told me to get lost and never show up at her doorstep again."

"But you didn't take no for an answer." Kat smiles beside me.

"Do I ever?" I wink at her, causing the blush on her cheeks to darken. "No, I refused to give up. I had seen with my very eyes what she could do, and I needed her expertise, more than I needed my next breath. So every night for a full month, there I was, offering her the same deal as the night before. I'm not sure if Cleo finally said yes because she was intrigued, or because she just wanted me out of her hair and this was the only way to go about it." I chuckle. "I brought her home, and that same night we went to work."

"Did it work?"

"I'll be honest. It took us a while to figure out which ones of her methods would work best on me. But once we figured it out, then yes, kitten. It worked wonders. Cleo saved me from myself. No matter how much gold and luxuries I gift her, I will never be able to repay the debt I owe Cleo. Never," I explain, recalling all those feelings Cleo was able to expunge from me.

When Katrina goes oddly quiet, I cover her hand with mine on the desk and give it a light squeeze.

"Did you love her?" she asks, her gaze lowered to our feet, unable to look me in the eye.

"I have only loved one woman my entire life and I have yet to stop. No, kitten. I did not love her."

She tilts her head upward and unnamed emotions coat the beautiful shade in her eyes.

"Did she love you?" she asks, her voice barely above a whisper.

"I believe the love we have for each other is mutual and strictly platonic. She's my family and I am hers."

Katrina nods as if understanding what I mean by that, but I see it in her eyes that there is something else weighing on her mind.

"Ask me."

Her brows pinch together in hesitation and it's only when I squeeze her hand again that she speaks her mind.

"I'm trying to wrap my head around everything you just said, but one thing still confuses me. You said that it took you both a while to figure out what type of methods worked on you. But didn't Cleo just offer sex? What possible methods could sex even have?"

"It wasn't just sex. There were plenty of times that fucking wasn't even on the menu. That didn't mean that they were any less effective. In fact, most of the things we did together that didn't involve intercourse were the ones I got the most benefit from."

When Kat still looks confused, I see a door opening up for me.

One that I thought was locked.

"You'd have to see it for yourself to fully understand. All I can tell you is that for a crowned prince of the south to have been riddled with such constricting emotions, was of no use to my kingdom. Cleo helped me shed that burden in order for me to once again be free. And I would gladly pay any ransom to ensure I'd never lose my freedom again."

I watch Katrina attentively as she takes it all in. Every honest morsel of it and the ending hook I dangled in front of her. So, when she opens her mouth to say the two words I was yearning to hear, I school my features to not let on how ecstatic I am that she took the bait.

"Show me."

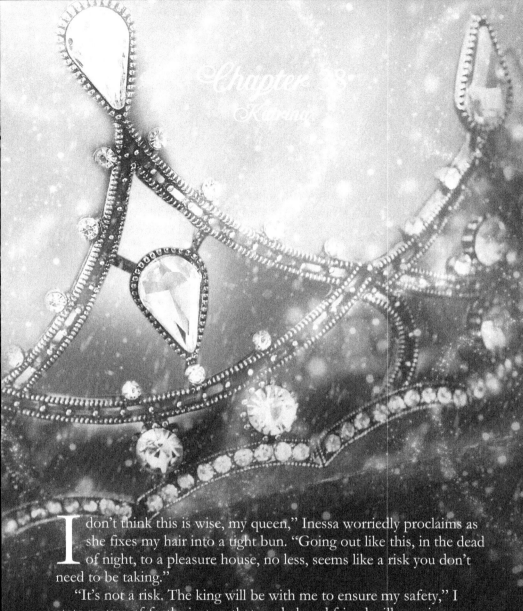

I don't think this is wise, my queen," Inessa worriedly proclaims as she fixes my hair into a tight bun. "Going out like this, in the dead of night, to a pleasure house, no less, seems like a risk you don't need to be taking."

"It's not a risk. The king will be with me to ensure my safety," I state matter-of-factly, just so that my beloved friend will remain clueless as to the nerves that are currently wrecking through my entire body.

"I think what Inessa is trying to say is that being alone with the king is a risk in itself," Anya explains with a playful hint to her tone as she continues sewing the black cape I requested to wear tonight.

"Fine." Inessa rolls her eyes. "That is exactly what I mean. The king doesn't inspire confidence. He's a slippery devil, that one."

"And if you two are going to go to a whorehouse, he's bound to get a whole lot slippier," Anya jokes before cutting the string with her teeth.

"Enough out of you," Inessa reprimands. "Those crude jokes are unbecoming to a lady. I blame your friend Cleo for being such a bad influence on you."

Anya's playful expression falls flat to the floor.

"I don't think Cleo is a bad influence on Anya," I defend my sensitive friend. "She's showing Anya how to tap into her own power."

"Power?" Inessa scoffs. "We are women, Your Highness. What power can we hold in a world ruled by men?"

"I say plenty. But then again, I'm the only queen of all of Aikyam, who all men have sworn their allegiance to, so what would I know on the matter?" I raise my brows at her.

"I'm sorry if I have insulted you, Your Highness, but not all of us can say the same. We can't rely on a crown to keep us safe," Inessa rebukes, never one to mix words. "It's all fine and well, Anya's behavior here in the south where cruder things are said, but once we return home, people will not be as understanding if they catch her saying such things."

My shoulders slump at how true her words are.

Here, Anya has managed to find happiness in her free-spirited ways.

But once we return home, she will have to bite her tongue or risk prosecution.

"Then all the more reason for me to go out into the city tonight and experience all the south has to offer. If I want to be a queen who will introduce change to my kingdom, one that ensures all people, of every walk of life, are treated equally and fairly, then what better place to learn from than Nas Laed? Here there is no gender bias or inequality of any kind. I say we have much to learn from the south, and I'm a willing pupil that yearns to be taught."

Inessa takes in my words, but still seems unconvinced.

"Speak, Inessa, since I know you're dying to," I blurt out.

"A person would have to be blind not to see how enamored you are with this… city. However, I need you to have a clear mind when making any decision. Yes, Nas Laed does seem to favor a freedom that we women aren't accustomed to, but I don't think that is the case in the entire realm. You were locked to your room in Braaka but Anya and I did venture out. And what we witnessed there could not be more opposite to what we found here."

I look to Anya for confirmation and am troubled when she nods.

"Inessa is right, Kat. There was no happiness in Braaka, only famine."

Inessa flings her arms up in the air as if finally vindicated.

"But there is no such lack here," I insist, deeply troubled by what they are insinuating.

"No. Here we are showered with abundance in all its forms. Freedom, food, and luxury. But while we devour all the sweet gifts Nas Laed has to offer, his kingdom starves. Like I said, Your Highness, King Teodoro is a slippery fellow. Take great care around him."

As if the villain himself heard his name being uttered, Teo knocks on my door and lets himself in.

"Are you ready, kitten? The night awaits," he says, all smiles.

Inessa gives me a knowing look while Anya hands me the finished black cape, a mist of sadness orbiting around her hourglass frame.

I put on the cape and pull the hood over my head, and tell Teo to lead the way. He's also wearing a similar-looking dark robe, one that ensures his face is covered.

"We'll ride on horseback to the city's gates but then we must walk the rest of the way there so as to not draw attention to us," he says when we step outside the palace and find two horses waiting for us.

I have this urgent need to ask him about what my handmaidens had discussed with me previously, but as he excitedly lifts me up to straddle my horse, I bite my tongue, knowing that now isn't the right time to bring up such politics.

As he planned, we ride to the city and leave our horses at the gate, walking down the busy streets to one of Nas Laed's most beloved brothels. I pull on my cape's hood to keep my hair covered as we pass a never-ending crowd.

"I didn't realize the city would be so alive at this late hour," I all but yell at him as I rush to keep to his hurried pace.

"Nas Laed never sleeps, kitten. Never," he says proudly, grabbing my hand so I don't get lost amongst the crowd.

"I'm starting to see that."

"Come. We're not too far now," Teo informs me with an eager smile.

Inessa's words of caution are still at the forefront of my mind, but they fade away when Teo stops at a red door, a lion's head on the handle. Teo doesn't waste any time pulling it, banging at it three times.

"Now what?" I ask impatiently.

"Now, we wait."

"Well, that sounds vague and ominous," I mutter under my breath sarcastically.

But just as I say the words, the red door flies open halfway, a pretty brunette with large brown eyes and nothing else under its arch. Her stunning eyes scan us up and down, and it's only when Teo flips his hood back and shows his face that she smiles and opens the door fully to let us in.

"Are you here to watch or…" she starts as her eyes linger at me once I've also pulled down my own hood. "Entertain?"

"Too early to tell." Teo winks at her, entwining his fingers with mine and pulling me into the pleasure den.

My heart is lodged in my throat as Teo walks his way around the lavish home, knowing exactly which hall leads to what.

"Let's start soft, shall we?" he whispers softly, pulling the pin Inessa dug into my hair to make it fall down my shoulders. "There. Much better. Come, kitten. We have so much to see and so little time."

I give him a curt nod, unable to form words as I'm too out of my depth to summon any.

I don't know what I expected, in all honesty.

Maybe poor lighting so people could live out their desires in the dark.

But the reality is the complete contrast of anything my imagination could have come up with. The home is bright, spacious and airy, a square open courtyard at the heart of it. Like the woman who greeted us, most of the people inside have discarded all their clothing, preferring to frolic around in the nude. People are drinking, eating, and laughing as they converse with each other in the courtyard, no hint of sexual tension at all in the air, save for their lack of clothing. It all looks so civilized that if I closed my eyes, I would think I was at some feast or celebration back in Tarnow.

"Are you ready?" Teo asks, pulling me away from the courtyard.

"Ready?" I parrot, not really understanding what he means.

"You came to learn, right? Well, there isn't much learning to be done out here. The fun is up there," he says, pointing to a staircase that leads to the second-floor balcony.

My throat is parched, and my chest feels like it's about to cave in on itself.

Long gone is the strong, fearless Winter Queen my sweet Salome gushed about.

I feel so inapt here. Like somehow someone will realize that I'm an imposter in the land of freedom and wonder and end up pointing a finger at me, ordering me to leave since it's clear I don't belong here.

Oh, gods be with me.

Lend me your ear and fortify my will with the northern winds from home.

Add eastern steel to my resolve and let me taste what true power feels like.

As if the gods themselves heard my prayer, a cold breeze runs all throughout the courtyard and kisses my cheeks. With my spine now ramrod straight, and my head held high as if my crown was placed on top of it, I let Teo lead me up the stairs, knowing that after I do this, I will never be the same woman again.

Once we step into the empty balcony, Teo points to the various closed doors on display and tells me to pick one. Not wanting my sudden bravery to waver, I pick the one in front of me.

"Nice and slow it is," Teo states with a conspiring smile before wrapping his hand on the doorknob and opening it.

I stay rooted to my spot as I look inside and see a similar scene like the one I witnessed yesterday between Anya and Cleo. Various men and women of every color, shape, and size, are currently busy with giving their various partners, no matter the gender, pleasure in any form they can think of. While yesterday there were only six people to watch, here, in this room, there are dozens. Some are laid on velvet pillows on the floor, or on large lounge chairs, while others prefer to stand as they bend their lovers over any hard surface they can find.

Teo pulls me inside and we begin to walk amongst the various couples—or whatever is the correct terminology to describe a slew of people screwing each other's brains out at the same time—and I realize that, like me, there are others just standing or sitting off to the side and watching. We stroll amongst the crowd of glistening limbs and body parts all wrapped up around each other. Women moan and wail as they find their release, while the men grunt and growl theirs. It's all so overwhelming how each one trusts that the other won't push further than the limits they are comfortable with. It's almost as if they are all in tune with each other's needs and are here to satisfy each one.

It's not the sex that gets me.

It's the blinding trust and faith that really makes an impression.

"Do you want to see more?" Teo asks, and this time I'm completely unafraid, eager for him to take me wherever he sees fit.

Because just like with the people here, I trust that Teo will not show me anything outside my comfort zone.

It's when he throws me a boyish smile, one that brings back all the memories we shared in our youth, that I realize that showing me this is his way of telling me that he trusts me too. That knowledge has my heart racing more than watching strangers have sex ever could.

Teo takes me back outside to the balcony and walks down the small corridor leading to the next door. Inside, I see men crawl on their hands and knees just for the pleasure of being humiliated by their lover. I watch women spit and slap their lovers, calling them every name known to mankind, only for their lovers to smile lovingly at them, thanking them for their abuse.

As we continue to open door after door, visiting room after room, I finally come to understand that arousal can be coaxed by a myriad of things and scenarios. I've watched men come from the sight of a woman's foot alone. I've watched women climax just by having her lover lick food off her body. Anything and everything can be used for sexual gratification; it all comes down to the person's likes and wants. I've seen couples reach nirvana as they used numerous objects that looked like a man's penis on each other. I've seen so much and yet there is a part of me that starts to wonder where I fit in.

Which room would serve me best?

"One more," Teo says once we find ourselves back on the balcony. He's nervous.

He's been such a calm force beside me all night, but now he's nervous.

"This is the one, isn't it? The room you met Cleo in," I stammer, suddenly feeling extremely anxious with how curious I am to see inside.

He nods sheepishly.

I squeeze his hand in mine and offer him a soft smile.

"Whatever it is, it's a part of who you are. And I want to see it."

"Be careful what you wish for, kitten," he replies, but grabs the doorknob just the same. I watch him take a deep breath, before turning the knob.

And what I find feels like coming home.

O n bated breath, I step inside the room filled with sounds of
pain and lust.

Places like this shouldn't exist out in the open like this.

They should be kept in the dark, like some secret only one person
knows about.

And yet, here we are.

Teo and I walk amongst the sinners that need a little pain to
experience an ounce of pleasure.

Right at the front of the room, women are gagged and bound as
their lovers take control of their bodies as they see fit. Some even have
blindfolds on, unaware of who is punishing them, always wondering if
it's the person they envision in their minds or some stranger who is
taking liberties with their bodies.

My own skin begins to heat as I watch these same women smile around their gags, as their lovers lick up the juices dripping down their legs while at the same time hitting them hard with a wooden paddle.

My core clenches with the words that flutter in the air surrounded by the infliction of pain.

Good girl.

That's my beautiful girl.

Take it, baby.

Look how good you take it.

Shut the fuck up and be a good girl and put Daddy's cock in your mouth.

Who's your master, baby?

Who owns you?

Good girl.

All of it is ridiculously obscene and highly erotic.

Every word that is uttered in this room is filthy and profane, and yet, it's all music to my ears.

This room is also more spacious than the others we've been in, and as we stroll further inside, it's understandable why that is. There are men and women tied up by ropes and chains to the walls and from the ceilings, each one with their own personal master to educate them on the ways of pain and pleasure.

"Cleo did this to you?" I ask, unable to pry my gaze away from the sight before me.

"She did," Teo confirms, his sight fixed on my face. "And then she taught me how to do it to her. It's like I told you this morning. When Cleo and I met, I was in a very dark place in my life, one ruled by misery and suffering."

"One could say this is a form of punishment too," I counter, intrigued with his own infatuation for pain.

"No. This is an escape. Cleo offered me a way out of the real suffering I had been in, one that I was too willing to grab hold of. She saved me," he explains passionately, as if he's reliving the first day he walked through the same door we did all over again.

"You found salvation in a place most consider a damnation to the soul."

"I did. And by that look on your face, I can tell you're just as curious about it as I was at the time. Aren't you, kitten?" he asks, my skin starting to tingle at the way his voice turned deep and throaty all of a sudden.

I nod, unable to mutter the word yes out loud.

"Would you like to try?"

I swallow the lump in my throat at his invitation.

"With… you?" I stutter, licking my dry lips.

"I would much prefer it to be with me, but you're a free woman, kitten. And like I keep reminding you, freedom comes with knowing how to wield your power any way you see fit. If there is someone else here that you would prefer to practice with, then that is your prerogative. Not mine."

"So if I want him," I point to a man who is currently leaving bite marks all over his lover's body, "all I have to do is walk over to him and you'd allow it?" I ask, testing him.

I need to be sure that this is not just one of Teo's games and that he's speaking from the heart.

"Free women don't need permission, Kat. From anyone," he says softly, but then leans in until we are but a hair's breadth away from each other, his expression deadly. "But choose me instead and that all changes when we start playing. Then you'll have to beg for my consent to even breathe."

My pussy clenches the emptiness inside it with just the way his voice dropped to a lethal octave. It's only when Teo takes a step back that I pull in oxygen to my lungs.

I haven't even accepted his offer and already my body is doing what he wants.

"I'm not having sex with you," I blurt out nervously.

"That's fine." He smiles slyly.

"I'm serious. I'm not," I say forcefully so he knows that I mean business.

"Like I said, whatever you want."

I scrutinize his face to see if he's lying or not, but with Teo, I never know.

"You can trust me," he adds, and to this I laugh. "Fine, don't trust me, but at least trust that I have enough experience to do this correctly and not hurt you. If you want, we can even have a safe word."

"What's a safe word?"

"It's a word that you pick that means stop," he explains, only adding to my confusion.

"That makes no sense. Why don't I just yell stop if I want you to stop?"

"Because there will be moments when it gets so intense that you'll yell out stop, but not really mean it."

"I always say what I mean."

"Trust me, kitten. Before the night is through, you'll yell much more than just stop. Best have a safe word just in case. It should be something simple and yet something that you don't use every day. Something you will remember easily, but not something that would come out in the throes of passion,"

"Fine. My safe word could be Tarnow. Does that work you?"

"As long as it works for you, then it's fine by me. Tarnow it is." He smiles like the cat who ate the canary.

Then it all hits me.

I didn't exactly say yes to his offer, but somehow have conceded to it anyway.

But that's not all that suddenly begins to weigh down on me. It's the fact that I'm about to do this in front of a room filled with strangers.

Am I that brave?

It takes all but two seconds to know that I'm not, nor will I ever be.

Exhibitionism apparently is not something I'm into. But I guess this place was built for that very purpose. To know what turns you on and what does not. Which means there must be some private rooms for those who prefer a more private setting.

I'm about to ask Teo as much when he pulls at our joint hands and starts leading me out of the room of sin.

"Where are we going?" I question him breathlessly as he dashes through the room in the direction to its exit.

"Where we can have a little more privacy, kitten. That's where."

Unable to break free from his hold, I let Teo lead the way until we are once again on the balcony. At first I think he's just going to find another door to open, but am surprised when we walk back down the staircase that leads to the courtyard. I try not to smile when I see a few familiar faces from upstairs, now drinking wine and talking animatedly with each other. I especially keep my grin in check when Teo bumps into one of the men that got off by acting like a dog who needed to be walked around on a leash.

To each their own, I guess.

After passing the courtyard and going back inside the house, Teo stops the same woman who opened the door for us earlier and whispers in her ear.

"I had a feeling you would be entertaining tonight, Your Majesty, so I saved you the perfect room for your endeavors."

She tilts her head for us to follow, me squeezing Teo's hand so he doesn't leave me behind.

"Shall I call someone to watch over you? Your friend seems like a novice," the naked brunette says, eyes lingering on me a little too long. "If Your Majesty prefers, I can take her place and she can watch. To learn," she adds the last bit as an afterthought.

"There will be no need for supervision or your assistance tonight, Jasmine. She's all I need," Teo retorts with a bit of a bite.

"Of course, Your Majesty," Jasmine says, doing a pitiful excuse for a curtsy before leaving us.

"Are you sure you wouldn't prefer Jasmine's company?" I ask, my own tone cold and snarky.

"This is all for you, kitten. No one else." He smiles. "Now are you ready to have some fun?"

Fun and pain shouldn't be synonymous, but in our case, it most certainly is.

I nod, biting the corner of my lip to keep the grin I want to let out at bay.

But when Teo opens the door to the dim room in front of us, all those foolish giddy thoughts fly out the window.

Right at its center is a table shaped like an X. There are ropes at the ends of each wooden board, and so many objects hanging around the walls that I get dizzy just looking at them. Between paddles and whips, the walls possess a playground of never-ending pain.

"If you want to leave, no one will judge you for it. Remember that shame is illusionary and therefore has no place here," Teo says beside me as I stand mute, taking the room in.

Sensing that I'm not yet ready to move, he walks in without me and stares at the walls to find the perfect object that will end up being my undoing. I shut my eyes when I see him pick up a black flogger with a black leather handle and equally black tresses. Just looking at it is intimidating.

But also exciting.

Slowly, I make my way to the odd-shaped table and run my fingers through the smooth, oak wood.

"I will be tied down here," I state more than ask.

"You will," Teo confirms.

"You'll tie me with these ropes," I add, fiddling with the coarse and scratchy material that is bound to leave a mark.

"Yes, again."

"And you'll use that," I point to the flogger in his hands, "on my body."

"Naked body," he corrects.

"Is there anything else that I might have left out that I don't know about?"

"You'll do it all while blindfolded," Teo says, surprising me.

"Blindfolded? Why?"

"Because that way you will be more in tune with your other senses. Not only that, but when you're deprived of sight, something happens inside you. Your inhibitions subside, and the real you emerges," he explains as he places the flogger on a nearby table.

"I am the real me," I assure him.

"You have no idea who you are, kitten. But after tonight, I promise you that you will."

"Is that what happened to you?" I ask, both because I'm trying to buy some time and also because I'm genuinely interested in knowing if he did something like this.

But instead of answering me, he takes off his cape and drops it to the floor and then proceeds to take off his shirt. I open my mouth to remind him that I'm the only one who should get undressed, when he stuns me silent by turning his back to me. There are a million little scars. Some that look like they were made with an actual whip.

I walk toward him and lightly brush the tips of my fingers over each mark.

"Cleo did this to you? And you let her?"

"Like I said, I was in a very dark place back then. These marks on my skin have nothing on the scars that are permanently carved into my soul."

He then pulls away from my touch and turns to face me, cupping my cheeks in his hands.

"I will not mark you like this, but for a few days you will be sore and bruised. There may be a few burn marks on your wrists and ankles too. Some light cuts on your breasts. I'm telling you this because I want you to consent to it still after knowing what your body is about to endure. What I'm about to do is not for the weak of heart. It is for warriors. Soldiers. And winter queens."

I chew on his words and go through every little detail and imagine myself wearing such badges of honor.

"I want this," I confess in a grave tone and proceed to untie my cape from my neck.

Teo turns his back to me once more, giving me my privacy to undress.

Not that it will make much of a difference.

He's going to see me naked the minute he turns around.

I drape off the summer dress and kick it to where Teo's clothes are on the floor.

"You can turn around now."

Teo does as instructed but he keeps his eyes lowered instead of looking at my naked frame.

"Lie on the table," he instructs with that low timbre voice that makes my heart palpitate.

I do as he commands and lie on the table. Sprawled out like this, I feel more vulnerable than I ever have been in my life. My cheeks feel flushed as I feel a heat pool in my lower belly.

But then I remember his advice about how we feel less inhibited when we are blindfolded, so I close my eyes and instantly feel more relaxed not being able to read Teo's face as he starts his preparations.

"I'm going to tie you up now."

I nod, my mouth feeling suddenly drier than the desert we passed to get to this city.

To his credit, Teo doesn't make some offhand comment or joke about my nudity or this peculiar predicament we find ourselves in. In fact, since we entered this house, he's been in total control of his emotions. It's like something has taken over my carefree friend and molded him into someone serious and direct.

"Does this hurt?" he asks, and I feel him tug at the rope that's wrapped around my wrist.

I shake my head.

"It itches a bit, but it doesn't hurt."

"It will," he advises with that same cool and collected tone he's prone to using here. "I'm going to put the blindfold on you now, so if you want to open your eyes, now is the time to do it."

"Are you going to be this authoritarian and domineering the whole time?"

"Yes," he says without missing a beat.

My heart does a double take and my insides begin to quiver.

"Okay," I reply, not really knowing what else to say.

But just as I feel him walk to where my head is at, my eyelids fling open.

"Why are you always telling me what you are about to do? Is that a part of... this?"

He nods.

"It's better that you know beforehand what is about to happen. That way if something pushes beyond your limits, you have enough time to say your safe word. Do you still remember what that is?"

"I doubt I'll forget the name of the place I grew up in."

"I'm going to ask you again. Do you remember your safe word?"

My eyes blink a few times before I'm able to say yes.

"Tarnow. My safe word is Tarnow."

"Good. Then let's begin, shall we?"

And then he puts the blindfold over my eyes, turning everything black as the veil he fastens around my head.

My ears try to pick up all the sounds around me, making a genuine effort to listen to Teo's footsteps. In my mind I imagine him picking up the flogger from the table and walking back to me, eyeing my naked body up and down and committing it to memory.

"I'm going to flog you once so you know what to expect. Do you understand?"

I nod, my anxiety as high as it's ever been.

And then I hear a whoosh followed by the feel of champagne bubbles tapping lightly at my skin just above my stomach.

"That kind of tickles." I laugh, my tense muscles instantly relaxing after seeing that my imagination was far worse than the real thing.

"It does… at first," he says before clearing his throat. "I'm going to do this again, but now I'll aim at your right breast."

"Okay."

When I hear another slice through the air and the tresses hit my sensitive nipple, I arch my back and let out a moan.

"Good, kitten. Just like that," Teo praises. "I'm going to go again, and this time I won't tell you where you'll be hit. And I won't stop either. Soon it will become very intense. I want you to push through it. But if you can't, you always have a way out."

"Safe word. I understand."

Just like he promised, the next time the black tresses hit my body, he doesn't warn me where. I let out a loud gasp when it hits the top edge of my pussy. And again, just like he said he would, he doesn't let up, hitting my other breast, followed by my thighs, then stomach. Every time, Teo finds a new place to assault, leaving me wondering where he's going to hit me next. The horsewhip is louder than its sting, but no less frightening. With the blindfold on me, I'm more aware of the sounds around me, so when I hear that familiar swoosh of the horsehair slice through the air, my body is already expecting its bite on my skin.

But as the minutes pass on, every slash brings with it a more punishing pain. My head begins to feel lightheaded as my flesh starts to complain about the abuse I'm willingly putting it under. More minutes pass, and with each one that does, the sensations become more intense.

Suddenly this game of ours has higher stakes.

Stakes that I'm not sure my body can pay the price for.

I have no idea how much time passes, only that it begins to feel like an eternity.

I'm both aroused and in utter misery, and I have no indication of which sensation is more prominent.

Tears start streaming down my face as I yell at Teo to stop.

Everything is heightened.

Sounds. Smells. Touch.

Everything.

"Stop! Stop! Stop!" I cry out.

"Purr for me, kitten, and I will."

My skin feels like it's burning alive, but it's the way my nipples harden with each bite of the whip that really has my heart drumming madly in my chest. With my legs spread this wide apart, I'm unable to rub my thighs together just to take some of the edge of.

Teo was right.

He knows what he's doing.

Oh, how I wish he didn't.

Because with each slash of the whip, the wetter I become, and my evident arousal begins to infiltrate the air around us.

"Do you remember your safe word?" I hear him ask, but his voice feels like it is coming from underwater—faint and garbled. "Nod, kitten, if you remember."

Safe word?

Safe word?

Tarnow!

Tarnow!

I nod profusely, finally remembering what we had agreed on.

"Do you want to say it now?" he asks, and I feel like he's throwing a trap for me.

If I say it, then all of this will disappear. Yes, my pain will vanish, but so will this fire inside me that craves to be extinguished by some other means.

I shake my head, and I can almost hear Teo smile.

He recommences with his punishment, and this time, I let myself enjoy every sting, every scratch, every little bruise inflicted on my feverish skin.

And it builds and it builds.

This light inside of me that threatens to blind me and everyone in its path.

"Teo!" I cry as if only he can save me from the light splitting me in two.

"Tell me what you want," he orders, that deep, husky voice of his doing nothing to simmer the fire inside of me.

I open my mouth, but no words come out.

I don't know what I want.

All I know is that whatever it is, I need it now.

Slash.

Slash.

Slash.

ARGH!

My back arches from the table, my body shaking so bad that I feel it no longer belongs to me.

"Tell me what you want and I'll give it to you," he continues to say, his calm tone the only thing that is keeping me tethered to the ground.

Slash.

Slash.

Slash.

OH, THE GODS!

"Tell me, kitten. Tell me and all of this can be over."

My brain can no longer comprehend words. My mind is suddenly a blank canvas. The only form of communication that still exists is the slashing sounds in the air and the marks of the whip on my skin. They write their poems on my flesh. Poems that only Teo gets to read.

Slash.

Slash.

Slash.

"I WANT TO COME!"

My breathing comes out in spurts as I wait for his cruel rejection or kind mercy. And when I feel the small cuts of the ends of the horsehair whip, tears begin to stream down the corners of my eyes. I'm about to wave the white flag of surrender and defeat and utter out the last word that I want to spill from my lips. But then my tears are accompanied by an unhinged laugh when I feel Teo's fingers play through my slick folds. It takes me a minute to recognize that I'm the one laughing. But all too soon do those wails of joy morph into wails of ecstasy as Teo finds my hidden pressure point and begins to flick it with the tips of his fingers just as his whip flicks against my sensitive flesh.

The combination of Teo's forbidden touch and the constant slash of his whip pushes me over the edge, and like a shooting star dropping from the night and plunging into the earth, I erupt. All of me convulses as I let the orgasm have its way with me. I give in to it and ride it out, praying that by the end of it, I'm still somewhat recognizable. For I fear that after this, I will never be the same. But just as I climb to its peak, my mind goes completely blank, protecting me from the fall.

And I cry.

And cry.

And cry.

Because up until tonight, I believed that power was just an illusion people said to themselves that they had.

This… this is true power.

To be able to shatter into a million tiny pieces and still feel whole, is the most powerful experience I've ever had. It's the relinquishing of power that ends up giving it back to me and ultimately setting me free.

After the shock of experiencing such a thing begins to fade, I feel Teo hurriedly rush to unknot the binds on my wrists and ankles. I don't move an inch; my body and soul are too eviscerated to move a muscle. When Teo finally has me free, he pulls the blindfold away from my eyes and then picks me up and cradles me in his lap.

"Shh, kitten. It's all over now. Shh, love."

I try to open my eyes, but even the dim lighting in this room is too bright for me.

"Shh, kitten. You did so good, love. So fucking good. I'm so proud of you."

More tears stream down my face at his praise, my heart preening at his words.

I snuggle into his chest, his scent invading my senses and comforting me. It's only when I shift my ass on his lap, that I feel his wet clothing underneath.

Again, I force myself to open my eyes, but all I can accomplish is a small sliver of an opening. Thankfully it's enough to see Teo's lips. The same lips that look so soft right now. My hand lifts of its own accord, as I run my thumb across his bottom lip.

"Teo," I rasp out, my voice still hoarse from all the loud wails I screamed out in the past hour.

"Hmm," he hums as he soothingly runs his fingers through my hair.

"Did you… did you come?"

"Yes, kitten. I did," he replies serenely. "How could I not when you came so fucking beautifully?"

Again, his words feel like butterfly kisses on my skin.

"Teo?"

"Yes, kitten. Tell me what you need," he asks, his voice remaining calm and sure, while I'm still swimming to the shores of my own sanity.

"I need you to kiss me," I hear myself say—no, beg him.

Again, he doesn't even wait to give me a response, leaning in to press a tender kiss to my lips.

When his lips part from mine, I let out a contented sigh and close my eyes, finally giving in to my slumber.

Chapter 40
Teodoro

The past seven nights have been filled with the loveliest music—the melody of my little kitten coming. I'll never tire of the sound she makes when she's reaching her peak toward the heavens.

To many, Nas Laed is paradise on earth.

But to me?

Nothing has me closer to feasting with the gods then watching my love come undone.

Like clockwork, after everyone has gone to bed, she knocks on my door, wearing her black cape, her silent way of telling me she wants to go out and play.

And every night, I oblige her.

I pick up my own dark cloak and entwine my hand in hers, without even uttering a word.

We never talk on our way into the city.

No words are shared as we walk the streets of it either.

It is only when we enter the pleasure house and lock ourselves in our favorite room that we become our true selves and are able to speak our minds freely.

I tell her what a good little kitten she is as I tie her up to a table, a chair, a wall, whatever my mood craves that night. And then after I've picked my poison of choice, I order her to purr for me as I mark her body repeatedly. Her fair porcelain skin turns the prettiest shade of pink and red with each love bite I inflict on her.

And purr, she does.

She wails and thrashes and begs for more until it's too much for her to take, needing the release that only my fingers can provide.

And each time she falls from the heavens back into my arms, she asks me the same questions.

Did you come?

Yes.

Will you kiss me?

Yes.

It's only after I've laid a chaste kiss to her lips that she succumbs to her exhaustion.

And every night, I carry her out of the pleasure house in my arms, a carriage already waiting for us at the door to take us home.

In all the times she's laid bare for me, opened herself up so beautifully to me, I have yet to touch her like I want to.

I have yet to kiss her like I *need*.

But tonight, things are going to be different.

Katrina has gotten a taste of who she truly is.

And now it's time she realizes who I am.

Chapter 41
Katrina

"Where is he?!" I shout out, furious, after I've swung Cleo's chamber's door open so fast that it hits the wall behind it with a loud thud.

"Your Highness!" Anya shrieks as she jumps off Cleo's bed and rushes to cover herself with a bedsheet.

Cleo isn't as shy, wrapping her hands behind her head on the pillow, uncaring that she is nude from the waist up.

"And by *he* you must mean…" she mocks with a sly grin that Teo must have taught her to do.

"You know damn well who I'm referring to. Your king! Where is he?!" I shout, feeling like I'm about to erupt with all the rage that is consuming my bloodstream.

Cleo just shrugs nonchalantly.

"I'm not his keeper, Your Highness. How am I to know where he is?"

I take a step closer to her bed and snarl.

"Don't give me that. You two are like two peas in a pod. If he's not on palace grounds, then you're the only one who knows where he's gone off to."

Cleo stretches her smile before tilting her chin toward one of the many windows that are still currently wide open to let the night breeze inside her room.

"By how the moon is hung up in the sky, I would venture a guess that it's well past midnight. I would have assumed *you'd* be more aware of his comings and goings at this late hour, Your Grace."

My cheeks heat up in both embarrassment and fury at her not-so-subtle insinuation.

Realizing that I won't get any answers here, I spin on my heel and head out the door.

I don't get far though when I hear a nervous Anya call out to my name.

"Kat! Kat!"

I halt my steps while fisting my hands at my sides to keep my temper in check and not take my rage out on one of my best friends.

"Can I help in any way? I can ask around for His Majesty if you need an audience with him," she says hurriedly while clutching at the bedsheet at her chest.

"No, Anya. That's fine. Thank you, though."

Sheer humiliation prevents me from telling her that I already interrogated Samir and his staff about whether any of them knew where their king had run off to this night.

"Are you sure?" she insists.

I nod, forcing a smile.

"Okay. Do you want me to come with you back to your room then? Maybe make you something to drink or eat? I can be good company if you need it," she says, genuinely concerned for my well-being.

That's my Anya.

She may speak before she thinks but she has a heart big enough to fit the entire world in.

"No, sweet friend. Go back to what you were doing. At least one of us should enjoy all the pleasures that the night brings." I wink at her.

Anya's cheeks blush bright red but it's the beaming smile that overtakes her whole face that ends up tempering my bad mood.

"Okay, then. Good night."

She's about to walk away when I reach for her hand to stop her.

"Are you happy, Anya? Does she make you happy?" I ask, sincerely worried that maybe she bit off more than she can chew with someone as savvy and experienced as Cleo.

But I have my answer when her green eyes light up and her smile splits her face in two.

"I've never known such happiness, Kat. Never."

When I hear the sincerity in her voice, I release her from my hold.

"I'm glad, sweet friend. Go. I won't keep you away from such happiness a minute longer. Go."

"Good night," she sings before rushing back into her lover's arms.

I, on the other hand, start walking back to my chambers, wrecked with so many contradicting emotions, it's hard to keep them straight in my head or my heart. But ultimately, one stands out more than the others—jealousy.

Where could he be?

Where could he have possibly gone to that is more important than… me?

And with that question banging at my head, follows more.

If he knew he had somewhere else to be tonight, wouldn't it have been the courteous thing to do to warn me? To say something to that effect?

We spent the whole day together, laughing and talking with each other about everything and nothing. It had been like it was before, back when I would wait impatiently for his visit up north. But throughout all that time I thought we were tapping into our youth, it didn't even cross his mind to warn me that our plans for tonight had changed.

Here in the south, we don't judge or warden the people we care about.

That's what he keeps reminding me.

When he first said those words to me, it had been liberating.

But now I understand that those words don't only apply to me.

They apply to him too.

Teo is a free man to do whatever he wants, whenever he wants to.

With whomever he desires.

As that bucket of ice water sinks in, forbidden images of what Teo might be doing with his so-called freedom corrupt my mind and crush my soul.

When I finally reach my chambers, I slam the door shut and fling myself on top of my bed, like a petulant child who was denied her dessert.

But as I turn to the side, and see Levi's letters piled on top of my dresser, my jealousy is quickly replaced with guilt.

Levi.

My heart.

What will he think of me when he finds out about what Teo and I have been up to? Especially since he made it very clear that there is no love lost between the two.

When word gets to the east that I've been...

What?

What have I been doing that is so wrong?

Letting a man, that at one point in my life I thought would be by my side forever as my wedded husband and king, punish me? That the sting of the paddle or the bite of tresses on my sensitive skin awakens something inside me that I didn't even know was there? Something that makes me feel more alive than I have ever been?

And then I remind myself of the whole reason I even traveled south in the first place. Did I not propose marriage to the worthiest contender? Doesn't that mean that I should explore every avenue that is offered to me? Shouldn't my decision be for the betterment of my people? To find an alliance that will benefit the north and, in the end, Aikyam more?

I can't make that kind of decision based on my heart's wants.

My kingdom needs to come first.

Lies.

Nothing but lies.

Sweet lies that hide an ugly truth.

I shut my eyes and pound the back of my head repeatedly on the mattress.

That's what I've been doing since all of this first started. I've been feeding myself lies, trying to find some crumb of logic that can justify my selfish betrayal. Some thread of hope that I can hold on to, with my nails and teeth, and never let go of. Anything to keep me in this state of denial that my urges and strong will aren't the real culprits of my impending downfall. But no matter how I try to spin it in my head, to downplay the damage that I've done, I know the fault is mine and only I should be the one to suffer for it.

My heart.

My Levi.

He'll never forgive me.

Not when I can't forgive myself.

It was reckless and foolish to be led astray like I have done since arriving in Nas Laed.

I'm not even sure why I did it.

Another lie.

It was because of him.

Teo.

He always did have that effect on me. To be reckless. Foolish. Brave.

When we were children, I would follow him to the edge of the earth if he so wished. That was the kind of pull he had over me. Nonsensical. Unsolicited. And oh-so addictive.

He made the ordinary feel extraordinary. It was his greatest gift. To make me believe I could fly when I only had a pair of arms instead of wings to do it.

At first I tried to hate him, as if my loathing would keep me safe from his spell.

Then I tried friendship. Friendship felt safe. After all, that was our beginning when we were young too.

But then Teo took me to the pleasure house, and suddenly our dynamics shifted again.

I could blame Levi for my curiosity.

How I would stare at myself in the mirror and brush the bruises he left on my skin with the tips of my fingers and spend hours marveling at them. I could curse him for sparking this desire in me. But in the end, that would just be me shifting the blame onto someone else, unwilling to admit to myself that this desire had always been inside me all along. It had been kept in a cage with glacier bars, trapping it in the cold.

Levi had found the key and twisted the lock open, but it was Teo who kicked the door in.

Teo set me free with his magnetic pull.

He swung it in the air and latched it around my neck, tightening around my throat to the point of suffocation until the only air I craved to breathe into my lungs was his scent. The way Teo toyed with my body, as if knowing exactly which buttons to press, had me in a trance of his making right from the start. And every night as Teo coaxed out one orgasm after the next, I wished that he would have singed my flesh with his heathen hands instead of a rod.

Isn't that the real reason why I'm so devastated that he left me tonight?

That somewhere deep inside, I believed to hold that same power over him as he held over me?

Nights and days have I spent imagining how good it would feel for him to drop his weapon of choice and ruin me with his body instead.

How empty and hollow I feel when our nights come to an end, and the only release I got was provoked by his harsh punishments.

I wanted him to take me and abuse me until I couldn't take it anymore.

I wanted him to use his hands.

His mouth.

His cock.

I wanted to feel him inside me as he moaned out my name.

I wanted it all.

But apparently, Teo doesn't.

And that stark truth has me devastated.

He left me.

For a second time in my life, he left me.

And suddenly I realize that it's not only my body that mourns his loss.

The heart that has already been claimed by another, suffers just the same.

Chapter 42
Teodoro

With both arms raised up high so my hands are clenched around the head of my doorframe, I stare at the woman sleeping peacefully in my bed.

I knew my little kitten wouldn't take tonight's absence lightly. I knew she would end up seeking me out to demand some kind of explanation or even curse me out for leaving her high and dry. But I never figured she'd be mad enough with me to sneak into my room and wait for me to arrive from wherever I had been off to.

Not that I'll ever tell her that all I did was walk my city's streets, solely thinking about her as I waited for the night to end. I needed to prove a point, and sometimes to do that, you have to snatch away any and all distractions from a person so they can realize the truth for themselves.

Katrina loves me.

She might not want to admit it yet to herself, but she does.

Otherwise, why would she be in my bed if she didn't care for me like that?

I tilt my head to the side and bite into my lip as I watch her moan in her sleep, rubbing her thighs against my mattress to ease the ache building up inside her. I don't even have to touch her to know she's wet. That whatever delicious dream she is having has her all hot and bothered.

I can smell her sweet arousal from here.

Hmm.

So many possibilities yet so little time to do them all.

No better time than the present, I always say.

Taking care to listen to my own advice, I gently close the door behind me, and with a smirk tugging at my lips, I walk over to my dresser and open the first drawer to pick out a few toys for us to play with. The first one I pick out is easy enough to choose, a silk scarf that I can use for rope since my kitten loves to be bound up and tied.

The next one I pick has me chuckling softly like a madman. A little toy Cleo bought for me when she tried to convince me that fucking a guy was the same as fucking a girl. Not that I was opposed to trying it, since I had participated in enough orgies with her for it to have piqued my interest. But in the end, I always favored a woman's loud wails of pleasure to a man's grunts in my ear.

In all fairness, I think the real reason Cleo gave me such a gift was because she thought I was lonely and needed some companionship from the male persuasion since I was always reminiscing about my youthful adventures with Levi and Atlas. The thing I had to clarify to her was that if I liked to recall those times so much, it was because I was as innocent as they were at the time.

I didn't have blood on my hands.

My innocence was still intact.

That was the real feeling I missed.

She dropped the subject after that, but I kept her gift just the same.

I store the small silver plug in my front pocket and search for my new favorite toy—the flogger I kept as a souvenir from the pleasure house from that first night Katrina and I were there.

My cock gets hard just thinking about it.

And tonight, I fully intend to use it.

On featherlight feet, I walk over to the bed and look over my Katrina once more. She's just in her nightgown, her robe nowhere in sight, which leads me to believe that she must have tossed and turned in her own bed, until she decided to call it quits and come to mine instead.

I dip my knee onto the mattress, staying perfectly still when she unexpectedly stirs in her slumber. After I'm sure she's fully asleep again, I hold in my breath and tug at the white string that is tied just above her breasts. Once it's nice and loose over her shoulders, I grab the hem of her nightgown and gently pull it down her slender frame.

"Much better," I whisper to myself as I slide off the bed, my little kitten now fully naked on top of it.

Now for the second part of my plan.

I pick the scarf off the floor and walk over to where Katrina's head lies on my pillow. Her lips are slightly parted open for breath, her chest heaving ever so slowly, making her breasts even more tantalizing to my eyes.

All in good time, Teo.

Gently, I pull her arms up over her head and proceed to tie her wrists together.

She must have waited for my return all night, because she doesn't wake at all while I prep her for what's about to happen.

I pull away and look at her, my mouth watering to sink its teeth into all the fair, porcelain skin. After I've taken off my shirt, I dip both of my knees on the mattress and place myself right at her waist. With the flogger in my hand, I lightly start to caress her skin with the tip of the tresses from neck to navel.

Katrina lets out a muffled sigh as the tresses kiss her nipples that instantly turn into two diamond studs with the light touch. I continue to stroke her whole body with the flogger while I aim my cock purposely to slide in between her wet folds, my crown hitting her sensitive clit.

"Oh gods," she moans out, her eyelids beginning to flutter open.

"No, pet. No gods here. Just heathens."

Katrina quickly stirs awake, her knee-jerk reaction to wipe the sleep out of her eyes. But when she sees that she can't because her wrists are tied together, she lets out a curse.

"What do you think you're doing?" she snaps.

"I can ask you the same thing," I retort while still covering my shaft with her juices. "You're the one that's in my bed, kitten. And when I see a beautiful woman in my bed, I can only assume she's a gift."

Her gaze turns thunderous as she stares me down.

"Is that your way of telling me that you've had many women in your bed?"

"Yes." I shrug nonchalantly. "I've had more than I can count."

She tries to flex her hips to push me off, but all that ends up doing is making my cock hit her clit just the way she likes it. Her eyelids can't help but to close, enjoying the sensation of skin to skin.

"I've had women of all ages, sizes, and colors. All more exquisite than the other," I continue on, as I flick the flogger with my wrist so it bites into her breast.

She hisses in pain, pleasure and hatred as I force her to hear how many women I've fucked.

"I've had them on their knees for me…"

Flick.

"I've had their legs wrapped around my shoulders…"

Flick.

"I've had them on all fours…"

Flick.

"I've fucked most of Nas Laed…"

Flick.

"Yet, I can't remember one face. Not one."

Flick.

"And that's because every time I come, it's you I see."

Katrina is all but panting, her eyes half-mast as she tries to look at my face.

"Now, kitten. I've let you have your fun. I've been patient and waited for you. That ends tonight. Tonight, I'm the one that gets to play."

"What… what are you going to do?" she asks on bated breath.

"I'm going to fuck every hole in your body with my toys. Then, after you've come so hard you can't see straight, I'm going to fuck that bratty mouth with my cock." I grin.

My words to anyone else would sound like a threat, but to my little kitten, they are the sweetest words she's ever heard.

Her heady gaze is all the answer I need that I have full consent to do with her as I see fit. Not wanting to delay myself the pleasure any longer, I lean down just enough that she can feel my breath fan her face.

"But to do that, you're going to be a good little kitten and open your mouth for me."

Katrina licks her lips, the anticipation of it all increasing her need to be ravished. Teasing me, she opens her mouth just a tad, her tongue peeking out to swipe over her bottom lip.

"Ah, kitten, you're going to have to open much wider than that," I taunt, before gripping her jaw and pushing her mouth open so that the leather handle of my flogger slides in nicely. Katrina's eyes go wide at the intrusion, as I begin to slide the makeshift dick in and out of her mouth.

"I want this stick to be nice and slick, kitten. Lavish it with your tongue as if it's my cock you are sucking."

The planted image is all she needs to moan out as she begins to suck at it like her life depends on it. Her eyelids close as she relaxes her throat, taking it as far as she's able to. I pull it out and lightly hit her lower lips, her tongue lapping at its head as if she can taste the phantom precum on it.

"That's a good little kitten. And good kittens get rewarded for sucking so beautifully," I tell her, as my head lowers toward one of her pink nipples and plucks it into my mouth.

Her back arches off the mattress, making me have to plant my hand on her stomach to push her back down. I release her nipple on a loud pop and then stretch my arm as far as it will go and slap her pussy.

"Argh!" she cries, her wail coming out muffled with her mouth full.

"Good kittens get rewards. Bad ones get punished."

She lets out a little moan before concentrating on sucking my toy again. When I see that it's nice and slick, I reward her again. I pull my silver plug out of my pocket and lean toward her face again as I shove it inside my mouth. Katrina's eyes glaze over at the forbidden sight of me sucking such a foreign object. Once I'm sure it's nice and wet, I pull it out of my mouth as well as the black handle out of hers. I then jump out of bed and grip the scarf that has Katrina's wrist bound into place and swivel her on the mattress, until her head is hung over its edge.

Her wide eyes look shocked as well as curious as to what I'm about to do next.

"Now, kitten. I'm going to fuck you nice and slow with my toys," I explain, my tone going darker. "And while I do that, I want you to be a good little kitten and stroke my cock with your hands. Understand?"

With the blood rushing to her head, it takes her a while to fully comprehend what's about to go down. But when she does, she nods furiously, her itching hands going to the string of my pants.

"Did I say we can start?" I ask, slapping her hands again and pinching her nipples simultaneously.

She hisses at the pain, her chest turning a gorgeous shade of red.,

"Remember the rules. If you play nice, so will I. If you don't then this can get very uncomfortable for you."

Even upside down I can see the idea bounce away in her head, thinking which one would she prefer, pain or pleasure. In the end, pleasure wins out.

She pulls her hands off me and lays there, waiting for my next command.

"Good. What a good little pet you are," I coo as I run my fingers up and down her chest. She lets out a small smile at the praise.

"Do you want your prize, pet?" I ask, my voice so deep with want it feels like it's not even my own.

"Yes," she pants, her tone just as desperate as mine.

I lean down and with my fingers, I begin to play with her slick pussy, flicking her clit like I would my flogger on her bare body. I only let up when Katrina's legs begin to shake, preferring to pick up my silver toy.

But first things first.

"Okay, kitten. Now you can free my cock. It's ready for you."

It's been fucking ready since I walked in the room, but Katrina doesn't need to know that.

As she begins to tug at the string of my pants again, I make sure that my toy slides through her folds to get it nice and soaked with her juices. When I feel air kiss my cock, no longer contained in its prison, I lean in and begin to toy with her little hole.

When she doesn't budge to do anything else, knowing she must wait for me to give her next instructions, I place a kiss on the tip of her clit, making her squirm with delight. I, on the other hand, curse myself for being so fucking foolish since now all I want is to eat her out and fuck the rest.

Hard and in pain, I order Katrina to stroke my cock with her hands to take the edge off. Of course, the minute she does and begins to pump my cock in her hands, I'm more desperate than I was after I had just a small taste of her pussy.

"Fuck this!" I groan, pushing myself up so I can pull her jaw forcedly open just so I can shove my cock down her throat.

"Oh, the gods!" I shout, uncaring that I just broke my number one rule—always be in control of every situation.

I start fucking her mouth as I lean back down, just so I can have another taste of her sweet nectar.

But the gods, she's sweet.

My tongue sinks itself in her cunt to taste her at the source, before I slide it back to her nub and lap at it with my tongue. Katrina's body writhes beneath mine so hard that I have no choice but to lift her thighs and wrap them around my shoulders just to keep her steady. Time stands still as I keep fucking her with my mouth as my little kitten deep-throats my cock.

When she's good and primed, I stretch my hands out to find my discarded toys again. With the flogger's handle in one hand and the silver plug in the other, I position them in their respective centers while my tongue thrashes at her clit.

It's only when I feel her come that I start fucking her for real. Her loud cry is muffled by my cock as I keep thrusting it into her hot mouth like tomorrow will never come while my toys have their way with her. From over my lashes, I watch as the silver plug is fully inserted in her hidden bud while I use my wrist to thrust the leatherbound handle in and out of her aching cunt.

The sensation of being defiled like this has both of us fiddling with the cords of insanity. All it would take is one hard tug for us to lose our minds and fall headfirst into the dark abyss. I plunge my cock deep down her throat, her gagging sounds only increasing my insatiable hunger for her. And then I feel the vixen using her own tongue to lavish my cock, sending me over the edge.

"Fuck!" I shout while savagely thrusting my cock and my toy repeatedly so deep inside her, I'm not sure where I end and she begins. Katrina's legs begin to tremble around my head, her own release splitting her wide open as she gushes in my face, making me lap every drop of her sweet nectar.

And as I follow her and come, I pull away from her pussy just to bite into her thigh to keep my own loud wail contained. Katrina follows my lead and drinks every drop of my cum, her tongue going to extreme efforts to lick me clean.

After the best fucking sex I've ever had, I only have the energy to pull the plug out of her ass and swing her body back to the bed so I can fall beside her. Her gaze is as sated as mine as she holds out her wrists for me to untie the knot that binds her. The instant she is free, she cuddles beside me, placing her head on my chest to hear my rapid heartbeat. I wrap my arm around her and hold her close, my nose smelling the floral scent of her hair.

This must be what true happiness feels like because I can't keep the fucking grin away from my face. Katrina tilts her head back just an inch and smiles when she sees it plastered on my face.

"You know," she starts, "most people just say sorry when they've messed up."

"Yeah?" I chuckle. "You don't like how I apologize?" I tease, making her smile widen from ear to ear.

"I didn't say that." She chews at her bottom lip. "I liked it well enough."

I cackle at that.

"Kitten, my face still has your juices all over it. You more than liked it. Trust me."

"Hmm. I guess we'll have to do that again just to make sure," she says, fluttering her eyelashes at me.

"Whatever my queen wants, she gets."

She throws me another bright smile before resting her head back on my chest.

I run my fingers through her hair until she falls asleep and let this feeling of contentment fill me with dreams of her—the only woman I ever loved.

Even in my slumber, I feel my dick getting hard. Katrina's ass continues to rub against it, like she's inviting it to spend the night in between her ass cheeks. I groan when she turns over, and sprawls her leg over my thigh, her hot pussy scorching my skin.

I pry my eyes open and am surprised when her silver gaze is staring back at me, fully awake. I open my mouth to say something, but she silences me when she places her index finger on my lips. My forehead creases in confusion, but then I let out a gruff rasp when my little kitten pulls herself off the mattress to straddle me.

My lids keep blinking as if trying to establish if this is a reality or simply another one of my dreams that she insists on haunting. But then she slides her finger in between my lips, demanding that I suck it as she rubs her pussy on my stomach. Never wavering my eyes from hers, I do as she silently commands and begin to suck at her digit, and when I feel her juices starting to drip on me, I grab her wrist and add two more of her fingers to the mix. Her head falls back as she dry humps me while fucking my mouth. I'm so fucking hard I'm about to come just like this.

But thankfully my kitten has other plans for me.

When I feel her cup my balls, my eyelids become so heavy it becomes hard to keep them open just to look at her. I hiss when I feel her nails run up and down my shaft, before grabbing it at its base and centering it to her opening.

The weight on my eyelids disappears as I realize what she is about to do.

"Don't ever disappear on me again," she threatens, pulling her fingers away from my mouth.

"Never," I promise, desperate for what's about to happen.

"Good. Because if you do that to me again, you can kiss my pussy goodbye."

"Bless the gods," I wail as she pushes herself down to the base. "Oh, fuck."

"Now be a good king, Your Grace, and just lie there as I fuck you. It's my turn to play."

Fuck!!!

Now this is a queen that knows how powerful she is and isn't afraid to use it.

I white-knuckle the bedsheet underneath me as Katrina begins to slowly lift herself off my cock, only to plunge down with all her might. Like me, she is merciless when she fucks, needing to get off while making her lover ache in delicious misery. But soon her tempo picks up, making me thank the gods for their small mercies.

"The gods, kitten. Just like that," I groan when she sinks her nails into my chest and carves her name on my soul.

Her full, mouthwatering breasts bounce up and down with each thrust, coaxing me to lift off the bed just far enough so I can suck on each nipple. Her hands leave my chest to run her fingers through my hair, pushing my face right in between her breasts. If her intention is to kill me by suffocating me like this, then no man will have a sweeter death. My arms lock her in place as I lick the beads of sweat dripping down the small sliver of skin in between her breasts.

She lets out a loud wail, releasing her fingers from my hair, and I use this to my advantage to bite at her sensitive flesh before sucking each one of nipples again, grazing them with my teeth. I then lift myself halfway off the bed, cradling her neck with one hand as I place the other on the small of her back, pushing my cock to sink itself deep into her hot, slick cavern.

Katrina's heavy breathing starts to come out in spurts, her forehead drenched as her brows pull together to keep herself steady. Seeing that my kitten needs a little hand, I grip her waist with both hands, flexing my hips forward and aiding her every thrust.

"Teo," she breathes out in my ear, the sound of my name falling from her lips making me lose all decorum.

I lick, suck, and bite her slender shoulder all the way up to her neck, before I plant my mouth to her ear.

"That's it, kitten. Fuck me with all you got. Let me feel that pussy strangle my dick with how good it feels inside of you."

And like the good girl she is, her pussy clenches around me with every filthy order I give her.

"Teo!" she screams, hurrying her pace and making me see fucking stars.

"You're so fucking close, kitten. I can feel how close you are. Tell me what you need. I'll fucking give it you. Just tell me what you need," I plead, so far gone that I'm having a hard time not coming myself.

"Kiss me, Teo. Kiss me," she begs on a sob.

I don't even have time to give her an answer; my lips already on hers before I even have time to think. Unlike the chaste kisses we shared after I punished her body with my toys, this kiss is ardent and desperate. It's a kiss that feels like a thousand little cuts are slicing away at my heart with how fucking perfect it is. She wraps her arms around my neck, while I swing my arms around her waist, both of us needing to be connected with each other in every way.

I feel the minute her orgasm hits her, making her body convulse in my arms. Unable to stop, my own release follows suit as I pound my cock into her soaked pussy with everything I still have inside me. Our kiss eats at our cries of ecstasy as we both ride the wave to a place where the gods feast and fuck up in the heavens.

And as we plunge back down to earth from our nirvana, fearful thoughts slither their way into my head, adding a cruel hue to the perfect moment we just shared.

What if she doesn't choose me?

What if after all we've been through, it's him that she wants?

And if that's the case, then how the fuck will I be able to ever let her leave me now?

I'll never survive it.

Never.

I'd rather Levi kill me than have to endure a life without Katrina in it.

We don't leave his chambers for three days straight.
I haven't seen a single person aside from his glorious face,
content in living in the bubble of pleasure and pain.

"ARGH!" I shout as I feel another drop of hot wax falling on my
back, while Teo has me bent over a table, fucking me from behind.

"Fuck, kitten," he moans from behind me as he thrashes inside of
me. "If only you knew how your pussy strangles my cock every time
you feel the burn of the candle wax.

He doesn't have to tell me.

I can feel it.

How my body betrays me in sucking him in anytime it feels just a
little hint of pain.

"That's it, kitten. Swallow me whole with your pussy," he demands,
his nails sinking into my hips as he thrusts deep inside of me.

"Oh the gods!" I wail when another drop hits the small of my back.

"Fucking gorgeous," he lets out as he places the candle back on the table in front of me.

I hold on tight to the table's edge, its rough surface scratching against my tender nipples. I feel Teo's cock stretching me out as he pounds into my core without restraint.

And then I feel something cold and slippery drip from my back down to the small hole of my ass. Teo's hands leave my hips and part my ass cheeks, making me feel that much more vulnerable to him.

"What... what are you doing?" I croak, too hot and needy for my words to come out strong and steady.

"Shh, kitten. Let me just see you."

I feel him lean back as he flexes his hips forward, not wanting to lose the rhythm he's got in place.

"Fuck, but what a pretty sight. Your virgin hole begging to be fucked while your whorish pussy takes my cock."

I feel myself clench around him as it always does when he talks such filth.

"I'm going to fuck this ass, kitten, and you're going to let me," he promises in a throaty rasp. "I almost wish I could stop what we're doing just to eat it out with my mouth and tongue and then fuck it raw. But first I have to prep it. Make it so that you can take my whole cock with ease. Just thinking about it has me ravenous."

Unable to give him a reply, all I do is push my ass back towards him with every punishing thrust.

"Gods, just like that, kitten," he curses, running the wetness of his spit around the circles of my forbidden hole.

"Does that feel good?"

Panting breathlessly, I nod.

"Yeah?" he groans. "And what about this?"

I feel a small pressure inside. Almost unnoticeable at first, until it intensifies, as if his whole finger is inside me.

"You're so fucking tight here. I barely have the tip in and already you're trying suck me in. My kitten is such a filthy slut. Needing all her holes filled."

And then he adds more pressure, breaking the breach and making my eyes roll to the back of my head.

"Teo!" I plead, so close that I think I'm going to lose my mind if he stops.

"I got you, kitten. I always got you."

Good to his word, his thrusts increase their speed as he hooks his digit inside me in a way that causes me to burst into rays of light all throughout the room.

"That's it, love. Come for me."

His loud command feels like a soft whisper on my heated flesh, kissing it ever so gently and stroking it until I shatter in his arms. I let my soul leave my body as I reach for the stars. Teo keeps his tight hold on my hip as my legs shake so profusely that if it wasn't for his steady hold on me and this table, they would surely buckle.

It's only after I've ridden my release to its full end that Teo lets out a loud groan and comes inside me. He instantly falls on my scorched back, pulling his digit out of my ass so that he can wrap both of his hands around my waist.

Our breathing is hard and erratic at first, taking us a while to get our bearings. Spent and utterly satisfied, my grin comes forth as I turn my head sideways to see Teo looking at me.

There's such tenderness in his amber gaze, such love, that a lump rises up my throat, and no matter how hard I try to swallow it down, it refuses to budge.

"Teo—"

"I love you," he says, cutting me off.

"Teo, wait—"

"No, I'm tired of waiting," he says adamantly, pulling me off the table and spinning me around in his arms. "You need to hear this. I love you. I'm in love with you. I always have been."

My heart races in my chest as Teo stares into my eyes.

"This is real, Katrina. You can't hide from it anymore, nor can you pretend that you don't feel the same. I love you. Do you understand that? I'm in love with you."

When he sees that I'm unable to give him the reply he wants to hear, he lets me go and begins to pace the room, head hung low as he tugs at his locks.

"Fuck. You still don't get it, do you?" he mumbles more to himself than to me. He then raises his head. "Wake the fuck up, Katrina. This, between us, is real. What we had when we were kids was real. I have known that you were the only woman for me before I even knew myself. And you," he points a menacing finger at me, "love me too. You can deny it to me, you can even lie to yourself that all you actually feel for me is lust and nothing more. But I know the truth. I feel it every time you kiss me. In every caress. I even feel it when you come on my cock. So don't stand there and say nothing. Instead, take a long look at what you've been trying to hide from yourself and fucking come to terms with it already. I love you and you love me. It's that simple."

"No, it's not," I finally manage to say.

Teo rushes toward me and instinctively, I take a step back, hitting the table behind me and halting his next step.

Teo's golden eyes widen as he stares at me.

"You're afraid," he accuses, shaking his head. "You're fucking terrified."

"I'm not," I deny, swallowing down hard.

"Yes, you are. Because if you admit that you love me, then you will also have to admit that you don't love *him*."

It's only when he conjures Levi's name that I take a step toward him.

"I do love him," I retort with an edge to my voice. "And don't you ever question my love for Levi again."

Teo's face pales and I watch all the blood leave his cheeks.

"That's not true. It can't be," he mutters under his breath.

"It is true," I snap with ice in my veins. "You can say that I'm in denial and that I'm hiding my true feelings from myself, but my love for Levi is undeniable and unquestionable."

Teo's expression turns lethal at my words.

"Yeah? How does he feel about you? How in love do you think he will be after he learns that I have fucked you every which way till Sunday, huh? Will he still love you once he finds out about our little games? How you gagged on my cock as I fucked you with my flogger's handle? Tell me, how understanding would the great king of the east be when he learns that his precious queen likes it rough and dirty? Likes to be tied up to be used and abused by the man he dreams of killing one day?"

"Who says that you're the only man I have ever let be rough with me? Or have you forgotten that when I came to you, my virtue had long been given to him."

Teo doesn't so much as flinch as he charges toward me and wraps his hand around my neck.

"The fuck did you just say?"

"You heard me," I challenge, my cold gaze piercing his heated one.

"You think he can satisfy you? You think he burns for you like I do? That his every waking minute is spent thinking about how best to serve you? How best to fucking love you?!"

"You have no idea what love is," I quip back, knowing it's a lie the minute the words spill from my lips.

"No, kitten. I know what love is because I have been tormented by it since the day I left you. I'm the fool to think you felt the same way," he breathes out, desperation and longing replacing the anger in his tone. His grip on my throat eases so that his hand slowly trails down my chest until it stops at my heart.

"I thought if I just made you remember... if I just awakened you to see what we could be like together, that you'd understand. There can never be anyone else for us, kitten. We're fated, you and I. It was always supposed to be us. Just us."

My heart feels like it's being torn apart with the devastation dimming his bright eyes.

"Teo, I—" But before I have time to finish my thought, someone knocks at the door.

"Go away," Teo replies, only for whoever is outside in the hall to bang at the door again. "I said go away." Another bang. "Curse the gods, but I told you to go away!" Teo yells as he turns around to open the door.

"My apologies, Your Highness, but this is important. Is the queen with you?" Anya asks, shifting nervously from one foot to another.

"There's your queen," he replies, widening his door so that Anya can look inside his room.

Anya immediately lowers her gaze to the floor when she realizes that both me and Teo are completely naked.

"I'm sorry, K—my queen. I didn't mean to interrupt."

"Well, you did. And we were having such a lovely time, weren't we, kitten?" Teo snorts sarcastically.

I look for something to put on and let out a sigh of relief when I find Teo's silk robe by the bed. I hurriedly put it on and rush to the door.

"Anya, is everything okay?" I ask, eyeing her up and down to see if she's hurt. "Is it Inessa?" I add when I confirm that Anya looks well, even if uncomfortable.

"Everything is fine, my queen. Both Inessa and I are fine."

"Then what's wrong?"

Anya discreetly looks up at Teo and then to me.

"You received a letter today, my queen. One that demands your immediate attention."

My anxious thoughts go immediately to my brother.

"Is it Elijah?" I ask worriedly, stretching my hand for Anya to deliver me the letter.

"No, my queen." She shakes her head, while pulling her arms from behind her back to show me an all too familiar green hydrangea seal. "The letter did not come from the north," she pauses to take a fortifying breath, "but the east."

Levi.

As if the man himself just raised a wedge in between us, I step away from Teo and leave his room.

"You're just going to leave?" he asks, pained.

"I am."

And then I turn my back on one love to see if I still have the love of another.

I sit cross-legged on the bed, staring at the green seal that taunts me so.

"Aren't you going to open it?" Anya asks inquisitively while biting at her thumb.

"Leave Her Majesty be, Anya. Stop being so impertinent," Inessa scolds, leaning against a wall, her gaze on mine.

"Fine. Then you read yours. I bet it's nice and juicy," Anya proclaims, skipping to her friend.

Inessa's cheeks instantly flush at her friend's light teasing.

"You got a letter too?" I ask, surprised.

"Not just any letter. A love letter." Anya wiggles her brows.

"Has anyone told you that you have a big mouth?" Inessa chastises her friend.

"Yes, you. Every single day." Anya giggles. "Now stop being a spoilsport and read it already. I'm dying to hear what romantic sonnets Brick has written to you."

"Brick?!" I all but choke. "Brick is who has been sending you love letters?"

Inessa looks like if she could dig a hole, she would crawl into it just to spare herself from this conversation.

"He has. Somehow he got it in that thick head of his that he's going to marry me someday," she explains, chewing nervously on her bottom lip.

"He has, has he?" I cock a brow, amused. "You didn't do anything that could have put such a notion in his head, did you?"

"She did!" Anya screeches in excitement. "She kissed him before we left—OUCH!" Anya shouts out in pain after Inessa pinches her arm again. "What did you do that for?"

"I was looking for something that would shut your big mouth up. Looks like I found it," Inessa mumbles.

"See, Kat? See what I have put up with for the past three days while you were locked away with the king in his chambers?" Anya pouts, but when she sees how her offhanded comment made me feel even more deplorable than I already do, she rushes to me. "Oh, I'm sorry, my queen. That came out all wrong. I didn't mean to offend."

"The queen is not offended, Anya. She can't be when it's the truth," Inessa interjects with a cold bite to her voice.

And then that's when I realize that Levi isn't the only one who is disappointed in my recent actions. Inessa is too.

"Are you cross with me?" I ask outright.

"You're my queen. Nothing you do could ever make me cross," she retorts evenly.

"Aye, I am your queen. But I am also your friend. Friends do disappoint one another at times."

"Curses," she mutters under her breath. "Levi gave you a heart and now you've grown soft on me."

At this, I laugh.

"Soft? Is that how you see me now?"

"I see a queen who is losing sight of her purpose. I see a queen that once had the arctic wind at her back and ice water in her veins. And now I'm not sure who this queen that stands before me is anymore."

"You mean you saw your own reflection and now that it's changed, your own limitations make it hard for you to comprehend that everything in the world evolves—even queens," I explain in an even tone.

"Yes, my queen. It's just that, before I could count on your cold, collected heart and mind to make the right choices. Now that both have thawed, I have yet to get used to this new Katrina of Bratsk."

"Well, acquaint yourself with her fast since she isn't going anywhere."

"Now it is I who have offended you," Inessa says, hanging her head down low with the reprimand.

I let out a long exhale.

"No, Inessa. You have not. Like I said, we are friends. If we can't speak the truth to one another, even when it's hard to hear, then what kind of friendship do we even have? I trust you, Inessa, to always keep me grounded even if, at times, all I want to do is fly away from this plane of existence."

"If that is the case, then please be patient with me as I tell you another truth that you might not like to hear," she advises sternly.

I prepare myself for her to berate me for my recent actions. For her to say atrocities regarding Teo and what she believes is a grave mistake that I'm making of even getting involved with him in such a way. But in the end, she surprises me with her next piece of advice, no less brutal than the words I thought I'd hear.

"You can keep staring at that letter all night long, Kat. It won't change what is inside it."

My gaze falls down to the letter lying inches in front of me, my heart hurting already without having read one word.

"I'm not sure I can," I admit on an anguished sob. "What if word has traveled east... what if he knows that me and Teo have... What will he think of me then?"

"No use in suffering beforehand, my queen. Life is cruel enough as it is without our thoughts making it even more so."

"Inessa's right. You have to open it, Kat. That's the only way you'll know," Anya chimes in consolingly.

I take a deep breath and pick the letter up in my hands.

"Do you need us to go? Give you some privacy?" Anya asks, concerned.

"No." I shake my head. "Can you just sit with me? Please?"

Both Anya and Inessa are quick to sit on either side of me on the bed. Anya begins to run her hand up and down my back to give me courage, while Inessa pats my knee, her own way of offering me the same.

When I crack the seal, the sound instantly feels ominous to me, as a hint to how my heart will break after I've read Levi's words. I close my eyes and take another deep breath, while praying to the gods to show me some mercy.

My dearest queen,

I hope this letter finds you well and in good health.

I fear I cannot say the same about me.

Your recent silence has been deafening, my love.

So deafening that the words left unsaid between us are all I seem to hear.

I was a coward in Braaka.

A foolish coward that believed if I didn't say the words then, your absence wouldn't hurt as much.

But the gods, they have been cruel in their lessons.

This time living without you has taught me that no words should be left unsaid, for who is to know when you'll have the chance again.

So here I am, grabbing what may be the last chance I ever have.

I love you, Kat.

Always and forever, I will love only you.

In the short time we spent together, you have given me more peace than a soldier like me could even think capable of having.

I have known love and have felt loved, and for that gift alone, I will be forever grateful to you and in your debt.

But I can't continue to pretend that your heart still belongs to me.

And I don't need to hear the rumors that have reached Arkøya from the south either to know that.

Your silence in these past few weeks has told me as much.

I don't resent you, my heart.

Never will you hear that of me.

You and Teodoro share a history, one that neither I nor Atlas were ever included in.

You loved him first, and while I wanted to be the one you loved last, I fear it's not to be.

How naïve I was to have thought those ties between you both had been forgotten.

That was my gravest mistake. One that I intend to repair by not making another.

If he is the one that you choose to keep, then I won't stand in your way, nor will I demand reparations for my broken heart.

I love you enough to only want your happiness, my queen.

I love you solely and completely, that if he is the man for you, then I won't keep my vow of killing him and taking him away from you.

Aye, Kat.

For before you came back into my life, my dreams were of him only.

Of killing the man who had a hand in destroying the world I so loved.

As fate would have it, the gods would test my resolve of my vow.

Test to see how far I would go to make it so.

Apparently, causing you any kind of pain is enough for me to become an oath breaker.

That is my choice and mine alone.

However, if your heart still has doubts, I would rather you know the truth from my lips before you make any final decisions.

The man that has captured your undivided attention, is not who he seems to be.

He's a villain.

One that uses his charm to seduce and blind the people that care about him from the truth.

I should know.

I loved him too once.

He had been my brother.

In all ways but blood, I loved and trusted him like a brother.

Even when sometimes we didn't see eye to eye, he was still my family.

He stopped being that when he stole my real family away from me.

Because if it wasn't for Teo and his father, my parents would still be alive to this day.

I watched as both of them died, while Teo did nothing.

I watched men violate my mother's dead corpse, and still he did nothing.

I watched his father plunge his sword through my father's heart before decapitating him, and still Teo did nothing.

Just stood there and smiled at my ruin.

These trespasses against me, I will never forgive or forget.

But for you, I will show leniency.

For you, my dearest Kat, I will show mercy when none was offered to me.

For you, my love, I will ensure your happiness, even if it means that his is also guaranteed.

That is my new vow to you.

One that I will protect and keep and lock away in my lifeless heart.

For what is a heart if it no longer has a reason for beating?

Your loyal servant,

whose heart will forever be faithfully yours,

Levi of Thezmaer

King of the east

Anya softly sobs beside me as I lay the letter to rest in front of me.

My watery-filled gaze blurs my vision as I reread each painful word over and over.

Again, and again until my heart can't take it anymore.

I turn to Inessa for strength, whose own crestfallen expression eats away at my soul.

I'm so overwhelmed by everything Levi has written down that it takes me a minute to make sense of all of it.

Not only has Levi forgiven me for being with Teo, but he's all but given us his blessing.

Blessing a union between the woman he loves and the monster that sat back and watched his parents being murdered.

All in the name of my happiness.

My feet move before I know it, jumping off the bed and wiping away the tears from my eyes.

"Inessa, I need a rider," I order, searching my room for my jewelry box.

"What are you looking for?" she asks, confused.

"Don't ask me that and find me a rider. Now, Inessa!" I beg, while still frantically searching the room.

Hearing the urgency in my voice, Inessa sprints out of the room.

"Kat, tell me what you are looking for. Maybe I'll know where it is," Anya rushes to say, not standing by my side.

"My mother's jewelry box. I need it and can't for the life of me remember where I put it last."

"I know where it is. I stored it away just to be safe," Anya explains, going to the other side of the room. She lowers herself on her hands and knees and stretches her arm under a dresser.

"Got it!" she exclaims, pushing my mother's jewelry box out of its hiding spot.

"Oh, thank the gods!" I clasp my hands in gratitude. "Here, give it here."

Anya hurriedly puts the antique jewelry box in my hands and I in turn place it on top of my bed, opening it immediately. It doesn't take me long to find what I'm looking for.

"Anya, get me a small purse or a satchel."

She nods and proceeds to open up drawer after drawer to find me what I need. As she plants a white silk purse in my hands, Inessa returns with my rider.

"Here, Your Highness. I got you your rider. The fastest in your service," Inessa proclaims, looking out of breath from running to find him for me.

"Thank you, Inessa," I say and walk over to the young man waiting for my instructions. "What's your name?"

"It's Mikhail, Your Highness," he says before bowing his head.

"Well, Mikhail, is it true you are the fastest rider that I brought with me from the north?"

"It is, my queen."

"Good, for I have a task to give you that is of most importance." I then place my mother's heart-shaped diamond necklace that I wore on the night Levi danced with me so long ago in the small purse and tie it with a string before handing it off to Mikhail. "I need you to ride east as fast as the wind will take you. I need this to be hand-delivered to

King Levi. Not his man or anyone else—only the king must lay eyes on it."

Mikhail nods.

"It shall be done."

"Good. Thank you."

"Is there a message that you wish me to give him?" he asks.

"There is. Please tell King Levi this, 'For what is a heart of any use if it's not in the hands of its rightful owner.' Understand? Do you need me to repeat it?"

"No, my queen."

"Then go and meet us in Huwen after it's done. Go, Mikhail! Go as fast as you can, for my very happiness depends on it."

Mikhail doesn't stand idly around and breaks into a fast sprint. If he rides as fast as he runs, then I'll be happy.

"What now? What are you to do?"

"Pack our belongings, for we head west as soon as we can manage it," I tell her.

"West?" Anya's eyes go big and fearful. "But we weren't to leave for another week."

"That was before."

Before I found out that the man I was falling in love with all over again had killed my king's parents.

Does he know you like to be tied up to be used and abused by the man he dreams of killing one day?"

At the time he said those words, they didn't make any sense to me. I brushed them off since I was too committed to the fight we were having. But now it all makes sense. All of it.

"Where are you going?" Anya all but shouts when I start heading out of the room like a woman possessed.

"To confront the villain in our midst."

The same one that tricked me into loving him again.

S he enters my room like a storm, ready to lay waste to anything in her path.

"Is it true?" she asks, her voice so cold that if I touched it, it would no doubt burn me.

"What is?"

"That you and your father killed Levi's parents?"

The black, gruesome shadow of guilt runs its fingers up my spine before gripping my neck from behind, sinking its ugly claws into me.

"I thought you knew," I lie, turning my back to her in favor of walking toward my window.

The bedsheets are still warm from our lovemaking, yet here she is calling me a murderer.

Not that I'm not.

I am what she accuses me of.

I am that traitor who damned his soul for love.

"Don't you fucking turn your back to me, Teodoro!" she curses, making me inwardly flinch with how angry she is at me.

Make this nightmare end, oh heavenly ones.

For my heart cannot take a second longer of her hate.

"Answer me!" she yells, pulling my arm so that I spin in her direction.

I put on a smile, the same one that hides my pain, and stretch it as wide as I can physically bear it.

"Oh my gods. You did, didn't you?"

My nails sink into my palms at the way she had held out hope that somehow, by some miracle, Levi was wrong.

He must have confessed everything to her in that wretched letter of his.

His last effort to win back her love.

The only thing that confuses me is why he didn't tell her before she journeyed south. Was the memory so hard to bear, that he couldn't even summon up the courage to tell his queen of my complicity in the horrors that occurred that night?

The answer to that question is an affirmative yes.

Like me, Levi must have buried that memory deep into the confinement of his soul where no one could see or touch.

"Was it all a ploy?" she asks, tears streaming down her cheeks in both anger and sorrow. "Was your plan to seduce me and then when crowned King of Aikyam, you'd find a way to get rid of me too?"

"Fuck your crown," I growl, my voice no longer my own.

She slaps me, tears free falling now.

"How I ever saw any beauty in you is mind-blowing to me now. You're a monster. A villain. A liar and a cheat! You never cared about me. You never cared about anyone except yourself. This was all a game to you. You play with people's lives and then sit back to enjoy the chaos you created. You murdered one of your best friend's parents. You watched them die and did nothing. And then to my shame, you won me over with that traitorous smile, all because you wanted to steal my birthright."

She goes to slap me again, but this time I catch her wrist before she makes contact with my cheek.

"You must be hard of hearing, kitten," I seethe. "I said fuck your crown. I never wanted it," I tell her truthfully, staring at those big silver pools she has for eyes that now only see a stranger. "It was never your crown. It was you. I wanted you."

She snatches her arm away, as if my words have brought another wave of pain intent to drown her with.

"Always the liar. You lie so beautifully that you almost had me convinced. You almost had me making the biggest mistake of my life."

My heart refuses to make a sound, even to beat at her sullen remark.

"How could I ever crown such a hideous monster? May the gods have mercy on your soul, Teodoro. For I am blessed that they showed me theirs by opening my eyes to the truth just in time. You are not who I thought you were. And the first thing I will do after I marry Levi is tell him he has my consent to seek his revenge on the man who had a hand in murdering his parents." She then leans closer to my ear, her arctic demeanor chilling me to the bone. "And then when he plunges his sword into that hollow black void you call a heart, I will take your example and do absolutely nothing. The last thing you will see is me not lifting a finger to help you."

She then pulls away, but not fast enough for me not to catch the flash of heartbreak mixed with all the hatred she now possesses for me pass through her gaze.

"As soon as my people are packed and ready, we shall leave Nas Laed at once. Farewell, Teodoro, for the next time I see you, I guarantee you that day will be your last."

And as I watch her back disappear from my sight, an old haunting memory takes her place.

Chapter 47
Teodoro

Sixteen Years Old

With my back pressed up against a wall, I hold my breath and keep as still as I possibly can, hiding from the two soldiers that are walking down the hall. I close my eyes, as if the darkness of sight will make it that they can't see me either. Once I hear them turn the corner, I let out a relieved exhale and take a peek at the hall to confirm that they are gone.

Once I've made sure the coast is clear, I sneak into the dimly lit corridor in search of Levi's chambers. Even though I've only been to Arkøya a handful of times, I count on my memory to show me the way. When I find the door that I believe will lead me to Levi, I gently pull it open just in case whoever is inside isn't one of my closest friends.

When I walk inside, the first thing that stands out for me is how the room is cool and gray compared to my warm colorful chambers back home. Like Levi himself, his chambers scream serious and grown up. Not that I'm surprised. I don't remember Levi ever acting like a child, even when he was one.

The second thing my gaze latches onto is the sound of shallow breathing coming from the bed in the center of the room. I walk over to the side just in case I made a mistake and got the chambers wrong. When I see Levi's face, sound asleep, I rush over to him.

"Levi… Levi… Levi," I whisper, hoping that the sound of my voice will be enough to wake him up from his slumber.

When he doesn't so much as stir, I grab his shoulder and begin shaking it.

"Levi!" I whisper-yell. "Wake up, you big oaf. I need you to wake up."

"Go away, Teo. I'm sleeping," he reprimands, slapping my hand off his shoulder.

Gods help me.

"I said get up," I seethe through my teeth, and with both hands I start to shake him

"The gods, Teo. What can be so important that it couldn't wait for you to tell me tomorrow?"

Because you'll be dead by tomorrow, I think to myself but refuse to say those horrid words out loud.

"Please, Levi. Just get up. Get dressed. We have to go," I insist, pulling the covers off him before turning around to search for his clothes. A hard task to accomplish since Levi apparently likes to sleep in total darkness aside from the moonlight coming through the glass of his window.

In the corner of the room, there is a set of clothes pressed and ready for him to use hanging on the arm of a chair. I rush over to grab the clothes and a pair of boots and then run back to his bed, where I find Levi still wiping the sleep from his eyes with his fists.

"Here. Put these on and be quick about it."

"Is this one of your games, Teo? Because I'm too exhausted for your pranks," he complains, looking at his clothes like he would rather push them to the floor just so he could get back into bed.

Fuck!

I place my hands on his shoulders and cling to them tightly.

"Do you love me, brother?" I ask, knowing this is the only way for him to hear the urgency in my voice.

"Teo, what the fu—"

"Levi, gods help me, just answer the question. Do you love me, brother?"

He nods.

"Of course. Sometimes you're a pain in the ass but you're still my family," he retorts without missing a beat.

"Then trust me when I tell you that I need you to put these clothes on, now! We don't have much time!"

His forehead creases in confusion, but thankfully he gets out of bed and starts getting dressed. I wait impatiently for him to hurry up, since time is of the essence. My father is still in the great hall having his *audience* with King Krystiyan, distracting him while his men do their dirty work. As soon as King Krystiyan finds out what is really happening under his roof, this whole castle will be a battleground, and before that happens, I have to make sure that Levi is as far away from here as possible, hidden away and kept safe.

"You are good?" I ask him after he's put his coat on.

"Confused, more like," he replies. "Just exactly what is this all about?"

"Do you still keep your horse in the back stable with the other servants?" I ask instead of answering his loaded question.

"I do. You know I prefer to groom my horse myself."

"Good. Let's go then and, for the love of the gods, don't make a sound," I order, creaking the door open.

Levi gives me a curt nod and silently follows me down the hall.

If memory serves me right, there is a door in the kitchen that will lead us to the back stables, so that's where we head off to. But just as we reach the ground level, Levi tugs at my sleeve to call my attention.

"Through that way it will take us longer. I know a shortcut," he announces, going in the opposite direction.

Shit.

"Wait! Levi, wait!" I all but yell after him.

Unfortunately for me, the stubborn ass just keeps to his route instead of the one I had planned out for us.

And then we hear it.

The loud clink of steel and metal.

Swords clashing away at the other.

Levi turns his head over his shoulder to stare in my direction, anger and confusion all rolled up into a haunting shade in his eyes.

"Don't!" I call out when Levi sprints away in the direction of the sound.

I run after him as fast as I can, Levi's tree trunks for legs leaving me in the dust. When I realize that the sword fighting sounds are coming from the great hall, my apprehension increases.

The fuck is going on?

I watch as Levi turns the corner and enters the hall before me, fear and trepidation chilling my bones. A few seconds later when I step into the room, my jaw slacks open at what I find.

My father panting for breath while on his hands and knees, Levi's father aiming the tip of his sword to his head. It's obvious that they were the two who we heard battling it out, King Krystiyan having bested my father.

But he doesn't finish him.

Instead, the east-born king just stares in my direction and that's when I see that one of my father's men has a dagger to Levi's throat.

"Let him go, Yusuf," King Krystiyan commands, never wavering his gaze from his son.

"I can't do that, old friend," my father rebukes, pushing himself off the floor and wiping the sweat off his brow with his sleeve.

"Friend? We are not friends anymore, Yusuf. Not when you come into my house and threaten me and mine."

"I didn't threaten you, Krystiyan. I merely stated a fact and gave you a choice to make. It's not my fault that you don't like the sound of either. Now, what will it be? Will you keep that sword on me or will you lay down your weapon and spare your son's life. Your call."

Krystiyan looks over at his son and drops his sword.

"You made the right decision," my father states with a smile before kicking the sword across the room.

"I've done what you asked, now release my son," King Krystiyan commands, balling his hands into two fists at his sides when one of my father's men forces him to his knees, while another stands behind him, holding a sword to his back.

"Unfortunately, I can't do that either, old friend," my father says, walking over to the table to pick up a cup of wine. He drinks it all, as if parched from battling the eastern king.

My father was never a strong fighter.

He's more of a politician than a king.

Which means his alliances can change as easily as the wind, depending on which side is more favorable to him.

And unfortunately for Levi's father, he's on the losing team.

My father then leans against the table, and crosses his arms over his chest, a disappointed scowl to his lips.

"You just couldn't play along, could you? You just had to cross that mad fuck and pull your troops home. That was foolish, old friend. By bringing your soldiers home, you showed King Orville your hand. If your men weren't out fighting his wars for him, then that could only mean one thing. You wanted them to fight your war instead."

"He wanted my wife, Yusuf! What was I to do?!"

"Give her to him," my father mocks with a nonchalant shrug. "Let him do whatever he wants with her and then bury her bones when it's over and done with. You're still a king in your prime, Krystiyan. You could marry another and start anew. And in a few years' time, after your young new bride has given you more sons, Daryna will be an afterthought for you. You won't even remember she ever existed."

Krystiyan spits on the floor in my father's direction.

"You're just as bad as he is," Levi's father berates. "Would it have been so easy for you to give up Nahla to him?"

At the mention of my mother's name, my father's expression turns lethal.

"Nahla is dead! The bitch died on me and left me without a wife! Do you know what that means? That instead of her head, King Orville could have asked for mine!"

"But he didn't. Otherwise, you wouldn't be here betraying me like this!" King Krystiyan shouts back just as menacingly.

"You're right," my father quips, more in control of his temper. "Our king did give me an option to keep my head, but it was my son, Teodoro, who wouldn't hear of it."

At the mention of my name, both men turn their attention to me. Worst of all, Levi does too.

Fuck.

I step farther inside the room and put on a smile since that's what my father will expect from me. I need to find a way out of this fucking mess, but I can't do that if the bastard thinks me disloyal.

"It's true. King Orville's proposition was unacceptable to me, and my lord, father and king, being the doting father that he is, granted my request to come up with a suitable alternative," I begin to explain.

"Which I did," my father cuts in for me. "I promised our northern sovereign that I would convince you to do the right thing and spare your life."

"And if I refuse?" King Krystiyan asks, his nostrils flaring.

"Oh, our king gave me instructions for that too," my father retorts. "I would think long and hard about what decision you make now, Krystiyan. For it may be your last."

"Father," Levi calls out, trying to get his father's attention while still thrashing to break free from my father's man's hold. When I see that the fucker cut him a little, blood starting to drip down his collar, it takes inhuman effort to keep rooted to my spot.

Still, I have to do something.

"My king," I bow my head to my father, placing my hand to my heart. "I can take the young prince back to his room so that you can continue your *negotiations*. "

The growl Levi lets out feels like a dagger to the chest.

No matter.

He might hate me now, but once I explain everything to him, he'll understand. Right now, my first priority is to keep him safe. And I can't do that if a blade is pressed against his throat.

I'm about to take another step, this time toward Levi, but my father puts that to a stop with his next remark.

"No need for that, Teodoro. I need the young prince here where he'll be of use to me."

"What use could he still have?" I ask, my gaze bouncing from my father's pleased face to the king that is on his knees with a sword at his back.

But just as my question hits the tense air around us, I hear a slew of footsteps drawing closer to the hall. My heart sinks to my stomach when four of my father's men drag Levi's mother into the hall from the main entrance opposite us. Her hair is disheveled, her face brutally beaten, and her nightgown torn up in places no queen should have bared.

"Mother!"

"Daryna!" Levi and his father shout in tandem.

Levi tries to break free, but the dagger at his throat prevents him to move.

His father, on the other hand, is quicker to get on his feet but not quick enough to rush toward his wife, my father's men holding him back.

"I'm... okay. I'm okay," Queen Daryna tries to assure, her bloody lip and bruised cheek saying otherwise.

"Fuck you, Yusuf! I'm going to kill you for this!" King Krystiyan shouts, his face growing red with rage.

"See..." my father starts with a sinister grin. "I don't think you are. I gave you a chance and you didn't take it. I'm sorry, old friend, but you forced my hand." And then my father gives his men a nod.

Everything after that happens in slow motion.

One of the men holding Queen Daryna hostage unsheathes his sword, Levi and his father screaming from the top of their lungs for him to stop as he raises the sword up high. But I can't hear a thing, only the ringing sound of the sword slicing into the air as Queen Daryna takes one final look at her son and husband and mouths, "I love you."

And then...

A lifeless head tumbles onto the floor, rolling over and over again until it comes to a dead stop. The piercing howls of misery coming out of King Krystiyan's mouth sound like a wounded animal's, his tears the only sign left of his humanity. The two men that are holding him down call for one of their friends to help since they're having trouble keeping him still.

But that dreadful sight isn't even the worst thing that is taking place in this hall—the same great hall where both King Krystiyan and Queen Daryna used to throw feasts and celebrations, its large space devoted to solely being reserved for occasions of happiness.

The same hall where, just a few hours ago, my father and I dined with them as friends.

No.

King Krystiyan suffering isn't the worst thing happening in this hall by a long shot.

The animals my father enlisted to accompany us east pick Queen Daryna apart, defiling her memory and body in any way they can. Some take turns fucking her dead, headless corpse, joking about how much easier it is to fuck her the second time now that she doesn't put up a fight. Then there is the circle of godless creatures that begin kicking her head around amongst them as if it's some toy to play with. They do this knowing that her son and husband are watching, taking pleasure in their pain.

Unable to watch, I turn my attention to my father, my blood boiling at how he just sits back and smiles at the chaos he's brought to this once happy home. But he must feel my eyes on him because he tilts his head my way and looks me dead in the eye.

Hating him with all my heart, I force a smile that mimics his own. Bile rises up my throat as he nods at me, as if proud of my reaction to what's happening to our friends. When he redirects his attention back to the nightmare he's conducted, my gruesome smile begins to slip from my lips, but not fast enough.

Levi's eyes look like two black pools of death staring me down.

And suddenly I see my own reflection in his eyes—me on my knees and Levi raising his sword, ready to swing at my neck.

Like a coward, I don't watch him cut me down and lower my gaze from his instead.

I'm not sure how long I stay like that… just staring at the ground, wishing I could unhear all the brutality that's being done and obscenities being laughed at.

Time stands still for me.

It could be minutes, hours, even days that we are all holed up in this room.

I find myself wishing that someone would interrupt these animals' fun.

Some east-born soldier or guard that sees this horror show and goes off to call the troops to aid their king.

But no one comes.

And as more of my father's men enter the great hall, looking like they've just been to war themselves, it dawns on me why that is.

I recall how my father wasn't in a rush to talk about the plans King Krystiyan had in regards to invading the north and taking King Orville off the throne. I recall how he said that he just wanted to be wined and dined by his friend, enjoy his family's company for the night, and that they could have their conversations after the queen, Levi, and I retired to our rooms. And even though I wasn't there to see, I'm sure my father stalled all conversations about his sovereign with King Krystiyan, until he was sure the hour was late enough for his men to be in position.

The east might hold the best and largest army the kingdom of Aikyam has, but Arkøya castle isn't guarded by such troops. Only forty to fifty guards at best patrol the castle's halls. And at this late hour, that number is probably cut by half, meaning the fifteen well-experienced men my father brought with us would be more than enough men to slay every tired and poorly alert guard on duty while the castle slept. By the morning we'll be gone, leaving this chaos for someone else to clean up.

"Enough." My father claps, putting an end to his men's fun. At first I think he's going to order us all to leave, since he got what he came for with Queen Daryna's death, but then quickly realize that my monster of a father still has more carnage to ensue.

He picks up his discarded sword from the floor and walks over to the defeated king of the east.

"This could have all been so simple. All you had to do was give your wife to the king and that would have been the end of that. But you always were stubborn when you thought you were in the right, Krystiyan. You were so blinded by your stubbornness that you let the wolves through your doors to steal her away from you anyway."

"It wasn't stubbornness that blinded me," Krystiyan spits out. "It was love, not stubbornness that kept me from sending my wife off to a king that has become unhinged in his grief. And it was friendship and loyalty that had me welcoming you into my home. Three sacred things you know nothing about and never will."

"Be that as it may, I'm the one still left standing. While you, old friend, are already dead."

And then, in the blink of an eye, my father drives his sword right through King Krystiyan's heart.

I stand there, shocked, as blood spurts out of Levi's father's chest and mouth, his gaze trying to find his son's face in the vast room just so he can have one last look at him. Levi's face looks like it's aged a millennium as he stands ramrod straight, shoulders squared, silent tears streaming down his face. When his father finally locks eyes with Levi, he grins a wide, bloody-toothed smile and then collapses on the floor, the breath of life no longer inside his body.

A cold sweat drips down my back when my father pulls out his sword and decapitates his friend. And when he sets his sights on Levi, I know which target he has in mind next.

"No!" I shout out, almost jumping in front of Levi.

"Teodoro—" my father starts with an annoyed tone, stepping closer to me.

"You can't kill him."

"And why not?"

Fuck!

Fuck!

"If you kill him then you'll be responsible for leaving the east without a king," I rush out to say, cringing when Levi snarls behind me.

"And that is my problem, why?" my father retorts, unbothered by my remark.

"Did King Orville ask you to kill him?" I ask, praying to all the gods that he didn't.

"Hmm, no. He didn't give me instructions on what to do with the young prince."

"King, Father," I correct. "Levi is king of the east now since you killed its predecessor. If you slay King Levi now, then you might as well order his troops to invade the north as well as the south. But keep him alive, and his people will stay faithful to the crown."

"And how will I manage that?" my father asks skeptically, not entirely sure that my plan has legs to stand on.

"Ask King Orville to send decrees across the eastern land, advising that King Krystiyan and Queen Daryna were slayed tonight for treason against him. Let him write that King Levi has been spared due to his loyal heart. And while it remains that way, both him and every man, woman, and child born in the east will be protected by King Orville's merciful rule."

My father ponders on it, tapping the tip of his sword on the side of his boot.

"What's to stop the young king from seeking out his revenge on his own?" my father counters, still trying to figure out if my plan has merit.

I turn my back on my father to face Levi.

"We remind him that death may sound like a blessing to him right now, but that there are still people in Aikyam that he loves. Friends that love him just as much. Remind him that King Orville knows exactly who these friends are and wouldn't bat an eye at taking them from him. Remind him of the lesson his father just taught him tonight—that there are far worse things than death."

"Fair enough. I'll leave the new king be. He's all the east has now anyway." My father snorts behind me like this is some kind of game to him. He then orders his men to grab the heads of the fallen king and queen since King Orville demanded proof of their demise.

But all of that passes by me since my eyes are still locked with Levi's. He doesn't have to utter a word, since I see all that he wishes to say so clearly written in his face.

I've not only lost a brother tonight, but I've lost my life, too.

For there will be a day of reckoning.

And when that day comes, I'm as good as dead.

Levi will come for me.

And his steel blade will be the instrument of my demise.

Of that, I am certain.

"Cleo, don't go in there!" I hear Anya shriek when her girlfriend barges into my room.

"Too late," I mumble when a pissed-off Cleo marches toward me. I should have known the minute I told Anya we were leaving, she would go running to her girlfriend to break the news. By the look on her face, she isn't too happy about it. "I see Anya has told you we're leaving."

"She did. My king informed me as well," Cleo tells me with an intimidating tone.

"Oh, so you've been with Teo. Good for you," I retort with a sneer.

Cleo looks like she's about to claw my eyes out when Inessa steps in front of me, putting herself in harm's way.

"I suggest you take your friend back to her room. It's too late an hour to request an audience with the queen," Inessa explains, using her own intimidating glare.

"First of all, Inessa, I'm not Anya's friend. I'm her girlfriend. Big fucking difference," Cleo rebukes. "And secondly, I *will* talk with your precious queen, because if she's leaving Nas Laed, then at least she'll leave with the full story, not just some watered-down version her boy toy from the east gave her."

Inessa's eyes widen to the point they're at severe risk of popping out of her head. No one has ever dared speak to me in that manner. No one save maybe Anya. I now understand why they get along so well. One says what she feels the minute she feels it, while the other has no filter whatsoever, no matter the company.

I place a comforting hand on Inessa's shoulder and give it a light squeeze.

"It's okay, Inessa. I'm fine to speak with Cleo."

I'm not actually fine, but I'm no longer mad with fury either. My furious rage of today's earlier events has long subsided, and in its place, only loathing and sorrow remains.

Hatred for the villain who stole Levi's parents away from him.

And sorrow for the lost love that had been blooming in my heart for such a man.

"Are you sure?" Inessa asks hesitantly while still eyeballing an angry Cleo.

"I'm positive," I reply, stepping around my overprotective friend. "Please, lead the way," I tell Cleo, sensing that it is best we talk in private where neither Anya nor Inessa can disturb us.

"Cleo—" Anya calls out nervously, fidgeting when we pass the door's threshold.

"It's okay, cherry. I promise I won't hurt your friend. I'm just going to talk to her." Cleo offers Anya a tender smile before leaning in and leaving a quick peck on her lips.

Anya instantly softens, waving us both goodbye as we walk down the hall.

"This way, Your Grace," Cleo says overtly sweetly as she ushers me to turn a corner.

"Your girlfriend isn't here anymore, Cleo, so you can drop the fake politeness," I say when Cleo opens a door for me. "It doesn't suit you."

"Oh, I'm well aware of that. Believe me, it's taking everything in me not to slap some sense into you, but I know how important you are to my girl and to my king."

"I guess I should be glad to see that that's the order of your loyalty." I scoff but then stop walking when Cleo stretches her arm in front of me, her palm flat on the wall beside me, preventing me from taking another step.

"It's not. I love Anya. I love her with all my heart. But Teo is Teo. He gave me this life. It's because of him I've even met Anya."

"Don't you mean it's because of me?" I raise a brow. "If I hadn't made the decision to journey south, then I'm afraid Anya wouldn't be here."

"That might be true, but I believe in fate. I believe that what's meant to be, even the gods can't interfere. Destiny is beyond their control."

"And you believe Anya is your destiny?" I ask, genuinely interested in her reply.

"She is," she deadpans.

"Fair enough. Then you have my blessing." I smile, only for it to drop flat on the floor when Cleo begins to laugh at me.

"Fuck, but you are the most pretentious, arrogant, conceited woman I have ever met!" She cackles.

"I beg your pardon?" I retort, outraged.

"Fucking stupid and short-tempered, too. I have no idea why he even loves you."

Rage starts bubbling in me again, the tips of my ears going red with it.

"For the love I have for Anya, I will not have your head for such an offensive remark," I seethe through gritted teeth, only for her to fake an exaggerated bow, continuing to mock me.

"Many apologies, Your Highness, but I couldn't give two fucks for your blessings or your mercy. For me to care, I'd have to respect you, which I don't. Since you've been here, I haven't seen one redeeming quality in you. Not one. I pegged you right from the start as the coldhearted bitch that you are, but both Anya and Teo assured me that you're so much more than the appearance you portray to the outside world. Frankly, I don't see it. To me, you are as the world says you are—the Winter Queen with a block of ice for a heart. But aside from your many flaws, I didn't think you'd be a fucking idiot on top of it. I thought you were more intelligent than that. But after what I heard tonight from both my king and my love, my opinion of you is even lower than it was before. Because only an idiot hears one side of a story and calls it the truth."

This woman has offended me more in the last minute than anyone has ever dared to in my entire life. But still, I pause from doing something regrettable because her last remark actually hits a chord within me.

"Only an idiot hears one side of a story and calls it the truth."

"Your king didn't seem very interested in telling me his side. In fact, he insinuated that he didn't need to since I already knew everything there was to know."

"Pardon my language, Your Highness, but you know jack shit."

"Cleo, I think we're well past me pardoning you for anything. You made it evidently clear that my opinion of you is none of your concern. So as a woman who talks so plainly and direct, please enlighten me. Tell me what I'm obviously missing, because as it stands, I can only arrive at one conclusion. Your king is no friend of mine, and therefore an enemy to the crown."

"An enemy? An enemy!?" she repeats like she's misheard me. "That man has done everything your fucking crown demanded of him. Every last thing, even when it cost him his soul. And you call him your enemy?"

I stand my ground and cross my arms over my chest.

"He once said something similar to that effect too. Tell me, Cleo, what sacrifices has Teodoro made for the crown that deserves such gratitude from me?"

Cleo's eyes turn pitch black as she takes two steps back away from me as if afraid of what she'll end up doing if she continues to stand so close to me.

"You want to hear about sacrifices? Then how about Teo being forced to send the north eighty percent of all the food grown here in the south every month?"

"What are you talking about?" I ask, confused.

"I'm talking about the thousands of deaths we have each year from starvation just to feed you and your northern kingdom. I'm talking about the millions of families all across this great land that work from sunup to sundown, only to come home to a bowl of broth soup and one measly slice of bread. And that's if they're lucky."

As Cleo tells me all this, I recall how Anya and Inessa made similar observations back in Braaka about the lack of food that they witnessed while roaming the streets of the city.

But Nas Laed isn't like that.

Here there is an abundance of everything. Especially food.

Cleo's exaggerating. She must be.

"You're wrong, Cleo. You must be. I would have known if there was such a high stipulation put on the south. You must be confused."

"I'm not." She shakes her head. "You want to know how I know what I'm telling you is the gods' truth? Because I myself lost two brothers to starvation," she explains with a stricken expression plastered to her face. "They were just wee little babes, still at my mother's bosom when they passed. Unfortunately, my mother was incapable of producing enough strong milk to feed them. A hard thing to do when you're starving yourself. When they perished, we couldn't even mourn them like they deserved since our time was best spent working the fields. There was food all around us, but we couldn't touch any of it, not even to save them. If we did, my whole family would have been killed for treason. My baby brothers died to feed strangers in some faraway glacier mountains and the greed of two kings who didn't give a fuck about their people. So don't tell me that I'm confused. I know exactly what I'm talking about."

I hear the grief in her voice. The hatred of the injustice of it all.

She's not lying to me.

Which only ends up confusing me more.

It's true that the north depends on those shipments to survive, but I would never condone such large amounts to be exported to us if I knew that the south was suffering for it. My kingdom needs food to thrive but not at the cost of all these southern lives, and not at the cost of children dying in their mothers' arms. The food sent to us is more than enough to be shared between both kingdoms equally.

But right now, it seems that even the small amount of food that the south does keep for itself is also not being distributed equally either. And the north can't be at fault for that.

Can it?

"I believe what you're telling me is true, but I still can't comprehend why I see this disparity here. Why is Nas Laed not suffering the same as the rest of the kingdom?" I ask, trying desperately to understand what the hell is going on here.

"That's because King Yusuf was rewarded by your father after he pleased him with a gift," Cleo explains, spitting Teo's father's name out like it's a curse.

"What kind of gift?"

"The gift of two traitorous heads—the king and queen of the east. The story goes that King Yusuf went to the north after his visit to the east and dropped their royal heads at your father's feet. And then the mad king danced on them."

I flinch at the image she just planted in my head.

"Your father was so happy with such an offering, he told King Yusuf that he could take a small percentage out of all the food that was transported to the north for himself and keep it for Nas Laed. That's why we live in abundance here, while the rest of our kingdom starves. The price for the food you've eaten since you arrived was paid for by your east-born king's parents' heads."

Bile rises up to my throat as I shake my head in denial, still not wanting to believe such a thing.

Not only did I betray my Levi, but I also benefited from his parents' deaths.

It's too much for me to take in.

Suddenly, I feel the world start spinning, my legs starting to buckle. I lean my temple against the wall and close my eyes, just so I can get my bearings and catch my breath.

"Oh no, you don't, Your Highness. Don't you dare pass out on me yet. I still got loads more to tell you," Cleo states, snaking her arm around my waist to keep me from falling to the floor.

Thankfully, she lets me take a minute, even telling me to breathe deep so I don't faint. I must be in an awful state if even Cleo is being kind to me. It's only after I feel the blood rush back to my face that I insist that she continue.

"Are you sure? Anya would never forgive me if you passed out because of something I said."

"Anya is not here, Cleo. You are. Remember? Now tell me all I need to know. Tell me everything Teodoro left out," I instruct with a leveled tone. She gives me a curt nod, and I might be hallucinating this, but even offers me a proud smile. "First, tell me why, even after King Yusuf died, Teo is still keeping the percentage of the food from our shipments only to feed the people living in his capital."

"You really are new to this whole queen business, aren't you?" She laughs. "Because, Your Highness, there are spies everywhere here."

"Spies? From where?"

"Well, I thought they were from the north but now that I'm talking to you, I'm not so sure anymore."

"I've never sent any spies to the south. I've never sent spies anywhere, period," I assure her.

Cleo keeps staring at me, trying to see if I have any tells that will reveal I'm lying to her. When she confirms that there isn't any and that I'm telling her the truth, she shrugs.

"Maybe they were sent by your father and the assholes just stayed here until you gave them further instructions. Who the fuck knows. All

I know is that both Teo and I have worked double time to send food to the neediest regions in the kingdom without causing too much attention to what we were doing."

"So Teo is helping his people?" I chew on my bottom lip.

"Of course, he is. Contrary to what you believe about him, Teo is no monster. He'll remain loyal to the north, but he'll do everything in his power to help the south too."

"Is that how my last few shipments disappeared? Because he used them to feed his people?" I ask, trying to make sense of all this.

"I have no idea what you're talking about. We've never missed a shipment to you. Ever."

Hmm.

That's not true, even if Cleo believes it is.

My forehead wrinkles as I wonder if there is more to this story that I still have yet to uncover.

But while I'm silently trying to connect the dots to this puzzle, Cleo seems to be anxious for us to move on to the next subject she wishes to talk to me about.

"Now, are we going to discuss your lover boy's letter accusing Teo of murdering his parents or what?"

I want to berate her for calling Levi that. I want to tell her that he's a king and demands respect. But then I remember that Cleo probably sees kings and queens all the same—as unhinged, greedy animals, much like my father and Teo's father were.

How could I have been so blind to all of this?

I worshiped my father.

I knew him to be ruthless, but I never imagined just how much.

"There was only ever one disease that ever cursed the kingdom of Aikyam. And that was your father."

Those had been Levi's exact words, and at the time, I wanted to defend my father from such an accusation, but now… now I'm starting to see that Levi was right all along.

My father plagued this kingdom and, unbeknownst to me, my people are still suffering even after all this time, despite my father being dead.

Cleo doesn't wait for me to respond, grabbing at my arm and pulling me to only the gods know where.

"Where are we going?"

"I want you to see something. I want you to see why Teo did what he did," Cleo says, her steps increasing in speed.

"No matter what you show me, there isn't a good enough reason to justify what Teo did."

"We'll see about that," she mumbles ominously. "First, tell me what you know. All of it."

"That my father went mad when my mother died. That he considered his vassals to be responsible for her death. And that he requested the other kings in his kingdom to send their queens to him as the price of their betrayal," I explain, hating each and every word that comes out from my mouth.

"Yeah, real peach, your father," Cleo interjects with a snide tone. "What else? What else do you know?"

"I know that King Krystiyan would never hand over his queen to my father, and that he would prefer going to war than put his wife in such jeopardy."

"Smart man. But not so smart that he didn't get himself killed," Cleo chimes in.

"The only reason he's dead in the first place is because he trusted the wrong people, Teo being one of them," I rebuke coldly, just as we stop at a door.

"You're right. Teo did betray King Krystiyan and your beloved Levi. But have you ever asked yourself why?"

"It doesn't matter why. Only that he did it."

"Oh, it matters, Your Highness. It fucking matters," she replies as she turns the knob to open the door in front of us.

I'm about to argue with her that there is absolutely nothing she can say or show me that could ever warrant such a betrayal, but as we start to venture inside the colorful, dimly lit room, I thin my lips when I realize we're in Zara's personal chambers, little Zara fast asleep in her bed.

"You want a reason that would explain someone doing such an atrocious act? How about a brother's love for his sister?"

"His sister?" My face blanches. "I thought little Zara was Teo's daughter."

"Well, you thought wrong. Not that I'm surprised. You're big on believing your own assumptions instead of just asking." Cleo rolls her eyes. "Zara is Teo's sister, not his daughter. Queen Nahla died giving birth to her," she explains, and suddenly I remember how surprised Teo was that I hadn't heard about Zara's mother's death.

Stupid, stupid Kat.

Maybe Cleo is right.

Maybe I do make assumptions in my head without bothering to investigate if they are true or not.

Curse the gods.

"Okay, so we've established that I was wrong. Still… what does Zara have to do with the death of the king and queen of the east?"

"You really disappoint me," Cleo mumbles on an exhale. "I want to think that if you just took the time to actually think about it, you would eventually get there, but since time is of the essence, I'll have to spell it out for you instead. Also, I would rather be entertaining my girlfriend than spend the rest of the night watching you struggle to put all the pieces together."

Cleo's words cut like a knife, but if I were in her shoes, I'd probably feel the same way.

"When your cunt of a father ordered every king to deliver his wife to him, and King Yusuf had none to offer, what do you think your father said was an appropriate substitute?"

My gaze instantly falls on the sleeping princess in front of me.

"Now, you're starting to see the full picture." Cleo smiles sarcastically. "And what do you think Teo's reaction was when his father informed him that he was going to ship his baby sister—his only link to his dead mother—to a madman bent on revenge?"

"Teo would never allow it. Never," I whisper, hot tears starting to sting at the corners of my eyes with the idea my father would have demanded such a sweet child as sacrifice.

"No, he wouldn't," Cleo confirms beside me. "So he did the only thing he could—told his father that he'd sacrifice himself instead. Of course, King Yusuf wouldn't hear of it. Teo was his firstborn son, next in line to the throne. So instead, he told Teo that he would negotiate with the northern king and ask him for an alternative. He offered to travel east so that he could persuade King Krystiyan to abide by King Orville's command to hand over his queen. Of course, what Teo didn't know was that the true forged deal between your father and his was the heads of both of Levi's parents. Teo didn't know, therefore he can't be held responsible for his father's actions. If that were the case, then you'd have to stand trial for your father's sins too. Which are many."

Oh Teo.

Why keep this from me?

Why not tell me the truth?

Did you think me so cold that I wouldn't forgive such an error of misjudgment?

"Where is he now? Teo?"

"Last time I saw him, he was walking the garden. I'm sure you'll find him there."

I give her a curt nod and begin to walk out of the room. But then I stop and glance over to Cleo again.

"Thank you. Thank you for telling me all of this."

"Someone had to. Might as well be me," she retorts, offering me a sincere smile.

I smile back at her before I leave the room and go in search of the boy I fell in love with when I was just a little girl.

Like Cleo advised, I find Teo sitting on a bench at the center of his garden, head hung low while staring at what looks to be a daisy in his palms. When I take a seat beside him, I feel his body tense up, but he never moves from his forlorn position. I pluck the daisy out of his hands and twirl it around with my fingers.

"We don't have these up north. They're simple in their beauty, aren't they?"

"Most beautiful things are," he mutters softly.

"It's astounding, isn't it? How the simplest things are always the ones that make the deepest impressions on us. A sunset. A snowflake. A smile. Even a lie."

Teo straightens his back and turns to face me.

"I always hated it when you lied to me," I continue on. "Even when we were younger and you used to fib just to get your way, I hated it. But what I hated more was when you kept the truth from me by omission. At least when you lied, I could tell that you were doing it. I was so obsessed with you that I had studied all your mannerisms. Especially the ones you used whenever you told a lie. But I could never tell when you were keeping a secret from me. I could never tell that. And it hurt me. It always hurt me when you did that. Because I felt that when you simply decided the truth was too painful for me to hear, that meant you thought I was weak. A fragile little thing that needed to be kept in the dark for her own good. You made me feel inferior to you when you did that."

"That was never my intention," he quickly defends, grabbing my hand in his and squeezing it tight. "However, by your tone, I see Cleo has been talking to you."

"She has."

"You know your handmaiden, Anya, is becoming a bad influence on her. Cleo didn't have such a big mouth before she came along," he says, trying to ease the tension between us.

"Noted." I let out a half-hearted smile, my way of meeting him halfway in attempting to lighten up the mood. But my attempts are in vain when I ask what I really want to know. "Why didn't you tell me? Why did you let me go off on you like that, not bothering to tell me what really happened that night with Levi's parents?"

"You didn't give me much of a chance, kitten." He smiles meekly.

"And you didn't make much of an effort either." He just shrugs at the accusation, as if it's of no importance. "There. That type of attitude is exactly what I'm talking about. If it was never your intention to make me feel less than, to make me feel weak, if that's true, then don't do it to me now. Don't omit anything, and don't lie. Give me the whole truth, no matter how gruesome and vile you think it is. I can take it."

"Well, maybe I can't, okay?!" he shouts, standing up to his feet. "Maybe I'm the one who can't face the horror of it all anymore. I can't relive it over and over again, like I have for so many years. It's taken too much from me as it is."

"But maybe if you just explain—" I start, only for him to cut me off.

"Explain what? That it was because of me that Levi's parents died so brutally like that? That his last memory of his mother is her decapitated body being raped and torn apart by savages? That his father sobbed and yelled as he watched them do that to her? I can't, Katrina! I just can't!"

My entire body trembles at his vivid accounts from that night, my tears no longer trapped inside me but streaming down my cheeks. The horror that both my loves went through is just too much to be put into words.

"It's my fault. Whether you believe it or not, it's all my fault," he cries, unable to keep his own heartbreak at bay.

I stand up from my seat and cup his cheeks in my hands.

"You were a boy. An innocent bystander in all of this. You had no way of knowing."

He flinches at my words.

"Didn't I?" he croaks. "If that were true, then why did I try so hard to get Levi out of the castle that night? Why did I wait for everyone to be asleep to go to his room and wake him up just so he could flee? No, kitten. I knew who my father was. Deep down, I knew he wasn't there on a diplomatic mission. He had his own agenda, and a part of me knew it. And I'll never be able to forgive myself for it either. Never."

"Teo," I sob, feeling the amount of pain and guilt that he went through. That he's still going through now. And suddenly, his desires to be punished all make sense. The scars on his back all make sense to me now. He needed his body to feel some form of pain just so it could overlap the pain he felt in his heart. That was the only way he found to escape the misery he had been trapped in. Even if only for a few blessed moments.

He shakes my hands off his face and steps back from me.

"No. Don't feel sorry for me. I'm the villain in the story, just like you accused me of. Don't forget that."

"You're not a villain, Teo. You're just another one of my father's victims. You are not at fault."

He closes his eyes, unable to stop the tears running down his face.

Ever so slowly, I walk to him, and lift his hand to place his palm on my cheek.

"I'm sorry I ever doubted your heart. I'm sorry for ever believing such a lie." I swallow hard. "And Levi will forgive you too, Teo. He will. He just needs to know the truth."

And it's hearing Levi's name that breaks him.

Teo falls to the floor, crying inconsolably.

I wrap my arms around him and just let him fall apart. All the while I tell him how he's not at fault. How this guilt isn't his to hold on to. How he is loved and cherished. I tell him all this while he weeps for the innocent boy who lost his whole self-worth that one fateful night.

I'm unsure how long we stay like this, kneeling on the floor, crying our eyes out, but I'm in no rush to move. Teo needs this. He needs someone to forgive him, even if he can't forgive himself yet. And when his tears begin to subside, I wipe them clean from his face with my hands.

"I thought I lost you," he stammers, his voice still raw.

"I did too," I admit, kissing away the remaining stubborn tears.

I watch his Adam's apple bob, a sliver of fear passing through his golden gaze.

"What? What are you thinking?" I ask, worried.

"Nothing, kitten. It's nothing."

"No, Teo. You were thinking of something. Tell me. Don't lie to me ever again, even if you think it's just to protect me from the truth."

I watch him swallow dryly, that trace of fear back in his gorgeous amber eyes.

"I have loved you all my life, Katrina. Know that first," he confesses, placing my hand on his heart. "But when you came into my room earlier today with all those accusations, I thought I was speaking with someone else. Someone I haven't seen in a long time."

"What are you talking about?"

"The woman that came into my room, bent on seeing me dead, wasn't the girl I fell in love with. She wasn't the woman that I still love."

"Who was she?" I stutter, feeling a cold chill run down my spine.

"She was more than just the Winter Queen. She was the spitting image of him—your father."

"Y ou want to stay? Here? In Nas Laed?" I ask, stunned, after Anya announces her desire to stay in the south instead of traveling west with Inessa and me.

But even as the question leaves my lips, I know what her answer will be. It's written all over her face.

"I do. Very much," she admits with a shy nod, still on her knees in front of where I'm seated.

"Because of Cleo?"

Another nod.

I gently pick up her chin and look her in the eyes.

"Is that wise, Anya? You've only just met her."

"I know." She blushes. "But she's… different. She makes me feel… special."

"You are special, sweet girl. I could have told you that," I tell her truthfully, feeling my own gaze going soft.

"It's not the same, my queen. I love you with all my heart. I would follow you to the edge of the earth—"

"Just not west," I finish for her.

"It will only be for the duration of your stay, my queen. Just a couple of months. Then when King Teodoro sets to go north, I'll go with him. Cleo too. And who knows, maybe by then you'll know who your heart belongs to, and maybe that will be King Teodoro and Cleo can stay with me in Tarnow," she says hopefully, but her wishful hopes are soon tarnished by Inessa's loud scoff.

"What about King Levi? Have you forgotten him so soon? Is our queen supposed to pick this king over another just because you fell in love?" Inessa is quick to reprimand, showing her outrage.

Anya tilts her head over to her friend, deep sorrow in her eyes.

"Are you asking that question because you honestly believe King Levi to be the better man for Kat, or are you just afraid that you will lose Brick if she chooses King Teodoro instead?"

Inessa widens her eyes in fury but slams her lips shut, refusing to answer that loaded question.

"I'm sorry, Inessa, but I'm not like you. I'm not frightened of love. I'll fight for it if I must. And I love Cleo."

Inessa frowns but refuses to voice her opinion any further.

Anya lets out a deep sigh and turns her attention back to me.

"If you command me to go with you, then I will. All I ask is that you think about it. Please. For me."

"Anya, if this is where you want to be, if this is where you have found happiness, then who am I to stand in the way?"

Anya's eyes go big before her arms swing around me, hugging me tightly while pressing her face on my lap.

"Thank you, Kat! Thank you! Thank you!" she screams in utter joy, jumping to her feet and racing out the door, knocking into Teo in the process.

"Beg your pardon, Your Majesty." She giggles, running off to find Cleo.

"What was that all about?" Teo laughs as he walks into my room.

"That was Anya being happy. Get used to it since apparently she's going to be living with you for a while. And Inessa and I couldn't be happier. Isn't that right, Inessa?"

Inessa just gives me a noncommittal nod of the head.

"I should go into the city to buy some things that will be needed for the lengthy journey ahead for us tomorrow. A month on the road, we are bound to run out of things if we don't properly prepare ourselves," she says, her dismissive tone telling me that she's not at all pleased with me.

"Very well. Go, but I would really love it if you came back before dinner so that we can have one last meal with our friend."

"As you wish, my queen." Inessa curtsies and bows to Teo before leaving the room with a gray cloud over her head.

"Well, she doesn't seem pleased that Anya's staying," Teo laughs, dropping on top of my bed.

"No, she isn't." I let out an exhale before getting out of my seat to join him on the bed.

"Does she not like Cleo? I know that she can be an acquired taste for some," Teo says after I've slid to lay beside him.

"I don't think Cleo is the problem. Inessa… she just doesn't trust easily. And leaving her friend behind where she can't look out for her makes her anxious."

"I can understand that. It's not easy to let go of someone you love," he utters, saddened, wrapping my pale blonde locks around his finger and tugging them lightly.

"You're not letting me go, Teo. This is just a little hiccup in our lives together," I reassure him, placing a tender kiss to his lips.

Teo pushes me back, binding my wrists above my head while hovering over me.

"Is that so? Does that mean you've chosen?" He grins excitedly.

"Chosen?" I laugh as he uses his nose to tickle the crook of my neck. "Chosen what?"

"A husband, kitten," he retorts animatedly, his excitement like a bucket of ice water over my amused disposition.

"I didn't say that."

Teo stops his playful antics and just stares down at me for an uncomfortable, pregnant pause. He then drops to my side, covering his eyes with his arm.

"You still haven't made up your mind. After all this time, you still have one foot here and the other back east. Funny how that is since tomorrow you're leaving me to head out fucking west!"

"You're upset." I chew my bottom lip, hating seeing him like this.

"Of course, I'm fucking upset, Katrina! You're fucking in love with another man!" he shouts, jumping off the bed to pace back and forth.

"It's true. I do love Levi and I never once hid that from you."

"Thank you for your honesty. I really fucking appreciate it," he retorts sarcastically.

I let out an exhale and go to my knees on the mattress.

"I love Levi, Teo, but that doesn't mean I love you any less. Because I do, Teo. I love you."

He stops his pacing and just stares at me.

"In all the times I fantasized about you saying those exact words to me, none of them ever included you saying you loved another man too."

"I can't control how I feel, Teo. I can't just make it go away. Love doesn't work like that."

"You want to know what doesn't work?" he counters, visibly upset. "Loving two kings at the same time. A heart isn't something you share like that."

Now I'm the one who is starting to get pissed off.

"Wait, so what happened to being free? Ever since I arrived here, you've been drilling into my head how free you and your people are, but this is a hard limit? So you're telling me that a woman can share her body with innumerous men at the same time as long as her heart isn't on the table? What kind of freedom is that if you are constricted in who you want to love?"

"It's not the same thing." Teo frowns.

"It is to me. I love you. I do. But I love Levi, too. And that's just something we'll have to deal with."

"You can't have us both, kitten. Levi will cut my throat before you even have the chance to ask," he explains in a pained tone.

"I'm not talking about Levi here. I want to know where your heart lies."

"With you. Always with you," he says defeatedly, as if my love is both a gift and a curse.

I hold out my hands for him to take.

"Then isn't that enough? For now at least?"

He bows his head and kisses the inside of my wrist.

"It will have to be." He sighs. "But I won't be making the journey west with you."

"Teo—" I try to pull my hands away from him, but he keeps his hold.

"You spoke your truth, now please do me the courtesy of allowing me to speak mine. I won't be following you west, not to hurt you or punish you for not choosing me. I'm not going because I prefer to remember you here… in our little slice of paradise. I've thought long and hard about this, kitten, and my mind is made up."

My heart sinks to the pit of my stomach as if he's already saying goodbye to me.

"Will you come up north once my visit with Atlas is over?" I ask, already dreading his response.

"I don't know," he answers truthfully. "I really don't know."

"What will happen to us then?"

He leans in and places a tender kiss on my temple.

"That, my queen, is a question only you can answer."

I stand back as Anya and Inessa bid their tearful goodbyes.

"I'm going to miss you," Inessa sobs in her friend's ear.

"Don't cry, Inessa. You'll make me cry if you do. It will only be for a couple of months. Soon I'll be back north with you," Anya tries to console as her own tears stream down her cheeks.

They both hug each other tightly, neither one wanting to let go.

It's Cleo's not-so-subtle clear of the throat that breaks the pair apart.

Inessa wipes at her tears, trying desperately to school her face to hold in her usual ice-cold, stone features.

"Take care of my friend. She has a tendency of getting herself in trouble, so she needs someone to look out for her."

"She's in good hands," Teo proclaims at their side.

Inessa gives him a short bow as a sign of her respect, but then leans into Cleo's ear while pretending to hug her too.

"If you hurt Anya in any way, I'll move heaven and earth to find you. Is that understood?"

Cleo just grins widely at the threat as the two pull away from each other.

"If that ever happens, I won't make it hard on you to find me."

Inessa offers everyone a parting farewell and rushes to the carriage that will take us west.

"Well, I guess it's my turn now." I smile, opening my arms for Anya to fall into.

"Take care of Inessa, okay? She might look strong and mean but she has a fragile heart that bruises easily. She's not like us, Kat. So please take care of her, okay?"

My heart softens at her words.

"I'm so going to miss you, sweet friend. You're the best of both of us and we will feel your absence terribly," I admit, getting choked up myself.

"I'll be home soon. I promise."

Even as she says it, I know how wrong that statement is.

Nas Laed is her home. This is where Anya belongs, not back up north in Tarnow.

But still, I put on a brave smile and hug her just as fiercely as Inessa did before me.

After we pull away from the hug, I turn my attention to the woman standing at her side, the woman that will in fact do everything in her power to make Anya happy.

"Are you about to threaten me too?" she jokes with a feline grin tugging at her lips.

"I wouldn't dream of it. I know that you will do right by my Anya. I know that you'll make her happy. That you have made her happy."

Cleo turns to Anya, her black eyes sparkling with love for my friend.

"And as long as she will have me, I will continue to do so."

"Then that's all I need to hear."

I pull Cleo into a hug too, but instead of the threat Inessa whispered in her ear, I give her my gratitude.

"Thank you for telling me the truth. I fear what would have happened if I had left Nas Laed not knowing the full story. And for that, I'll always be in your debt."

"You're welcome, my queen," she retorts sincerely, and offers me a bow like a true lady belonging to the southern court.

And then I turn to my Teo, who looks just as dashing as any king could possibly look.

"I don't want to say goodbye," I admit, when he takes my hands and kisses my knuckles.

"Neither do I," he says, his voice sounding just as vulnerable as I feel.

Unable to control myself, I jump into his arms and hold on to him as if my life depends on it. He runs his fingers through my hair, kissing it any way he can.

"I love you so much, kitten. So fucking much," he says, holding me tightly.

"I love you too. I always have," I admit on a strangled sob. "Please, Teo, come north when it's time. Please."

He doesn't answer me and instead, pulls me away just far enough to kiss me.

I taste the saltiness of our tears as our mouths become one.

But all too soon does he break the kiss and take a step back.

"Go, kitten. While I still have the nerve to let you walk away from me. Go!"

"I love you," I cry out as I rush to the carriage and lock myself in. I bang at the ceiling, my order for this train to start moving west.

I open the small curtain and watch as my taste of paradise begins to slip through my fingers. Anya waves at us, while still crying her eyes out, Cleo holding her close so she doesn't get trampled by the horses passing her by.

But it's Teo's face that I memorize most.

Please, oh heavenly ones, bring him back to me.

Let this not be the last time I see him.

With that prayer in my thoughts and Teo no longer in my view, I sit back into my seat, and hold Inessa's hand.

"This is the last time we will say goodbye to the people we love, Inessa. The last time."

First Levi.

And now Anya and Teo.

I don't think my heart could handle another goodbye.

"Maybe we'll be too distracted in the west to miss them," Inessa says, trying to find something positive to say.

"You sound like Anya," I tease her.

"I wish that were true. I'm not sure what I'm going to do without her. Do you really think she'll come home?"

I shake my head.

"I didn't think so either," Inessa mutters with a sad frown on her face.

"But she's happy. Take comfort in that, dear friend. Our sister is happy," I state warmly, squeezing her hand reassuringly.

"She is, isn't she?" Inessa wipes at her tears. "That's all we can ever aspire to be. Happy."

Truer words have never been spoken.

But where does my happiness lie?

Is it in the soft green meadows of the east with Levi?

Or is it in the hidden oasis with Teo?

These questions have yet to be answered.

But right now, my destiny forges me to go neither east nor south.

West is where it lies.

So to the west I must go.

And soon after that challenge is done with, I can finally go home.

Epilogue
Atlas

Dearest brother,

I hope this letter finds you well and in good spirits.

For what I am about to confide requires a patient heart and a cool, collected mind to fully understand its meaning. I pray to the gods that this letter finds you in such a mood, for I fear the alternative.

I have never been one to measure my words, therefore I won't insult you by doing it now.

The rumors are true.

I have failed you, dear brother.

In our quest for vengeance and mayhem, I lost sight of my purpose and discarded it in favor of a new one—a better one. One that just might be the answer to our deepest desires—to undo years of tyranny without shedding one drop of innocent blood.

I don't need to be standing by your side to know that your interest has been piqued, as has your pessimistic nature, finding such a promise all but false.

But hear me now, and hear me true, sweet brother.

I am no liar.

Nor have I ever been.

So if I tell you I have found another way to bring us the peace that we so crave, then it's because I have.

Katrina is our way.

Our only way to ensure union and everlasting peace to our people and our kingdoms.

Katrina is still ours, Atlas.

In every way that counts, she is still the girl we were devoted to in all ways.

I vow that it is true.

Do not continue on this path of revenge, for the target in question is not at fault.

A daughter should not be held accountable for the father's sins.

Neither should a son.

Welcome our love and protect her in the west so she may return home to me.

This I beg of you, Atlas.

Please.

Let no harm come to her, for she is my heart.

The same heart that loves you like my own flesh and blood.

Swear it to me true, and I will believe you.

Your loyal brother in lasting peace,
Levi of Thezmaer
King of the east

I fist the scroll in my hand, feeling my rage bubbling through.
Weak.
I'm surrounded by weakness.
I breathe hard through my nose, as Levi's messenger shifts from one foot to the other, waiting for my response.
I crack my neck from side to side and step off my throne to take the three stairs down to where he stands.
"Tell your king that I trust in his wisdom and shall abide by his counsel." I force a fake smile.
"Anything else, Your Majesty?" he asks, beads of nervous sweat streaking down his brow.
I shake my head.
"That is all."
"Very well, Your Majesty. I shall depart at once."
"Good man," I praise, tapping him on the shoulder. "Go. I'm sure your king is anxious for the news."
The young messenger bows before leaving my hall to run back east where his weak, pathetic excuse for a king awaits.
I walk over to my fireplace and run my fingers over the small box that rests on its mantle. I flick the lid open and pull out a wooden boat and stare at it. It's the same one Levi sent me not a couple of months back, swearing that nothing would change the course of our plans.
Oh Levi.
How disappointed I am in you, brother.
We spent all these years strategizing and planning the north's demise, and all it took was bedding Kat for you to lay down your vengeful sword.
I thought you were made of tougher steel than that.
Tsk. Tsk.
No pussy tastes as sweet as revenge.
Oh well. As the saying goes, if you want something done right, then you must do it yourself.
I grin at the thought.
My eyes wander the hall and I call one of my squires standing by.
"Yes, Your Highness?"
"Bring me some wine. Tonight, we celebrate."

The young lad eyes me curiously as I fiddle with the toy ship in my hand.

"May I ask, Your Grace, what are we celebrating?"

My sinister smile crests my lips and widens on my face.

"We're about to kill the Winter Queen of the north. Is there a happier cause to celebrate?"

The young boy mimics my smile and hurries off to fetch me my wine.

See, Levi.

The east might have forgiven the north's transgressions.

But here in the west?

We never forgive or forget what was done to us.

Katrina of Bratsk will take her last breath here.

Even if I have to strangle her myself.

That, I swear to you, my traitorous brother.

For judgment day is upon us, and I welcome its wrath.

And with that righteous thought in my head, I throw Levi's boat into the fire where it belongs.

**To be continued in
The Winter Kissed Kings**

Thank you so much for reading The Frost Touched Queen.

If you enjoyed this book, please consider leaving an honest, spoiler-free review.

It may only take you a minute to write, but reviews are how books get noticed by other readers.

By writing a small review, you are opening the door for my love stories to be enjoyed by so many others.

I'd also love it if you would check out my website at https://www.ivyfoxauthor.com/ and I invite you to join my Facebook Reader's Group at https://www.facebook.com/groups/188438678547691/

Much love,

Ivy

xoxo

Ivy Fox Novels

Reverse Harem / Why Choose Romance

The Privileged of Pembroke High
A High School Bully Romance (Completed Series)

Rotten Love Duet
A Mafia Romance (Completed Series)

Bad Influence Series
A Forced Proximity Romance (Interconnected Standalone Series)

Contemporary Romance / New Adult

The Society
Secret Society Romance (Completed Series)

The King - After Hours Series
Office Romance

Cowrites And Collaborations

Binding Rose - Mafia Wars Series
Mafia Reverse Harem Romance (Completed Series)

Co-Write with C.R. Jane
Breathe Me Duet
Second Chance Romance (Completed Series)

The Love & Hate Duet
Stepbrother Bully Romance

Co-Write with K.A. Knight
Deadly Love
Stalker Dark Romance (Completed Series)

ABOUT THE AUTHOR

Ivy Fox is a USA Today bestselling author of angst-filled, contemporary romances, some of them with an unconventional #whychoose twist.

Ivy lives a blessed life, surrounded by her two most important men—her husband and son, but she also doesn't mind living with the fictional characters in her head that can't seem to shut up until she writes their story.

Books and romance are her passion.

A strong believer in happy endings and that love will always prevail in the end, both in life and in fiction.

Printed in Great Britain
by Amazon